T4-ACM-940

REFERENCE -- NOT TO BE
TAKEN FROM THIS ROOM

ENNIS AND NANCY HAM LIBRARY
ROCHESTER COLLEGE
800 WEST AVON ROAD
ROCHESTER HILLS, MI 48307

THE NEW INTERNATIONAL COMMENTARY ON
THE NEW TESTAMENT — F. F. BRUCE, *General Editor*

THE EPISTLE TO THE ROMANS

THE EPISTLE TO THE ROMANS

THE ENGLISH TEXT WITH INTRODUCTION,
EXPOSITION AND NOTES

by

JOHN MURRAY

*Professor of Systematic Theology, Westminster Theological Seminary
Philadelphia, Pennsylvania*

VOLUME II
Chapters 9 to 16

WM. B. EERDMANS PUBLISHING CO.
GRAND RAPIDS, MICHIGAN

© WM. B. EERDMANS PUBLISHING CO. 1965

All rights reserved

PRINTED IN THE NETHERLANDS

CONTENTS

Editor's Preface vii
Author's Preface ix

INTRODUCTION xi

   Purpose of Chapters 12–16 xi
   Purpose of Chapters 9–11 xii
   Summary of Contents xv

TEXT, EXPOSITION AND NOTES

   ROMANS IX 1
      XIV. The Unbelief of Israel 1
      XV. Vindication of God's Faithfulness and Righteousness 8

   ROMANS X 46
      XVI. The Righteousness of Faith 46

   ROMANS XI 65
      XVII. The Restoration of Israel 65
         A. The Remnant and the Remainder . . . 65
         B. The Fulness of Israel 75
         C. The Fulness of the Gentiles and the Salvation of Israel 91
         D. The Doxology 104

   ROMANS XII 109
   XVIII. The Christian Way of Life 109
         A. Manifold Practical Duties 109

   ROMANS XIII 145
         B. The Civil Magistrate 145
         C. The Primacy of Love 158
         D. The Approaching Consummation . . . 165

CONTENTS

ROMANS XIV 171
      E.   The Weak and the Strong 171

ROMANS XV 197
      F.   Christ's Example 197
      G.   Jews and Gentiles One 203
  XIX. Paul's Gentile Ministry, Policy, and Plans . 208

ROMANS XVI 225
    XX. Greetings and Closing Doxology 225
      A.   Paul's Own Greetings 225
      B.   Warnings against Deceivers 234
      C.   Greetings of Friends 238
      D.   Doxology 240

APPENDIX A.   Romans 9:5 245

APPENDIX B.   Leviticus 18:5 249

APPENDIX C.   The Authorities of Romans 13:1 252

APPENDIX D.   Romans 14:5 and the Weekly Sabbath . . 257

APPENDIX E.   The Weak Brother 260

APPENDIX F.   The Integrity of the Epistle 262

INDEXES 269

EDITOR'S PREFACE

Ever since the appearance of Volume I of Professor Murray's Commentary on Romans we have looked forward eagerly to the publication of Volume II. Now it lies before us, and the patience with which we waited for it is amply rewarded. Professor Murray has devoted the same degree of meticulous and unhurried care to the exposition of Chapters 9–16 as he did to the exposition of Chapters 1–8. Whether he is engaged in the interpretation of the theological arguments of Chapters 9–11, or in the practical application to present-day life of the ethical injunctions of the chapters that follow, or in the elucidation of the textual problems that beset the study of the conclusion of the Epistle, he takes all the factors into consideration and expresses his judgment in terms which command the reader's respect. Above all, he is concerned to bring out Paul's meaning, without trying to make him say what the commentator himself, or the twentieth-century climate of opinion, would prefer him to say. Thus the user of this commentary will be greatly helped towards hearing and obeying the Word of God spoken through the Apostle to the Gentiles.

I need say nothing by way of introducing Professor Murray to his readers. Dr. Stonehouse did all that was necessary in this regard in the Editor's Preface to Volume I, and Professor Murray is already well enough known by his other publications among those who appreciate Reformed theology. But I do esteem it an honour to be associated editorially with a work of this high quality—the work, moreover, of a fellow-Scot who worthily maintains the noble tradition of theological exegesis which has for long been one of the glories of our native land.

F. F. BRUCE
General Editor

AUTHOR'S PREFACE

Several years have passed since the publication of Volume I, Chapters 1 to 8, of this commentary. I wish to express to the Wm. B. Eerdmans Publishing Company my deep appreciation of the patience shown to me during this interval and I also extend my warmest thanks for all the courtesies conferred upon me by the Company.

I gratefully acknowledge indebtedness to the following publishers for permission to quote from the copyrighted books cited: Wm. B. Eerdmans Publishing Company, Grand Rapids—F. F. Bruce: *The Epistle of Paul to the Romans* (1963), *Commentary on the Epistle to the Colossians* (1957); John Calvin: *The Epistle of Paul to the Romans* (1961) as translated by Ross Mackenzie; Harper & Brothers, New York—C. K. Barrett: *A Commentary on the Epistle to the Romans* (1957); The Westminster Press, Philadelphia—Oscar Cullmann: *Christ and Time* (1950); Charles Scribner's Sons, New York—Oscar Cullmann: *The State in the New Testament* (1957); Lutterworth Press, London—Franz J. Leenhardt: *The Epistle to the Romans* (1961).

I submit this volume for publication in gratitude to God for the privilege of attempting by his grace to make some contribution to a better understanding of this portion of his precious Word. Exposition of the Word of God is an arduous task. It is also great joy. No undertaking is more sacred. For that reason it is demanding. But by the same token it is rewarding. It is the voice of the eternal God we hear in Scripture and his glory is revealed. When the day will dawn and the day star arise in our hearts, we shall find no discrepancy between the witness of Holy Scripture and the glory then manifested. This faith demands the care and reverence with which Scripture should be handled and it undergirds the confidence with which its testimony is to be received and obeyed.

JOHN MURRAY

Philadelphia, March 25, 1964

INTRODUCTION

Purpose of Chapters 12–16

If chapters 12 to 16 had immediately succeeded chapter 8 in this epistle, the sequence would accord with a pattern easily understood and consonant with the order that we might expect. As observed in the commentary that follows, the section extending from 12:1 to 15:13 deals with concrete and practical duties devolving upon believers. These are particularly concerned with their relations to one another in the community and fellowship of the saints. Also, since believers sustain relations to other men and institutions, Paul deals with the conduct that becomes saints in the exercise of their societal and political responsibilities. In the latter part of chapter 15 the apostle sets forth his missionary policy and plans in pursuance of his Gentile ministry. It is highly appropriate that he should do this in a letter to the church or churches at Rome.

Since Paul was not the agent in founding the church at Rome, it might seem that the more expanded reflection on his policy as apostle of the Gentiles is his apology for addressing an epistle to the saints at Rome and for the boldness with which he had written (*cf.* 15:15). The evidence furnished by the epistle does not support this construction. At the outset of the epistle his apology is concerned with the delay in fulfilling his earnest desire to visit Rome (1:11–13) and he insists that as much as lay in him he was ready to preach the gospel there (1:15). He takes occasion to resume that same subject in chapter 15 and gives additional information explanatory of the delay in fulfilling his desire and intent (15:22–26). Furthermore, as the greetings in chapter 16 indicate, Paul had many friends at Rome and among these were close associates in the work of the gospel. These friends and particularly such co-labourers as Aquila and Prisca would be ardently desirous that Paul should go to Rome and we may reasonably suppose that this desire was expressed to and concurred in by the Christian community in the imperial city. There may have been urgent communications to that effect. Hence the assurance of desire and purpose in chapter 1, reiterated and expanded in chapter 15.

There was another reason for delineating his missionary policy and plans. Rome occupied an important place in his projected itineraries for the extension of his Gentile ministry. It was necessary, therefore, that his visit to Rome be set in the context of this broader vision of pursuing his labours to the western bounds of Europe (15:28). And not only so. It was necessary to define more clearly the character of his visit to Rome lest the saints there should entertain wrong notions respecting the purpose or length of his visit. Rome was to be but a resting place on his way to Spain and the church at Rome would send him forth on his new missionary undertaking (15:24, 28).

Chapter 16 is largely devoted to greetings (16:1–16; 21–23). There are also the final warnings against corrupters of the gospel (16:17–20) and a closing doxology eminently consonant as respects length and content with the character and scope of the epistle as a whole (16:25–27).

Purpose of Chapters 9–11

But what of chapters 9 to 11? It might seem that there is discontinuity in this portion of the epistle and its length appears to aggravate the question raised. It is only as we fail to discern or overlook the relation that these chapters sustain to the thesis of this epistle that any thought of irrelevance or discontinuity is entertained. On closer inspection this part of the epistle is seen to bring to climactic vindication the thesis stated in 1:16, 17 and correlative doctrines unfolded later in chapters 1 to 8. If this section of the epistle were absent, there would be a hiatus leaving us with unanswered questions and the corresponding perplexity. It is not that we may demand or expect answers to all questions. But in this instance we may be profoundly grateful that the supreme author of Scripture inspired the apostle to deal with questions so germane to the grand theme of this epistle and urgently pressing upon the minds of intelligent readers.

It is, however, not merely the questions which emerge from this epistle that are answered in chapters 9 to 11. They are the questions which the biblico-theological perspective derived from the whole of Scripture necessarily provokes. It is noteworthy to what an extent Paul appeals to the Old Testament in this part of the epistle. This appeal shows that the subjects with which he deals are those which have their roots in the Old Testament and are, therefore, to be understood in the light of the apostle's interpretation and application. In other words, the apostle, writing in the full light of the fulfilment which the advent of Christ brought and by the inspiration of the Spirit of Pentecost, furnishes us with the orientation in terms of which the prophetical Scriptures are to be understood.

Furthermore, these chapters delineate for us the worldwide design of God in reference to Jew and Gentile. They disclose to us in a manner that is without parallel in the New Testament revelation the ways in which God's diverse providences to Jew and Gentile react upon and interact with one another for the promotion of his saving designs. It is as the apostle leads us on through this delineation and reaches the climax at 11:32: "For God hath shut up all unto disobedience, that he might have mercy upon all" that we with him reach the apex of adoring wonder and exclaim: "O the depth of the riches both of the wisdom and the knowledge of God!" That Paul, at the conclusion of the section of the epistle concerned, should have occasion to burst forth in such unsurpassed exclamatory doxology is of itself demonstration that the themes of these chapters are the fitting sequel to the great theses of the gospel developed in the first eight chapters.

The question encountered at the beginning of chapter 9 is one that arises from the terms in which the theme of the epistle is stated. The gospel "is the power of God unto salvation to every one that believeth; to the Jew first, and also to the Greek" (1:16). "To the Jew first." It is this priority that appears to be contradicted by the large-scale unbelief and apostasy of Israel. The priority of relevance and application seems to have no verification in the sequel of history. Hence the necessity of dealing with the question which Jewish unbelief poses. This, of itself, would be sufficient reason for chapters 9 to 11. But this is not the only angle from which the coherence can be shown. In the earlier chapters Paul had made appeal to Abraham as the "father of all them that believe" (4:11) and in this context refers to the promise given to Abraham (4:13). Although all the implications of this promise are not reflected on in the context in which this reference occurs, nevertheless these implications cannot be forgotten nor the questions pertinent thereto suppressed. So in chapter 9 when we read: "But it is not as though the word of God hath come to nought" (9:6), it is the word of promise to Abraham that is in view.

In chapters 9 to 11 the apostle deals with these questions which emerge from the themes of the earlier part of the epistle as these are related to Israel's unbelief. In summary, his answers are that the promise to Abraham and to his seed was not to all proceeding from Abraham by natural descent. It is to the *true* Israel the promises are made and the purpose of God according to election stands fast (9:6–13); there is always a remnant according to the election of grace (11:5, 7). In this remnant the word of the promise is fulfilled. So it is not as though the word of God has come to nought. This constitutes the first answer to the problem of the mass unbelief of Israel and of their casting away. But it is not the whole answer. The apostle proceeds in chapter 11 to unfold another aspect of God's counsel respecting Israel. In chapter 9 it is sufficient to demonstrate that Israel's unbelief and rejection were not *total*; there was a remnant. In chapter 11:11–32 Paul discloses what at 11:25 he calls "this mystery" that the rejection of Israel is not *final*. There is a further implication of the Abrahamic covenant which the future will verify and vindicate, an implication that goes beyond the reserving of a remnant in all generations. As a result of the covenant with Abraham a favour and love on God's part toward Israel *as a people* are still in exercise. They are beloved for the fathers' sake, and this is so even though they are alienated from God's favour and blessing (11:28). The privileges of Israel enumerated in 9:4, 5 have abiding relevance because "the gifts and the calling of God are not repented of" (11:29). In accordance with these implications of the covenant promise there will be restoration of Israel to the faith and blessing of the gospel. This Paul calls "their fulness" (11:12), a fulness in overt contrast with their trespass and loss and, therefore, characterized by a proportion that will be commensurate in the opposite direction. He also calls this their "receiving" and it is likewise in contrast with their "casting away" (11:15). It is their grafting in again into their own olive tree (11:23, 24). Finally, the restoration is expressed in these terms: "all Israel shall be saved" (11:26).

In this unfolding of the prophecy and promise of Israel's

reclamation Paul not only shows how the Abrahamic covenant as it respects Israel will be fulfilled and finally vindicated but he also shows how the counsel of God respecting the Gentiles is interwoven with the various phases of Israel's history. The trespass of Israel is the riches of the world, their loss the riches of the Gentiles, their casting away the world's reconciliation (11:12, 15). Again, the fulness of Israel and their receiving will bring incomparably greater blessing to the Gentile world. And not only so. The blessing accruing to the Gentiles from Israel's loss, on the one hand, and from Israel's fulness and restoration, on the other, reacts upon Israel to the promotion of their salvation. They are thereby provoked to jealousy (11:11) and the fulness of the Gentiles marks the terminus of Israel's hardening (11:25). Thus is delineated for us God's worldwide design for the realization of his saving purposes. What chapter 11 provides is an insight into the divine philosophy of history as it pertains to the salvation of Jew and Gentile. When we gain this perspective we must exclaim with Paul, "O the depth of the riches both of the wisdom and the knowledge of God!" (11:33).

Summary of Contents[1]

XIV. THE UNBELIEF OF ISRAEL — 9:1–5.
XV. VINDICATION OF GOD'S RIGHTEOUSNESS AND FAITHFULNESS — 9:6–33.
XVI. THE RIGHTEOUSNESS OF FAITH — 10:1–21.
XVII. THE RESTORATION OF ISRAEL — 11:1–36.
    A. *The Remnant and the Remainder* — 11:1–10.
    B. *The Fulness of Israel* — 11:11–24.
    C. *The Fulness of the Gentiles and the Restoration of Israel* — 11:25–32.
    D. *The Doxology* — 11:33–36.
XVIII. THE CHRISTIAN WAY OF LIFE — 12:1–15:13.
    A. *Manifold Practical Duties* — 12:1–21.
    B. *The Civil Magistrate* — 13:1–7.
    C. *The Primacy of Love* — 13:8–10.

---

[1] Continued from Summary of Contents of Chapters 1–8, Volume I, p. xxii.

D. *The Approaching Consummation* — 13:11–14.
E. *The Weak and the Strong* — 14:1–23.
F. *Christ's Example* — 15:1–6.
G. *Jews and Gentiles One* — 15:7–13.
XIX. PAUL'S GENTILE MINISTRY, POLICY, AND PLANS — 15: 14–33.
XX. GREETINGS AND CLOSING DOXOLOGY — 16:1–27.
A. *Paul's own Greetings* — 16:1–16.
B. *Warnings against Deceivers* — 16:17–20.
C. *Greetings of Friends* — 16:21–23.
D. *Doxology* — 16:25–27.

Romans IX

XIV. THE UNBELIEF OF ISRAEL
(9:1–5)

9:1–5

1 I say the truth in Christ, I lie not, my conscience bearing witness with me in the Holy Spirit,
2 that I have great sorrow and unceasing pain in my heart.
3 For I could wish that I myself were anathema from Christ for my brethren's sake, my kinsmen according to the flesh:
4 who are Israelites; whose is the adoption, and the glory, and the covenants, and the giving of the law, and the service *of God*, and the promises;
5 whose are the fathers, and of whom is Christ as concerning the flesh, who is over all, God blessed for ever. Amen.

1, 2 "I say the truth" would have been sufficient certification on the apostle's part to arrest the attention of his readers (*cf*. I Tim. 2:7). But Paul adds what gives ultimate sanction to the veracity of assertion; it is "in Christ" he speaks the truth about to be stated. "In Christ" here refers to union with Christ. It is not a formula of adjuration nor in this instance is he appealing to the agency of Christ. Union with Christ is the orbit within which his emotions move and the spring from which they proceed. Thus the thing spoken of as "the truth" derives its impulse and the guarantee of its propriety from this union. If we ask: why this form of certification? there are two reasons that may reasonably be suggested. (1) Paul's denunciation of Jewry in the earlier part of the epistle must not be regarded as estrangement from his kinsmen. (2) This form of certification is necessary to support the almost unparalleled optative with which he continues, "I could wish that I myself were anathema from Christ" (vs. 3). But, in any case, it is characteristic of the apostle to support his statements by this formula (*cf*. 14:14; II Cor. 2:17; 12:19; Eph. 4:17; I Thess. 4:1).

The negative "I lie not" is likewise added, according to Paul's pattern, to emphasize the veracity of his utterance (*cf.* II Cor. 11:31; Gal. 1:20; I Tim. 2:7). The truth stands in absolute antithesis to the lie, and, as Christ is "the truth", what receives its impulse and guarantee from union with him cannot partake of the lie (*cf.* I John 2:21, 27). In Godet's words, "in the eyes of Paul there is something so holy in Christ, that in the pure and luminous atmosphere of His felt presence no lie, and not even any exaggeration, is possible".[1]

It would seem that the apostle had said enough to certify his truthfulness. It is the more striking, therefore, that he should appeal to the witness of his conscience. A glance at Paul's appeal to conscience elsewhere in his epistles will evince that the clause appended, "my conscience bearing witness with me in the Holy Spirit", is not superfluous (*cf.* Acts 23:1; II Cor. 1:12; 4:2; 5:11; I Tim. 1:5, 19; 3:9; II Tim. 1:3; Tit. 1:15). Conscience is the activity by which we judge ourselves and bring our own conduct under moral and religious scrutiny. Conscience may approve or disapprove. When it approves we have a good or pure conscience (*cf.* Acts 23:1; I Tim. 1:5, 19; 3:9; Heb. 13:18; I Pet. 3:16, 21). When conscience disapproves and convicts of sin then we have a bad or guilty conscience (*cf.* John 8:9; Rom. 2:15; Tit. 1:15; Heb. 10:22). It is to the approval of conscience that Paul here appeals. He states this, however, in terms of the confirmatory witness borne by conscience. It is most significant that he regards this witness as borne "in the Holy Spirit". Just as the certification of his earlier assertion is derived from union with Christ, so the veracity of the witness of his conscience is certified by the Holy Spirit. It is only as we are indwelt by the Spirit and live in the Spirit, only as our minds are governed by the Spirit may we be assured that the voice of conscience is in conformity with truth and right. "In Christ" and "in the Holy Spirit" are correlative and mutually dependent in Paul's thinking and they are introduced in these consecutive clauses for the purposes indicated and in appropriate connections.

The truth referred to in verse 1 is now stated: "I have great sorrow and unceasing pain in my heart". That Paul should have

---

[1] F. Godet: *Commentary on St. Paul's Epistle to the Romans* (E. T., Edinburgh, 1881), II, p. 131.

adduced the ultimate sanctions of veracity to certify his own subjective state of mind points up the seriousness of that which constrains this state of mind and the relevance of his anguish to the situation in view. In a word, Paul's sorrow is the reflection of the gravity pertaining to Israel's unbelief. The intensity of the apostle's sorrow, as Liddon observes, is marked by its greatness, its continuance, and its depth.[2]

3 "Anathema from Christ"[3] means to be separated from Christ and devoted to destruction (*cf.* LXX, Lev. 27:28, 29; Deut. 7:26; 13:16, 18; Josh. 6:17; 7:1, 11, 12). In the New Testament "anathema" has similar force and means accursed (*cf.* Acts 23:14; I Cor. 12:2; 16:22; Gal. 1:8, 9). Any difficulty attaching to this verse cannot be relieved by toning down the force of the expression. It means to be abandoned to perdition. Did Paul then wish to be thus devoted to destruction and separated from Christ?

It would not be proper to refer this clause to the past attitude of the apostle when he was persecuting Christ and the church. His opposition to Christ could not with any warrant be construed as wishing himself anathema from Christ. Neither can we suppose that Paul considered it possible for him to be separated from Christ. This would contradict the assured confidence expressed in the preceding chapter (8:38, 39). Furthermore, the expression does not mean that he *actually* wished or prayed that he would be anathema from Christ. The tense used in the Greek is well expressed by the version in the words "I could wish".[4] It is hypothetical to the effect that if it were possible and of avail for the salvation of his kinsmen he would be willing to be accursed on their behalf. The intensity of the apostle's love for his own people

---

[2] H. P. Liddon: *Explanatory Analysis of St. Paul's Epistle to the Romans* (New York, 1897), p. 148.
[3] The reading ὑπὸ τοῦ Χριστοῦ, supported by D G, is not to be followed. ἀπό is strongly attested.
[4] ηὐχόμην is Imperfect and clearly expresses this idea in other instances in the New Testament. *Cf.* E. DeWitt Burton: *Syntax of the Moods and Tenses in New Testament Greek* (Edinburgh, 1955), § 33; F. Blass and A. Debrunner: *A Greek Grammar of the New Testament and Other Early Christian Literature* (E. T., Chicago, 1961), § 359; G. B. Winer: *A Grammar of the Idiom of the New Testament* (E. T., Andover, 1892), p. 283. Examples given by Burton are Acts 25:22; Gal. 4:20; Phm. 13, 14. *Cf.* also J. B. Lightfoot: *St. Paul's Epistle to the Galatians*, *ad* 4:20; M. J. Lagrange: *Épître aux Romains* (Paris, 1950), p. 225; F. F. Bruce: *The Epistle of Paul to the Romans* (Grand Rapids, 1963), *ad loc.*

is hereby disclosed. It is love patterned after the love of the Saviour who was made a curse and sin for the redemption of men (*cf.* Gal. 3:13; II Cor. 5:21). "It was, therefore, a proof of the most fervent love that Paul did not hesitate to call on himself the condemnation which he saw hanging over the Jews, in order that he might deliver them."[5] "It is objected that the wish must thus be irrational... but the standard of selfish reflection is not suited to the emotion of unmeasured devotedness and love out of which the apostle speaks."[6] The use of the term "brethren" bespeaks the bond of affection which united the apostle to his kinsmen. "According to the flesh" is added to show that those for whom he had concern were not contemplated as brethren in the Lord (*cf. contra* 14:10, 13, 15, 21; 16:14) but it also expresses what is implicit in the term "kinsmen" and supplies an additional index to the bond of love created by this natural, genetic relationship.

4, 5 The attachment to Israel is not due merely to natural ties. It is accentuated by the place Israel occupied in the history of revelation. Apart from this identity the great question with which the apostle proceeds to deal would not have arisen. Hence he proceeds to enumerate the distinguishing privileges of the Jewish people.

The first mentioned is that they were "Israelites". This name harks back to Genesis 32:28 and is reminiscent of the dignity bestowed upon Jacob in the reception of the name "Israel", a dignity conferred also upon his seed (*cf.* Gen. 48:16; Isa. 48:1). Although Paul is jealous for the distinctions drawn in verses 6, 7 that they are not all Israel who are of Israel and that natural descent does not constitute the "seed", yet he in no way discounts the advantages belonging to ethnic Israel (*cf.* 3:1, 2; 11:28). The term "Israelite" conveniently expressed this distinguishing character (*cf.* John 1:47; Acts 2:22; 3:12; 5:35; 13:16; 21:28; Rom. 11:1; II Cor. 11:22; and "the stock of Israel" in Phil. 3:5).

"Adoption" is the filial relation to God constituted by God's grace (*cf.* Exod. 4:22, 23; Deut. 14:1, 2; Isa. 63:16; 64:8; Hos. 11:1; Mal. 1:6; 2:10). This adoption of Israel is to be distinguished from that spoken of as the apex of New Testament privilege

---

[5] John Calvin: *The Epistle of Paul the Apostle to the Romans* (E. T. by Ross Mackenzie, Grand Rapids, 1961), *ad loc.*

[6] Heinrich A. W. Meyer: *Critical and Exegetical Handbook to the Epistle to the Romans* (E. T., Edinburgh, 1881), II, *ad loc.*

9:1–5 THE UNBELIEF OF ISRAEL

(8:15; Gal. 4:5; Eph. 1:5; *cf.* John 1:12; I John 3:1). This is apparent from Galatians 4:5, for here the adoption is contrasted with the tutelary discipline of the Mosaic economy. Israel under the Old Testament were indeed children of God but they were as children under age (*cf.* Gal. 3:23; 4:1–3). The adoption secured by Christ in the fulness of the time (Gal. 4:4) is the mature, full-fledged sonship in contrast with the pupilage of Israel under the ceremonial institution. This difference comports with the distinction between the Old Testament and the New. The Old was preparatory, the New is consummatory. The adoption of the Old was propaedeutic. The grace of the New appears in this, that by redemption accomplished and by faith in Christ (*cf.* Gal. 3:26) all without distinction (*cf.* Gal. 3:28) are instated in the full blessing of sonship without having to undergo tutelary preparation corresponding to the pedagogical discipline of the Mosaic economy.

"The glory" should be regarded as referring to the glory that abode upon and appeared on mount Sinai (Exod. 24:16, 17), the glory that covered and filled the tabernacle (Exod. 40:34–38), the glory that appeared upon the mercy-seat in the holy of holies (Lev. 16:2), the glory of the Lord that filled the temple (I Kings 8:10, 11; II Chron. 7:1, 2; *cf.* Ezek. 1:28). This glory was the sign of God's presence with Israel and certified to Israel that God dwelt among them and met with them (*cf.* Exod. 29:42–46).

"The covenants"—[7] the plural could refer to the two distinct covenantal administrations to Abraham (Gen. 15:8–21; 17:1–21). Though these two covenant dispensations are closely related yet the distinctions in respect of time, character, and purpose are not to be overlooked. It is more reasonable, however, to regard the plural as denoting the Abrahamic, Mosaic, and Davidic covenants. No feature of Israel's history marked their uniqueness as the recipients of redemptive revelation more than these covenants. The progressive covenantal disclosure advanced apace with the fulfilment of redemptive promise (*cf.* Exod. 2:24; 6:4, 5; Deut. 8:18; Luke 1:72, 73; Acts 3:25; Gal. 3:17–19; Eph. 2:12).

---

[7] The singular ἡ διαθήκη, though supported by P⁴⁶, B, D, G and other authorities, is not probably to be preferred. Internal evidence would favour the plural. In citing the privileges of Israel we should expect mention of more than one covenant and, besides, "the covenant" without any further specification would be so unusual as to be ambiguous, and this we would not expect (*cf.* Eph. 2:12 and the plural "promises" in this same verse).

"The giving of the law" refers to the Sinaitic promulgation and "the service of God" to the worship of the sanctuary (*cf.* Heb. 9:1, 6). "The promises" are those which found their focus in the Messiah (*cf.* Gal. 3:16). "The fathers" would certainly include Abraham, Isaac, and Jacob (*cf.* 4:1, 11, 12, 16, 17; 9:10; 15:8; Acts 3:13, 25). But it would not be proper to restrict the denotation to these patriarchs (*cf.* Mark 11:10; Acts 2:29; I Cor. 10:1; Heb. 1:1; 8:9). The next clause would require the inclusion of David. In 1:3 Paul had spoken of Jesus as "born of the seed of David according to the flesh". It would not appear reasonable to exclude the father expressly mentioned in 1:3.[8] Thus we should have to extend the line beyond Jacob and conclude that the fathers of distinction in redemptive history from Abraham onwards are in view. The term could be used to designate those whose names are in an outstanding way associated with the unfolding of Israel's covenantal history, a history that reached its climax in Christ, "born of the seed of David according to the flesh" and "constituted the Son of God with power, according to the spirit of holiness, by the resurrection from the dead" (1:3, 4).

"Of whom is Christ as concerning the flesh." At this point there is a change in the relationship. After "Israelites" all the privileges mentioned are stated as *belonging* to the Jewish people. Even "the fathers" are represented thus. But when Paul reaches the climax he does not say that Christ belonged to them but that Christ came from the Jewish stock.[9] The antecedent of "whom" is not "the fathers" but the Israelites. "Concerning the flesh" has the same import as the similar expression in 1:3 (*cf.* comments at that point). The next two clauses are to be taken as referring to Christ and defining what he is in his divine identity as Lord of all and God blessed for ever (see Appendix A, pp. 245ff., for fuller treatment of this disputed question). It is altogether appropriate that there should be this reflection upon the supereminent dignity of Christ at this climactic point in the enumeration of Israel's privileges. The chief reason for the apostle's anguish was the

---

[8] It may well be that "the fathers" in 11:28 should be restricted to Abraham, Isaac, and Jacob in view of 11:16. But the denotation in 11:28 does not decisively determine the same in 9:5. *Cf. contra* F. A. Philippi: *Commentary on St. Paul's Epistle to the Romans* (E. T., Edinburgh, 1879), II, p. 67; Meyer: *op. cit., ad loc.*; Bruce: *op. cit., ad loc., et al.*

[9] The ἐξ ὧν is to be noted in this case in distinction from the simple ὧν in two instances preceding.

rejection on Israel's part of that which brought to fruition the covenantal history which constituted their distinctiveness. The gravity of this rejection was pointed up by the uniqueness of Jesus' person. In view of the situation with which the apostle is dealing there could not be any context in this epistle which would more appropriately, if not necessarily, call for the declaration of Christ's supreme dignity.

XV. VINDICATION OF GOD'S FAITHFULNESS AND RIGHTEOUSNESS
(9:6–33)

9:6–13

6 But *it is* not as though the word of God hath come to nought. For they are not all Israel, that are of Israel:
7 neither, because they are Abraham's seed, are they all children: but, In Isaac shall thy seed be called.
8 That is, it is not the children of the flesh that are children of God; but the children of the promise are reckoned for a seed.
9 For this is a word of promise, According to this season will I come, and Sarah shall have a son.
10 And not only so; but Rebecca also having conceived by one, *even* by our father Isaac—
11 for *the children* being not yet born, neither having done anything good or bad, that the purpose of God according to election might stand, not of works, but of him that calleth,
12 it was said unto her, The elder shall serve the younger.
13 Even as it is written, Jacob I loved, but Esau I hated.

6, 7 Literally rendered "But it is not such that the word of God has failed" and means that the case is not such that the faithfulness of God is impugned. The question arises: what in the preceding context requires this reservation? Some have found this in verses 4 and 5 and have supposed that "the word of God" alluded to is the word of threatening.[10] It is to be borne in mind, however, that the leading thought of the preceding verses is the grief the apostle entertains. The certifications we found in verse 1 are for the purpose of assuring the veracity of what is stated in verse 2, and verse 3 demonstrates the intensity of the apostle's anguish. Verses 4, 5 are attached to verse 3 for the purpose of explaining this grief and the zeal for Israel. However significant is the catalogue of privileges enumerated in verses 4, 5 it must not

---

[10] *Cf.* James Morison: *An Exposition of the Ninth Chapter of Paul's Epistle to the Romans* (Kilmarnock, 1849), pp. 164ff.

be dissociated from its purpose in relation to verses 2, 3. Hence it is to the apostle's grief that the reservation of verse 6 is to be attached. This grief is the reflection in Paul's consciousness of an objective situation; it has compelling grounds and its reality is certified by ultimate sanctions. In the context of the history referred to in verses 4, 5, the anticlimax of Israel's unbelief and of Paul's anguish incident thereto might appear to contradict the covenant promises of God. It is this inference that Paul denies. The word of God has not fallen to the ground.

"The word of God" should be understood in a more specific sense and not in the sense of Scripture as a whole or of the word of the truth of the gospel. It is the word of promise in the covenants alluded to in verse 4. Covenant in Scripture is synonymous with oath-bound promise and the statement here is to the same effect as saying "God's covenant has not come to nought". Then the reason is given: "they are not all Israel who are of Israel". Those "of Israel" are the physical seed, the natural descendants of the patriarchs. It is not necessary to identify "Israel" here as Jacob specifically. It makes no difference to the sense whether we regard "Israel" as those descended from Jacob or go back further to include Abraham and Isaac. The main thought is that of children according to the flesh. In the other expression, "they are not all Israel", obviously the denotation is much more limited and the thought is that there is an "Israel" within ethnic Israel. This kind of distinction appears earlier in this epistle in connection with the term Jew and circumcision (2:28, 29). If the terms of the present passage were applied to the earlier the formulae would be, "they are not all Jews who are of the Jews" and "they are not all circumcised who are of the circumcision". Thus we have been prepared by the patterns of Paul's thought and usage for what we find here in 9:6.

The Israel distinguished from the Israel of natural descent is the *true Israel*. They are indeed "of Israel" but not coextensive with the latter. It is in accord with our Lord's usage to make this kind of distinction within a designated class. He distinguished between those who were disciples and those *truly* disciples (*cf.* John 8:30–32). He spoke of Nathanael as "truly an Israelite" (John 1:47). If we use Paul's own language, this Israel is Israel "according to the Spirit" (Gal. 4:29) and "the Israel of God" (Gal. 6:16), although in the latter passage he is no doubt including the people of God of all nations. The purpose of this distinction is to show that the covenantal promise of God did not have respect to Israel after the flesh but to this *true* Israel and that, therefore, the unbelief and rejection of ethnic Israel as a whole in no way interfered with the fulfilment of God's covenant purpose and promise. The word of God, therefore, has not been violated. The argument of the apostle here is not *in principle* different from that which we find earlier in this epistle. There is a parallel between his present contention and his polemic that "not through the law was the promise to Abraham or to his seed" (4:13) and that the children of Abraham were those "who walk in the steps" of Abraham's faith (4:12). Now the interest is centred upon a coordinate facet of truth that not through natural descent are the promises inherited and that God's covenant promise was not made so as to include all of ethnic Israel. Thus the exclusion of Israelites from God's covenant favour does not negate the word of the oath.

In verse 7 Paul continues to support this same distinction and expressly carries it back to the seed of Abraham. He is still speaking of those "of Israel" and now draws the distinction in terms of that between "Abraham's seed" and "children". In this instance "Abraham's seed" denotes the natural posterity and "children" is equivalent to the *true* Israel, and in that sense the *true* children as inheritors of the promise. Later on these children are called "children of God" (vs. 8) and this fixes their identity even though in verse 7 they are contemplated simply as the *true* children of Abraham.

The foregoing differentiation is now supported by appeal to Scripture. "In Isaac shall thy seed be called" (Gen. 21:12).[11] Isaac must here be taken of the person and not collectively. Thought is focused on the choice of Isaac in contrast with Ishmael: the proposition to be demonstrated is that natural descent does not make children in the sense of *true* children, children to whom the promise belongs. The choice of Isaac to the exclusion of Ishmael is sufficient to prove this thesis. Furthermore, it may not be taken for granted that "thy seed" in this instance is to be understood

---

[11] The literal rendering is: "In Isaac shall a seed be called to thee". The reference does not appear to be to the descendants of Isaac but to Isaac himself as the son of promise. The *true* seed of Abraham will in every instance be such after the pattern or principle thus exemplified in Isaac as distinct from Ishmael.

collectively. The English rendering creates the impression that "seed" is here collective. But it may well be understood in the sense "Isaac shall be thy seed" and "seed" understood in this case in contrast with "Abraham's seed" and in the sense of *true* seed.[12] If we take "seed" in verse 7b collectively, then the meaning is that in Isaac will your true descendants be reckoned, as Sanday and Headlam take it. If this is the intent the central thought of the passage, namely, that natural descent does not make children of God and of promise, cannot be suspended at this point any more than in the case of Abraham. The meaning, on this supposition, would have to be that in reckoning the true seed from Isaac the same principle of differentiation would have to apply to Isaac's seed as was operative in the case of Isaac himself. That is to say, the collective "seed" are not those descended from Isaac but those "of Isaac" who like him are children of the promise. But we may not be dogmatic to the effect that "thy seed" in this case is collective; it may be singular and personal.

8, 9 "That is" at the beginning of verse 8 means that what had been said is now explicated still further. "The children of the flesh" has the same import and extent as "Abraham's seed" in verse 7. "The children of God" has the same reference as "children" in verse 7. But now there is the additional definition whereby their identity as those brought into the adoptive relation to God is clearly indicated (*cf.* 8:16, 17, 21; Phil. 2:15). "The children of the promise" are the same as the children of God and this designation is placed in contrast with "the children of the flesh". The latter are those born after the flesh but the children of the promise are those who derive their origin from the promise of God. The promise in this instance is the promise given to Abraham, quoted in verse 9 and drawn from Genesis 18:10, 14. Isaac was born in pursuance of that promise. To that promise the faith of Abraham attached itself (*cf.* 4:19–21). In the case of Ishmael there were no such factors. He was begotten, conceived, and born in accordance with natural procreative powers. It is this radical difference in the birth of the respective sons that

---

[12] *Cf.* Philippi: *op. cit., ad loc.*; Liddon: *op. cit.*, p. 157; Charles Hodge: *Commentary on the Epistle to the Romans, ad loc.* Sanday and Headlam are insistent that "seed" is here collective; *cf.* W. Sanday and A. C. Headlam: *A Critical and Exegetical Commentary on the Epistle to the Romans* (New York, 1926), *ad loc.*

is summed up here in the word "promise". Isaac was a child of promise. This same criterion is used to define the differentiation that is maintained between those who are "of Israel" and the *true* Israel (vs. 6), between "Abraham's seed" and the *true* children (vs. 7), between the children of the flesh and the children of God (vs. 8), and between the natural seed and the *true* seed (vss. 7, 8). In the sequence of thought, therefore, this word "promise" specifies that which is explanatory of the sustained distinction between the more inclusive and the restricted use of the various terms "Israel", "seed", and "children". In each case the restricted use is defined by what is implicit in God's promise. This brings us back to verse 6: "But it is not as though the word of God hath come to nought". The "word of God" is God's covenant promise.[13] It has not come to nought because it contemplates those whose identity is derived from that same covenant promise. The seed to whom the promise was given or, at least, the seed whom the promise had in view are those in whom the promise takes effect; they are "children of the promise".[14]

10–13 In these verses appeal is made to another instance of the same kind of differentiation in patriarchal history. The thesis being established, it must be remembered, is that not by natural descent did the descendants of Abraham become partakers of God's covenant grace and promises. This was proven in Abraham's own sons in the differentiation between Isaac and Ishmael. But it was not only in Abraham's sons that this discrimination appeared; it enters also into Isaac's own family. The argument of the apostle becomes cumulative as it proceeds. There are new factors exemplified in Isaac's family that do not appear in the case of Abraham's sons and these considerations point up more forcefully and conclusively the differentiation that must be recognized in the fulfilment of God's covenant purposes. These considerations may be listed as follows.

1. If the discrimination which God's covenant promise contemplates were exemplified only in the case of Isaac in the history

---

[13] This is also borne out by verse 9: "This is a word of promise". The genitive ἐπαγγελίας is appositional, the word that consisted in the promise.
[14] "κατὰ τὸν καιρὸν τοῦτον is shown clearly by the passage in Genesis to mean 'at this time in the following year,' i.e. when a year is accomplished" (Sanday and Headlam: *op. cit., ad loc.*).

of the patriarchs, then the proposition, "they are not all Israel who are of Israel", would not have as much ostensible support. It could be pleaded that the promise, "in Isaac shall thy seed be called", guarantees that the promise is to all of Isaac's seed without distinction. The fact that differentiation becomes operative within Isaac's seed shows that the same discrimination exemplified in the case of Isaac himself continues within his progeny.

2. Ishmael was the son of the bondmaid, not of the freewoman. The discrimination, therefore, appeared to reside in a natural factor and this reason would appear to detract from the interest which is paramount in this whole passage, namely, the pure sovereignty of the discrimination which the covenant promise implies. This consideration connected with Ishmael as the son of Hagar is completely eliminated in the case of Esau and Jacob as the sons of Rebecca. The sons are of the same mother and she a freewoman.[15] This is still more accentuated by the fact that they were conceived by her at the same time and their foetal development was concurrent.

3. Though Esau and Jacob were twins, yet Esau was the firstborn. The choice of Jacob went counter to the priority which primogeniture would have required. This illustrated still further the sovereignty of the discrimination in actual operation.

4. The apostle draws attention not only to these foregoing facts that Rebecca "conceived by one, even by our father Isaac" but also to the fact that the oracle which bespoke the discrimination was uttered *before the children were born* and before they had done anything good or evil. The word of God to Abraham, quoted in verse 7 with respect to Isaac, reflects a radically different situation (*cf.* Gen. 21:8–12). As was noted earlier, the thesis of the apostle in this passage that physical descent does not determine the objects of God's covenant promise is parallel to his earlier contention that "not through the law was the promise to Abraham or to his seed" (4:13).[16] This is demonstrated in the present passage: the oracle

---

[15] It may not be irrelevant to note that Isaac had only one wife.

[16] Philippi claims that τέκνα τῆς σαρκός (vs. 8) reflects on this, that "in consonance with the more comprehensive notion of the word σάρξ in Paul" the term refers "to the entire sphere of sensuous, visible profession upon which man might possibly found a claim of right in the presence of God" (*op. cit.*, p. 86).

was spoken to Rebecca[17] before the children did good or evil. This shows that the discrimination did not proceed "of works, but of him that calleth" (vs. 11). "Not of works" and "not of natural descent" are correlative and point to the same principle. Thus the apostle can adduce the one in an argument that is mainly concerned with the other without any sense of incongruity.

There are three features of this passage which require special comment. The first is that the discrimination expressed in the oracle is said to be "that the purpose of God according to election might stand". This is the first time that "election" is expressly mentioned in this passage. Previously the emphasis fell on "promise" as the principle of differentiation and implicit in this term is the sovereign will and grace of God. Promise is in contrast with natural descent and with any right or privilege arising therefrom. Thus promise as a determining factor is coordinate with election. But now the accent falls on election or, more accurately, "the purpose of God according to election". In order to gain the import of this clause several observations are necessary.

1. The oracle spoken to Rebecca[18] is directed to the end of establishing the purpose of God according to election. Verse 11 is not a parenthesis but, syntactically, stands in close relation to verse 12. It is in pursuance of God's electing purpose that the disclosure was made to Rebecca before the children were born. The electing purpose is the plan of God which the oracle serves to bring to expression and fruition.

2. The immutability of the electing purpose is intimated in the words "might stand".[19] The false inference drawn from the unbelief of Israel, namely, that "the word of God hath come to nought" (vs. 6), the apostle is refuting in this passage. In verse 11 he is asserting the security and immovability of the electing purpose in eloquent contrast to the supposition that the word of

---

[17] Why Rebecca received the promise rather than Isaac it may be vain to speculate. It is, however, to be noted that the deception she designed and practised serves also to demonstrate the sovereign grace of God as overcoming and going counter to all human demerit.

[18] The construction in verses 10–12 is not easy to determine. Probably the best proposal is that $Ρεβεκκα\ ἐξ\ ἑνὸς\ κοίτην\ ἔχουσα$ is to be taken as nominative absolute and thus provides the introduction to what is stated in verses 11, 12a and the antecedent of $αὐτῇ$ in verse 12b.

[19] The present tense $μένῃ$ may more adequately express the "abiding condition" (Philippi, *ad loc.*). The purpose of God always stands firm.

9:6–33 GOD'S FAITHFULNESS AND RIGHTEOUSNESS VINDICATED

God could be invalidated, the word of God being understood as referring to his covenant promise and purpose.

3. There are various ways of construing the words "the purpose of God according to election". It has been assumed that, since the election and the purpose are eternal and, therefore, before time, there cannot be any order of priority whereby election could be conceived of as prior to purpose or purpose as prior to election.[20] This consideration that the electing purpose is supratemporal does not, however, rule out the thought of priority; there can be priority in the order of thought and conception quite apart from the order of temporal sequence. We find this elsewhere in Paul (*cf.* 8:29; Eph. 1:4–6). The preposition rendered "according to" in the version frequently expresses in Paul's epistles and elsewhere the thought of priority as that in accordance with which something occurs, whether it be the order of time or simply that of logical relationship (*cf.* 8:28; Gal. 1:4; 2:2; 3:29; Eph. 1:5, 11; II Tim. 1:9; Heb. 2:4; I Pet. 1:2). Hence there is no reason why, in the present instance, the purpose of God should not be conceived of as the purpose determined in accordance with election and election would be prior in the order of causation. The purpose would be that which springs from election and fulfils its design. This is the interpretation that has most in its favour on the grounds of usage and Paul's teaching elsewhere. But, since the purpose could be thought of as that which comes to expression in election, dogmatism would not appear to be warranted. In any case, the whole expression cannot mean less than electing purpose. It is a purpose characterized by election and an election with determinative purpose. Both terms, "election" and "purpose", must be given the full force of their biblical and particularly Pauline connotation.

4. The question now is: what is this electing purpose? It is maintained by several commentators older and more recent that the election of which Paul here speaks is not that of individuals but of Israel as a people and that he is thinking not of the destiny of

---

[20] ἡ κατ' ἐκλογὴν πρόθεσις, says Meyer, "can neither be so taken, that the ἐκλογή *precedes* the πρόθεσις in point of time (comp. viii. 28), which is opposed to the nature of the relation, especially seeing that the πρόθεσις pertains to what was antecedent to time... nor so that the ἐκλογή follows the πρόθεσις". The ἐκλογή, he continues, "must be apprehended as an essential *inherent* of the πρόθεσις, expressing the *modal character* of this divine act" (*op. cit., ad loc.*).

individuals but in terms of collectives.[21] This thesis requires expanded examination.

(*a*) It is true that the Scripture speaks of the election of Israel as a people and in numerous passages it is the relationship of God to the people collectively that is in view (*cf.* Deut. 4:37; 7:7, 8; 10:15; 14:2; I Kings 3:8; Psalm 33:12; 105:6, 43; 135:4; Isa. 41:8, 9; 43:20–22; 44:1, 2; 45:4; Amos 3:2). In fact, so much was Paul aware of this and of all its implications that the problem with which he is dealing in this chapter presupposes this election of Israel as a people. The catalogue of privileges mentioned in verses 4, 5 is but a fuller and more pointed way of harking back to the "election" of Israel. We need go no further than the clause "who are Israelites" to be reminded of what the apostle has in view: it is Israel's election.

(*b*) There is no doubt but the oracle to Rebecca contemplated more than the individuals Esau and Jacob. This lies on the face of the Old Testament passage from which Paul quotes in verse 12. "And the Lord said unto her, Two nations are in thy womb, and two peoples shall be separated from thy bowels: and the one people shall be stronger than the other people; and the elder shall

---

[21] "In the context the apostle is not speaking of that specific plan of election in accordance with which he elects certain individuals... He is speaking of a totally different scheme of election,—that scheme, to wit, in accordance with which he selected from among the various races, which sprang out of the loins of Abraham, the peculiarly favoured Messianic seed" (Morison: *op. cit.*, p. 212). With respect to the names Jacob and Esau, Leenhardt says, "the names mentioned certainly do not connote individuals so much as peoples who are thus named after their eponymous ancestors, according to Old Testament practice. It is best to understand the names in this way, since the argument which they are quoted to support concerns the destiny of Israel as a whole, and not the destiny of individuals who compose Israel. Paul thinks in terms of collectives" (Franz J. Leenhardt: *The Epistle to the Romans* [E. T., London, 1961], p. 250). *Cf.* F. F. Bruce: *op. cit., ad* 9:13; Ernst Gaugler: *Der Römerbrief* (Zurich, 1952), II Teil, pp. 38f.; G. C. Berkouwer: *Divine Election* (Grand Rapids, 1960), pp. 210–217; Herman Ridderbos: *Aan de Romeinen* (Kampen, 1959), pp. 227–231. Karl Barth's view of election is so diverse that it could not properly be examined without taking into account his more extensive treatment of the subject in *Church Dogmatics.* The following quotation, however, illustrates the dialectic in terms of which election is construed: "He [God] makes himself known in the parable and riddle of the beloved Jacob and hated Esau, that is to say, in the secret of eternal, twofold predestination. Now, this secret concerns not this or that man, but all men. By it men are not divided, but united. In its presence they all stand on one line—for Jacob is always Esau also, and in the eternal 'Moment' of revelation Esau is also Jacob" (*The Epistle to the Romans*, [E. T., London, 1933], p. 347).

serve the younger" (Gen. 25:23). It is also apparent from the context of what Paul quotes from Malachi 1:2, 3 (vs. 13) that the peoples of Israel and of Edom are contemplated (*cf.* Mal. 1:1, 4, 5). In terms of biblical teaching it could not be otherwise. Human relationships and the relations of God to men are governed by the principle of solidarity and in the history of redemption it could not be otherwise than that the election of Jacob and the rejection of Esau should have had radical bearing upon their respective progenies. In other words, it would be contrary to the principles that govern history according to the biblical witness to suppose that the election of such a pivotal personage in the history of salvation as Jacob would have any other sequel than the election of Israel as a people. The only question is therefore: is this the exclusive interest of the apostle in this passage? Is the case such that the phrase "the purpose of God according to election" is not applied in this context to the sphere of individual destiny? The following data bear upon this question and supply the answer.

(i) The two components of the phrase should be given the meaning which the usage of Paul determines. There is, first of all, the term "election". Not only the noun but also the verbal forms have to be taken into account. With respect to the noun it is possible that in 11:28 it is used with reference to the election of Israel collectively. This passage as well as 11:5, 7 will be discussed later. In the other one remaining passage in Paul (I Thess. 1:4) it refers unquestionably to election to everlasting life (*cf.* II Pet. 1:10). The term "elect" occurs more frequently and, apart from 16:13 where it is used in a specialized sense but with the implication of elect in the ultimate sense, all the instances[22] refer to particular election to salvation and life (8:33; Col. 3:12; II Tim. 2:10; Tit. 1:1; *cf.* Matt. 22:14; 24:22, 24, 31; Mark 13:20, 22, 27; Luke 18:7; I Pet. 1:1; 2:9; Rev. 17:14). The verb "to elect" occurs infrequently in Paul and probably Ephesians 1:4 is the only directly relevant passage where it refers unmistakably to soteric election (*cf.* Mark 13:20; James 2:5). This application of the term in its various forms to the election unto salvation makes it indefensible to understand it in another sense unless there is a compelling contextual reason. There is, secondly, the term "purpose". This term when used with reference to God uniformly

---

[22] I Tim. 5:21 is not included because it refers to the elect angels.

denotes the determinate will of God (8:28; Eph. 1:11; 3:11; II Tim. 1:9). Thus the whole expression means nothing less than the determinate will of God in election and all that is involved in the expression is confirmed by the verb of which it is the subject, "might stand".

(ii) The thesis that Paul is dealing merely with the election of Israel collectively and applying the clause in question only to this feature of redemptive history would not meet the precise situation. The question posed for the apostle is: how can the covenant promise of God be regarded as inviolate when the mass of those who belong to Israel, who are comprised in the elect nation in terms of the Old Testament passages cited above (Deut. 4:37 *et al.*), have remained in unbelief and come short of the covenant promises? His answer would fail if it were simply an appeal to the collective, inclusive, theocratic election of Israel. Such a reply would be no more than appeal to the fact that his kinsmen were Israelites and thus no more than a statement of the fact which, in view of their unbelief, created the problem. Paul's answer is not the collective election of Israel but rather "they are not all Israel, who are of Israel". And this means, in terms of the stage of discussion at which we have now arrived, "they are not all elect, who are of elect Israel". As we found above, there is the distinction between Israel and the *true* Israel, between children and *true* children, between the seed and the *true* seed. In such a distinction resides Paul's answer to Israel's unbelief. So now the same kind of distinction must be carried through to the problem as it pertains to the collective, theocratic election of Israel. In terms of the debate we are now considering we should have to distinguish between the elect of Israel and elect Israel. The conclusion, therefore, is that when Paul says "the purpose of God according to election" he is speaking of the electing purpose of God in a discriminating, differentiating sense that cannot apply to all who were embraced in the theocratic election. This is to say the clause in question must have a restrictive sense equivalent to "Israel" as distinguished from "of Israel" in verse 6.

(iii) In 11:5, 7 the same term for election is again used: "a remnant according to the election of grace" (11:5); "the election obtained it, and the rest were hardened" (11:7). The apostle is dealing with the remnant of ethnic Israel who had obtained the righteousness of faith. Hence the "remnant" and "the election" are those conceived of as possessors and heirs of salvation. The election, therefore, is one that has saving associations and implications in the strictest sense and must be distinguished from the election that belonged to Israel as a whole. It is this concept of election that accords with the requirements of Paul's argument in 9:11 and its context. Since it appears without question in 11:5, 7, we have this additional confirmation derived from Paul's own usage in the general context to which 9:11 belongs.

(iv) The clause, "not of works, but of him that calleth", is closely related to the clause in question. Whatever may be the precise connection, the two clauses are intended to express correlative ideas. But "calling" in Paul's usage, when the call of God is in view and when applied to the matter of salvation, is the effectual call to salvation (*cf.* 8:30; 9:24; I Cor. 1:9; 7:15; Gal. 1:6, 15; 5:8, 13; Eph. 4:1, 4; Col. 3:15; I Thess. 2:12; 4:7; 5:24; II Thess. 2:14; I Tim. 6:12; II Tim. 1:9).[23] If the Pauline concept of God's call is to govern our exegesis, it must be given in this instance (9:11) the definition that the total evidence requires. This is all the more necessary when it is conjoined with the negative "not of works"; this stresses the freeness and sovereignty as well as efficacy which are in such prominence elsewhere in connection with God's call. Since, therefore, the clause that is correlative with that bearing on election has this strictly soteric import, "the purpose of God according to election" cannot be given any lower significance and understood of election merely to privilege such as Israel as a people enjoyed.

For all these reasons the interpretation which regards the election as the collective, theocratic election of Israel as a people must be rejected and "the purpose of God according to election" will have to be understood as the electing purpose that is determinative of and unto salvation and equivalent to that which we find elsewhere (Rom. 8:28-33; Eph. 1:4; I Thess. 1:4 *et al.*).

The second feature of this passage (vss. 10-13) that needs to be considered is the clause "not of works, but of him that calleth" (vs. 11). The question is that of its relation to what immediately

---

[23] The same is true of κλῆσις and κλητός (*cf.* 1:6, 7; 8:28; I Cor. 1:2, 24, 26; Eph. 1:18; 4:1, 4; Phil. 3:14; II Thess. 1:11; II Tim. 1:9; Heb. 3:1; II Pet. 1:10). Matt. 22:14 apparently refers to the external call of the gospel. Rom. 11:29 is discussed at that point (p. 101).

precedes.[24] It would appear that it may best be taken as an additional characterization of the electing purpose of God and emphasizes or confirms what is intrinsic to the purpose of God, namely, that it does not proceed from nor is it conditioned by the human will but by the determinate will of God (*cf.* Eph. 1:5, 11). In order to express this negatively no formula is more suited than "not of works" and to express it affirmatively no concept is more appropriate than that denoted by calling. The sovereign initiative and agency of God are nowhere more in evidence than in the call. God alone calls and its definition derives no ingredient from human activity. We see, therefore, how congruous is this amplificatory clause with what precedes whether we take it more particularly with "might stand" or, preferably, with the electing purpose.

The third feature of this passage requiring more detailed comment is the appeal to Malachi 1:2, 3 in verse 13: "Jacob I loved, but Esau I hated". There are two questions that arise in the interpretation.

1. Does this apply to the individuals Jacob and Esau or simply to the nations springing from Jacob and Esau? It must be observed that in Malachi 1:1–5 the peoples of Israel and Edom are distinctly in view. The prophecy is introduced as "the burden of the word of the Lord to Israel" (vs. 1) and verses 3–5 clearly refer to the Edomites, to the desolation of their country, and as the people against whom the Lord hath indignation for ever. This collective or ethnic reference is parallel to what we find in connection with the preceding oracle spoken to Rebecca, as noted earlier. Thus there is no doubt that this word as originally spoken had application to the nations of Israel and Edom. It must not be assumed, however, from this patent fact that the question of its relevance to the individuals Jacob and Esau is thereby determined and determined for the most part negatively. Certain considerations must be kept in mind.

(*a*) Although the respective peoples proceeding from Jacob and Esau are in the forefront in Malachi 1:1–5 (*cf.* also Gen. 25:23), yet we may not discount the relevance to Jacob and Esau themselves. Why was there this differentiation between Israel and Edom? It was because there was differentiation between

---

[24] Philippi rightly criticizes what he quotes from Luther to the effect that the clause is to be attached to ἐρρέθη αὐτῇ.

Jacob and Esau. It would be as indefensible to dissociate the fortunes of the respective peoples from the differentiation in the individuals as it would be to dissociate the differentiation of the individuals from the destinies of the nations proceeding from them. So the question cannot be dismissed: what is the character of the differentiation as it affects the individuals, Jacob and Esau?

(*b*) As observed in connection with verse 11, the differentiation which belongs to Israel as a whole in virtue of the theocratic election does not meet the question the apostle encounters in this whole passage, namely, the unbelief of the mass of ethnic Israel. There must be another factor at work which will obviate the inference that the word of God has come to nought. This factor is found in the particularity of election, that is, in a more specific and determinative election than is exemplified in the generic election of Israel as a people. So now, in terms of *love*, the only criterion that will meet the demands of the situation is a more specific love than that exemplified in the love that distinguished Israel as a people from Edom as a people. The conclusion, therefore, must be that in respect of the persons Jacob and Esau Paul pushes his analysis and application of love and hate to their ultimate in order to discover the kind of differentiation that will satisfy the demands of the problem with which he is dealing. As he had done earlier with God's electing purpose so he now does with the love of God for Jacob.[25]

2. The next question is the meaning of the love and hate of which Jacob and Esau are respectively the objects. It has been maintained that the word "hate" means "*to love less, to regard and treat with less favour*".[26] Appeal can be made to various passages where this meaning holds (*cf.* Gen. 29:32, 33; Deut. 21:15; Matt. 6:24; 10:37, 38; Luke 14:26; John 12:25).[27] It would have to be admitted that this meaning would provide for the differentiation which must be posited. Without embarking on the question of God's love for the reprobate, this view would imply that Esau was not the object of that love which God exercised toward Jacob, namely, the specific distinguishing love which alone would account for the differentiation. The text, it must be said, could not mean

---

[25] *Cf. contra*, e.g., Sanday and Headlam: *op. cit., ad* 9:11; F. F. Bruce: *op. cit., ad* 9:12, 13; Philippi: *op. cit., ad* 9:13.
[26] Charles Hodge: *op. cit., ad* 9:13.
[27] Prov. 13:24 is sometimes cited also. But it is questionably relevant.

anything less than this. Esau could not be the object of the love borne to Jacob for, if so, all distinction would be obliterated, and what the text clearly indicates is the radical distinction.

It is, however, questionable if this privative notion adequately expresses the thought in either Hebrew or Greek as it applies to our text. It can readily be suspected that in the original context, as it pertains to the Edomites (Mal. 1:1–5), the mere absence of love or favour hardly explains the visitations of judgment mentioned: "Esau I hated, and made his mountains a desolation, and gave his heritage to the jackals of the wilderness" (vs. 3); "they shall build, but I will throw down; and men shall call them the border of wickedness, and the people against whom the Lord hath indignation for ever" (vs. 4). These judgments surely imply disfavour. The indignation is a positive judgment, not merely the absence of blessing. In Scripture God's wrath involves the positive outflow of his displeasure. What we find in Malachi 1:1–5 is illustrated by instances in the Old Testament where God's hatred is mentioned and where either persons or things are the objects (*cf.* Psalms 5:5; 11:5; Prov. 6:16; 8:13; Isa. 1:14; 61:8; Jer. 44:4; Hos. 9:15; Amos 5:21; Zech. 8:17; Mal. 2:16). The divine reaction stated could scarcely be reduced to that of not loving or loving less. Thus the evidence would require, to say the least, the thought of disfavour, disapprobation, displeasure. There is also a vehement quality that may not be discounted. We must not predicate of this divine hate those unworthy features which belong to hate as it is exercised by us sinful men. In God's hate there is no malice, malignancy, vindictiveness, unholy rancour or bitterness. The kind of hate thus characterized is condemned in Scripture and it would be blasphemy to predicate the same of God. But there is a hate in us that is the expression of holy jealousy for God's honour and of love to him (*cf.* Psalms 26:5; 31:6; 139:21, 22; Jude 23; Rev. 2:6). This hate is the reflection in us of God's jealousy for his own honour. We must, therefore, recognize that there is in God a holy hate that cannot be defined in terms of not loving or loving less. Furthermore, we may not tone down the reality or intensity of this hate by speaking of it as "anthropopathic" or by saying that it "refers not so much to the emotion as to the effect".[28] The case is rather, as in all virtue, that this holy hate in us is patterned after holy hate in God.

[28] Philippi: *op. cit., ad* 9:13.

It is difficult for us to find terms adequately to express this holy hate as it is exercised by us. It is still more difficult to express this hate as it belongs to God. And it is not to be supposed that an appeal to the analogy between our holy hate and that of God resolves for us the precise character of the hate specified in the proposition, "Esau I hated". The hate of verse 13 belongs to the transcendent realm of God's sovereignty for which there is no human analogy. The purpose of appeal to holy hate in us is merely for the purpose of showing that even in us men there is a hate that is entirely distinct from malicious and vindictive hatred. It is in this direction that we are to construe God's hate and we may not tone it down to a negative or comparative notion.

On the basis of biblical patterns of thought and usage, therefore, the statement "Esau I hated" is not satisfactorily interpreted as meaning simply "not loved" or "loved less" but in the sense that an attitude of positive disfavour is expressed thereby. Esau was not merely excluded from what Jacob enjoyed but was the object of a displeasure which love would have excluded and of which Jacob was not the object because he was loved. This quotation by Paul from Malachi 1:2, 3 is for the purpose of elucidating or confirming what had just been quoted from Genesis 25:23. It must, therefore, be construed as having relevance to the same situation as that to which the oracle to Rebecca applies. Since the oracle points to a discrimination that existed before the children were born or had done good or evil (vs. 11), so must the differentiation in the present instance. Thus the definitive actions denoted by "loved" and "hated"[29] are represented as actuated not by any character differences in the two children but solely by the sovereign will of God, "the purpose of God according to election" (vs. 11). In accord with what we have found above, however, respecting biblical usage it must be interpreted as hate with the positive character which usage indicates, a hate as determinative as the unfailing purpose in terms of which the discrimination between Jacob and Esau took place. In view of what Paul teaches elsewhere respecting the ultimacy of the counsel of God's will, it would not be proper to say that the ultimate destinies of Jacob and Esau were outside his purview. Besides, in this passage (vss. 6–13) the apostle is making the distinction between the *true* Israel and Israel after

---

[29] The aorists are to be noted.

the flesh, between *true* children and children by descent, between the *true* seed and the natural seed. He is doing this to show that the covenant promise of God has not failed. The promise comes to fruition in the *true* Israel, in the remnant according to the election of grace. It would nullify the whole argument and interest of the passage to suppose that the *true* Israel, the *true* seed, are not conceived of as partakers of the promise in the fullest soteric sense. The appeal to the electing purpose of God, to the oracle spoken to Rebecca in pursuance of that purpose, and to the word "Jacob I loved, but Esau I hated" is for the purpose of confirming this same distinction between those who are partakers of the promise and those who are not. To suppose that the final word of differentiation in this passage is not intended to bear out the distinction between salvation and the coming short of the same is to suppose something that would make this word irrelevant to the apostle's thesis. We are compelled, therefore, to find in this word a declaration of the sovereign counsel of God as it is concerned with the ultimate destinies of men.

9:14–18

14 What shall we say then? Is there unrighteousness with God? God forbid.
15 For he saith to Moses, I will have mercy on whom I have mercy, and I will have compassion on whom I have compassion.
16 So then it is not of him that willeth, nor of him that runneth, but of God that hath mercy.
17 For the scripture saith unto Pharaoh, For this very purpose did I raise thee up, that I might show in thee my power, and that my name might be published abroad in all the earth.
18 So then he hath mercy on whom he will, and whom he will he hardeneth.

14–16 In verses 6–13 Paul's argument is that God's faithfulness to his covenant is not to be judged by the extent to which those physically descended from Abraham are partakers of salvation. God's faithfulness is vindicated by the fact that the covenant promise contemplates those who had been sovereignly chosen by God to be possessors and heirs of his covenant grace. The purpose of God according to election stands firm and this insures that the covenant promise has not come to nought. The word of God has not failed. So these verses are a vindication of God's veracity. At verse 14 the apostle deals with another objection that is anticipated or that might be urged. It is the question of the justice of God. The two questions asked are similar to those of 3:5. The form of the second question is in this case different and points up the ultimate and decisive question of justice. "Is there unrighteousness with God?"[30] A negative answer is implied and Paul answers with the strongest form of denial at his disposal.[31] The thought of injustice with God is so intolerable that it must be dismissed with abrupt and decisive denial. Verse 15 is an appeal to Scripture in support of "God forbid". As illustrating Paul's conception of the place of Scripture it is significant that in answering so basic a question as that of God's justice he should be content to adduce the witness of Scripture. He quotes from Exodus 33:19.[32] This is God's answer to Moses' request, "Show me, I pray thee, thy glory" (Exod. 33:18) but, perhaps of greater relevance, to the anxiety of Moses expressed in verses 13–16 that he should find favour in God's sight and that God's presence would prove that Israel were God's people separated from all other people upon the face of the earth. Although Paul quotes this word without in any way restricting its application to the question at issue, the force is increased when we take into account the particular occasion on which it was spoken. The favour shown to Moses is hereby certified to proceed from God's sovereign mercy. Even Moses and with him God's people can lay no claim to any favour; it is altogether a matter of God's free choice and bestowment.

It is not necessary to press the distinction between the two terms "have mercy" and "have compassion". There are two emphases in the text. The first is the reality, security, and effectiveness of God's mercy. This is accented by the two parallel clauses, the one expressing his favour in terms of mercy, the other in terms of compassion. The second emphasis is primary. It is not so well expressed in English unless we render "on whom" as "on whomsoever", accentuating God's free and sovereign choice.[33]

---

[30] The form παρὰ τῷ θεῷ emphasizes the blasphemy of the suggestion.
[31] On the negative μὴ γένοιτο see comments on 3:4, 6 (Vol. I, pp. 93f., 97).
[32] With a slight difference of spelling in the verb οἰκτίρω the question is verbatim as in the LXX.
[33] The emphasis is upon the ὃν ἄν.

In this context we may not tone down the soteric import. This is Paul's answer to the question of justice that arises from the sovereign discrimination on God's part on which Paul had based his argument in verses 6–13. This differentiation, as shown above, is concerned with the realization of God's covenant promise in those who are the beneficiaries of the election of grace. If lesser import were given to the mercy and compassion of God, the apostle's answer would fall short of the question with which he is dealing.

The all-important aspect of verse 15 is that in support of the "God forbid" of verse 14 the mercy of God is not a matter of justice to those who are partakers of it but altogether of free and sovereign grace. This is true whether the mercy be viewed as the theocratic election of Israel to covenant privileges or, in terms of what is the apostle's particular interest, as the mercy that is unto salvation. Justice presupposes rightful claims, and mercy can be operative only where no claim of justice exists. Since mercy alone is the constraining consideration, the only explanation is God's free and sovereign determination. He has mercy as he pleases. This is the emphasis of Exodus 33:19 and to this Paul makes his definitive appeal. Back of this thesis is the polemic of the apostle in the earlier part of the epistle for the principle of grace.

Verse 16 can be regarded as the inference drawn from the Scripture quoted in verse 15 but it is preferably regarded as a statement of what is involved in the truth just asserted. The relation would then be as follows: if God has mercy on whomsoever he wills, "then it is not of him that willeth, nor of him that runneth, but of God that hath mercy". The emphasis falls here on the exclusion of man's determination as the negative counterpart to God's exercise of mercy. The first negation refers to human volition, the determination belonging to man's will; the second refers to man's active exertion (*cf.* I Cor. 9:24, 26; Gal. 2:2; 5:7; Heb. 12:1). The mercy of God is not an attainment gained by the most diligent labour to that end but a free bestowal of grace. No statement could be more antithetic to what accrues from claims of justice or as the awards of labour.

17, 18 Here another proof from Scripture is introduced. The most distinctive feature of this passage is that it expressly mentions the opposite of mercy. Verses 15, 16 had referred only to the exercise of mercy. If all men were the recipients of this mercy there would be no interference with the sovereignty of its exercise. It would have been of God's free choice that he determined to make all men its beneficiaries. We could not but think, however, of differentiation in the bestowal of mercy in such a context as this because it is with such the apostle is dealing. So in this second appeal to Scripture the negative of mercy is expressly stated—"whom he will he hardeneth" (vs. 18). The sovereignty of which the apostle is speaking is, therefore, not an abstract sovereignty but that which was concretely exemplified in the history connected with Moses in the twofold exercise of this determinative will of God, "he hath mercy on whom he will, and whom he will he hardeneth". In view of the sustained emphasis on the free, sovereign will of God we must recognize that this sovereignty is just as inviolate in the hardening as it is in showing mercy. Otherwise the relevance to the subject in hand would be impaired. This is but another way of saying that the sovereignty of God is ultimate in both cases and as ultimate in the negative as in the positive.

The way in which the instance of Pharaoh is introduced is again significant for the apostle's use of Scripture. The words quoted are the word of God spoken to Pharaoh through Moses. But here the formula is not "he saith", as in verse 15, but "the scripture saith", indicating that this has the same effect as "God saith".

The word quoted (Exod. 9:16) is that spoken through Moses after the sixth plague, that of boils upon man and beast. In view of the preceding verse (Exod. 9:15), the verse quoted could be understood of the preservation of Pharaoh from being cut off from the earth in that particular instance by the pestilence of boils. But the term that Paul uses here, "raise up",[34] is one that is used in the Greek Old Testament in the sense of raising up on the scene of history for a particular purpose (*cf.* Numb. 24:19; II Sam. 12:11; Job 5:11; Hab. 1:6; Zech. 11:16). So, with many commentators, the quotation is best taken here as referring to the position Pharaoh occupied by the providence of God on the scene of history and to the role he played in connection with the redemption of Israel from Egypt. The adamant opposition of

---

[34] The verb ἐξεγείρω used by Paul differs from the LXX and is closer to the Hebrew "caused thee to stand".

Pharaoh became the occasion for the display of God's great power in the plagues visited upon Egypt and particularly in the distruction of Pharaoh's hosts in the Red Sea and the passage of Israel as on dry land. That God's name was thus published abroad in all the earth is abundantly verified and this signal manifestation of his power is the theme of Scripture elsewhere (*cf.* Exod. 15:13–16; Josh. 2:9, 10; 9:9; Psalms 78:12, 13; 105:26–38; 106:9–11; 136:10–15).

In verse 18 we have the same kind of explicatory conclusion as we found in verse 16: "So then he hath mercy on whom he will". This is to the same effect as verse 15 in its emphasis upon God's sovereignty in the exercise of his mercy. But there is the new feature in this case, that the sovereign and determinative *will* of God is mentioned and bears the emphasis. Like verse 15 it is a statement that has general application to God's exercise of mercy; whoever is the recipient of mercy owes this favour to God's sovereign will. The main question in this verse is the kind of action implied in the words "whom he will he hardeneth". Like verse 15 and the first part of verse 18 this is a statement with general application to every case that falls into this category. But since this verse is an inference from verse 17 or, preferably, an explication of what is involved in the providence of God referred to in verse 17, we must regard Pharaoh as an example and the example particularly in view. As Moses, in this context, exemplifies mercy, so Pharaoh hardening. Furthermore, since the hardening of Pharaoh's heart is so frequently mentioned in the general context from which verse 17 is taken, there can be no doubt but Pharaoh's hardening is in view. What then is this hardening?

The harshness of the term could be relieved by the view that God is said to do what he permitted. God allowed Pharaoh to harden his own heart but the action of hardening was Pharaoh's own. Analogy could be appealed to in support of such an interpretation (*cf.* II Sam. 12:11; 16:10; Psalm 105:25). As Hodge says, "from these and similar passages, it is evident that it is a familiar scriptural usage, to ascribe to God effects which he allows in his wisdom to come to pass".[35]

There can be no question but Pharaoh hardened his own heart. Although the instances are comparatively few in which the activity

[35] *Op. cit., ad loc.*

of Pharaoh is expressly mentioned (*cf.* 7:13; 8:32(28); 9:34), yet they are sufficient. But, preponderantly, the terms are to the effect that the Lord hardened Pharaoh's heart (*cf.* Exod. 4:21; 7:3; 9:12; 10:1, 20, 27; 11:10; 14:4, 8). The term used by Paul is the same term as occurs in each of these latter instances in the Greek Old Testament.[36] With this sustained emphasis on the Lord's action it would not be proper to dismiss the interpretation that God did harden Pharaoh's heart unless there were compelling biblical grounds to the contrary. A contextual consideration and the teaching of Paul earlier in this epistle constrain the conclusion that God's action is in view. The text is concerned with the sovereignly determinative will and action of God. This is patent in connection with his mercy: "he hath mercy on whom he will". The determinative will comes to effect in the act of having mercy. These same emphases must be carried over to the hardening: "whom he will he hardeneth". The parallel must be maintained; determinative will comes to effect in the act of hardening. Furthermore, Paul had prepared us for such a conception by his teaching in 1:24, 26, 28 where he deals with judicial abandonment to lust, to the passions of dishonour, and to a reprobate mind (*cf.* comments on these verses). Thus a positive infliction on God's part is the only interpretation that fits the various considerations.

The hardening, it should be remembered, is of a judicial character. It presupposes ill-desert and, in the case of Pharaoh, particularly the ill-desert of his self-hardening. Hardening may never be abstracted from the guilt of which it is the wages. It might appear that the judicial character of hardening interferes with the sovereign will of God upon which the accent falls in this text. It would be sufficient to say that this cannot be the case in the counsel with which the apostle is dealing. It is impossible to suppress or tone down the sovereign determination of God's will any more than in the first part of the verse, as noted earlier. But it should also be observed that the sin and ill-desert presupposed in hardening is also presupposed in the exercise of mercy. Both parts of this verse rest upon the premise of ill-desert. Indeed, the whole argument of the apostle in this section in refutation of the objection that there is unrighteousness with God (vs. 14) is conducted on the premise that salvation is not constrained by the

---

[36] σκληρύνω.

dictates of justice, that it proceeds entirely from the exercise of sovereign mercy, that God has mercy on whomsoever he wills. The differentiation, therefore, overtly expressed in verse 18, is altogether of God's sovereign will and determination. In reference to the judicial act of hardening the sovereignty consists in the fact that all, because of the sin and ill-desert presupposed in mercy as well as in final judgment, deserve to be hardened and that irretrievably. Sovereignty pure and simple is the only reason for the differentiation by which some are consigned to hardening while others equally ill-deserving are made the vessels of mercy. There is thus no escape from sovereignty in the will to harden or in the action which brings this will to effect. Hence Paul can say without any more reserve than in the case of mercy, "whom he will he hardeneth".

9:19-26

19 Thou wilt say then unto me, Why doth he still find fault? For who withstandeth his will?
20 Nay but, O man, who art thou that repliest against God? Shall the thing formed say to him that formed it, Why didst thou make me thus?
21 Or hath not the potter a right over the clay, from the same lump to make one part a vessel unto honor, and another unto dishonor?
22 What if God, willing to show his wrath, and to make his power known, endured with much longsuffering vessels of wrath fitted unto destruction:
23 and that he might make known the riches of his glory upon vessels of mercy, which he afore prepared unto glory,
24 *even* us, whom he also called, not from the Jews only, but also from the Gentiles?
25 As he saith also in Hosea,
I will call that my people, which was not my people; And her beloved, that was not beloved.
26 And it shall be, *that* in the place where it was said unto them, Ye are not my people,
There shall they be called sons of the living God.

The objection here is one that arises from the assertion at the end of verse 18 that God hardens whom he will. If God determinatively wills to harden men and puts that will into effect, how can

9:6-33 GOD'S FAITHFULNESS AND RIGHTEOUSNESS VINDICATED

those subjected to this hardening be condemned? Are they not in that state by the will of God? This question is reinforced by the consideration that no one can frustrate this will of God. The will of which Paul is speaking in the preceding context and which the objector has in view is not the will of precept but the will of determinate purpose. The way in which the objection, as it pertains to the irresistibility of this will, is stated should be noted. We might expect the question to be: who *can* resist his will? But the tense used has the force of a present condition and is properly rendered: "who withstandeth his will?" The objector implies that in the premises of the apostle's teaching there is no one who has placed himself in the position of withstanding God's will. It is not necessary to particularize the objector as Philippi does and say that Paul is "thinking of an arrogant Jew, such as alone he has to do with in the whole of the present exposition".[37] The objection is the common one, inevitably encountered when dealing with reprobation. How can God blame us when we are the victims of his irresistible decree?

20 The answer is the appeal to the reverential silence which the majesty of God demands of us. The eloquence of the contrast between "O man" and "God" must be observed. On this contrast the other emphases rest. The conjunction rendered "nay but" (*cf.* 10:18; Luke 11:28; Phil. 3:8) in this instance serves to correct the self-vindication implied in the preceding questions. Based on the contrast between man in his weakness and ignorance and God in his majesty the emphasis falls on *thou*: who art *thou?* And then the presumption of man's attitude appears in the arrogance of replying against God. The method of answering the objection is similar to what we found earlier in 3:6. There Paul's appeal was to the universal judgment as an ultimate datum of revelation. When we are dealing with ultimate facts categorical affirmation must content us. So here, when dealing with the determinate will of God, we have an ultimate on which we may not interrogate him nor speak back when he has uttered his verdict. Who are *we* to dispute his government?

The apostle's answer is significant not only as illustrating his method and the assumptions upon which this method is based but

---
[37] *Op. cit., ad loc.*

also for what he does not say. If, in the matter concerned, the determinative will of God were not ultimate, if the differentiation of verse 18 were not due solely to God's sovereign will, then the apostle would have to deny the assumption on which the objection is based. This he does not do. In Calvin's words: "Why, then, did he not make use of this short answer, but assign the highest place to the will of God, so that it alone should be sufficient for us, rather than any other cause? If the objection that God reprobates or elects according to His will those whom He does not honour with His favour, or towards whom He shows unmerited love—if this objection had been false, Paul would not have omitted to refute it."[38]

The latter part of verse 20 goes more conveniently with verse 21.

21 The thought here is the reproduction of what we find repeatedly in the Old Testament (*cf.* Isa. 29:15, 16; 45:9; 64:8, 9; Jer. 18:1–6). God's sovereign right, pleaded here after the pattern of the potter's right over the clay, belongs to God as Creator in the disposal of his creatures as creatures. It must be borne in mind, however, that Paul is not now dealing with God's sovereign rights over men as men but over men as sinners. He is answering the objection occasioned by the sovereign discrimination stated in verse 18 in reference to mercy and hardening. These, it must be repeated, presuppose sin and ill-desert. It would be exegetically indefensible to abstract verse 21 and its teaching from these presupposed conditions. In other words, Paul is dealing with God's actual government and with the sovereign determinations of his will actualized in this government. The same is true of the Old Testament passages of which verse 21 is reminiscent. Suffice it to refer to Isaiah 64:7, 9 which supplies the context of verse 8.

The similitude is that of the potter making vessels of different character from the same lump of kneaded clay, one to serve a high purpose, another a purpose less noble. No one questions his right to make these distinctions. He has not merely the power; he has the *authority*. There is no warrant for the interpretation or objection that Paul represents God as esteeming mankind as clay and dealing with men accordingly. He is using an analogy and the

---

[38] *Op. cit., ad loc.*

meaning is simply that, in the realm of his government, God has the intrinsic right to deal with men as the potter, in the sphere of his occupation, deals with clay. But the kind of differentiation is as great as is the difference between God and the potter, on the one hand, and between men and clay, on the other.

22-24 These verses are an unfinished sentence (*cf.* Luke 19:42; John 6:62; Acts 23:9). Literally the Greek terms are "but if" and their force is properly rendered by "what if", as in the version, or, as Sanday and Headlam observe, "like our English idiom 'what and if'".[39] Understood thus the three verses are an expansion and application of what underlies the analogy appealed to in verses 20b, 21. If God in the exercise of his sovereign right makes some vessels of wrath and others vessels of mercy what have we to say? It is a rhetorical way of reiterating the question of verse 20.

The interpretation of these verses may more suitably be discussed in the order of the following details.

1. "Vessels of wrath" and "vessels of mercy" are best regarded in terms of verse 21. The potter makes vessels for certain purposes. So here the vessels are *for* wrath and mercy.[40] It is true that they are vessels deserving wrath but this cannot apply in respect of mercy to the vessels of mercy. Hence both should be taken in a sense that can apply to both. This view is to the same effect as that of Calvin who says that vessels are to be taken in a general sense to mean instruments and therefore instruments for the exhibition of God's mercy and the display of his judgment.[41]

2. The participle "willing" has been interpreted in two ways: "because willing" or "although willing". In the former case the thought would be that because God wishes to give more illustrious display of his wrath and power he exercises his longsuffering. In the latter case the meaning would be: although God wills to

---

[39] *Op. cit., ad loc.*
[40] δέ at the beginning of verse 22 is transitional, not adversative. As Godet says it is "the transition from the figure to the application" (*op. cit., ad loc.*). *Cf. contra* Sanday and Headlam: *op. cit., ad loc.*
[41] *Op. cit., ad loc.*; *cf. contra* Sanday and Headlam who maintain that "'destined for God's anger' would require σκεύη εἰς ὀργήν: and the change of construction from the previous verse must be intentional" (*ibid.*). This is not necessary. "Vessels of mercy" corresponds to εἰς τιμήν and "vessels of wrath" to εἰς ἀτιμίαν.

execute his wrath he nevertheless restrains and postpones the execution from the constraint of longsuffering. In the one case longsuffering serves the purpose of effective display of wrath and power, in the other case longsuffering inhibits the execution of the just desert. In favour of the latter it could be said that according to 2:4 God's longsuffering is a manifestation of the goodness of God directed to repentance and could hardly be represented as the means of promoting the demonstration of God's wrath. Before reaching a decision on this question other considerations bearing on the interpretation of verses 22, 23 have to be taken into account.

3. The governing thought of these verses, as of the preceding, is the twofold way in which the sovereign will of God comes to expression. This is apparent from several considerations but from none more than from the two designations, "vessels of wrath" and "vessels of mercy". This same emphasis upon God's determinative will must be present in the word "willing" at the beginning of verse 22. It harks back to verse 18 and also to the term "will"[42] in verse 19. So "willing" is not simply wishing but determining.

4. It would not be proper to suppress the parallel[43] between "to show his wrath, and to make his power known" (vs. 22) and "that I might show in thee my power" (vs. 17). There is surely reminiscence of the latter in the former. Hence what God did in the case of Pharaoh illustrates what is more broadly applied to vessels of wrath in verse 21. Pharaoh was raised up and hardened, in the sense explained above, for the purpose of demonstrating God's power and publishing his name in all the earth. If we interject the term "forbearance", we must say it was exercised in this case in order that God's great power might be displayed. From this consideration, namely, that of the parallel, there appears to be a compelling reason to subordinate the longsuffering of verse 22 to the purpose of showing his wrath and making his power known. If we bear in mind the determinate purpose of God upon which the accent falls and that those embraced in this purpose are vessels of wrath and therefore viewed as deserving of wrath to the uttermost, the "much longsuffering" exercised towards them is not deprived of its real character as such. It is only because God is forbearing that he delays the infliction of the full measure of ill-

---

[42] βούλημα refers to determinate purpose in verse 19.
[43] *Cf.* Lagrange: *op. cit., ad* 9:22.

desert. Furthermore, the apostle has in view the unbelief of Israel and the longsuffering with which God endures their unbelief. He is reminding his unbelieving kinsmen that God's longsuffering is not the certificate of God's favour but that, awful though it be, it only ministers in the case of those who are the vessels of wrath to the more manifest exhibition of their ill-desert in the infliction of God's wrath and the making known of his power. In the light of these considerations the participle "willing" (vs. 22a) can and should preferably be understood in the sense "because willing" rather than "although willing". The total thrust of the context indicates the subordination which the former alternative implies.

5. The "willing" (vs. 22), as indicated already, has a twofold reference. The first is "to show his wrath, and to make his power known". The second is "that he might make known the riches of his glory upon vessels of mercy" (vs. 23).[44] This is parallel to other expressions earlier in this chapter, especially to verses 16b, 18a. But no expression used hitherto is of comparable richness. The same term is used for making known as is used in verse 22 for making known his power upon vessels of wrath. Yet there is an eloquent contrast in respect of what is made known. Now it is "the riches of his glory". God's glory is the sum of his perfections and "the riches" refer to the splendour and fulness characterizing these perfections. It is to be borne in mind that in the bestowal of mercy there is no prejudice to any of God's attributes. But it is not this negative that bears the emphasis. It is that the perfections are magnified in the work of mercy and in no action is there so effulgent an exhibition of God's glory (*cf.* Psalm 85:9–11; Rom. 11:33; Eph. 1:7, 12, 14; 2:4, 7; 3:8, 16; Col. 1:27; I Tim. 1:11). Glory in this instance is not to be identified with the glory mentioned at the end of verse 23. The latter is the glory bestowed, the former the glory of God manifested. The correlation, however, is noteworthy. The grandeur of believers' bliss will consist in the fact that therein the richness of God's glory will be manifest and it would fall short of "glory" if this were not the case.

---

[44] There is no good reason for opposing this construction. καὶ ἵνα has this force in Greek, especially after such verbs as willing. *Cf.* William F. Arndt and F. Wilbur Gingrich: *A Greek-English Lexicon of the New Testament and Other Early Christian Literature* (Chicago, 1957), *ad* ἵνα, II, 1, a. The change from the infinitive γνωρίσαι (vs. 22) to ἵνα γνωρίσῃ (vs. 23) is, therefore, no obstacle.

6. The vessels of wrath are "fitted unto destruction". The question disputed is whether they are represented as fitted or prepared by God for destruction or whether they are viewed as fitting themselves for destruction. It is true that Paul does not say that God prepared them for destruction as he does in the corresponding words respecting the vessels of mercy that "he afore prepared" them unto glory. It may be that he purposely refrained from making God the subject. However, we may not insist that God is not viewed as fitting them for destruction. In verse 18 there is the agency of God in hardening. In verses 22, 23 the analogy of verse 21 is being applied and the vessels of wrath correspond to the potter's vessel unto dishonour which he prepares for this purpose. They are also vessels of wrath and, therefore, as observed above, vessels for wrath, and wrath corresponds to destruction. For these reasons there is nothing contrary to the teaching of the context if we regard God as the agent in fitting for destruction. At the same time we may not dogmatize that the apostle intended to convey this notion in this case. The main thought is that the destruction meted out to the vessels of wrath is something for which their precedent condition suits them. There is an exact correspondence between what they were in this life and the perdition to which they are consigned. This is another way of saying that there is continuity between this life and the lot of the life to come. In the general context of the apostle's thought there is no release from human responsibility nor from the guilt of which perdition is the wages.

7. The vessels of mercy God "afore prepared unto glory". In this case there is no question as to the agent. The vessels of wrath can be said to fit themselves for destruction; they are the agents of the demerit which reaps destruction. But only God prepares for glory. The figure of the potter is applied without reserve; vessels unto honour correspond to vessels prepared unto glory. The "afore prepared" points to the parallel truth indicated in "fitted unto destruction" that there is continuity between the process of operative grace in this life and the glory ultimately achieved. The glory meted out is something for which the precedent state and condition prepared the vessels of mercy (*cf.* II Tim. 2:20, 21).

8. Verse 24 must be understood in the light of the differentiation which permeates this whole passage from verse 6 onwards. This differentiation is the answer to the objection that the word of God

might appear to have come to nought. It is the differentiation which the purpose of God according to election causes to be, exemplified in "Jacob I loved, but Esau I hated", vindicated in God's sovereign prerogative to have mercy on whom he will and to discriminate between vessels of wrath and vessels of mercy. Since the apostle is not thinking abstractly nor dealing merely with the past, he brings this to bear upon the concrete situation which he encounters and upon the way in which God's sovereign will unto salvation is realized in the present. So he says "even us, whom he also called, not from the Jews only, but also from the Gentiles". This is the conclusion to what in English has been rendered as a question (vss. 22–24) with the implied answer that we have no reply against God (*cf.* vs. 20). Paul applies what he had said respecting vessels of mercy prepared beforehand unto glory to actual experience in his own case and that of others. He finds in the call of Jews and Gentiles the illustration of God's working grace.

Although in verses 22, 23 there is not direct reference to the decretive foreordination of God in the expressions "fitted unto destruction" and "afore prepared unto glory", it is not possible to dissociate verse 24 from the earlier passage in which calling is given its locus in relation to predestination (8:28–30). Never in Paul is calling anything else than according to purpose and, therefore, the mention of calling in this passage harks back to the sovereign will and purpose of God repeatedly appealed to in the preceding verses. Thus the predestinarian background cannot be denied.

Calling here has the same meaning as elsewhere, the effectual call to salvation (1:7; 8:28, 30; I Cor. 1:9; Gal. 1:15; II Tim. 1:9). It is neither necessary nor proper to think that the preparation mentioned in verse 23 preceded the actual call.[45] The call would rather be the inception of the preparatory process.

The reference to both Jews and Gentiles is all-important. That there should be the called from Jewry belongs to the argument of the passage as a whole. The covenant promise has not failed but comes to effect in the *true* Israel, the *true* children, the *true* seed (*cf.* vss. 6–9, 27, 29; 11:5, 7). This is expressed in the words "not from the Jews only". The form, however, signifies that the covenant

---

[45] *Cf. contra* E. H. Gifford: *The Epistle of St. Paul to the Romans* (London, 1886), *ad* 9:24 who says: "We here see that the preparation mentioned in v. 23 preceded the actual call".

promise and the electing grace of God have broader scope than Jewry. So "but also from the Gentiles" is added. In 4:12–17 the interest of the apostle differs from that of the present passage. There the polemic is focused upon justification by faith in opposition to works; here the interest is the fulfilment of the covenant promise. But there is a close relationship between the two passages, as may be seen particularly from 4:16. Basic in Paul's thought is the promise given to Abraham that in his seed *all the families of the earth* would be blessed.

25, 26 These verses are an appeal to Old Testament passages in confirmation of the call of the Gentiles, drawn from Hosea 2:23; 1:10.[46] There might appear to be a discrepancy between the purport and reference of these passages in the prophecy and as applied by Paul. In Hosea they refer to the tribes of Israel and not to the Gentile nations. There should be no difficulty. Paul recognizes that the rejection and restoration of Israel of which Hosea spoke have their parallel in the exclusion of the Gentiles from God's covenant favour and then their reception into that favour. Of Israel it had been said "Lo-ruhamah; for I will no more have mercy upon the house of Israel" (Hos. 1:6). But this is not the final word. God will again betroth in lovingkindness and "in the place where it was said unto them, Ye are not my people, it shall be said unto them, Ye are the sons of the living God" (Hos. 1:10). So it is with the Gentiles, once forsaken of God but later embraced in covenant love and favour. The same procedure is exemplified in both cases and Paul finds in the restoration of Israel to love and favour the type in terms of which the Gentiles become partakers of the same grace.[47] "In the place where" (vs. 26) may best be taken as referring in Paul's application to "every place, where the people had been regarded as aliens, they

---

[46] Verse 26 is a verbatim quotation of the LXX and with the exception of ἐκεῖ, which nevertheless is implied, is a literal rendering of the Hebrew (Hos. 2:1 in both Hebrew and LXX). But verse 25 does not exactly correspond to the Hebrew or LXX of Hosea 2:23. The LXX is a rather close rendering of the Hebrew which in translation reads: "And I will sow her to me in the earth, and I will have mercy upon her who had not obtained mercy, and I will say to them who were not my people, Thou art my people, and he will say, Thou art my God". Paul has retained the thought but has adapted the actual terms. It may be that the reason is to assimilate the thought of Hosea 2:23 more closely to the terms of Hosea 1:10 which is quoted verbatim in verse 26.

[47] *Cf.* Meyer, Hodge, Sanday and Headlam: *op. cit., ad* 9:25.

9:6–33 GOD'S FAITHFULNESS AND RIGHTEOUSNESS VINDICATED

should be called the children of God".[48] Thus "the utterance *of God* ... is conceived, in the plastic spirit of poetry, as *resounding in all Gentile lands*".[49] "I will call" in this case should be understood not precisely in the sense of "called"in verse 24 but as "named". It is the new denomination that is expressed and the significance resides in the designation "my people" (*cf.* Numb. 6:27). The various designations, "my people", "beloved", "sons of the living God" express differing aspects of the new relationship and, correlative with the effectual call (vs. 24), are all soteric in their import.

9:27–33

27 And Isaiah crieth concerning Israel, If the number of the children of Israel be as the sand of the sea, it is the remnant that shall be saved:
28 for the Lord will execute *his* word upon the earth, finishing it and cutting it short.
29 And, as Isaiah hath said before,
Except the Lord of Sabaoth had left us a seed, We had become as Sodom, and had been made like unto Gomorrah.
30 What shall we say then? That the Gentiles, who followed not after righteousness, attained to righteousness, even the righteousness which is of faith:
31 but Israel, following after a law of righteousness, did not arrive at *that* law.
32 Wherefore? Because *they sought it* not by faith, but as it were by works. They stumbled at the stone of stumbling;
33 even as it is written,
Behold, I lay in Zion a stone of stumbling and a rock of offence:
And he that believeth on him shall not be put to shame.

27–29 In the two preceding verses the call of the Gentiles had been supported by and represented as the fulfilment of Old Testament promises. In these three verses the Isaianic witness is adduced to confirm Paul's thesis that the covenant promise did not contemplate or guarantee the salvation of all ethnic Irsael.

---

[48] Hodge: *op. cit., ad* 9:26.
[49] Meyer: *op. cit., ad* 9:26.

This is the proposition with which Paul began: "they are not all Israel, that are of Israel" (vs. 6). It is the thesis implicit in the statement of verse 24, "not from the Jews only". If all Jews were *ipso facto* heirs of the promise, this *form* of statement, identical with "also of the Gentiles" and coordinate with it, could not be used. The apostle is showing now from the Old Testament that prophecy itself had spoken of the remnant and of the seed as those to whom salvation belonged and apart from whom the nation would have suffered the destruction of Sodom.

Verses 27, 28 are taken from Isaiah 10:22, 23.[50] This passage occurs in the context of the Lord's indignation executed upon Israel through the instrumentality of Assyria as the rod of God's anger and the staff of his indignation (*cf.* Isa. 10:5). From the desolation only a remnant of Israel would escape. This is spoken of as the return of "the remnant of Jacob, unto the mighty God" (vs. 21). Paul's quotation follows the Greek version with some modification and contraction. In verse 22 he changes "the people of Israel" to "the number of the children of Israel" and verse 23 he condenses. These adaptations do not interfere with the sense. In all cases, as Philippi says, "the fundamental thought is still this, that in the destruction of Israel and the salvation merely of a holy remnant, a divine judicial punishment is carried out".[51] Here again Paul finds in escape from the Assyrian conquest an example of God's government of Israel as it applies to the actual situation with which he is dealing. This scripture demonstrates that God's promises do not pertain to the mass of Israel but are fulfilled in the remnant.

The main thought of verse 28[52] is the efficacy with which God accomplishes his word and the decree of which the word is the utterance. It is the emphasis of Isaiah 14:24: "Surely as I have thought, so shall it come to pass; and as I have purposed, so shall it stand". "Finishing it" refers to accomplishment, "cutting it short" to the expeditious despatch with which the accomplishment takes place. The reference in Isaiah 10:22b, 23 is to the thorough-

---

[50] "His description of Isaiah as *exclaiming*, and not speaking, is deliberately intended to arouse greater attention" (Calvin: *op. cit., ad loc.*).
[51] *Op. cit., ad loc.*
[52] The addition after συντέμνων of the words ἐν δικαιοσύνῃ ὅτι λόγον συντετμημένον found in D G and some versions and in the textus receptus is not supported by P⁴⁶, ℵ, A, B, 1739 and some others. These words are found in these identical terms in the LXX of Isaiah 10:23.

9:6-33 GOD'S FAITHFULNESS AND RIGHTEOUSNESS VINDICATED

ness and the despatch with which God's punitive judgment will be executed. Also, so widespread will be the destruction that only a remnant will escape. This same emphasis should be understood in the apostle's quotation. The salvation of the remnant and the significance of the remnant are thrown into bold relief by the dark background of judgment with which this salvation is contrasted (*cf.* Amos 3:12).

Verse 29 is quoted from Isaiah 1:9 and adheres to the Greek version without modification. The only difference from the Hebrew is that "a little remnant" is rendered "a seed" in the Greek. In Paul's teaching here "seed" and "remnant" have the same denotation. "Seed", occurring here for the first time after verse 8, points back to that same meaning, namely, the seed who are partakers of the promise. The reference to the remnant is to the same effect as in verse 27 but the accent of the two verses differs. In verse 27 it is that only a remnant will be saved, in verse 29 that the remnant is the preserving seed apart from which the nation would have been given up to utter destruction. Both verses are closely related to the thought of verse 28. That only a remnant is saved points up the severity and extent of the judgment executed. That a remnant is saved is the evidence of the Lord's favour and the guarantee that his covenant promise has not failed. It should be noted that it is by God's gracious action that a seed is maintained: "except the Lord of Sabaoth had left us a seed". In accord with the sustained stress upon the sovereign will and determinate purpose of God in the preceding context the same is still applied to the reservation of a remnant and the preserving of a seed.[53]

30-33 In verses 6-13 the apostle showed that the unbelief and rejection of ethnic Israel as a whole did not invalidate God's covenant promise; the promise had respect to and was realized in the election of grace. In verses 14-18 he had vindicated this procedure by appeal to the sovereignty of God's mercy. In verses 19-29 he had answered the objection that God's sovereign determinations relieved men of responsibility and blame. This

---

[53] The verb ἐγκαταλείπω and the substantive ὑπόλειμμα express similar ideas and the latter is the result of God's action in the former.

section closes with proof that the Old Testament itself and the plan of God disclosed therein had in view only a remnant as the partakers of salvation. This remnant, spoken of also as the seed, brings us back to verse 8. Thus a unity of conception ties all these verses (vss. 6–29) together and the paramount consideration pleaded by the apostle is the differentiation which God in the exercise of his sovereign will determines, a differentiation also which insures that his covenant promise never falls to the ground. The electing purpose stands fast; there is the remnant according to the election of grace.

In verses 30–33, however, a new aspect of the situation with which Paul is dealing comes into view. The emphasis upon the sovereign will of God in the preceding verses does not eliminate human responsibility, nor is the one incompatible with the other. It is not as if God's sovereign will runs athwart all that obtains in the sphere of human will and action. The case is rather that what occurs in the one realm is correlative with what occurs in the other, not because the human will governs and determines God's will but because God's will is concerned with men there is a correspondence between what God wills and what men subjectively are. It is with the latter Paul deals in verses 30–33.

"What shall we say then?" is the same form of question as in verse 14 (*cf.* 3:5; 4:1; 6:1; 7:7; 8:31). It scarcely agrees with the construction of the whole passage to regard what follows as anything else than the direct answer to this question. The question arises in connection with the unbelief of Israel so much in the forefront in verses 1–3. But alongside of this unbelief there is also the faith of Gentiles (vss. 25, 26). This diversity provokes the question: What are we to make of it? The answer is given in a form that accentuates the anomaly; the outcome is so different from what God's dealings in the past with the respective peoples would lead us to expect. This strange outcome is that Gentiles not following after righteousness gained righteousness and that Jews, though following righteousness, did not attain to it.

When Gentiles are said not to follow righteousness, there is allusion to the fact that they were outside the pale of special revelation and had been abandoned to their own ways (*cf.* 1:18–32; Acts 14:16; 17:30). But thought is focused on what is central to the theme of this epistle in the earlier chapters and again in Chapter 10, namely, that they did *not seek after the righteousness of justification*. It is not that they were destitute of all moral interest (*cf.* 2:12–15) but that the matter of justification and of the righteousness securing it was not their pursuit. On the other hand, Israel unto whom the oracles of God had been committed did pursue this righteousness. We may not tone down this statement. As possessors of special revelation, epitomized in the Abrahamic covenant, the matter of righteousness with God unto justification was focal in their interest; it was central in their religion. It is this contrast that points up the tragedy of the sequel. Gentiles attained to this righteousness and Israel failed to arrive there.

The change of form used in verse 31 must not, however, be overlooked. Israel is said to "follow after a law of righteousness". This should not be taken as referring to the righteousness of the law, that of works. "Law" in this case is similar to its use in 3:27b; 7:21, 23; 8:2 and means principle or rule or order. Israel is represented as pursuing that order or institution which was concerned with justification. But Israel came short of gaining the righteousness to which that institution bore witness; "they did not arrive at that law"; they did not attain to what was provided in the institution that was their glory. We sense the importunity of the question: why? This is Paul's question: "wherefore?" Verses 32, 33 are the answer.

This answer is already anticipated in verse 30: the Gentiles are said to have "attained to righteousness, even the righteousness which is of faith". In this instance it was necessary to define the righteousness as that of faith because the apostle does not in this context return to the subject of the righteousness to which the Gentiles attained. In verse 32 the question is why *Israel* did *not* attain to the same. The indictment is a reiteration of the thesis set forth earlier in the epistle, especially in 3:27–4:25. No further exposition is necessary other than to observe the way in which the antithesis is stated: "not of faith but as of works".[54] "As of works" indicates the conception entertained by Israel respecting the way by which justification was to be secured and the kind of righteousness constituting this justification. The misapprehension was total. Hence the failure.

---

[54] νόμον after ἔργων is weakly attested and, besides, robs the antithesis of its pungency. The version, furthermore, weakens this force by inserting unnecessarily "it were".

The latter part of verse 32 is an expansion of this fatal error in the terms of an Old Testament figure. The Scripture had forewarned of the stumbling which constituted Israel's fall. There is neither need nor warrant to weaken the meaning of the term "stumbled" as if it referred merely to irritation or annoyance.[55] It clearly refers to a fall and "the stone of stumbling" (Isa. 8:14), as the stone over which one stumbles, confirms this interpretation. If the figure of running a race is present in verses 30, 31 and carried on in verse 32, then the picture is the graphic one of stumbling over the hurdle and failing to gain the prize.

Verse 33 is a fuller confirmation from the Old Testament of the allusion to Isaiah 8:14 in verse 33. The quotation is a combination of two passages of different purport in their original contexts (Isa. 8:14; 28:16). In the former the Lord of hosts is said to be "for a stone of stumbling and for a rock of offense to both the houses of Israel". According to the latter the "stone, a tried stone, a precious corner-stone" is laid in Zion for a foundation and serves the purpose of giving stability and security. Paul takes parts of both passages, weaves these parts together into a unit, and by this abridgement and combination obtains the diverse thought of both passages. This twofold aspect he applies to the subject with which he is dealing, the failure of Israel and the attainment of the Gentiles. He thus shows that the Scripture had foretold in effect the twofold outcome. The main interest, however, is confirmation of the stumbling of Israel. It is this tragedy that looms high in the apostle's concern, as is apparent from the preceding and succeeding contexts.[56]

It cannot be doubted that Paul applies both passages to Christ. This is all the more significant in the case of Isaiah 8:14 for there it is the Lord of hosts who is spoken of as being for a stone of stumbling. The apostle had no hesitation in applying to Christ passages which pertained to the Lord of hosts. Since these passages are applied to Christ (*cf.* also Matt. 21:42; Mark 12:10; Luke 20:17; Acts 4:11; I Pet. 2:6–8), the faith mentioned in verses 30, 32 is the faith specified in verse 33 as believing upon Christ. It is the faith of resting upon him and in the context (*cf.* vss. 30, 31) is viewed

---

[55] *Cf.* John 11:9, 10; Rom. 14:13, 20, 21; I Cor. 8:9; I Pet. 2:8.
[56] The twofold reaction is set forth more fully in I Pet. 2:6–8 where the passages are more fully quoted. This is the best commentary on Paul's more condensed quotation and more summary use of both passages.

particularly as the faith directed to justification. The righteousness attained is that of faith in contrast with works. The effect, "shall not be put to shame", taken from Isaiah 28:16, varies from the Hebrew. The latter says: "he that believeth shall not be in haste". Paul in quoting follows the rendering of the Greek translators. The rendering should not be regarded as importing an idea alien to the thought of the Hebrew. The idea expressed by the Greek is that the believer will not be confounded, he will not have occasion to be ashamed of his confidence. And the Hebrew may express the closely related thought that he will not flee in disappointment.

Romans x

XVI. THE RIGHTEOUSNESS OF FAITH
(10:1–21)

10:1–8

1 Brethren, my heart's desire and my supplication to God is for them, that they may be saved.
2 For I bear them witness that they have a zeal for God, but not according to knowledge.
3 For being ignorant of God's righteousness, and seeking to establish their own, they did not subject themselves to the righteousness of God.
4 For Christ is the end of the law unto righteousness to every one that believeth.
5 For Moses writeth that the man that doeth the righteousness which is of the law shall live thereby.
6 But the righteousness which is of faith saith thus, Say not in thy heart, Who shall ascend into heaven? (that is, to bring Christ down:)
7 or, Who shall descend into the abyss? (that is, to bring Christ up from the dead.)
8 But what saith it? The word is nigh thee, in thy mouth, and in thy heart: that is, the word of faith, which we preach:

1 In this chapter the apostle is concerned with the same subject as that dealt with in the latter part of the preceding chapter. In 9:32, 33 the stumbling of Israel consisted in seeking righteousness by works and not by faith. This is but another way of saying that they sought to establish their own righteousness and did not subject themselves to the righteousness of God, the way it is stated in 10:3. Thus there is no break in the thought at 10:1. It should be noted, however, that into the midst of this treatment of the guilt of Israel the apostle interjects what reminds us of the way in which the whole subject of the unbelief of Israel had been introduced (9:1–3). The terms he uses now do not have the intensity used earlier. But it is the same heartfelt, deep-seated solicitude

10:1-21 THE RIGHTEOUSNESS OF FAITH

for his kinsmen according to the flesh. The address with which he begins, "Brethren", is one charged with emotion and affection and draws our attention to a solicitude, expressed in the words that follow, for those who are outside of the fellowship which the term "brethren" implies.

The word rendered "desire" is more properly translated "good-pleasure" (*cf.*, with reference to God, Matt. 11:26; Luke 2:14; 10:21; 12:32; Eph. 1:5, 9; Phil. 2:13 and, with reference to men, Rom. 15:26; II Cor. 5:8; 12:10; I Thess. 2:8; 3:1; II Thess. 2:12). We are reminded of Ezekiel 18:23, 32; 33:11, in which God proclaims it to be his good-pleasure that the wicked turn from his evil way and live. So here Paul asserts the good-pleasure, the delight of his heart with reference to Israel. This is joined with supplication to God for Israel.[1] "That they might be saved" expresses that to which the good-pleasure of his heart and his supplication were directed. The sorrow and pain of heart (9:1) were not, therefore, emotions of hopeless melancholy; they were joined with goodwill toward Israel and the outgoing of specific entreaty to God on their behalf to the end that they might be saved. Here we have a lesson of profound import. In the preceding chapter the emphasis is upon the sovereign and determinative will of God in the differentiation that exists among men. God has mercy on whom he wills and whom he wills he hardens. Some are vessels for wrath, others for mercy. And ultimate destiny is envisioned in destruction and glory. But this differentiation is God's action and prerogative, not man's. And, because so, our attitude to men is not to be governed by God's secret counsel concerning them. It is this lesson and the distinction involved that are so eloquently inscribed on the apostle's passion for the salvation of his kinsmen. We violate the order of human thought and trespass the boundary between God's prerogative and man's when the truth of God's sovereign counsel constrains despair or abandonment of concern for the eternal interests of men.

2, 3 When Paul says "I bear them witness" he is making

---

[1] The reading αὐτῶν is supported by P⁴⁶, ℵ, A, B, D, G, by several versions and fathers; τοῦ 'Ισραήλ ἐστιν by K, L, P, and the mass of the cursives. It is easy to understand how in the course of transmission the longer reading would have been substituted for the simple αὐτῶν in order to make specific the reference which is unquestionably clear from the context.

allowance for the religious interest which Israel possessed and accords to them the credit due on this account. They have "zeal for God". No one knew better than the apostle what such zeal was; in no one had it risen to greater intensity (*cf.* Acts 26:5, 8; Gal. 1:14). Hence he knew from personal experience the state of mind and conscience with which he credited his kinsmen and his "witness" to that effect takes on added meaning for that reason. The adversative, "but not according to knowledge", points to the criterion by which "zeal for God" is to be judged. Zeal is a neutral quality and can be the greatest vice. It is that to which it is directed that determines its ethical character. The criterion, therefore, is "knowledge". The term used here is one that often expresses the thorough knowledge that is after godliness to be distinguished from the knowledge that puffs up (*cf.* I Cor. 8:1; 13:2, 8 with Eph. 1:17; 4:13; Phil. 1:9; Col. 1:9; 3:10; I Tim. 2:4; II Tim. 2:25; 3:7; Tit. 1:1).[2] Verse 3 gives the reason why their zeal was not according to knowledge and explains what this lack of knowledge was: they did not know God's righteousness. It is not merely that they did not acknowledge this righteousness while at the same time knowing that it was that to which the Scriptures bore witness; they did not apprehend that which had been revealed. This concept of "God's righteousness" is that introduced at 1:17 and unfolded still further at 3:21, 22 (*cf.* the exposition at these points). In opposition to God's righteousness Israel sought to establish their own. Thus again Paul institutes the antithesis between a God-righteousness and a human righteousness, a righteousness with divine properties in contrast with that derived from human character and works. This is the theme developed in the early part of the epistle. Just as in 9:11, 30–32 there is distinct allusion to what had been argued at length in 3: 21–5:21, so here also. The basic error of Israel was misconception respecting the righteousness unto justification. The righteousness of God as the provision for man's basic need is here viewed as an ordinance or institution requiring subjection. To this ordinance

---

[2] It is, however, unwarranted to draw a hard and fast line of distinction between γνῶσις and ἐπίγνωσις in the usage of the New Testament as if the former always fell short of the richness and fulness of ἐπίγνωσις and the latter always referred to the knowledge that is unto life (*cf.* for γνῶσις Luke 1:77; Rom. 15:14; I Cor. 1:5; II Cor. 2:14; 4:6; 6:6; 8:7; Eph. 3:19; Col. 2:3; II Pet. 1:5, 6; *cf.* for ἐπίγνωσις coming short of fulness Rom. 1:28; 3:20 and for ἐπιγινώσκω Rom. 1:32; II Pet. 2:21).

10:1-21 THE RIGHTEOUSNESS OF FAITH

Israel did not subject themselves.[3] It is the "zeal for God" that places in bolder relief the tragedy of Israel's failure to attain to the law of righteousness. And the sin of ignorance is accentuated when by not knowing we miss the central provision of God's grace. How contrary to the popular notion that ignorance is an excuse and good intent the norm of approbation.[4]

4 This verse gives the reason for the thesis of verse 3 that God's righteousness and not man's is the institution of God: "Christ is the end of the law". This has been taken in the sense that the purpose of the law is fulfilled or realized in Christ. The term rendered "end" does on occasion have this meaning (*cf.* Luke 22:37; I Tim. 1:5). It is also true that if law is understood in the sense of the Mosaic institution, then this institution is fulfilled in Christ (*cf.* Gal. 3:24). Furthermore, the righteousness which Christ has provided unto our justification is one that meets all the requirements of God's law in its sanctions and demands. There are, however, objections to this interpretation.

1. Though the word "end" can express aim or purpose, preponderantly, and particularly in Paul, it means termination, denoting a terminal point (*cf.* Matt. 10:22; 24:6, 14; Mark 3:26; Luke 1:33; John 13:1; Rom. 6:21; I Cor. 1:8; 15:24; II Cor. 1:13; 3:13; 11:15; Phil. 3:19; Heb. 6:11; 7:3; I Pet. 4:7).[5]

2. If "end" means purpose then we should expect the apostle to say that the purpose of the law is Christ,[6] the reason being that, on this assumption, the purpose of the law would be the main thought and the real subject of the sentence. But this would give an awkward if not impossible construction as will appear from the

---

[3] ὑπετάγησαν is the form of the aorist passive (*cf.* 8:20; I Cor. 15:28; I Pet 3:22) but since the passive and middle often have the same forms this form should be taken as aorist middle. To regard it as passive would yield a virtually impossible sense. In other instances (*cf.* James 4:7; I Pet. 2:13; 5:5) the passive is not impossible but these are preferably taken as middle after the pattern of the middle in other instances and forms (*cf.* Col. 3:18; Tit. 3:1; I Pet. 3:1, 5).

[4] "Away then with those empty equivocations about good intention. If we seek God from the heart, let us follow the way by which alone we have access to Him. It is better, as Augustine says, to limp in the right way than to run with all our might out of the way" (Calvin: *op. cit.*, *ad* 10:2).

[5] If Paul meant purpose or aim there were other terms at his disposal that would have expressed the thought more adequately and less ambiguously as, *e.g.*, τελείωσις or πλήρωμα.

[6] τέλος is surely predicate not subject. In I Tim. 1:5 it is subject but in that case the thought and construction require it to be.

49

translation that would be required: "The end of the law is Christ for righteousness to every one that believeth".

3. In this epistle and in the context the antithesis is between the righteousness of the law as that of works and God's righteousness as the righteousness of faith. The next verse is the clearest demonstration of this antithesis and of the meaning we are to attach to the apostle's concept of the law as the way of attaining to righteousness (*cf.* also 3:20, 21, 28; 4:13, 14; 8:3; 9:32). The view most consonant with this context is, therefore, that the apostle is speaking in verse 4 of the law as a way of righteousness before God and affirming the relation that Christ sustains to this conception. The only relation that Christ sustains to it is that he terminates it.

4. It needs to be noted immediately, however, that a qualification is added: "to every one that believeth". This qualification implies that only for the believer is Christ the end of the law for righteousness. Paul does not mean that the erroneous conception ceased to be entertained. That was sadly not the case, as verse 3 proves. It is, Paul says, for every one who believes that Christ is the end of the law, and his whole statement is simply to the effect that every believer is done with the law as a way of attaining to righteousness. In this consideration we have an added reason for the interpretation given. If Paul were speaking of the purpose of the law as fulfilled in Christ, we would expect the absolute statement: "Christ is the end of the law for righteousness", and no addition would be necessary or in place.

The foregoing observation regarding the force of the apostle's statement bears also upon an erroneous interpretation of this verse, enunciated by several commentators to the effect that the Mosaic law had propounded law as the means of procuring righteousness. [7]

It is strange that this notion should be entertained in the face of Paul's frequent appeal to the Old Testament and even to Moses and the Mosaic law in support of the doctrine of justification by grace through faith (*cf.* 3:21, 22; 4:6–8, 13; 9:15, 16; 10:6–8;

---

[7] *Cf.*, *e.g.*, Meyer who says: "τέλος νόμου, which is placed first with great emphasis, is applied to Christ, in so far as, by virtue of His redemptive death... the divine dispensation of salvation has been introduced, in which the basis of the procuring of salvation is no longer, as in the old theocracy, the Mosaic νόμος, but faith, whereby the law has therefore ceased to be the regulative principle for the attainment of righteousness" (*op. cit., ad loc.*)

10:1–21 THE RIGHTEOUSNESS OF FAITH

15:8, 9; Gal. 3:10, 11, 17–22; 4:21–31). There is no suggestion to the effect that in the theocracy works of law had been represented as the basis of salvation and that now by virtue of Christ's death this method had been displaced by the righteousness of faith. We need but reflect again on the force of the proposition in question: *for the believer* Christ is the end of the law for righteousness. Paul is speaking of "law" as commandment, not of the Mosaic law in any specific sense but of law as demanding obedience, and therefore in the most general sense of law-righteousness as opposed to faith-righteousness.

5–8 The antithesis which had been developed in verses 3, 4 the apostle finds enunciated in the books of Moses. That is to say, Moses speaks of the righteousness which is of the law and defines what it is and he also speaks of the righteousness of faith. For the former Leviticus 18:5 is quoted and for the latter Deuteronomy 30:12, 14. The general purpose of this appeal to these passages is apparent. In characteristic manner Paul adduces the Old Testament witness to support his thesis. At least he derives from Scripture illustrations of the antithesis instituted in the preceding verses and thus confirms from the Jewish Scriptures themselves the argument he is conducting. But there are difficulties connected with the particular passages quoted, especially in the application which Paul makes.

The difficulty with the first (Lev. 18:5) is that in the original setting it does not appear to have any reference to legal righteousness as opposed to that of grace. Suffice it to say now that the formal statement Paul appropriates as one suited to express the principle of law-righteousness. It cannot be doubted but the proposition, "The man that doeth the righteousness of the law shall live thereby", is, of itself, an adequate and watertight definition of the principle of legalism. (See Appendix B, pp. 249 ff., for fuller discussion.)

Since Paul in verses 6–8 does not introduce the allusions to Deuteronomy 30:12–14 with such a formula as "Moses writeth" (vs. 5) or "Isaiah hath said" (9:29) but with the more unusual expression "The righteousness of faith saith"[8], it could be argued

---

[8] There is no reason why the version should have intruded "which is" in the translation.

51

that he is not here adducing Scripture proof but making his own independent assertion. Also, since he does not quote with close adherence to the Hebrew or Greek but makes alterations and intersperses his own comments which have no parallels in the passage concerned, it has been maintained that here is not strictly *quotation* in support of his argument but "a free employment of the words of Moses, which the apostle uses as an apt substratum for his own course of thought" so that "the independent dogmatic argument" finds only a formal point of support in the Deuteronomic passage.[9] But since there is patent allusion to and partial quotation from Deuteronomy 30:12–14 and since the formula, "the righteousness of faith saith", is immediately followed by quotation (Deut. 30:12), it is difficult to escape the thought that in this passage the apostle finds the language of faith and appeals to it as confirmation of the righteousness of faith as much as Leviticus 18:5 expresses the principle regulative of law-righteousness. The type of adaptation and application we find in this instance is not wholly diverse from what we find in other instances (*cf.* 9:25, 26 and vs. 5 preceding).

We should not perplex the difficulties of this passage by supposing that the apostle takes a passage concerned with law-righteousness and applies it to the opposite, namely, faith-righteousness. It is true that Moses is dealing with the commandments and the statutes which Israel were charged to obey. Of this commandment he speaks when it is said, "it is not too hard for thee, neither is it far off" (Deut. 30:11), and the protestations of the verses that follow are all in confirmation of the nearness and practicality of the covenant ordinances. It would be a complete misconstruction of Deuteronomy to interpret it legalistically. The whole thrust is the opposite (*cf.* Deut. 7:7ff.; 9:6ff.; 10:15ff.; 14:2ff.; 15:15f.; 29:9f., 29; 32:9; 33:29). The words in question, therefore, do not find their place in a legalistic framework but in that of the grace which the covenant bespoke. Their import is that the things revealed for faith and life are accessible: we do not have to ascend to heaven nor go to the utmost parts of the sea to find them. By revelation "they belong to us and our children for ever" (Deut. 29:29) and therefore nigh in our mouth and in our heart. This truth Paul finds exemplified in the righteousness of faith and

---

[9] Philippi: *op. cit., ad loc.*

10:1-21 THE RIGHTEOUSNESS OF FAITH

he applies it to the basic tenets of belief in Christ. These same tenets were a stumblingblock to unbelieving Israel. Thus, when we think of the truth expressed in Deuteronomy 30:12-14, we can see the appropriateness of the use of this passage to show that the same tenets over which the Jews stumbled are the tenets which verify to the fullest extent the truth of the passage from which the apostle quotes. As we proceed we shall discover this relevance.

When Paul says "the righteousness of faith saith", he is personifying the same (*cf.* Prov. 1:20; 8:1; Heb. 12:5). It is to the effect of saying "Scripture says with reference to the righteousness of faith". The main question in verse 6 is the meaning of Paul's own statement: "that is, to bring Christ down" and in verse 7: "that is, to bring Christ up from the dead".

The former has been interpreted to mean: Christ has ascended up to heaven, and the preceding question is the retort of unbelief: who can ascend up to heaven to establish contact with him? This makes good sense of itself but it does not accord with the unbelief of Israel that hovers in the background in this context nor does it suit that which follows in succeeding verses. It is better, therefore, to take the statement as implying that Jesus never came down from heaven and the preceding question as the taunt of unbelief. What Paul is insisting on is the accessibility, the nearness of revelation. That Christ came down from heaven and tabernacled among men is the most signal proof of this fact. We dare not say: who shall ascend to heaven to find the truth? For this question discounts the incarnation and is a denial of its meaning. In Christ the truth came to earth.

The other statement: "that is, to bring Christ up from the dead" (vs. 7) should be interpreted as a denial of the resurrection. The question: "who shall descend into the abyss?"[10] echoes the same kind of unbelief as that of verse 6. It is to the effect: who shall go down to the abyss to find the truth? The abyss as representing that

---

[10] The abyss in this instance may most suitably be taken as the synonym of *sheol* and the latter is frequently in the Old Testament "the grave". As in Matt. 11:23; Luke 10:15 heaven is contrasted with *hades*, so here heaven is contrasted with the abyss and, since it is in reference to Jesus' resurrection that the question is asked, the abyss can most conveniently denote what *sheol* and *hades* frequently denote in the Old Testament. In the LXX ἄβυσσος is very frequently the rendering of the Hebrew תהום the "deep" and in the singular and plural applied to the depths of the sea. In LXX Psalm 70:20 we have "the depths of the earth".

which is below is contrasted with heaven as that which is above. The question, as the language of unbelief, discounts the significance of Christ's resurrection. For the latter means that Jesus went to the realm of the dead and returned to life again. We do not need to go down to the abyss to find the truth any more than we need to ascend to heaven for the same purpose. For as Christ came from heaven to earth so also did he come again from the lower parts of the earth (*cf.* Eph. 4:9) and manifested himself to men.

Verse 8 is the assertion of what is the burden of Deuteronomy 30: 12–14 and is, with slight alteration, quotation of verse 14. Paul now specifies what this word is: it is "the word of faith, which we preach". So the word of Deuteronomy 30:14 is applied directly to the message of the gospel as preached by the apostles.[11] "The word of faith" is the word to which faith is directed,[12] not the word which faith utters. It is the word *preached* and therefore the message which brings the gospel into our mouth and heart.

10:9–15

> 9 because if thou shalt confess with thy mouth Jesus *as* Lord, and shalt believe in thy heart that God raised him from the dead, thou shalt be saved:
> 10 for with the heart man believeth unto righteousness; and with the mouth confession is made unto salvation.
> 11 For the scripture saith, Whosoever believeth on him shall not be put to shame.
> 12 For there is no distinction between Jew and Greek: for the same *Lord* is Lord of all, and is rich unto all that call upon him:
> 13 for, Whosoever shall call upon the name of the Lord shall be saved.
> 14 How then shall they call on him in whom they have not believed? and how shall they believe in him whom they have not heard? and how shall they hear without a preacher?
> 15 and how shall they preach, except they be sent? even as it is written, How beautiful are the feet of them that bring glad tidings of good things!

---

[11] As in verses 17, 18 (*cf.* Eph. 5:26; I Pet. 1:25) the term for word is ῥῆμα.

[12] τῆς πίστεως is objective genitive.

10:1–21 THE RIGHTEOUSNESS OF FAITH

9–11 There are various ways of summarizing the gospel message and of stating the cardinal elements of faith. The way adopted in a particular case is determined by the context and suited to the angle from which the gospel is viewed. In this passage attention is focused upon the lordship and the resurrection of Christ, confession that Jesus is Lord and belief that God raised him from the dead. It appears that the conjunction at the beginning of verse 9 means "that" rather than "because"; it specifies what is in the mouth and in the heart, confession of Jesus' lordship and belief of the resurrection, respectively. The order which the apostle follows corresponds to that of verse 8, "in thy mouth, and in thy heart", the order followed in the text quoted (Deut. 30:14).

The confession "Jesus as Lord" or "Jesus is Lord" refers to the lordship which Jesus exercises in virtue of his exaltation (*cf.* 1:4; 14:9; I Cor. 12:3; Eph. 1:20–23; Phil. 2:11; also Matt. 28:18; Acts 2:36; 10:36; Heb. 1:3; I Pet. 3:21, 22). This lordship presupposes the incarnation, death, and resurrection of Christ and consists in his investiture with universal dominion.[13] It can readily be seen how far-reaching are the implications of the confession. On several occasions Paul had reflected earlier in this epistle on the significance of Jesus' resurrection (*cf.* 1:4; 4:24, 25; 5:10; 6:4, 5, 9, 10, and the exposition at these points). In this instance the accent falls upon believing in the heart that God raised him. The heart is the seat and organ of religious consciousness and must not be restricted to the realm of emotions or affections. It is determinative of what a person is morally and religiously and, therefore, embraces the intellective and volitive as well as the emotive. Hence believing with the *heart* that God raised Jesus means that this event with its implications respecting Jesus as the person raised and the exceeding greatness of God's power as the active agency has secured the consent of that which is most decisive in our persons and is correspondingly determinative of religious conviction. The effect of this confession and belief is said to be salvation—"thou shalt be saved". We are not to regard confession and faith as having the same efficacy unto salvation. The contrast between mouth and heart needs to be observed. But we may not tone down the importance of confession with the

---

[13] "The whole acknowledgement of the heavenly κυριότης of Jesus as the σύνθρονος of God is conditioned by the acknowledgement of the preceding descent from heaven, the incarnation of the Son of God" (Meyer: *op. cit., ad loc.*).

mouth. Confession without faith would be vain (*cf.* Matt. 7:22, 23; Tit. 1:16). But likewise faith without confession would be shown to be spurious. Our Lord and the New Testament in general bear out Paul's coordination of faith and confession (*cf.* Matt. 10:22; Luke 12:8; John 9:22; 12:42; I Tim. 6:12; I John 2:23; 4:15; II John 7). Confession with the mouth is the evidence of the genuineness of faith and sustains to the same the relation which good works sustain (*cf.* 12:1, 2; 14:17; Eph. 2:8–10; 4:1, 2; James 2:17–22).

In verse 10 the order is inverted; faith is mentioned first and then confession. This shows that verse 9 is not intended to announce the order of priority whether causal or logical. Obviously there would have to be belief with the heart before there could be confession with the mouth. This verse is explanatory of the preceding. A few features deserve comment. (1) Literally the rendering would be: "For with the heart it is believed unto righteousness, and with the mouth it is confessed unto salvation". This can be taken, as in the version, as equivalent to "one believes" and "one confesses". But the subjects can be taken over from the preceding verse and so the resurrection would be the subject of "is believed" and the lordship of Christ of "is confessed". This would particularize the tenets believed and confessed as in verse 9. It may be, however, that Paul intended a more general statement and focused attention upon the heart as the organ of faith and the mouth as the organ of confession. "Heart" and "mouth" have the positions of emphasis. In either case this emphasis must not be overlooked, and thus again the stress falls upon the necessity of confession with the mouth as well as belief of the heart. (2) There is a specification in this verse that does not appear in verse 9. Faith is unto *righteousness*, confession is unto *salvation*, whereas in verse 9 salvation is said to be the common effect of both. In accord with 9:30–33; 10:2–6 the righteousness contemplated must be that which is unto justification and it is consonant with the teaching of the epistle throughout that faith should be represented as the instrument. Thus when Paul becomes more analytic than in verse 9 we find what we would expect—that faith is directed to *righteousness* (for exposition *cf. ad* 1:16, 17; 3:22; 4:1–12 *passim*). Confession is unto salvation as faith is unto righteousness. This cannot mean confession to the exclusion of faith. Such a supposition would be contrary to verse 9 and other passages (*cf.* 1:16; Eph. 2:8).

10:1–21 THE RIGHTEOUSNESS OF FAITH

It does, however, draw attention to the place of confession with the mouth. Confession verifies and confirms the faith of the heart.

Verse 11 is another appeal to Isaiah 28:16 (*cf.* 9:33) with the insertion on the apostle's part of "whosoever". This emphasis, implied though not expressed in Isaiah, is supplied in anticipation of verses 12, 13.

12, 13 "For there is no distinction" gives the reason for the "whosoever" of verse 11. Upon the absence of differentiation in respect of sin and condemnation, on the one hand, and opportunity of salvation, on the other, Paul had repeatedly reflected (*cf.* 1:16; 3:9, 19, 22, 23, 29, 30; 4:11, 12; 9:24). The distinctive feature of this text is the reason given in the latter half. In 3:29, 30 the oneness of God is given as the reason why God justifies Jews and Gentiles through faith. Here in verse 12 the same kind of argument is derived from the lordship of Christ: "the same *Lord* is Lord of all".[14] That Christ is in view should be apparent from the immediately preceding context as well as from Paul's usage in general (*cf.* vs. 9). When it is said that he "is rich unto all that call upon him", the thought is not so much that of the riches that reside in Christ (*cf.* Eph. 3:8) as that of the readiness and fulness with which he receives those who call upon him. Verse 13 is again confirmation from the Old Testament (Joel 2:32; Heb. and LXX 3:5). This formula "call upon the name of the Lord" is a characteristic Old Testament way of expressing the worship that is addressed to God and applies specifically to the worship of supplication (*cf.* Gen. 4:26; 12:8; 13:4; 21:33; 26:25; I Kings 18:24; II Kings 5:11; Psalms 79:6; 105:1; 116:4, 13; Isa. 64:7). Joel 2:32 has the same significance as belongs to it elsewhere. When Paul applies the same to Christ this is another example of the practice of taking Old Testament passages which refer to God without qualification and applying them to Christ. It was the distinguishing mark of New Testament believers that they called upon the name of the Lord Jesus (*cf.* Acts 9:14, 21; 22:16; I Cor. 1:2; II Tim. 2:22) and therefore accorded to him the worship that belonged to God alone. In the present text the formula is applied to initial faith in Christ but should not be restricted to the act of commitment to Christ which believing in Christ specifically denotes.

---

[14] αὐτός is subject and κύριος is predicate.

Calling upon the name of the Lord is a more inclusive act of worship that presupposes faith.

14, 15 These two verses are obviously related to the preceding. They are an analysis of the process involved in calling upon the Lord's name. But in the development of the apostle's thought they sustain a closer relation to what follows and prepare for the statement in verse 16: "But they did not all obey the gospel". The logical sequence set forth in these two verses scarcely needs comment. The main point is that the saving relation to Christ involved in calling upon his name is not something that can occur in a vacuum; it occurs only in a context created by proclamation of the gospel on the part of those commissioned to proclaim it. The sequence is therefore: authorized messengers, proclamation, hearing, faith, calling on the Lord's name. This is summed up in verse 17: "faith is of hearing, and hearing through the word of Christ".

The faith referred to in the first part of verse 14 is the faith of trust, of commitment to Christ,[15] and the proposition implied in the question is that there must be this trust in Christ if we are to call upon his name. The richness of calling upon Christ is thus again indicated and means that there is the relinquishment of every other confidence and abandonment to him as our only help (*cf.* Psalm 116:3, 4; Jonah 2:2). In the next clause, "how shall they believe him[16] whom they have not heard?", it is not likely that any weaker sense is given to the word "believe" than in the preceding clause though the construction differs.[17] A striking feature of this clause is that Christ is represented as being heard in the gospel when proclaimed by the sent messengers. The implication is that Christ speaks in the gospel proclamation. It is in this light that what precedes and what follows must be understood. The personal commitment which faith implies is coordinate with the encounter with Jesus' own words in the gospel message. And the dignity of the messengers, reflected on later, is derived from the fact that they are the Lord's spokesmen. In the last clause of verse 14 the apostle is thinking of the institution which is the ordinary and most effectual means of propagating the gospel,

---

[15] The εἰς goes with ἐπίστευσαν. ἐπικαλέω takes a direct object, as in verses 12, 13.
[16] There is no need to insert the preposition "in" before "him".
[17] That is to say "believe" is not to be given the bare sense of crediting.

namely, the official preaching of the Word by those appointed to this task.[18] Verse 15 reflects on the necessity of God's commission to those who undertake this office. The presumption of arrogating to oneself this function is apparent from what had just been stated. Those who preach are Christ's spokesmen and only the person upon whom he has laid his hand may act in that capacity. But if the emphasis falls on the necessity of Christ's commission, we may not overlook the privilege and joy involved in being sent. It is the sanctity belonging to the commission that enhances its dignity when possessed. This is the force of the quotation which the apostle appends, derived from Isaiah 52:7 but an abridgement of the same and expressing its central feature. In the original setting the passage is one of consolation to Israel in the Babylonish captivity and may well be regarded as the prophecy of restoration (*cf.* vss. 4, 5, 9, 10). It has broader reference and can be applied to the more ultimate salvation accomplished by the Messiah. In its immediate reference the messenger is viewed as swift-footedly[19] coming over the mountains with the good tidings of peace and salvation to Zion. The feet are said to be beautiful because their movements betray the character of the message being brought. The essential thought the apostle expresses by saying, "how beautiful are the feet of them that preach good tidings!" The purpose is to declare the inestimable treasure which the institution of gospel proclamation implies, a treasure that consists in the sending of messengers to preach the Word of Christ. The word from Isaiah is thus applied to that of which the restoration from Babylon was typical. And as the prophecy found its climactic fulfilment in the Messiah himself so it continues to be exemplified in the messengers whom he has appointed to be his ambassadors (*cf.* II Cor. 5:20).

10:16–21

16 But they did not all hearken to the glad tidings. For Isaiah saith, Lord, who hath believed our report?

---

[18] "By this very statement, therefore, he has made it clear that the apostolic ministry..., by which the message of eternal life is brought to us, is valued equally with the Word" (Calvin: *op. cit., ad loc.*).
[19] *Cf.* Franz Delitzsch: *Biblical Commentary on the Prophecies of Isaiah* (E. T., Edinburgh, 1881), II, *ad Isa.* 52:7.

17 So belief *cometh* of hearing, and hearing by the word of Christ.
18 But I say, Did they not hear? Yea, verily,
Their sound went out into all the earth,
And their words unto the ends of the world.
19 But I say, Did Israel not know? First Moses saith,
I will provoke you to jealousy with that which is no nation,
With a nation void of understanding will I anger you.
20 And Isaiah is very bold, and saith,
I was found of them that sought me not;
I became manifest unto them that asked not of me.
21 But as to Israel he saith, All the day long did I spread out my hands unto a disobedient and gainsaying people.

16, 17 At verse 16 the apostle returns to that subject which permeates this section of the epistle, the unbelief of Israel. "But they did not all obey the gospel". Although stated in a way that would hold true if only a minority had been disobedient, yet the mass of Israel is viewed as in this category. In the next part of the verse the paucity of the number of the obedient is implied in the question quoted from Isaiah. The unbelief of Israel is corroborated by the word of the prophet: "Lord, who hath believed our report?" (Isa. 53:1). Paul quotes from the Greek version. The term for "report" is the same as appears twice in verse 17 and is there rendered "hearing". It is apparent that in verse 16 this term must mean message or report, namely, that which was heard. It is not impossible to carry over this same meaning to verse 17 and the thought would be that faith arises from the message proclaimed and this message is through or consists in the word of Christ. But it is preferable to take the word in verse 17 in the sense of hearing. It is characteristic of Paul to change from one shade of meaning to another in the use of the same term in the same context (*cf.* 14:4, 5, 13). The verb corresponding to the term in question is used of hearing in verse 14 and again in verse 18. On the assumption that the act of hearing is the sense in verse 17 there are two observations. (1) That faith comes from hearing is a reiteration of what is implied in verse 14: "how shall they believe him whom they have not heard?" and means that there cannot be faith

10:1-21 THE RIGHTEOUSNESS OF FAITH

except as the gospel is communicated in proclamation and comes within our apprehension through hearing.[20] (2) It might seem to be redundant to add the second clause of verse 17. For is not the word of Christ that which constitutes the gospel of which Paul had been speaking in verses 14–16? There is, however, an eloquent reiteration of what is implied but is now expressly stated to be "the word of Christ" in order to eliminate all doubt as to what is encountered in the gospel proclamation. It is the word in the sense used in verse 8, but the special interest now is to show that this word is that which Christ speaks (*cf.* John 3:34; 5:47; 6:63, 68; 12:47, 48; 17:8; Acts 5:20; Eph. 5:26; 6:17; I Pet. 1:25).

18 It might appear from verse 17 that hearing produces faith or at least that hearing is used in the sense of hearkening. The present verse obviates this misapprehension. "But I say, Did they not hear?" The answer is in effect: yes indeed they heard but, nevertheless, they did not hearken. In order to support the universalism of the gospel proclamation Paul quotes from Psalm 19:4 in the exact terms of the Greek version (LXX, Psalm 18:5). It has raised a difficulty that the psalmist here speaks of the works of creation and providence and not of special revelation. Was this due to a lapse of memory or to intentional artifice?[21] It is not necessary to resort to either supposition. We should remember that this psalm deals with general revelation (vss. 1–6) and with special revelation (vss. 7–14). In the esteem of the psalmist and in the teaching of Scripture throughout these two areas of revelation are complementary. This is Paul's own conception (*cf.* Acts 17:24–31). Since the gospel proclamation is now to all without distinction, it is proper to see the parallel between the universality of general revelation and the universalism of the gospel. The former is the pattern now followed in the sounding forth of the gospel to the uttermost parts of the earth. The application which Paul makes of Psalm 19:4 can thus be seen to be eloquent not only of this parallel but also of that which is implicit in the parallel, namely, the widespread diffusion of the gospel of grace. Its sound

---

[20] We are not to regard the apostle as excluding or disparaging other means of communication. But this is an index to the special place accorded to the *preaching* of the gospel.
[21] *Cf.* Leenhardt: *op. cit., ad loc.*

goes out to all the earth and its words to the end of the world. It cannot then be objected that Israel did not hear.

19–21 At the beginning of verse 19 the same form of expression is used as in verse 18, the only difference being that Israel is now specified and the word "hear" is changed to "know": "But I say, Did Israel not know?". As verse 18 is concerned with the question whether or not Israel *heard*, so verse 19 is concerned with the question whether or not Israel *knew*. The answer to the first was that Israel did hear; so to the second it is that Israel did know.[22] The only question is: *what* did Israel know? The answer is indicated in the quotations which follow (Deut. 32:21; Isa. 65:1, 2). The first is quoted as in the Greek version, which is close to the Hebrew, with the exception that the object of the verbs is changed from the third person plural to the second person. This word from the Song of Moses appears in a context in which Israel is being upbraided for unfaithfulness and perversity. This context corresponds to the situation with which Paul is dealing. The meaning of the quotation, particularly as interpreted and applied by the apostle, is that Israel would be provoked to jealousy and anger because another nation which had not enjoyed God's covenant favour as Israel had would become the recipient of the favour which Israel had despised. This implies the extension of gospel privilege to all peoples, the particular truth emphasized in verse 18. But the distinctive feature of verse 19 is not the universal diffusion of the gospel; it is the provocation of Israel as the by-product of this diffusion. Strangers and aliens will become partakers of covenant favour and blessing. This, therefore, is what Israel *knew*; they had been apprized and forewarned of the outcome, that the kingdom of God would be taken from them and given to a nation bringing forth its fruit. All the more forceful as proof of this knowledge is the appeal to the word of Moses.[23] Nothing could have more cogency for Israel than the testimony of Moses.

---

[22] In μὴ 'Ισραὴλ οὐκ ἔγνω the μή implies a negative answer to the negative οὐκ ἔγνω and a negative of the negative is the positive, "Israel did know". An alternative possibility is that μή is used in the sense "perhaps"; Paul, that is to say, envisages an interlocutor as saying, "Perhaps Israel did not know."

[23] πρῶτος could be understood as stylistic. This is the first instance that Paul adduces. But it should rather be taken as referring to the fact that Moses was the first to bear witness to the provoking of Israel to envy.

10:1-21 THE RIGHTEOUSNESS OF FAITH

The next passage quoted to confirm the thesis that Israel knew is Isaiah 65:1. There is a transposition of the two clauses in the apostle's quotation but otherwise it adheres substantially to the Greek version. The lesson for Israel is that they had been informed by God through the prophet that favour would be shown to the Gentiles. The way in which this quotation is introduced implies that Isaiah had spoken with forthrightness and, since God is directly the speaker in this prophecy, the words "is very bold" point to the plainness with which the reception of the Gentiles had been foretold. There is a close similarity between this verse and 9:30. The Gentiles had not followed after righteousness. This is correlative with the terms now used that they had not sought or asked after the Lord.[24] As faith is said to be the way of attaining to righteousness in 9:30, so now the grace of God is manifest in the bestowal of what was not asked for or sought.

Verse 20 must not be dissociated in interpretation and application from verse 21. It is the contrast that is particularly relevant to the present interest. The contrast is that between the favour shown to the Gentiles and the disobedience of Israel. The aggravated character of the latter is made apparent by the terms that are used to express God's longsuffering and lovingkindness: "All the day long did I stretch out my hands". In Gifford's words, "it is a picture of *the everlasting arms* spread open in unwearied love".[25] The overtures of grace are not merely represented as rejected but as made to "a disobedient and gainsaying people". The perversity of Israel, on the one hand, and the constancy and intensity of God's lovingkindness, on the other, are accentuated by the fact that the one derives its character from the other. It is to a disobedient and contradicting people that the outstretched hands of entreaty are extended. The gravity of the sin springs from the contradiction offered to the overtures of mercy.

In this chapter the apostle is dealing with the failure of Israel. His analysis begins with the indictment that their zeal was not according to knowledge, that they were ignorant of God's righteousness and did not subject themselves to it. He continues this accusation by noting that they did not give obedience to the

---

[24] The paradox of being found when not sought indicates the sovereignty of grace.
[25] *Op. cit., ad loc.*

gospel. But the climax is reached in verse 21 when Israel is characterized as a disobedient and gainsaying people. The apostle demonstrates the inexcusableness of Israel and does so by appeal to their own Scriptures. They had heard the gospel. They knew beforehand the design of God respecting the call of the Gentiles. They had been forewarned of the very situation that existed in Paul's day and with which he is concerned in this part of the epistle. Verse 21 brings us to the terminus of the condemnation. We may well ask: what then? Is this the terminus of God's lovingkindness to Israel? Is verse 21 the last word? The answer to these questions chapter 11 provides.

ROMANS XI

XVII THE RESTORATION OF ISRAEL
(11:1-36)

A. THE REMNANT AND THE REMAINDER
(11:1-10)

11:1-10

1 I say then, Did God cast off his people? God forbid. For I also am an Israelite, of the seed of Abraham, of the tribe of Benjamin.
2 God did not cast off his people which he foreknew. Or know ye not what the scripture saith of Elijah? how he pleadeth with God against Israel:
3 Lord, they have killed thy prophets, they have digged down thine altars; and I am left alone, and they seek my life.
4 But what saith the answer of God unto him? I have left for myself seven thousand men, who have not bowed the knee to Baal.
5 Even so then at this present time also there is a remnant according to the election of grace.
6 But if it is by grace, it is no more of works: otherwise grace is no more grace.
7 What then? That which Israel seeketh for, that he obtained not; but the election obtained it, and the rest were hardened:
8 according as it is written, God gave them a spirit of stupor, eyes that they should not see, and ears that they should not hear, unto this very day.
9 And David saith,
Let their table be made a snare, and a trap,
And a stumblingblock, and a recompense unto them:
10   Let their eyes be darkened, that they may not see,
And bow thou down their back always.

1   The question posed by the unbelief of Israel as a people

pervades this section of the epistle.[1] It comes to the forefront at various points and in different forms (*cf.* 9:1-3, 27, 29, 31, 32; 10:2, 3, 21). At 11:1 another aspect of the same question is introduced. At 9:6ff. the apostle dealt with what might appear to be the effect of Israel's unbelief, namely, that God's word of promise had come to nought, at 9:14ff. with the question as it pertains to God's justice. Now the question is whether the apostasy of Israel means God's rejection of them. It is not, however, in these terms that the question is asked. It is asked in a way that points up the gravity of the issue and anticipates what the answer must be: "did God cast off his people?" The answer, as repeatedly in this epistle (*cf.* 3:4, 6, 31; 6:2, 15; 7:7, 13; 9:14), is the most emphatic negative available. The ground for this negative answer is implicit in the terms used in the question. For Paul's question is in terms that are reminiscent of the Old Testament passages which affirm that God will not cast off his people (I Sam. 12:22; Psalm 94:14 (LXX 93:14); *cf.* Jer. 31:37).

The second part of verse 1 is an additional reason for the negative reply. There are two views of the force of the apostle's appeal to his own identity as an Israelite, of the seed of Abraham and of the tribe of Benjamin. One is that, since he is of Israel, his acceptance by God affords proof that God had not completely abandoned Israel.[2] The appeal to his own salvation would be of marked relevance because of his previous adamant opposition to the gospel (*cf.* Gal. 1:13, 14; I Tim. 1:13-15). The unbelief of Israel (*cf.* 10:21) had been exemplified in no one more than in Saul of Tarsus. The mercy he received is proof that God's mercy had not forsaken Israel. On this view, "of the seed of Abraham, of the tribe of Benjamin" would serve to accentuate his identity as truly one of that race with which he is now concerned. The other view is that the appeal to his own identity is the reason given for the *vehemence* of his negative reply "God forbid" and, therefore, the reason why he recoils from the suggestion that God had cast off his people.[3] His own kinship with Israel, his Israelitish identity,

---

[1] The addition of ὃν προέγνω after τὸν λαὸν αὐτοῦ in P46, A, D* is no doubt an insertion following the pattern of verse 2 and should not be accepted as genuine.

[2] Perhaps the most pronounced exponent of this view is Philippi in *op. cit., ad loc.*; *cf.* also Luther, Calvin, Hodge, Godet, Liddon, Gaugler, *et al.*

[3] *Cf.* particularly Meyer: *op. cit., ad loc.* but also Sanday and Headlam, Gifford, and apparently C. H. Dodd.

constrains the reaction, "may it not be". More meaning can be attached to "of the seed of Abraham, of the tribe of Benjamin" on this interpretation. These additions would drive home the depth of his attachment to Israel and emphasize the reason for his revulsion from the proposition that God had cast off his people. Both views are tenable and there does not appear to be enough evidence to decide for one against the other.

2 It might seem that no more than what is stated in the second part of verse 1 would have been necessary to answer the question at the beginning. But the negative reply is now confirmed by direct denial. The denial is in the express terms used in the question with the addition of the clause "which he foreknew". The qualification which this clause provides offers the strongest reason for the denial; the "foreknowing" is the guarantee that God has not cast off his people. The question on which expositors are divided is whether the clause applies to the people of Israel as a whole or whether it is to be understood restrictively as applying only to the elect of Israel in distinction from the nation as a whole.[4] The strongest consideration in support of the latter view is the appeal on the part of the apostle to the differentiation and, therefore, to the restriction involved in particular election in verses 4–7. It may not be doubted but it is the election of a remnant from Israel (vs. 5) that offers proof that God had not cast off Israel as a people. The same type of argument is present in this chapter as is found earlier in 9:6ff. In 9:6ff. the proof that the word of God had not failed resides in the differentiation between the true Israel and those of Israel, between the true seed and those of mere descent. So in the present instance the election of grace is the demonstration that Israel as a people had not been completely cast off by God. But it is not apparent that the qualifying clause in 11:2 must be understood as referring only to the specific and particular election of verses 4–7. As noted above, it is Israel as a whole that is in view in verse 1.[5] The answers in the latter part of verse 1 apply to Israel as a whole. The first part of verse 2 is the direct reply unfolding what is implicit in the latter

---

[4] The arguments in support of this interpretation are most ably presented by Hodge: *op. cit., ad loc.*; *cf.* Calvin, Haldane, *et al.* and *contra* Meyer, Philippi, Liddon, Gifford, Godet, Sanday and Headlam.
[5] Likewise in 10:21 it is the people as a whole who are in view.

part of verse 1. It would be difficult to suppose that the denotation is abruptly changed at the point where this direct denial is introduced. It is more tenable, therefore, to regard "his people" (vs. 1) and "his people which he foreknew" (vs. 2) as identical in their reference and the qualifying clause in verse 2 as expressing what is really implied in the designation "his people". If Israel can be called God's "people", it is only that which is implied in "foreknowledge" that warrants the appellation. There should be no difficulty in recognizing the appropriateness of calling Israel the people whom God foreknew. Israel had been elected and peculiarly loved and thus distinguished from all other nations (*cf.* the evidence adduced and comments thereupon under 9:10–13, pp. 12ff). It is in this sense that "foreknew" would be used in this case.[6] Paul then proceeds to adduce an example from the Old Testament. This instance is relevant because it provides a parallel to the situation with which he is dealing and furnishes a fitting illustration of what is his main interest in succeeding verses, namely, that notwithstanding widespread apostasy in Israel there is "a remnant according to the election of grace".

"Or know ye not" is an arresting way of indicating what the readers are assumed to know or, at least, ought to know and is a favourite expression in Paul (*cf.* 6:16; I Cor. 3:16; 5:6; 6:2, 3, 9, 15, 16, 19, and also to the same effect Rom. 6:3; 7:1). "Of Elijah" refers to that section of Scripture which deals with Elijah and in the Greek, for this reason, reads "in Elijah". Elijah's pleading with God against Israel is not to be understood as making intercession to God for Israel but, as the term "against" indicates, refers to the appeal made against Israel and therefore to the *accusation* quoted in verse 3 from I Kings 19:10, 14.

3, 4 Apart from inversion of order and some abridgement the quotation in verse 3 follows the Hebrew and Greek of the passage concerned. The particular interest of these verses is focused in the reply to Elijah's complaint and the relation of this answer to the apostle's theme. The answer[7] (vs. 4) is taken from I Kings 19:18.

---

[6] See 8:29 for the meaning of προέγνω. It has inherent in itself the differentiating ingredient. But in this instance it has the more generic application as in Amos 3:2 and not the particularizing and strictly soteric import found in 8:29 (*cf.* πρόγνωσις in I Pet. 1:2).

[7] χρηματισμός is used only here in the New Testament but for the corresponding verb *cf.* Matt. 2:12, 22; Acts 10:22; Heb. 8:5; 11:7. The answer is the oracular reply; *cf.* Sanday and Headlam: *op. cit.*, *ad loc.*

11:1-10 THE REMNANT AND THE REMAINDER

The reproduction, though conveying the thought, is modified from both the Hebrew and the Greek in accord with the freedom the apostle applies in other cases. The oracle is not merely that there were seven thousand left who had not bowed to Baal. Emphasis is placed upon God's action; he had reserved these. And Paul introduces the thought that God had kept *for himself* the seven thousand.[8] There is the note of efficacious grace and differentiation. The effectiveness of the discrimination is indicated by the way in which the result of God's preserving grace is stated: they are men of such sort that they did not bow the knee to Baal.

Though the number corrects Elijah's mistaken estimate of the situation and is far in excess of what his complaint would imply, yet it should be noted that the seven thousand were only a remnant. This fact underscores the widespread apostasy in Israel at that time and points to the parallel between Elijah's time and the apostle's. This is a consideration basic to the use Paul makes of the Old Testament passage. Notwithstanding the apostasy of Israel as a whole, yet there was a remnant, though only a remnant, whom God had kept for himself and preserved from the idolatry of Baal's worship. This example is adduced to prove that God had not cast off Israel as his chosen and beloved people. The import, therefore, is that the salvation of a small remnant from the total mass is sufficient proof that the people as a nation had not been cast off.

5, 6 From the parallel situation in the days of Elijah Paul makes the application to his own time and concludes that there is a remnant according to the election of grace. According to the argument there is a necessity for a remnant, however widespread may be Israel's unbelief and apostasy. The necessity resides in the fact that Israel God had loved and elected. For that reason they are "his people which he foreknew". That he should utterly cast them off is incompatible with electing love. The guarantee that this abandonment had not occurred is not denial of the widespread apostasy with its resultant rejection on God's part but the existence

---

[8] "There is nothing in the Hebrew corresponding to the words '*for myself*' (ἐμαυτῷ), which St. Paul adds to bring out more emphatically the thought that the remnant is preserved by God Himself for His own gracious purpose" (Gifford: *op. cit., ad loc.*).

of a remnant. Therefore, since God's "foreknowledge" cannot fail of its purpose, there is always a remnant. The seven thousand in Elijah's day exemplify the operation of this principle because it was a time of patent and aggravated apostasy in Israel. But as it was in Elijah's day so also is it now.

The idea of a remnant is present in verse 4.[9] In 9:27 this notion appears in the quotation from Isaiah 10:22. Now, however, the term is used expressly to designate the distinctive segment of Israel defined by the election of grace. The precise form of expression is that there has come to be a remnant according to the election of grace[10] and this means that the distinguishing identity of those thus characterized proceeds from God's gracious election. This description of the source shows of itself that the differentiation finds its whole explanation in the sovereign will of God and not in any determination proceeding from the will of man. Either term bears this implication and the combination "the election of grace" makes the emphasis cumulative. In verse 6 the apostle adds further definition of what is implicit in the expression "election of grace", and he does so by setting up the antithesis between grace and human performance. If grace is conditioned in any way by human performance or by the will of man impelling to action, then grace ceases to be grace. This verse as specifying the true character of grace in contrast with works serves the same purpose at this point as does "not of works, but of him that calleth" in 9:11 (*cf.* also Eph. 2:8b).[11]

7–10 "What then?" is the way of asking: what is the conclusion to be drawn from what precedes? The situation in view with respect to which the question is asked is that dealt with in the six verses preceding. The apostle is concerned with the apostasy of Israel as a whole. This constrains the question: has God therefore cast off his chosen people? The answer is negative but not negative in such a way as to deny the empirical fact of Israel's apostasy. The answer finds its validation in the fact that there is still a

---

[9] λεῖμμα (vs. 5) is cognate with κατέλιπον (vs. 4).
[10] The perfect γέγονεν has this force.
[11] Verse 6 ends with οὐκέτι γίνεται χάρις in P⁴⁶, ℵ*, A, D, G, and other uncials as well as several versions. The longer ending is supported by ℵᶜ, L, and most of the cursives. B has a shorter form of the longer ending. The longer ending expands the thought of the shorter form of verse 6 and was probably a marginal note that found its way into the text in the course of transmission.

11:1-10 THE REMNANT AND THE REMAINDER

remnant of Israel whom God has elected and reserved for himself. This is just saying that the negative answer is demanded because of the differentiation between the mass and the remnant. The answer to "what then?" is, therefore, a summary assessment of the total situation unfolded in verses 1-6 and viewed from the perspective of Israel's *failure* as the way of interpreting the unbelief with which the whole passage is concerned. The way of stating Israel's failure—"that which Israel seeketh for, that he obtained not"—is similar to, and substantially to the same effect as, what we found already in 9:31, 32; 10:2, 3. It is reasonable to infer that what Israel is represented as seeking for, though not stated in this verse, is the righteousness mentioned in 9:31; 10:3. This righteousness Israel did not obtain and the reason is given in 9:32; 10:3.

When Paul says "the election obtained it" he means the elect. But he uses the abstract noun in order to lay stress on "the idea rather than on the individuals"[12] and thus accentuates the action of God as the reason. "The election", in the evaluation of the situation given in this verse, is parallel to "I have left for myself seven thousand men" in verse 4 and "a remnant according to the election of grace" in verse 5 and fulfils the same purpose in pointing to the act of God's grace by which is obviated the inference that God has cast off his people. What the elect have obtained is the righteousness of God and with it God's favour and acceptance.

"The election of grace" and "the election" of verses 5 and 7 must refer to the particular election of individuals in distinction from the theocratic election referred to in "his people" (vs. 1) and "his people which he foreknew" (vs. 2). This distinction we found earlier in the exposition of 9:10-13. But the reasons for the same conclusion in this context are to be noted. (1) There is sustained differentiation in the whole passage, in verse 4 between the mass of Israel and the seven thousand, in verse 5 between the mass and the remnant, in verse 7 between the hardened and the election. We are compelled to inquire as to the source, implications, and consequences of this distinction. (2) The election is said to be "of grace" (vs. 5) and the apostle in verse 6 is careful to define the true character of grace in contrast with works. When Paul emphasizes grace in this way it is the grace unto salvation that is in view (*cf.* 3:24; 4:16; 5:20, 21; Gal. 2:21; Eph. 2:5, 8; I Tim.

---

[12] Sanday and Headlam: *op. cit., ad loc.*

1:14; II Tim. 1:9). (3) "The election" (vs. 7) is said to have obtained it and, as noted above, the thing obtained cannot be anything less than the righteousness unto eternal life (*cf.* 5:18, 21). (4) The seven thousand (vs. 4) are said to have been kept for God himself and as not having bowed a knee to Baal. As characterizations these imply a relation to God similar to the obtaining of righteousness, favour, and life of verse 7. These reasons render it impossible to think of the election as anything other than the election unto salvation of which the apostle speaks elsewhere in his epistles (*cf.* 8:33; Eph. 1:4; Col. 3:12; I Thess. 1:4; II Tim. 2:1; Tit. 1:1). These considerations derived from this context are confirmatory of what we have found above regarding the election referred to in 9:11.

"The rest were hardened." The contextual emphasis upon election as entirely of grace and therefore upon the free and sovereign will of God as the determining cause of the differentiation involved requires us to apply in this case the same doctrine stated earlier in 9:18: "so then he hath mercy on whom he will, and whom he will he hardeneth".[13] Furthermore, ultimate issues are bound up with this hardening. There are several reasons for this conclusion. (1) Election is bound up with the issue of righteousness unto life and therefore with salvation; hardening as the antithesis cannot have a less ultimate issue in the opposite direction. (2) The hardened are those in view in verse 7 when we read: "that which Israel seeketh for, that he obtained not"; "obtained not" means coming short of the righteousness that is unto life and therefore of salvation. (3) The parallel in 9:18 means, because of the antithesis, that the hardened are not the partakers of God's mercy and thus not of the salvation of which mercy is the only explanation.

The subject of the hardening is not mentioned in this verse as in 9:18. But, as we shall discover in the verses which follow, there does not need to be doubt that the same subject, namely, God is in view as in 9:18. We may not abstract this hardening from the sustained indictment brought against Israel in the preceding context. "Israel, following after a law of righteousness, did not arrive at that law. Wherefore? Because they sought it not by

---

[13] In 9:18 the verb is σκληρύνω; in 11:7 it is πωρόω which can be rendered "blinded" (*cf.* II Cor. 3:14). But the meaning is not essentially different. Both terms refer to moral and religious insensitivity.

11:1–10 THE REMNANT AND THE REMAINDER

faith, but as it were by works" (9:31, 32). "Being ignorant of God's righteousness, and seeking to establish their own, they did not subject themselves to the righteousness of God" (10:3). "But they did not all hearken to the glad tidings" (10:16). "But as to Israel he saith, All the day long did I spread out my hands unto a disobedient and gainsaying people" (10:21). It is judicial hardening and finds its judicial ground in the unbelief and disobedience of its objects. This does not, however, interfere with the sovereign will of God as the cause of the differentiation which appears here as at 9:18. The elect have not been the objects of this hardening. But the reason is not that they had made themselves to differ. Election was all of grace and the elect deserved the same hardening. But of mercy (9:18) and of grace (vss. 5, 6) they were not consigned to their ill-desert. Thus grace as the reason for differentiation and unbelief as the ground of the judicial infliction are both accorded their proper place and emphasis.

In verses 8–10 Old Testament passages are adduced to support and confirm the proposition in verse 7 that "the rest were hardened". Verse 8 is for the most part taken from Deuteronomy 29:4 (LXX 29:3). Instead of the negative form of Deuteronomy, "the Lord hath not given you a heart to know", the positive form, "God gave them a spirit of stupor",[14] is adopted and this corresponds more closely to Isaiah 29:10 where God is the agent in pouring out the spirit of deep sleep. This form is taken over because the apostle wishes to represent the hardening as wrought by God himself. The action of God is likewise carried over to the two clauses which follow. He gave eyes so that they would not see and ears so that they would not hear.[15] God's hardening of Israel in Paul's day is parallel to that in the days of Moses and Isaiah. Verses 9 and 10 are taken from Psalm 69:22, 23 (LXX 68:23, 24) and with slight modification in verse 9 follows the terms of the Greek version. The messianic reference of Psalm 69:21 is apparent (*cf.* Matt. 27:34, 48). In the succeeding verses we have David as

---

[14] πνεῦμα κατανύξεως may best be taken as a spirit characterized by stupor. As Gifford says, "'*spirit*' is used for the pervading tendency and tone of mind, the special character of which is denoted by the Genitive which follows" (*op. cit., ad loc.*).

[15] "Unto this very day" may be compared with Stephen's indictment, "ye do always resist" (Acts 7:51).

God's mouthpiece uttering imprecatory curses.[16] The words "snare", "trap",[17] and "stumblingblock" are closely related and distinction of meaning is not to be pressed. The combination serves to enforce the purpose and effect of turning "their table" into the opposite of its intent. The table stands for the bounties of God's providence placed upon it and the thought may be that those concerned are conceived of as partaking of these gifts in ease and content but instead of peaceful enjoyment they are caught as in a trap or snare (*cf.* Dan. 5:1, 4, 5), overtaken by the judgments of God. In any case the table as intended for comfort and enjoyment is turned to be the occasion of the opposite. The word "recompense" bespeaks the retribution meted out and therefore confirms the judicial character of the hardening (vs. 7) and of the spirit of stupor (vs. 8). The judicial blinding, already expressed in verse 8, is reiterated in the first part of verse 10 in stronger terms. The last clause in verse 10 differs from the Hebrew though identical with the Greek version. It is difficult to know whether the figure of a back bowed down portrays the bondage of slaves bending under a heavy burden or represents the bowing down under grief, especially that of terror. The Hebrew, "make their loins continually to shake", suggests the latter.

The application of these Old Testament passages to the unbelief of Jewry in Paul's day has relevance surpassing anything that could have been true in Israel's earlier history. The movements of redemptive revelation and history had reached their climax in the coming and accomplishments of Christ, and the contradiction (*cf.* 10:21) which Israel offered correspondingly climaxed the gravity of the sin which had been exemplified in the successive stages of Israel's history.

---

[16] "In this, as in Ps. cix and Ps. cxxxix. 21 'Do not I hate them, O Lord, that hate Thee?' the Psalmist regards the enemies of the Theocracy as his own, and his own enemies as enemies only so far as they fought against the Divine order of the world. The imprecations, therefore, are only the form which 'Thy Will be done' necessarily assumes in the presence of aggressive evil. They are a prayer that the Divine Justice might be revealed in action for the protection of the cause of Truth and Righteousness against its enemies. So far are they from being 'peculiar to the moral standard of Judaism,' that they are, as here, deliberately adopted by the inspired teachers of Christianity" (Liddon: *op. cit.*, p. 202).

[17] καὶ εἰς θήραν is added by Paul.

B. THE FULNESS OF ISRAEL
(11:11–24)

11:11-15

11 I say then, Did they stumble that they might fall? God forbid: but by their fall salvation *is come* unto the Gentiles, to provoke them to jealousy.
12 Now if their fall is the riches of the world, and their loss the riches of the Gentiles; how much more their fulness?
13 But I speak to you that are Gentiles. Inasmuch then as I am an apostle of Gentiles, I glorify my ministry;
14 if by any means I may provoke to jealousy *them that are* my flesh, and may save some of them.
15 For if the casting away of them *is* the reconciling of the world, what *shall* the receiving *of them be*, but life from the dead?

11, 12 In the preceding verses the thesis is that although Israel as a whole had been disobedient yet a remnant was left and therefore God had not cast off his people. Israel's rejection was not *complete*. The thesis in the verses which follow is that the rejection is not *final*. Both considerations–not complete but partial, not final but temporary–support the proposition that God had not cast off his people.

"I say then", as in verse 1, is Paul's way of introducing a question intended to obviate a conclusion which might seem to follow from what precedes. The question: "did they stumble that they might fall?" is answered with the usual emphatic negative, "God forbid". It cannot be doubted but the mass of Israel stumbled (*cf.* 9:32, 33), and it cannot be doubted that this meant a fall with the gravest consequences (*cf.* vss. 7–10). So neither the stumbling nor the corresponding fall[18] is denied. What then is the

---

[18] If πέσωσιν is taken to mean "fall utterly and permanently" (*cf.* Philippi and Liddon), then what would be denied would be the permanent rejection of Israel and in this way, as Philippi says, "the apostle intimates by anticipation the closing thought of the subsequent exposition" (*op. cit., ad loc.*). This does not appear to be the thought at this point. Surely those who stumbled did fall with ultimate consequences. Is not the denotation of those in view the same as those mentioned in verse 7: "the rest were hardened"? And is not Paul thinking here of those contemplated in verse 22: "toward them that fell, severity"? The interpretation, therefore, appears to be required that what Paul is reflecting on here is the more ultimate and gracious design of God in the stumbling and fall of the mass of Israel at the time with which he was dealing.

meaning of the negative reply? The construction supplies the answer. The question is not: "did they stumble and fall?" To that question an affirmative answer would be required. Everything here turns on the clause, "that they might fall". The negative answer means that the purpose of their stumbling was not that they might fall but was directed to and designed for another end, the end immediately appended in the latter part of the verse. This purpose is not viewed as that entertained by Israel when they stumbled as if they stumbled with the intent of thereby promoting the salvation of the Gentiles. It is on God's purpose the apostle is reflecting and the purpose of Israel in stumbling is not within the purview of the passage either negatively or positively. We are here advised, therefore, of the overriding and overruling design of God in the stumbling and fall of Israel. This is that "by their fall salvation is come unto the Gentiles, to provoke them to jealousy". The rendering is unfortunate. It is "by their trespass" rather than "by their fall". What is in view is the stumbling of Israel, their rejection of Christ as Saviour. This was their trespass and it is by this that salvation came to the Gentiles. This development is exemplified in Jesus' prediction and in the history of the apostolic era (*cf.* Matt. 8:12; 21:43; Acts 13:46; 18:6; 28:28). The same fact is referred to again in verses 15, 25. The salvation of the Gentiles is itself of sufficient magnitude to evince the gracious design fulfilled through the trespass of Israel and therefore sufficient to warrant denial of the proposition that Israel stumbled merely for the purpose that they might fall. In the construction of the sentence, however, the salvation of the Gentiles is subordinate to another design. This subordination is not to depreciate the significance of the Gentiles' salvation. To this Paul returns repeatedly later on. But it is striking that this result should here be represented as subserving the saving interests of Israel. It is "to provoke them to jealousy". Several observations are to be elicited from this latter part of verse 11.

(1) The ethnic distinction between the Gentiles and Israel appearing earlier in these chapters (*cf.* 9:25, 26, 30, 31; 10:19, 20) is here again brought to the forefront. The saving design contemplated in "to provoke them to jealousy" has in view, therefore, the salvation of Israel viewed in their distinct racial identity. This obviates any contention to the effect that God's saving design does not embrace Israel as a racial entity distinguished by the place

which Israel occupied in the past history of redemption. While it is true that in respect of the privileges accruing from Christ's accomplishments there is now no longer Jew or Gentile and the Gentiles "are fellow-heirs, and fellow-members of the body, and fellow-partakers of the promise in Christ Jesus through the gospel" (Eph. 3:6), yet it does not follow that Israel no longer fulfils any *particular* design in the realization of God's worldwide saving purpose. (2) Paradoxically, the unbelief of Israel is directed to the restoration of Israel's faith and the fall of Israel to their reclamation. We already anticipate Paul's adoring amazement: "O the depth of the riches both of the wisdom and the knowledge of God!" (vs. 33). (3) Provoking to jealousy[19] is not an unworthy incentive to repentance and faith. It is here incorporated in God's design. Later (vs. 14) the apostle says that he conducts his ministry to the Gentiles with the same end in view. The idea is that the Jews observing the favour and blessing of God bestowed upon the Gentiles and the privileges of the kingdom of God accruing therefrom will be moved to emulation and thereby induced to turn to the Lord. It is eminently proper to emulate such gifts as the faith of the gospel secures. (4) The unbelief of Israel is ordained to promote the salvation of the Gentiles. But this implied faith on the part of the Gentiles is not, in turn, to be prejudicial to Israel's salvation; it is to promote the same.

In verse 12 the translation should again be: "now if their trespass is the riches of the world". The trespass is the same as in verse 11b and pointing back to the stumbling of verse 11a. Verse 12 is the beginning of an *a fortiori* argument and uses the fact stated in verse 11b to press home the greater result that will accrue for the Gentile world by the faith of Israel in contrast with their unbelief. "The riches of the world" is the salvation that has come to the Gentiles by the trespass (unbelief) of Israel and in this verse "the world" and "the Gentiles" are synonymous in their denotation.[20] Since this is so the accent must largely fall upon the distinction between "trespass" and "loss". At least it would be difficult to explain the virtual repetition "the riches of the world" and "the riches of the Gentiles" unless distinction resides in that

---

[19] In using this term Paul harks back to Moses' word in Deut. 32:21 quoted at 10:19.

[20] This does not mean that no purpose is served by varying the expression. κόσμος serves to emphasize the ethnic universalism.

with which these are conjoined respectively. The word rendered "loss" has been variously interpreted. The rendering "diminishing" (AV) is not supported by usage and the only apparent reason for adopting the same is that it provides a fitting contrast with fulness. The evidence indicates that the term means defeat, overthrow, discomfiture (*cf.* Isa. 31:8; 51:7; I Cor. 6:7; II Pet. 2:19, 20).[21] Besides, "diminishing" would not agree with the parallels in the passage. If "diminishing" were in view this would apply only to the small number of the remnant. But that of which Paul is speaking here is that which has befallen the mass of Israel, their stumbling and fall (vs. 11a), their trespass (vss. 11b, 12a); and so the "loss" must be that of the mass of Israel and not anything characterizing the remnant. Furthermore, the meaning "defeat" is sufficiently distinct from trespass to warrant and explain the sequence, "their trespass the riches of the world and their defeat the riches of the Gentiles". What is in view is the great loss, as by overthrow in battle, sustained by Israel when the kingdom of God was taken from them. They are viewed after the figure of a defeated host and deprived of their heritage.[22]

"How much more their fulness." There should be no question but this is the fulness of Israel as a people. The stumbling was theirs, the fall was theirs, theirs was the trespass, and theirs the loss. The fulness, therefore, can have no other reference. What is "their fulness"? This word has a variety of meanings and applications. It often means the plenitude or totality. It can be the full complement. In this instance it is not merely contrasted with "loss" but also with "trespass". Whatever might be the precise term by which to express the import here, it is obvious that the condition or state denoted is one that stands in sharp contrast with the unbelief, the trespass, and the loss characterizing Israel when the apostle wrote. It points, therefore, to a condition marked by antithesis in these respects. This means that Israel is contemplated

---

[21] *Cf.* Frederick Field: *Notes on the Translation of the New Testament* (Cambridge, 1899), pp. 160f.; Lagrange: *op. cit.*, p. 276; Gaugler, *op. cit.*, p. 183; Philippi: *op. cit.*, pp. 193ff. The only other instance of ἥττημα in the New Testament is I Cor. 6:7 but *cf.* ἡττάομαι in II Pet. 2:19, 20 and in LXX ἥττημα in Isa. 31:8 and the verb in Isa. 8:9; 13:15; 19:1; 20:5; 30:31; 31:4; 33:1; 51:7; 54:17.

[22] It would not be altogether out of the question to regard loss in verse 12 as parallel to the fall of verse 11 (πέσωσιν) just as trespass (παράπτωμα, vs. 12) corresponds to the stumbling (ἔπταισαν) of verse 11.

as characterized by the faith of Christ, by the attainment of righteousness, and by restoration to the blessing of God's kingdom as conspicuously as Israel then was marked by unbelief, trespass, and loss. No word could serve to convey the thought of the thoroughness and completeness of this contrast better than the term "fulness". For if "fulness" conveys any idea it is that of completeness. Hence nothing less than a restoration of Israel as a people to faith, privilege, and blessing can satisfy the terms of this passage. The *argument* of the apostle is not, however, the restoration of Israel; it is the blessing accruing to the Gentiles from Israel's "fulness". The "fulness" of Israel, with the implications stated above, is presupposed and from it is drawn the conclusion that the fulness of Israel will involve for the Gentiles a much greater enjoyment of gospel blessing than that occasioned by Israel's unbelief. Thus there awaits the Gentiles, in their distinctive identity as such, gospel blessing far surpassing anything experienced during the period of Israel's apostasy, and this unprecedented enrichment will be occasioned by the conversion of Israel on a scale commensurate with that of their earlier disobedience. We are not informed at this point what this unprecedented blessing will be. But in view of the thought governing the context, namely, the conversion of the Gentiles and then that of Israel, we should expect that the enlarged blessing would be the expansion of the success attending the gospel and of the kingdom of God.

13, 14 The two preceding verses have been concerned with the grace bestowed upon the Gentiles by Israel's unbelief and with the promise of greater blessing for the Gentiles when Israel turns to the Lord. The salvation of the Gentiles is thus the theme. In now addressing the Gentiles directly[23] Paul is impressing upon them the significance for their own highest well-being of Israel's conversion. There can be no segregation of interest. As apostle of the Gentiles (*cf.* 1:5; 12:3; 15:15, 16; Gal. 2:7-9; Acts 26:17, 18), his labours to fulfil that ministry in no way conflict with the interests of Israel. The more this ministry to the Gentiles is crowned with success the more is furthered the cause of Israel's salvation. This is why he says "I glorify my ministry" as apostle of the

---

[23] The clause "that are Gentiles" is not restrictive as might appear. Paul is addressing his readers as Gentiles. It is hard to suppress the inference that the Christian community at Rome was preponderantly Gentile.

Gentiles. The reason for this intimate relationship is that which had been stated in verse 11 respecting the purpose and providence of God, that the salvation of the Gentiles is directed to the end of moving Israel to jealousy. This same aim the apostle now states to be his own in the magnifying[24] and promoting of his Gentile ministry. What was said above (vs. 11) respecting the propriety of this impulsion applies in this case to the motivation of the apostle.

In verse 12 a mass restoration of Israel is in view. But here in verse 14 Paul does not say that his activity in provoking Israel to jealousy is in order that the fulness of Israel may be attained. He is much more modest. What he strives for is to stir up this emulation and "save some of them".[25] The same affection for his kinsfolk and zeal for their salvation, voiced on earlier occasions (*cf.* 9:2, 3; 10:1), appear again in this verse. But his zeal does not spill over into any excessive claims for the success of his ministry nor does he presume to state how his ministry of provoking to jealousy is related either causally or temporally to the "fulness" of Israel.

15 Although the apostle does not state in verse 14 how his ministry is causally related to the "fulness" of Israel, there is nevertheless a close relation between verses 13, 14 and verse 15. This is indicated by the terms with which verse 15 begins, "for if". The thesis in this section (vss. 11ff.) is that the apostasy of Israel is not final. This consideration provides the apostle with the incentive to pursue his ministry to the Gentiles and to glory in that office. For the more successful is that ministry the more Israel's salvation is promoted by their being moved to jealousy, and the salvation of Israel reacts for the more abundant blessing of the Gentiles. Thus the thought of verse 12 is reiterated in verse 15 and resumed in this instance in order to support the emphatic assertion of his ministry to the Gentiles in verses 13, 14. Though there is this reiteration in verse 15 the different terms are significant.

---

[24] The expression "glorify my ministry" involves the zealous pursuit of the Gentile ministry. But the term "glorify" does not itself express this; it means that he exalts his office.

[25] Since the provoking to jealousy is a factor in the conversion of Israel (vs. 11) and since Paul pursues his ministry to that end, his saving of some no doubt contributes to the "fulness" of Israel. But this he does not say.

11:11–24 THE FULNESS OF ISRAEL

For the first time Paul speaks of the "casting away"[26] of Israel. Hitherto he had spoken of their disobedience, their stumbling, their trespass, their defeat. The thought of rejection by God is no doubt implied, especially in the term "defeat". The accent falls, however, upon the action or failure of action on Israel's part. Now the accent is placed upon the action of God in having cast off Israel. The kingdom of God was taken from them (cf. Matt. 21:43). And just as the stumbling and trespass refer to the mass of Israel, so must the rejection. When the rejection is said to be the reconciling (preferably reconciliation) of the world, this is parallel to the result expressed in verses 11, 12, namely, the salvation of the Gentiles, the riches of the world, and the riches of the Gentiles. The term, however, has its own specific meaning and this is germane to the teaching of this verse in distinction from verses 11, 12. "Reconciliation" is contrasted with "casting away". The latter means rejection from the favour and blessing of God and reflects therefore on the attitude of God to Israel and the relation he sustains to them. So the accent falls distinctly upon God's attitude and action thereanent. Reconciliation is in contrast and likewise reflects on the attitude, relation, and action of God. The Gentiles are viewed as previously alienated from God and excluded from his favour. By God's action this alienation was exchanged for reconciliation and the attitude of disfavour exchanged for favour. This is a clear index to that on which the term "reconciliation" focuses attention.

In this verse again we have an *a fortiori* argument as in verse 12. The "receiving" is contrasted with the "casting away" and must, therefore, mean the reception of Israel again into the favour and blessing of God. In terms of the whole passage, as noted repeatedly, this must refer to Israel as a whole and implies that this restoration is commensurate in scale with Israel's rejection, the restoration of the mass of Israel in contrast with the "casting off". Again the accent falls on the action of God, in this case that of grace in contrast with judgment, and on the changed attitude of God to the mass of Israel. This restoration of Israel will have a marked beneficial effect, described as "life from the dead". Whatever this result may be it must denote a blessing far surpassing in its

---

[26] ἀποβολή means more than loss (cf. Philippi: op. cit., ad loc.). Any harshness belonging to the term is not to be eliminated. The meaning is fixed by the contrast with πρόσλημψις.

proportions anything that previously obtained in the unfolding of God's counsel. In this respect it will correspond to the effect accruing from the fulness of Israel (vs. 12).

The change of construction in verse 15 as compared with verse 12 is noteworthy. Paul does not say "how much more their receiving" as in verse 12 he says "how much more their fulness". In verse 12 we have to infer what the "how much more" has in view; it is not expressly defined. But in verse 15 we read instead: "what shall the receiving of them be, but life from the dead?" and thus the greater blessing is specified for us. What is this "life from the dead"?

It must be accorded its full force as that which brings "the reconciliation of the world" to climactic realization. There is a note of finality belonging to the expression. Many commentators ancient and modern regard it as denoting the resurrection, holding that nothing less than this consummatory event can satisfy the climactic character involved nor accord with the actual terms, "life from the dead".[27] It cannot be doubted that the resurrection from the dead and the accompanying glories would provide the fitting climax to the unfolding of God's saving counsels with respect to Jew and Gentile so much in view in this context. Furthermore, the actual terms, "life from the dead", could denote resurrection. There are, however, weighty considerations which, to say the least, indicate that the foresaid interpretation is not proven. (1) While it is true that the word used for "life" can refer specifically to the resurrection (cf. John 5:29; 11:25; II Cor. 5:4) and the corresponding verb likewise to the act of rising from the dead or of having risen (cf. Matt. 9:18; Luke 20:38; John 4:50, 51; 11:25; Rom. 14:9; II Cor. 13:4; Heb. 7:25; Rev. 1:18;

---

[27] "The πρόσλημψις of the still unconverted Jews, Paul concludes, will be of such a kind..., will be of so glorious a character (comp. Eph. i. 18), that it will bring with it the last most blessed development, namely, the life beginning with the resurrection of the dead in the αἰὼν ὁ μέλλων, the ζωὴ αἰώνιος, which has the awakening from death as its causal premiss" (Meyer: *op. cit., ad loc.*). "The climacteric nature of the event to be expected as the issue of the unfolding ways of God forbids to tone down this phrase (ζωὴ ἐκ νεκρῶν) to the purely-metaphorical, making it fall within the terms of mere spiritual revival. 'Life from the dead' must refer to the resurrection specifically so named, and so understood it presupposes the beginning of the closing act of the eschatological drama" (Geerhardus Vos: *The Pauline Eschatology* [Princeton, 1930], pp. 87f.). *Cf.* Barrett: *op. cit., ad loc.*; Lagrange: *op. cit., ad loc.*; as the preferred interpretation Sanday and Headlam: *op. cit., ad loc.*

2:8; 20:5), and while the term used for "dead" frequently refers to literal death, yet these same terms are also used in the figurative sense of spiritual life and death. "Life" frequently denotes the new life in Christ (*cf.* Acts 11:18; Rom. 5:18; 6:4; 8:6; II Cor. 2:16; Eph. 4:18; Phil. 2:16; I John 3:14; 5:11-13). The corresponding verb also is used in this religious sense (*cf.* Rom. 6:10, 11, 13; 8:12, 13; 10:5; II Cor. 5:15; I John 4:9). The word "dead" has also this same figurative meaning on many occasions (*cf.* Luke 15:24, 32;[28] Rom. 6:11, 13; Eph. 2:1, 5; Col. 2:13; Heb. 6:1; 9:14; James 2:17; Rev. 3:1). It is significant that so many of these instances occur in Paul's epistles and not a few in the epistle to the Romans. Most noteworthy is Romans 6:13: "but present yourselves unto God, as alive from the dead, and your members as instruments of righteousness unto God". The expression "alive from the dead" is as close to "life from the dead" as could be when the verb "live" is substituted for "life".[29] But "alive from the dead" refers not to the resurrection but to newness of life in Christ. (2) If Paul meant the resurrection, one wonders why he did not use the term occurring so frequently in his epistles and elsewhere in the New Testament to designate this event when referring both to the resurrection of Christ and to that of men (Rom. 1:4; 6:5; I Cor. 15:12, 13, 21, 42; Phil. 3:10; *cf.* Acts 4:2; 17:32; 23:6; 24:15, 21; 26:23; Heb. 6:2; I Pet. 1:3).[30] This expression "resurrection from the dead" is the standard one with Paul and other New Testament speakers and writers to denote the resurrection. It could be that Paul varied his language in order to impart an emphasis appropriate to his purpose. But no such consideration is apparent in this case, and in view of his use of the terms "life" and "dead", particularly in this epistle, we would expect the word "resurrection" in order to avoid all ambiguity if the apostle intended the expression in question to denote such. Besides, nowhere else does "life from the dead" refer to the resurrection and its closest parallel "alive from the dead" (6:13) refers to spiritual life.

For these reasons there is no place for dogmatism respecting the

---

[28] Luke 15:24, 32 is cited not because it has precisely the same reference as "dead" in the other passages but because it illustrates a non-literal use of the term.
[29] ἐκ νεκρῶν ζῶντας as compared with ζωὴ ἐκ νεκρῶν.
[30] ἀνάστασις.

interpretation so widely held that the resurrection is in view. The other interpretation, that of an unprecedented quickening for the world in the expansion and success of the gospel, has much to commend it. The much greater blessing accruing from the fulness of Israel (vs. 12) would more naturally be regarded as the augmenting of that referred to in the preceding part of the verse. Verse 15 resumes the theme of verse 12 but specifies what the much greater blessing is. In line with the figurative use of the terms "life" and "dead" the expression "life from the dead" could appropriately be used to denote the vivification that would come to the whole world from the conversion of the mass of Israel and their reception into the favour and kingdom of God.[31]

11:16-24

16 And if the firstfruit is holy, so is the lump: and if the root is holy, so are the branches.
17 But if some of the branches were broken off, and thou, being a wild olive, wast grafted in among them, and didst become partaker with them of the root of the fatness of the olive tree;
18 glory not over the branches: but if thou gloriest, it is not thou that bearest the root, but the root thee.
19 Thou wilt say then, Branches were broken off, that I might be grafted in.
20 Well; by their unbelief they were broken off, and thou standest by thy faith. Be not highminded, but fear:
21 for if God spared not the natural branches, neither will he spare thee.
22 Behold then the goodness and severity of God; toward them that fell, severity; but toward thee, God's goodness, if thou continue in his goodness: otherwise thou also shalt be cut off.
23 And they also, if they continue not in their unbelief, shall be grafted in: for God is able to graft them in again.
24 For if thou wast cut out of that which is by nature a wild olive tree, and wast grafted contrary to nature into a good olive tree; how much more shall these, which are the natural *branches*, be grafted into their own olive tree?

---

[31] *Cf.* Calvin, Philippi, Hodge, Gifford, Godet, Leenhardt: *op. cit., ad loc.*; H. C. G. Moule: *The Epistle of St. Paul to the Romans* (New York, n. d.), *ad loc.*; David Brown: *The Epistle to the Romans* (Edinburgh, n. d.), *ad loc.*

11:11-24 THE FULNESS OF ISRAEL

16 The idea of this verse is drawn from Numbers 15:17–21. The first of the dough given unto the Lord meant the consecration of the whole lump. In the application of this figure "the firstfruit" is the patriarchs rather than the remnant. The firstfruit and the lump are parallel to the root and the branches. The root is surely the patriarchs. Furthermore, in verse 28 Israel are said to be "beloved for the fathers' sake". In the one case it is the consecration belonging to Israel, in the other it is the love borne to Israel. But both are derived from the patriarchal parentage. Here again we are apprized of the distinguishing character of Israel in the relation of God to them and of his counsel respecting them. This fact of consecration derived from the patriarchs is introduced here by the apostle as support for the ultimate recovery of Israel. There cannot be irremediable rejection of Israel; the holiness of theocratic consecration is not abolished and will one day be vindicated in Israel's fulness and restoration.

17–21 The figure of the tree with its root and branches is continued throughout these five verses and also in verses 22–24. The figure of the olive tree to describe Israel is in accord with the Old Testament usage (*cf.* Jer. 11:16, 17; Hos 14:6).[32] The act of judgment upon Israel spoken of in verse 15 as the "casting away" is now represented as breaking off of branches. This is the appropriate representation in terms of the figure now being used. The expression "some of the branches" does not seem to agree, however, with the fact that the mass of Israel had been cast away. It is a sufficient answer to this difference to bear in mind that the main interest of the apostle now is focused on the grafting in of the Gentiles and the cutting away of Israel and it is not necessary to reflect on the extent to which the latter takes place.

Israel with its rootage in the patriarchs is viewed as the cultivated olive tree (*cf.* vs. 24) and the Gentiles as the wild olive. The latter is grafted into the former. It would press the language and the analogy too far to think of the wild olive as grafted in its entirety into the good olive. As indicated in verse 24 the *branches* of the wild olive are viewed as grafted in. It is not necessary to debate at length the question arising from the kind of olive-culture to which Paul here refers. The common form of tree-culture is to

---

[32] *Cf.* also Psalm 80:8–16; Isa. 5:1–7; John 15:1ff.

take a shoot from a good tree and graft it into the young tree so that the latter might derive from the fatness of the graft the vitality necessary to fruitbearing. That to which Paul refers is the reverse of this practice. It has been shown, however, that grafting from a wild olive to a cultivated olive was a practice also followed for certain purposes[33] and that Paul could have been acquainted with this type of olive-culture and have applied it in this instance. But even if the apostle were not alluding to a practice known to him and even supposing that he was aware of the discrepancy between common practice and the figure he uses, this would not in the least interfere with the propriety of his figure. He could be interpreted as using an analogy diverse from the usual pattern of olive-culture in order to make more striking the super-natural character of the ingrafting in the application of his figure. It should be remembered that Paul is dealing with what he says is "contrary to nature" (vs. 24). Besides and more to the point is the consideration that he conceives of the branches that were broken off as grafted in again into the olive from which they were taken (vss. 23, 24), something out of the question in horticulture.

Two statements in verse 17 bear significantly upon the warning directed to the Gentiles in subsequent verses. The first is: "grafted in among them". The privilege enjoyed by Gentiles is one in this intimate association with Jews; there is always the remnant according to the election of grace. The way in which the breaking off is stated, namely, "some of the branches were broken off" accentuates the fact that not all were. The second is: "partaker of the root and fatness of the olive tree". Gentiles are reminded that they draw all the grace they enjoy from the tree whose root is Israel's patriarchs. Gentiles and Jews partake together of the privilege that stems from the same root.[34] This same lesson is pressed home more forcefully in verse 18: "it is not thou that bearest the root, but the root thee". The warning is then issued: "boast not against the branches". The branches in this case must be the branches broken off, for in verse 19 the Gentile is represented as saying, "branches were broken off that I might be grafted

---

[33] *Cf.* W. M. Ramsay: "The Olive-Tree and the Wild-Olive" in *The Expositor*, Sixth Series, Vol. XI (1905), pp. 16–34, 152–160.

[34] τῆς ῥίζης τῆς πιότητος, supported by ℵ*, B, is the more difficult reading and the insertion of καί can be explained as an attempt to relieve the difficulty. τῆς πιότητος when taken as a genitive of quality is quite intelligible.

11:11–24 THE FULNESS OF ISRAEL

in". The boasting condemned is the arrogance and presumptuous confidence to which believing Gentiles are liable when they consider the place of privilege and honour they occupy in the kingdom of God by the displacement of Israel. The self-adulation can be sensed in the contrasts of verse 19, between "broken off" and "grafted in", between "branches" and "I".[35] A streak of contempt for the Jew may also be detected. It is not difficult to find parallels in the life of the church. The person who is called upon to fill a place vacated by the exercise of discipline upon another is liable to gloat self-righteously over this advancement and look with disdain upon the fallen.

In verse 20 the reference to the unbelief of the branches broken off harks back to the repeated mention of the stumbling and trespass of Israel (9:32; 10:21; 11:11, 12) and reminds us again of the judicial character of the hardening (11:7) and "casting away" (11:15). The observation that "by their unbelief they were broken off" is made in this instance, however, to emphasize that by which Gentiles have come to stand and occupy a place in the olive tree, namely, by faith. The main interest of the context is to rebuke and correct vain boasting.[36] The emphasis falls on "faith" because it is faith that removes all ground for boasting. If those grafted in have come to stand by faith,[37] then all thought of merit is excluded (*cf*. 9:32; 11:6). "Where then is the glorying? It is excluded. By what manner of law? of works? Nay: but by the law of faith" (3:27). Furthermore, the accent on faith and the contrast with unbelief serve to enforce the necessity of maintaining this faith and of taking heed lest by the presumptuous confidence which is its opposite the Gentiles may fall under the same judgment. In faith there is no discrimination. The gospel is the power of God unto salvation to every one that believes (*cf*. 1:16; 3:22). In unbelief there is no respect of persons (*cf*. 2:11). God did not spare the natural branches and neither will he spare the Gentiles (vs. 21). If they continue not in faith, they also will be cut off (vs. 22). It is noteworthy that the attitude compatible with and promotive of faith is not only lowliness of mind but one of fear

---

[35] Note the ἐγώ expressing the egoism and vainglory of this boasting.

[36] That against which Paul is warning is that for which Israel fell and the same judgment will overtake the Gentiles if they fall into the same kind of self-righteous confidence (*cf*. 9:32, 33; 10:3, 21).

[37] It is not necessary to suppose that "stand" refers to standing in the olive tree, though this is not an entirely impossible figure.

(vs. 20). Christian piety is constantly aware of the perils to faith, of the danger of coming short, and is characterized by the fear and trembling which the high demands of God's calling constrain (*cf.* I Cor. 2:3; Phil. 2:12; Heb. 4:1; I Pet. 1:17). "Let him that thinketh he standeth take heed lest he fall" (I Cor. 10:12).[38]

22 This is an appeal to Gentiles to consider the import of the twofold action of God delineated in the preceding verses, the breaking off and the grafting in. It is the lesson of conjunction in God of goodness and severity, a conjunction which cannot be restricted to execution but must apply also to the disposition of which execution is the expression. This can readily be seen in the case of "goodness"; it refers to the lovingkindness characterizing him by which he is actuated in the dispensing of favour. Although the word for severity occurs only here in the New Testament,[39] yet it denotes that which is involved in his wrath and retributive justice (*cf.* 1:18; 2:4–16).[40] The conditional clause in this verse, "if thou continue in his goodness", is a reminder that there is no security in the bond of the gospel apart from perseverance. There is no such thing as continuance in the favour of God in spite of apostasy; God's saving embrace and endurance are correlative. In another connection Paul enunciates the same kind of condition. We are reconciled to God and assured of being presented holy and unreprovable only if we "continue in the faith, grounded and stedfast, and not moved away from the hope of the gospel" (Col. 1:23; *cf.* Heb. 3:6, 14). The "goodness" in which the Gentile must continue is the goodness of God referred to in the preceding clause as bestowed. It is not here the ethical uprightness which the believer must exhibit and which is involved in perseverance. The thought is that he must continue in the enjoyment of God's goodness and is identical with that of Acts 13:43 where the devout are urged to "continue in the grace of God". The implication, however, is that this continuance is conditioned upon the lowliness of mind and the stedfast faith upon which the accent falls in the preceding verses. There is the note of *severity* in the way by which

---

[38] The insertion of μήπως before οὐδέ in verse 21 in accord with P[46], D, G *et al.* would weaken the categorical statement.
[39] *Cf.* for the adverb II Cor. 13:10; Tit. 1:13.
[40] This complementation of goodness and severity is characteristic of the Old Testament (*cf.* Psalm 125:4, 5; Isa. 42:25–43:1; 50:10, 11; Nah. 1:5, 6).

11:11-24 THE FULNESS OF ISRAEL

the alternative is expressed: "otherwise thou also shalt be cut off", a severity with the same character and decisiveness as that mentioned in the earlier part of the verse.

23, 24 The alternatives stressed in the preceding verse and applied with warning to the Gentile believers in the privileged position they occupy are now applied to Israel in their fallen condition but applied in the direction of encouragement and hope. Thou (Gentile) wilt be cut off if thou dost not continue in *faith*; they (Israel) will be grafted in if they do not continue in *unbelief*. No assurance is given in this verse that Israel will desist from unbelief; the stress falls on the certainty of the complementation, faith and grafting in, if and when Israel turn to faith. The last clause in the verse gives the reason why they will be grafted in, more particularly the reason why the grafting in will not fail when unbelief is renounced. The emphasis falls upon the power of God. Different views are held as to the reason for this emphasis. In verse 24 the argument is that it is more natural for Israel to be grafted into their own olive tree than for Gentiles taken from a wild olive to be grafted contrary to nature into a good olive. Thus there would appear to be no need to stress the power of God once the unnatural grafting in of the Gentiles is assumed as it is in the preceding verses. The best view, it would appear, is that the appeal to the power of God in verse 24 is to obviate or answer what is liable to be, if not actually is, the assumption entertained by Gentiles, when actuated by the presumptuous confidence condemned in the preceding verses, that Israel, once disinherited and cast off, cannot again be established in God's covenant favour and blessing. It is the assumption that to restore Israel is contrary to the implications of their "casting away" (vs. 15) and that consequently grafting in again would violate the divine ordinance. This Paul contradicts by saying "God is able". Though the power of God is placed in the forefront, underlying the exercise of power is the recognition that the grafting in again is consonant with his counsel and the order he has established.[41] The erroneous assumption Paul meets directly by appeal to God's omnipotence and verse 24 is an additional *argu-*

---

[41] In δυνατός there is no necessary reflection upon the fact that faith is the gift of God (*cf.* Eph. 2:8; Phil. 1:29).

ment to offset the fallacious inferences drawn from the rejection of Israel.

The point of the argument in verse 24 is obvious. If God's action of grace in the reception of the Gentiles is analogous to the unnatural ingrafting of branches from a wild olive into a cultivated olive, how much more compatible to receive Israel again after the pattern of grafting cultivated branches into a cultivated olive. There are, however, two observations. (1) It is to be noted that the figure is not that merely of grafting branches of a cultivated olive into a cultivated olive; it is that of grafting in the branches of the same olive. This is the force of "grafted into their own olive tree". The thought of compatibility in receiving Israel again is thus accentuated. The doctrine involved in this argument is the one pervading this passage, that the provisions of God's redemptive grace for Jew and Gentile have their base in the covenant of the fathers of Israel. To use Paul's figure here, the patriarchal root is never uprooted to give place to another planting and thus it continues to impart its virtue to and impress its character upon the whole organism of redemptive history. The ingrafting of Israel is for this reason the action which of all actions is consonant with the unfolding of God's worldwide purpose of grace. This signally exemplifies the great truth that the realization of God's saving designs is conditioned by history. (2) It is in the light of the foregoing that we should understand the "how much more" of verse 24. The thought is not attached in a restricted sense to the power of God stressed in verse 23 as if it were *easier* for God to graft in Israel than to graft in Gentiles. It is the "how much more" of consonance with the basic Israelitish character of the covenant in terms of which salvation comes to the world.

C. THE FULNESS OF THE GENTILES AND THE SALVATION OF ISRAEL (11:25-32)

11:25-32

25 For I would not, brethren, have you ignorant of this mystery, lest ye be wise in your own conceits, that a hardening in part hath befallen Israel, until the fulness of the Gentiles be come in;
26 and so all Israel shall be saved: even as it is written, There shall come out of Zion the Deliverer; He shall turn away ungodliness from Jacob:
27 And this is my covenant unto them, When I shall take away their sins.
28 As touching the gospel, they are enemies for your sake: but as touching the election, they are beloved for the fathers' sake.
29 For the gifts and the calling of God are not repented of.
30 For as ye in time past were disobedient to God, but now have obtained mercy by their disobedience,
31 even so have these also now been disobedient, that by the mercy shown to you they also may now obtain mercy.
32 For God hath shut up all unto disobedience, that he might have mercy upon all.

25 The words, "For I would not, brethren, have you ignorant", as in other instances (1:13; I Cor. 10:1; 12:1; II Cor. 1:8; I Thess. 4:13), draw attention to the importance of what is about to be said and the necessity of taking full account of it. The apostle is still speaking to Gentiles and has in view the liability to erroneous assumptions and vain conceits on their part. This is evident from the purpose for which he gives them the disclosure concerned, namely, "lest ye be wise in your own conceits" (*cf.* vss. 18-21). The disclosure he is about to make he calls a "mystery". This term appears frequently in Paul's epistles but this is the first occasion in this epistle and it occurs again in 16:25. The latter instance virtually furnishes a definition.[42] We are liable to

---
[42] *Cf.* exposition at 16:25.

associate with the term the idea of secrecy or of unintelligible mysteriousness. This is not the meaning in Paul's use of the term. As appears in 16:25, there is in the background the thought of something hid in the mind and counsel of God (*cf.* Eph. 3:9; Col. 1:26, 27) and therefore not accessible to men except as God is pleased to make it known. But, as is obvious in this verse, it is not the hiddenness that defines the term but the fact that something has been *revealed* and thus comes to be known and freely communicated. Paul is jealous that his readers be not ignorant of the mystery and therefore that they know it. But, in addition to the emphasis upon revelation and knowledge, "mystery" draws attention to the greatness and preciousness of the truth revealed. In several instances the unsurpassed sublimity of that denoted by mystery is apparent (*cf.* I Cor. 2:7; 4:1; 15:51; Eph. 1:9; 3:3, 4; 5:32; Col. 1:27; 2:2; 4:3; I Tim. 3:16).[43] It is not necessary to suppose that the revelation in this instance (vs. 25) was given only to Paul.[44] The truth denoted as "this mystery" is that "hardening in part hath befallen Israel, until the fulness of the Gentiles be come in". Both elements are clearly expressed: the hardening of Israel is partial not total,[45] temporary not final, "in part" indicating the former, "until the fulness of the Gentiles be come in"

---

[43] *Cf.* Sanday and Headlam: *op. cit.*, p. 334.

[44] In Eph. 3:5 Paul associates other apostles and prophets with himself as organs of revelation. Besides, Paul's appeal to the Old Testament for confirmation (vss. 26, 27) shows that the truth denoted by "mystery" was not entirely undisclosed in the Old Testament. It is upon the fulness and clarity of the revelation that the accent falls in the New Testament disclosure.

[45] "In part" does not refer to the degree of hardening but to the fact that not all were hardened (*cf.* vss. 7, 17). The last clause in this verse should surely be taken as referring to a point of eventuation that brings the hardening of Israel to an end. There is not good warrant for the rendering: "while the fulness of the Gentiles is coming in". It is true that in Heb. 3:13 ἄχρις οὗ has the meaning "while". But there it is used with the present tense καλεῖται and no other rendering is possible. In Acts 27:33 the conjunction would likewise mean "while": "while the day was coming on". In Luke 21:24 it would not yield an impossible sense to render the clause with ἄχρι οὗ: "while the times of the Gentiles are being fulfilled". But this is an unnatural rendering and, to say the least, questionable in view of the aorist passive subjunctive πληρωθῶσιν. In every other instance in the New Testament, whether used with the aorist or future, the meaning "until" is the necessary rendering and indicates a point of eventuation or a point at which something took place (*cf.* Acts 7:18; I Cor. 11:26; 15:25; Gal. 3:19; Rev. 2:25). Hence in Rom. 11:25 it would require a departure from pattern to render the clause other than "until the fulness of the Gentiles will come in". The context makes this the necessary interpretation of the force of the clause in question.

11:25–32 FULNESS OF GENTILES AND SALVATION OF ISRAEL

the latter. The restoration of Israel was implied in verse 24 but not categorically stated. Now we have express assurance. The word "mystery" is itself certification of the assurance which divine revelation imparts.

The partial hardening of Israel will have a terminus. This is marked as "the fulness of the Gentiles". What is this "fulness"? The term as applied to Israel (vs. 12) has the complexion of meaning appropriate to that context. It is contrasted with their trespass and loss. Without doubt the present context yields its own complexion to the term as applied to the Gentiles. But it would not be proper to discard the basic meaning found in verse 12. There "fulness", like the "receiving" in verse 15, refers to the mass of Israel in contradistinction from a remnant, the mass restored to repentance, faith, the covenant favour and blessing of God, and the kingdom of God. In other words, the numerical cannot be suppressed. To exclude this notion at verse 25 would not be compatible with the indications given in this chapter as to the import of the term in question. To say the least, we would expect that the "fulness" of the Gentiles points to something of enlarged blessing for the Gentiles comparable to that expansion of blessing for Israel which "their fulness" (vs. 12) and their "receiving" (vs. 15) clearly involve.

There are, in addition, other considerations which have to be taken into account, derived from the immediate context. (1) The verb, of which "the fulness of the Gentiles" is the subject, namely, "be come in", is the standard term in the New Testament for entering into the kingdom of God and life (*cf.* Matt. 5:20; 7:13; 18:3; Mark 9:43, 45, 47; Luke 13:34; John 3:5; Acts 14:22).[46] The thought is, therefore, that of Gentiles entering into the kingdom of God. The perspective is that of the future, at least from the standpoint of the apostle. The only way whereby those who had already entered could be included is to suppose that "the fulness of the Gentiles" means the total number of elect from among the Gentiles, a supposition that will be dealt with presently. The chief point now is, however, that it is impossible to exclude from the expression "be come in" the thought of numbers entering God's kingdom. (2) In the words "hardening in part" there is an intimation of the numerical. Not all were hardened;

---

[46] Sometimes the verb is used absolutely as here.

there was always a remnant; the hardening was not complete. (3) "All Israel" in verse 26, as will be noted, refers to the mass of Israel in contrast with a remnant. In view of these considerations it would be indefensible to allege that to the expression "the fulness of the Gentiles" no thought of numerical proportion may be attached.

It has been maintained that the designation means the full tale of the elect from among the Gentiles[47] or the added number necessary to make up the full tale of elect Gentiles. On this view the signal for the restoration of Israel would be the completion of the full number to be saved from the Gentiles. Admittedly, "fulness" could *of itself* denote such completion. But contextual considerations militate against this interpretation. (1) Israel's "fulness" (vs. 12) cannot be the total of the elect of Israel. The "fulness" is contrasted with Israel's trespass and loss and must refer to the restoration to faith and repentance of Israel as a whole. The total number of the elect of Israel or the number necessary to make up this total would not provide this contrast nor express the restoration which the passage requires. The total number of the elect or the number remaining to make up that total would require nothing more than the total of a remnant in all generations. Verse 12, however, envisions a situation when it is no longer a saved remnant but a saved mass. Applying this analogy in the use of the term "fulness" in verse 12 to the instance of verse 26 we are, to say the least, pointed in the direction of an incomparably greater number of Gentiles entering into the kingdom of God. But, in any case, the "fulness" of Israel cannot mean simply the full tale of the elect of Israel nor the added complement necessary to complete that tale. And so there is no warrant to impose that concept upon the same term in verse 25. The evidence is decidedly against it. (2) The idea that "fulness" means the added number necessary to complete the elect of the Gentiles would agree with the expression "be come in". But the view that "fulness" means the full tale of elect Gentiles does not comport with the perspective indicated in the clause "until the fulness of the Gentiles be come in", the reason being that this clause refers to an entering in that takes place in the future and provides this perspective. The full tale includes those who had already entered in and it would be

---

[47] *Cf.* Barrett: *op. cit., ad loc.*

unnatural to speak of those who had entered in as contemplated in such an expression as "until they have entered in". Thus the interpretation "full tale" is ruled out. But even if we adopt the view that "fulness" means the added number, a view compatible with "be come in", we have still to reckon with the analogy of verse 12, namely, that "fulness" intimates a proportion such as supplies contrast with what goes before. In other words, we cannot exclude from "fulness" the enhancement and extension of blessing which "fulness" in verse 12 necessarily involves. In this case this increase would have to be interpreted in terms of entering into the kingdom of God and this, in turn, means a greatly increased influx of Gentiles into God's kingdom. (3) In verse 12 the fulness of Israel is said to bring much greater blessing to the Gentiles. As observed above, the interpretation most consonant with the context is the greater expansion of the blessing mentioned in the same verse as the riches of the world and of the Gentiles. But if "the fulness of the Gentiles" means the full tale of the elect of Gentiles, then the fulness of Israel would terminate any further expansion among the Gentiles of the kind of blessing which verse 12 suggests.

The contextual data, therefore, point to the conclusion that "the fulness of the Gentiles" refers to blessing for the Gentiles that is parallel and similar to the expansion of blessing for Israel denoted by "their fulness" (vs. 12) and the "receiving" (vs. 15).

It could be objected that the foregoing interpretation brings incoherence into Paul's teaching. On the one hand, the "fulness" of Israel brings unprecedented blessing to the Gentiles (vss. 12, 15). On the other hand, "the fulness of the Gentiles" marks the terminus of Israel's hardening and their restoration (vs. 25). But the coherence of these two perspectives is not prejudiced if we keep in mind the mutual interaction for the increase of blessing between Jew and Gentile. We need but apply the thought of verse 31 that by the mercy shown to the Gentiles Israel also may obtain mercy. By the fulness of the Gentiles Israel is restored (vs. 25); by the restoration of Israel the Gentiles are incomparably enriched (vss. 12, 15). The only obstacle to this view of the sequence is the unwarranted assumption that "the fulness of the Gentiles" is the consummation of blessing for the Gentiles and leaves room for no further expansion of gospel blessing. "The fulness of the Gentiles" denotes unprecedented blessing for them but does not exclude even greater blessing to follow. It is to this subsequent blessing that the restoration of Israel contributes.[48]

It must not be forgotten that the leading interest of the apostle in verse 25 is the removal of the hardness of Israel and their conversion as a whole.[49] This is the theme of verses 11–32. It is stated expressly in verse 12, is reiterated in different terms in verse 15, and is resumed again in verse 25. In verses 17–22 Paul found it necessary to warn Gentiles against vain boasting. But he returns to the theme of Israel's restoration at verse 23, pleads considerations why Israel could be grafted in again in verses 23, 24, and in verse 25 appeals to divine revelation in final confirmation of the certainty of this sequel. This prepares us for the interpretation of verse 26.

26, 27 "And so" with which verse 26 begins indicates that the proposition about to be stated is either one parallel to or one that flows from the revelation enunciated in the preceding verse. It means "and accordingly", continuing the thought of what precedes or drawing out its implications.[50] "All Israel shall be saved" is the proposition thus involved. It should be apparent from both the proximate and less proximate contexts in this portion of the epistle that it is exegetically impossible to give to "Israel" in this verse any other denotation than that which belongs to the term throughout this chapter. There is the sustained contrast between Israel and the Gentiles, as has been demonstrated in the exposition preceding. What other denotation could be given to Israel in the preceding verse? It is of ethnic Israel Paul is speaking and Israel could not possibly include Gentiles. In that event the preceding verse would be reduced to absurdity and since verse 26 is a parallel or correlative statement the denotation of "Israel" must be the same as in verse 25.[51]

---

[48] "We must remember, that Paul is here speaking as a prophet, ἐν ἀποκαλύψει, 1 Cor. xiv. 6, and therefore his language must be interpreted by the rules of prophetic interpretation. Prophecy is not proleptic history" (Hodge: *op. cit.*, p. 588).

[49] Together with Israel's restoration goes also the great advantage accruing to the Gentiles from this restoration (*cf.* vss. 12, 15).

[50] The force of καὶ οὕτως could also be that it introduces something correlative with what precedes.

[51] "It is impossible to entertain an exegesis which takes 'Israel' here in a different sense from 'Israel' in verse 25" (F. F. Bruce: *op. cit., ad loc.*; *cf. contra* Calvin: *op. cit., ad loc.*). It is of no avail to appeal, as Calvin does, to Gal.

11:25-32 FULNESS OF GENTILES AND SALVATION OF ISRAEL

The interpretation by which "all Israel" is taken to mean the elect of Israel, the true Israel in contrast with Israel after the flesh, in accord with the distinction drawn in 9:6, is not tenable for several reasons. (1) While it is true that all the elect of Israel, the true Israel, will be saved, this is so necessary and patent a truth that to assert the same here would have no particular relevance to what is the apostle's governing interest in this section of the epistle. Furthermore, while true that the fact of election with the certainty of its saving issue is a truth of revelation, it is not in the category that would require the special kind of revelation intimated in the words "this mystery "(vs. 25). And since verse 26 is so closely related to verse 25, the assurance that "all Israel shall be saved" is simply another way of stating what is expressly called "this mystery" in verse 25 or, at least, a way of drawing out its implications. That all the elect will be saved does not have the particularity that "mystery" in this instance involves. (2) The salvation of all the elect of Israel affirms or implies no more than the salvation of a remnant of Israel in all generations. But verse 26 brings to a climax a sustained argument that goes far beyond that doctrine. Paul is concerned with the unfolding of God's plan of salvation in history and with the climactic developments for Jew and Gentile that will ensue. It is in terms of this historical perspective that the clause in question is to be understood. (3) Verse 26 is in close sequence with verse 25. The main thesis of verse 25 is that the hardening of Israel is to terminate and that Israel is to be restored. This is but another way of affirming what had been called Israel's "fulness" in verse 12, the "receiving" in verse 15, and the grafting in again in verses 23, 24. To regard the climactic statement, "all Israel shall be saved", as having reference to anything else than this precise datum would be exegetical violence.[52]

6:16. In the present passage there is the sustained contrast between Israel and the Gentiles. There is no such contrast in the context of Gal. 6:16. Although Calvin regards "all Israel" as referring to all the people of God including Jews and Gentiles, yet he does not exclude the restoration of Israel as a people to the obedience of faith. "When the Gentiles have come in, the Jews will at the same time return from their defection to the obedience of faith. The salvation of the Israel of God, which must be drawn from both, will thus be completed, and yet in such a way that the Jews, as the first born in the family of God, may obtain the first place" (*op. cit., ad loc.*; *cf.* also his comment *ad* 11:15).

[52] Besides, how anticlimactic in this context would be the general truth implicit in all of Paul's teaching that all the elect will be saved!

97

If we keep in mind the theme of this chapter and the sustained emphasis on the restoration of Israel, there is no other alternative than to conclude that the proposition, "all Israel shall be saved", is to be interpreted in terms of the fulness, the receiving, the ingrafting of Israel as a people, the restoration of Israel to gospel favour and blessing and the correlative turning of Israel from unbelief to faith and repentance. When the preceding verses are related to verse 26, the salvation of Israel must be conceived of on a scale that is commensurate with their trespass, their loss, their casting away, their breaking off, and their hardening, commensurate, of course, in the opposite direction. This is plainly the implication of the contrasts intimated in fulness, receiving, grafting in, and salvation. In a word, it is the salvation of the mass of Israel that the apostle affirms. There are, however, two reservations necessary to guard the proposition against unwarranted extension of its meaning. (1) It may not be interpreted as implying that in the time of fulfilment every Israelite will be converted. Analogy is against any such insistence. The apostasy of Israel, their trespass, loss, casting away, hardening were not universal. There was always a remnant, not all branches were broken off, their hardening was in part. Likewise restoration and salvation need not include every Israelite. "All Israel" can refer to the mass, the people as a whole in accord with the pattern followed in the chapter throughout.[53] (2) Paul is not reflecting on the question of the relative proportion of saved Jews in the final accounting of God's judgment. We need to be reminded again of the historical perspective in this section. The apostle is thinking of a time in the future when the hardening of Israel will terminate. As the fulness, receiving, ingrafting have this time reference, so must the salvation of Israel have. Therefore the proposition reflects merely on what will be true at this point or period in history.

As is characteristic of this epistle and particularly of chapters 9–11, appeal is made to Scripture for support (*cf.* 9:12, 15, 17, 25, 27, 29, 33; 10:5, 8, 11, 18, 19, 20, 21; 11:8, 9). The first part of the quotation is from Isaiah 59:20, 21 and the last part derived from

---

[53] "πᾶς must be taken in the proper meaning of the word: 'Israel, as a whole, Israel as a nation,' and not as necessarily including every individual Israelite. *Cf.* I Kings xii. 1... 2 Chron. xii. 1... Dan. ix. 11" (Sanday and Headlam: *op. cit., ad loc.*).

11:25-32 FULNESS OF GENTILES AND SALVATION OF ISRAEL

Jeremiah 31:34.[54] There should be no question but Paul regards these Old Testament passages as applicable to the restoration of Israel. In the earlier portions of this section of the epistle Scripture had been adduced to support various theses and arguments. There may be veiled allusion to the conversion of Israel on some of these occasions (*cf.* 10:19; 11:1, 2). But this is the first instance of express appeal to Scripture in support of the large-scale reclamation and it is questionable if there is even oblique reference in these earlier passages. This express application is an index to the principle of interpretation which would have to be applied to many other Old Testament passages which are in the same vein as Isaiah 59:20, 21, namely, that they comprise the promise of an expansion of gospel blessing such as Paul enunciates in verses 25, 26.[55] The elements of these quotations specify for us what is involved in the salvation of Israel. These are redemption,[56] the turning away from ungodliness, the sealing of covenant grace, and the taking away of sins, the kernel blessings of the gospel, and they are an index to what the salvation of Israel means. There is no suggestion of any privilege or status but that which is common to Jew and Gentile in the faith of Christ.

The clause, "this is my covenant unto them", warrants further comment. Apart from 9:4, where the patriarchal covenants are mentioned, this is the only reference to covenant in this epistle. In

---

[54] In Isa. 59:20 the Greek differs from the Hebrew in the second clause. Paul quotes the Greek verbatim but the Hebrew reads "and unto them that turn from transgression in Jacob". The first clause in Paul's quotation does not exactly correspond to either the Hebrew or Greek. The former reads "to Zion" or "for Zion" (לְצִיּוֹן) and the Greek renders this quite properly "on behalf of Zion" (ἕνεκεν Σιων). But Paul renders "out of Zion", as in Psalm 14:7 (LXX 13:7). There should not be any great difficulty. The preposition involved in Hebrew is capable of both renderings and Paul was at liberty to use the one he did. Both significations are true, that the Redeemer came out of Zion and for its deliverance. The accent in Paul's teaching in this passage is on what the Redeemer will do *for* Zion. But in the first clause the thought is focused on the relation of the Redeemer to Zion after the pattern of 9:5. This is germane to the total emphasis of this context and underscores the relevance of the Redeemer's saving work to Israel as a people.

[55] *Cf.* Psalms 14:7; 126:1, 2; Isa. 19:24, 25; 27:13; 30:26; 33:20, 21; 45:17; 46:13; 49:14–16; 54:9, 10; 60:1–3; 62:1–4; Mic. 7:18–20. This is more particularly apparent when Isa. 59:20, 21 is seen to provide the basis for 60:1–3 and in 54:9, 10 the same emphasis upon covenant faithfulness appears as in 59:20, 21 which is the text to which the apostle here appeals.

[56] גָּאַל used in the Hebrew is one of the standard terms with redemptive meaning in the Old Testament.

accordance with the biblical conception of covenant as oath-bound confirmation there is here certification of the faithfulness of God to his promise and the certainty of fulfilment. We cannot dissociate this covenantal assurance from the proposition in support of which the text is adduced or from that which follows in verse 28. Thus the effect is that the future restoration of Israel is certified by nothing less than the certainty belonging to covenantal institution. It is to be observed that the other clauses coordinate with the one respecting covenant refer to what God or the Deliverer will do. In a way consistent with the concept of covenant the accent falls upon what God will do, upon divine monergism. In Isaiah 59:21 the covenant is stated in terms of perpetual endowment with the Spirit and words of God, another index to the certitude which covenant grace involves.[57]

28, 29 The first clause of verse 28 has reference to what the apostle had noted earlier in verses 11, 12, 15. The only feature calling for additional comment is the force of the word "enemies". This is not to be understood subjectively of the enmity entertained by Jews toward Gentiles or by Gentiles toward Jews. It refers to the alienation from God's favour and blessing. This is proven by the contrast with "beloved" in the next clause. "Beloved" must be beloved of God. "Enemies" has in view the same relationship as is denoted by "casting away" in verse 15 where it is contrasted with reconciliation and receiving, both of which mean reception into the favour and blessing of God. Hence "enemies" points to that rejection of Israel with which Paul is dealing throughout this chapter. It was the occasion of bringing the gospel to the Gentiles. As in the context, Gentiles are being addressed.

The second clause in verse 28 raises more difficulty. It must be observed that the two clauses refer to relationships of God to Israel that are contemporaneous. Israel are both "enemies" and "beloved" at the same time, enemies as regards the gospel, beloved as regards the election. This contrast means that by their rejection of the gospel they have been cast away and the gospel had been given to the Gentiles but that nevertheless by reason of

---

[57] It is worthy of note that although Paul distinguishes between Israel and Israel, seed and seed, children and children (*cf.* 9:6–13) he does not make this discrimination in terms of "covenant" so as to distinguish between those who are in the covenant in a broader sense and those who are actual partakers of its grace.

11:25–32 FULNESS OF GENTILES AND SALVATION OF ISRAEL

election and on account of their relation to the fathers they were beloved. "The election" in this instance is not the same as that in 11:6, 7. In the latter the election belongs only to the remnant in distinction from the mass who had been rejected and hardened and so denotes the particular election which guarantees the righteousness of faith and salvation. But in this instance Israel as a whole are in view, Israel as alienated from the favour of God by unbelief.[58] The election, therefore, is the election of Israel as a people and corresponds to the "people which he foreknew" in verse 2, the theocratic election. This is made apparent also by the expression "for the fathers' sake". It is another way of saying what had been said in terms of the firstfruit and the root in verse 16. "Beloved" thus means that God has not suspended or rescinded his relation to Israel as his chosen people in terms of the covenants made with the fathers. Unfaithful as Israel have been and broken off for that reason, yet God still sustains his peculiar relation of love to them, a relation that will be demonstrated and vindicated in the restoration (vss. 12, 15, 26).

It is in this light that verse 29 is to be understood. "The gifts and the calling of God" have reference to those mentioned in 9:4, 5 as the privileges and prerogatives of Israel. That these "are not repented of" is expressly to the effect that the adoption, the covenants, and the promises in their application to Israel have not been abrogated. The appeal is to the faithfulness of God (*cf.* 3:3). The veracity of God insures the continuance of that relationship which the covenants with the fathers instituted, another index of the certitude belonging to covenantal confirmation.

30, 31 The apostle is still addressing the Gentiles. Verse 30 is a repetition in different terms of what had been stated already in verses 11, 12, 15, 28 that the Gentiles had become the partakers of God's mercy by the disobedience of Israel. Verse 31, though not without parallel in the preceding verses (*cf.* vss. 11b, 14, 25b), expressly enunciates the relation which the salvation of the Gentiles sustains to the restoration of Israel. The salvation of the Gentiles was promoted by the disobedience of Israel. But it is the reverse of this that obtains in the promotion of Israel's salvation.

---

[58] "He is not, we must remember, dealing now with the private election of any individual, but the common adoption of a whole nation" (Calvin: *op. cit., ad loc.*)

It is by the mercy shown to the Gentiles,[59] not by their disobedience or defection, that Israel's conversion is realized. The grace of God's plan for the salvation of Jew and Gentile is shown by this progression, and the occurrence on three occasions of the terms for mercy in these two verses (*cf.* 9:15, 16) brings more clearly into focus the emphasis upon God's sovereign beneficence in the whole process here described. We are thus prepared for the statement of God's merciful design in verse 32.

32 In the two preceding verses the triple occurrence of the terms for mercy brings to the forefront the place that God's mercy occupies in the salvation of men. But no less noteworthy is the triple reference to disobedience. The lesson is obvious. It is only in the context of disobedience that *mercy* has relevance and meaning. Mercy is of such a character that disobedience is its complement or presupposition and only as exercised to the disobedient does it exist and operate. It is this truth that comes to expression in verse 32 in terms of the providential *action* of God. It is not simply that men are disobedient, are therefore in a condition that gives scope for the exercise of mercy, and by God's sovereign grace become the objects of mercy. The accent now falls upon the determinate action of God. He "hath shut up all unto disobedience". It is so ordered in the judgment of God that all are effectively inclosed in the fold of the disobedient and so hemmed in to disobedience that there is no possibility of escape from this servitude except as the mercy of God gives release. There is no possibility of toning down the severity of the action here stated.

It is, however, the severity that exhibits the glory of the main thought of this verse. It is "that he might have mercy upon all". The more we reflect upon the implications of the first clause the more enhanced becomes our apprehension of the marvel of the second. And it is not mere correlation of disobedience and mercy that we have now; it is that the shutting up to disobedience, without any amelioration of the severity involved, is directed to the end of showing mercy. The former is for the purpose of promoting the latter. The apostle advances from the thought of complementation to that of subordination. If we are sensitive to

---

[59] τῷ ὑμετέρῳ ἐλέει is to be construed with the ἵνα that follows; *cf.* the same construction in II Cor. 2:4b; Gal. 2:10.

the depths of the design here stated, we must sense the unfathomable, and we are constrained to say: God's way is in the sea and his paths in the great waters: his footsteps are not known (*cf.* Psalm 77:19). This was the reaction of Paul himself. Hence the exclamations: "O the depth of the riches both of the wisdom and knowledge of God! how unsearchable are his judgments, and his ways past finding out!" (vs. 33). It is not the reaction of painful bewilderment but the response of adoring amazement, redolent of joy and praise. When our faith and understanding peer to the horizons of revelation, it is then our hearts and minds are overwhelmed with the incomprehensible mystery of God's works and ways.

In terms of Paul's own teaching (*cf.* 2:4–16; 9:22; II Thess. 1:6–10) it is impossible to regard the final clause in verse 32 as contemplating the salvation of all mankind. The context determines the scope. The apostle is thinking of Jews and Gentiles. In the preceding context he had dealt with the differentiating roles of Jew and Gentile in the unfolding of God's worldwide saving purpose (*cf.* vss. 11, 12, 15, 25–28). Even in the two preceding verses this differentiation is present to some extent. Gentiles obtained mercy by Israel's disobedience and Israel obtains mercy by the mercy shown to the Gentiles. But in verse 32 the emphasis falls upon that which is common to all without distinction, that they are shut up to unbelief and fit objects for that reason of *mercy*. This, however, is no more all without exception than do verses 30 and 31 apply to all Gentiles and Jews nor verse 26 to all of Israel past, present, and future. Thus "mercy upon all" means all without distinction who are the partakers of this mercy. Although the first clause of verse 32 is true of all without exception (*cf.* Gal. 3:22), it is not apparent that in this instance Paul is reflecting upon that fact but, after the pattern of the context and in accord with the last clause, emphasizing that Gentiles and Jews without any difference are shut up to disobedience.

D. THE DOXOLOGY
(11:33–36)

11:33–36

33 O the depth of the riches both of the wisdom and the knowledge of God! how unsearchable are his judgments, and his ways past tracing out!
34 For who hath known the mind of the Lord? or who hath been his counsellor?
35 or who hath first given to him, and it shall be recompensed unto him again?
36 For of him, and through him, and unto him, are all things. To him *be* the glory for ever. Amen.

33–36 The theme of verses 33, 34 may be stated as the incomprehensibility of God's counsel. The terms "unsearchable" and "past tracing out" indicate this. It is a mistake, however, to think that God's incomprehensibility applies only to his secret, unrevealed counsel. What God has not revealed does not come within the compass of our knowledge; it is inapprehensible. What is not apprehended is also incomprehensible. But the most significant aspect of incomprehensibility is that it applies to what God has revealed. It is this truth that is conspicuous in this passage. What constrains the doxology is the revealed counsel, particularly that of verse 32. The apostle is overwhelmed with the unfathomable depth of the scheme of salvation which has been the subject of discourse in the preceding context. Besides, the riches and the wisdom and the knowledge of God which he views as a great deep are not unrevealed. They are the riches of grace and mercy, the deep things of God revealed by the Spirit, and the wisdom not of this world disclosed to the saints (*cf.* I Cor. 1:24; 2:6–8). Furthermore, the judgments that are unsearchable and the ways past tracing out are those of which the apostle had given examples.

It is not certain to how much of the preceding part of the epistle this doxology is intended to be the conclusion. It could be the whole of the epistle up to this point. There is an obvious transition at the end of this chapter to concrete and practical application in

11:33-36 THE DOXOLOGY

the spheres of Christian life and behaviour. The doxology is a fitting conclusion to all that precedes. It could also be the climax to this well-defined section of the epistle (9:1–11:36). There can be no dogmatism on this question. If a preference might be suggested it is for the second of these alternatives. The question of Israel is the one with which this section began. The apostle had dealt with various facets of God's counsel as they bear upon the unbelief and rejection of Israel. In the latter part of chapter 11 (vss. 11ff.) he comes to deal with Israel in relation to God's worldwide redemptive design and shows how both the rejection of Israel and their restoration promote the salvation of the nations of the earth. Casting his eye on the future unfolding of this saving design he sees the fulness of both Gentiles and Israel, and these in their conditioning of one another. It is this sequel of abounding grace that is the final answer to the problem of Israel, a sequel that is brought to fruition by God's mercy and by that alone. In the unfolding of this prophetic survey he places even the unbelief of Israel in the perspective of God's merciful design and not only the unbelief of Israel but that of all nations and makes the astounding statement of verse 32. This is the grand climax. It is this climax in particular that evokes the doxology and the latter is thus directly related to the theme of this section (9:1–11:32).

The word "riches" in verse 33 could be taken, as in the version, to denote the riches of God's wisdom and knowledge. When Paul uses this term, most frequently he speaks of the riches of some attribute of God or of his glory (*cf.* 2:4; 9:23; Eph. 1:7; 2:7; 3:16) or of the riches of something else (*cf.* II Cor. 8:2; Eph. 1:18; 2:4; Col. 1:27; 2:2). But he can also speak of God's riches directly (Phil. 4:19) as also of the riches of Christ (Eph. 3:8; *cf.* II Cor. 8:9). Hence the three terms can be taken as coordinate and so the rendering would be: "O the depth of the riches and the wisdom and the knowledge of God". In this event the "riches" would have in view particularly God's grace and mercy upon which so much stress falls in the preceding context. The challenge of verse 35a would thus find its appropriate antecedent and reason in the word "riches", and this would be the strongest argument in favour of the second rendering. On the other hand, it could be said that the riches of God without any specification would be expected to include wisdom and knowledge and, since these are mentioned separately, the intent of the apostle was to characterize God's wisdom and knowledge by the exclamation "O the depth of the riches". Furthermore, the apostle proceeds to speak of God's judgments and ways and then utters the challenges of verse 34 which are concerned with knowledge and wisdom in that order. There is good reason, therefore, why the accent in these two verses should be placed upon wisdom and knowledge. For in God's providential ordering of events to their designed end (*cf.* vs. 32) it is the wisdom and knowledge of God that come to the forefront for adoration and admiration. The question, however, may not be settled with certainty. Both renderings are appropriate to the context.

Knowledge refers to God's all-inclusive and exhaustive cognition and understanding, wisdom to the arrangement and adaptation of all things to the fulfilment of his holy designs. In God these are correlative and it would be artificial to press the distinction unduly. His knowledge involves perfect understanding of interrelationships and these, in turn, are determined by his wisdom; the relations of things exist only by reason of the designs they are to promote in his all-comprising plan.

"Judgments" can be used in the sense of decisions or determinations. This meaning appears frequently in the use of the corresponding verb (*cf.* 14:13b; I Cor. 2:2; 7:37; 11:13; II Cor. 2:1; Tit. 3:12). But preponderantly, if not uniformly, in the New Testament "judgment" refers to judicial decisions or sentences. In the preceding contexts there are several examples of this kind of judgment on God's part (*cf.* 9:18, 22; 11:7b, 8–10, 20–22, 25, 32). Thus God's judicial acts may be in view. In any case these may not be excluded. The "ways" of God are not to be understood in the restrictive sense of the ways of God revealed for our salvation and direction (*cf.* Matt. 21:32; Luke 1:76; Acts 13:10; 18:25, 26; Rom. 3:17; I Cor. 4:17; Heb. 3:10). They refer in this instance to God's dealings with men and are to be understood inclusively of the diverse providences in which his decretive will is executed. God's judgments are unsearchable and his ways past tracing out (*cf.* Eph. 3:8). The praise of the riches of God's wisdom and knowledge preceding is eloquent witness to the contrast between God's knowledge and ours. It is of our understanding Paul speaks when he says unsearchable and past tracing out. But it is the *depth* of God's wisdom and knowledge that makes it so for our understanding.

11:33-36 THE DOXOLOGY

Verses 34, 35 are confirmation drawn from the Old Testament after the pattern so frequently occurring in this section of the epistle. Verse 34 is practically a verbatim quotation from the Greek version of Isaiah 40:13. This quotation may attach itself to wisdom and knowledge in verse 33, though in reverse order. "Who hath known the mind of the Lord?" witnesses to the unfathomable depth of God's knowledge. "Who hath been his counsellor?" implies that God alone, without dependence on any creature for counsel, devised the plan of which providence is the execution. With change of person from the first to the third, verse 35 appears to be from Job 41:11 (Heb. 41:3).[60] As indicated above, this may refer back to God's riches (vs. 33). This is not necessary, however, and may be artificial. In the preceding context there has been repeated appeal to the grace and mercy of God and no instance is more relevant than the climax which introduced the doxology (vs. 32). God is debtor to none, his favour is never compensation, merit places no constraints upon his mercy. The three rhetorical questions, all implying a negative answer, have their positive counterparts in the self-sufficiency, sovereignty, and independence of God. This truth finds its reason in what brings the doxology to its own climax: "For of him, and through him, and unto him, are all things" (vs. 36).

Verse 36 should be compared with other Pauline texts in which similar sentiments are expressed (I Cor. 8:6; Eph. 4:6; Col. 1:16; *cf.* Heb. 2:10). The view of older interpreters, however, that there is reference in this text to the Father as the one *of* whom are all things, the Son as the one *through* whom are all things, and the Holy Spirit as the one *unto* whom are all things is without warrant. The fallacy can be readily seen in the fact that the Holy Spirit is not represented elsewhere as the person of the Godhead unto whom by way of eminence are all things. Paul is here speaking of God inclusively designated and understood and not by way of the differentiation evident in other passages (*cf.* I Cor. 8:6; Eph. 4:5, 6). Of God as the Godhead these ascriptions are predicated. He is the source of all things in that they have proceeded from him;

---

[60] In both Hebrew and LXX the text is Job 41:3. Paul here does not follow the LXX. He is closer to the Hebrew which reads literally: "who has anticipated me that I should make recompense?" This thought Paul reproduces in his rendering. The LXX has τίς ἀντιστήσεταί μοι καὶ ὑπομενεῖ. The ἀντιστήσεται could be derived from the Hebrew verb קדם but otherwise there appears to be no similarity to the Hebrew.

he is the Creator. He is the agent through whom all things subsist and are directed to their proper end. And he is the last end to whose glory all things will redound. The apostle is thinking of all that comes within the created and providential order. God is the Alpha and the Omega, the beginning and the end, the first and the last (*cf*. Prov. 16:4; Rev. 4:11). And to him must not only all glory be ascribed; to him all glory will redound.

ROMANS XII

XVIII. THE CHRISTIAN WAY OF LIFE (12:1–15:13)

A. MANIFOLD PRACTICAL DUTIES (12:1–21)

12:1, 2

1 I beseech you therefore, brethren, by the mercies of God, to present your bodies a living sacrifice, holy, acceptable to God, *which is* your spiritual service.
2 And be not fashioned according to this world: but be ye transformed by the renewing of your mind, that ye may prove what is the good and acceptable and perfect will of God.

A change of theme is apparent at the beginning of this chapter. That the apostle is concerned with the subject of sanctification is evident from the outset. "Be ye transformed by the renewing of your mind" (vs. 2) is exhortation to the sanctifying process and the terms used are specially adapted to a definition of that in which this process consists. Paul did not, however, postpone to this point in the epistle his teaching on the subject of sanctification. Chapters 6–8 had been concerned with that topic, and the basis of sanctification as well as the exhortations particularly relevant thereto had been unfolded in 6:1–7:6. What then is the difference between these earlier chapters and that to which we are introduced at chapter 12? At this point the apostle comes to deal with concrete practical application. It is important to note the relationship and to appreciate the priority of the aspect developed in 6:1–7:6. It is futile to give practical exhortation apart from the basis on which it rests or the spring from which compliance must flow.

The basis and spring of sanctification are union with Christ, more especially union with him in the virtue of his death and the power of his resurrection (*cf.* 6:2–6; 7:4–6). It is by this union with Christ that the breach with sin in its power and defilement was effected (*cf.* 6:14) and newness of life in the efficacy of Jesus' resurrection inaugurated (*cf.* 6:4, 10, 11). Believers walk not after the flesh but after the Spirit (*cf.* 8:4). And not only is there this virtue in the death and resurrection of Christ but, since union with Christ is permanent, there is also the virtue that constantly emanates from Christ and is the dynamic in the growth unto holiness. The Holy Spirit is the Spirit of the ascended Lord (*cf.* 8:4, 9). Hence, when Paul at 12:1 enters the sphere of practical application, he does so on the basis of his earlier teaching. The formula with which he begins, "I beseech you therefore" (*cf.* I Cor. 4:16; Eph. 4:1; I Tim. 2:1), points to a conclusion drawn from the preceding context and although the climactic exclamation of the preceding verses in adoration of the riches of God's free and unmerited grace is of itself sufficient to constrain the exhortation with which chapter 12 begins yet it would not be feasible to exclude the whole more doctrinal parts of the epistle, especially the part devoted to sanctification, from that which underlies the "therefore" of 12:1. This illustrates what is characteristic of Paul's teaching, that ethics must rest upon the foundation of redemptive accomplishment. More specifically stated it is that ethics springs from union with Christ and therefore from participation of the virtue belonging to him and exercised by him as the crucified, risen, and ascended Redeemer. Ethics consonant with the high calling of God in Christ is itself part of the application of redemption; it belongs to sanctification. And it is not as if ethics is distinct from doctrine. For ethics is based on ethical teaching and teaching is doctrine. A great deal of the most significant doctrine is enunciated in the teaching concerned with the most practical details of the Christian life.

1, 2 It is important to observe that when the apostle enters upon practical exhortation he deals first with the human body—"present your bodies a living sacrifice". It has been maintained that he uses the term "body" to represent the whole person so that the meaning would be "present your persons". Undoubtedly there is no intent to restrict to the physical body the consecration here enjoined. But there is not good warrant for taking the word "body" as a synonym for the whole person. Paul's usage elsewhere would indicate that he is thinking specifically of the body (*cf.* 6:6, 12;

12:1-21 MANIFOLD PRACTICAL DUTIES

8:10, 11, 23; I Cor. 5:3; 6:13, 15-20; 7:4, 34; 9:27; 15:44; II Cor. 5:6, 8, 10). A study of these passages will show how important was the body in Paul's esteem and, particularly, how significant in the various aspects of the saving process. It is not without necessity that he should have placed in the forefront of practical exhortation this emphasis upon consecration of the body. In Greek philosophy there had been a depreciation of the body. The ethical ideal was to be freed from the body and its degrading influences. This view of the body runs counter to the whole witness of Scripture. Body was an integral element in man's person from the outset (*cf.* Gen. 2:7, 21-23). The dissolution of the body is the wages of sin and therefore abnormal (*cf.* Gen. 2:17; 3:19; Rom. 5:12). The consummation of redemption waits for the resurrection of the body (*cf.* Rom. 8:23; I Cor. 15:54-56; Phil. 3:21). Hence sanctification must bring the body within its scope. There was not only a necessity for this kind of exhortation arising from depreciation of the body but also because indulgence of vice closely associated with the body was so prevalent and liable to be discounted in the assessment of ethical demands. It is in the light of this practical situation that the injunction of the apostle is to be appreciated. Paul was realistic and he was aware that if sanctification did not embrace the physical in our personality it would be annulled from the outset.

What is Paul's injunction? "Present your bodies a living sacrifice." The language is that of sacrificial ritual. The difference, however, is striking. Any animate offering in the Old Testament ritual had to be slain and its blood shed. The human body is not presented to be slain. It is true that in union with Christ believers were put to death (*cf.* Rom. 6:2; 7:4, 6) and this also applies to the body of sin (*cf.* Rom. 6:6). But it is not this body of sin or sinful body that they are to present as a living sacrifice. Romans 6:13 is the index to Paul's meaning here: "Neither present your members as instruments of unrighteousness to sin, but present yourselves to God as those alive from the dead and your members instruments of righteousness to God". It is a body alive from the dead that the believer is to present, alive from the dead because the body of sin has been destroyed. The body to be presented is a member of Christ and the temple of the Holy Spirit (*cf.* I Cor. 6:15, 19). It is possible that the word "living" also reflects on the permanence of this offering, that it must be a constant dedication.

"Holy, acceptable to God." Holiness is contrasted with the defilement which characterizes the body of sin and with all sensual lust. Holiness is the fundamental character and to be well-pleasing to God the governing principle of a believer. These qualities have reference to his body as well as to his spirit and show how ethical character belongs to the body and to its functions. No terms could certify this fact more than "holy" and "well-pleasing to God". When we take account of the sexual vice in all its forms, so prevalent in Paul's day as well as in ours, we see the contradiction that it offers to the criteria which are here mentioned.

"Your spiritual service." The term used here is not the term which is usually rendered by the word "spiritual" in the New Testament. Reasonable or rational is a more literal rendering. No doubt the presenting of the body as a living sacrifice is a spiritual service, that is to say, a service offered by the direction of the Holy Spirit (*cf.* I Pet. 2:5). But there must have been some reason for the use of this distinct term used nowhere else by Paul and used only once elsewhere in the New Testament (I Pet. 2:2). The service here in view is worshipful service and the apostle characterizes it as "rational" because it is worship that derives its character as acceptable to God from the fact that it enlists our mind, our reason, our intellect. It is rational in contrast with what is mechanical and automatic. A great many of our bodily functions do not enlist volition on our part. But the worshipful service here enjoined must constrain intelligent volition. The lesson to be derived from the term "rational" is that we are not "Spiritual" in the biblical sense except as the use of our bodies is characterized by conscious, intelligent, consecrated devotion to the service of God. Furthermore, this expression is very likely directed against mechanical externalism and so the worship is contrasted, as H. P. Liddon says, "with the external ceremonial of the Jewish and heathen cultus".[1] In any event the term in question shows how related are our bodies and the service they render to that which we characteristically are as rational, responsible beings.

The introductory words of this verse must not be overlooked. They bespeak the tenderness of the appeal. As in I John 2:1 we sense the bowels of earnest solicitude on John's part so here in Paul. "I beseech you therefore, brethren." It is the appeal of

---

[1] *Op. cit.*, p. 229.

loving relationship. But the heart of the exhortation resides in the expression "by the mercies of God". These are the tender mercies of God, the riches of his compassion (*cf.* II Cor. 1:3; Phil. 2:1; Col. 3:12) and are made the plea to present our bodies a living sacrifice. Paul can appeal to the severity of God's judgment in his pleas for sanctification (*cf.* Rom. 8:13; Gal. 6:8). But here we have the constraint of God's manifold mercies. It is the mercy of God that melts the heart and it is as we are moved by these mercies of God that we shall know the constraint of consecration as it pertains to our body (*cf.* I Cor. 6:20). The tenderness of Paul's plea is after the pattern of that which he pleads as the impelling reason.

The leading thought of verse 2 is the pattern of behaviour. In connection with the concrete and practical details of life there is no more searching question than that of the patterns of thought and action which we follow. To what standards do we conform? We know how disconcerting it is to break with the patterns of behaviour that are common in the social environment in which we live. It is to be understood that we should not violate the customs of order, decency, and kindliness. Later in this chapter Paul enjoins: "If it be possible, as much as in you lieth, be at peace with all men" (vs. 18; *cf.* Heb. 12:14). But there are patterns that must not be adhered to. This is the force of "be not fashioned according to this world".

Three things are to be noted about this injunction. (1) It is negative. The Pauline ethic is negative because it is realistic; it takes account of the presence of sin. The pivotal test of Eden was negative because there was liability to sin. Eight of the ten commandments are negative because there is sin. The first evidence of Christian faith is turning from sin. The Thessalonians turned to God from idols to serve the living God (I Thess. 1:9). (2) The term used for this "world" is "age". Its meaning is determined by the contrast with the age to come. "This age" is that which stands on this side of what we often call eternity. It is the temporal and the transient age. Conformity to this age is to be wrapped up in the things that are temporal, to have all our thought oriented to that which is seen and temporal. It is to be a time-server. How far-reaching is this indictment! If all our calculations, plans, ambitions are determined by what falls within life here, then we are children of this age. Besides, this age is an evil age (*cf.* I Cor. 2:6, 8; Gal. 1:4) and if our fashion is that of this age then the iniquity characteristic of this age governs our life. The need for the negative is apparent. (3) The term rendered "fashioned", though it may not of itself reflect upon the fleeting and passing character of this present age, does nevertheless draw our attention to the difference between the pattern of which we are to divest ourselves and the pattern after which we are to be transformed.[2] There is nothing abiding in that by which this age is characterized. "The world is passing away and the lust thereof: but he who does the will of God abides for ever" (I John 2:17). We must have patterns that abide, patterns that are the earnest of and are continuous with the age to come. We do well to examine ourselves by this criterion: are we calculating in those terms which the interests and hopes of the age to come demand?

"But be ye transformed by the renewing of your mind." The term used here implies that we are to be constantly in the process of being metamorphosed by renewal of that which is the seat of thought and understanding. If there is any suggestion of the fleeting fashions of this age in the preceding clause, there is here reflection upon the deep-seated and permanent change wrought by the process of renewal. Sanctification is a process of revolutionary change in that which is the centre of consciousness. This sounds a fundamental note in the biblical ethic. It is the thought of progression and strikes at the stagnation, complacency, pride of achievement so often characterizing Christians. It is not the beggarly notion of second blessing that the apostle propounds but that of constant renewal, of metamorphosis in the seat of consciousness. We must relate the expression here used to Paul's fuller statement of this same process of transformation. "But we all, with unveiled face beholding as in a mirror the glory of the Lord, are transformed into the same image from glory to glory, even as from the Lord the Spirit" (II Cor. 3:18).

The practical and experiential outworking of this renewal of the mind is indicated by that to which the renewal is directed—"that ye may prove what is the good and acceptable and perfect will of God". To "prove" in this instance is not to test so as to find out whether the will of God is good or bad; it is not to examine (*cf.*

---

[2] *Cf.* J. B. Lightfoot: *Saint Paul's Epistle to the Philippians* (London, 1908), p. 130.

I Cor. 11:28; II Cor. 13:5). It is to approve (*cf.* Rom. 2:18; Phil. 1:10). But it is this meaning with a distinct shade of thought, namely, to discover, to find out or learn by experience what the will of God is and therefore to learn how approved the will of God is. It is a will that will never fail or be found wanting. If life is aimless, stagnant, fruitless, lacking in content, it is because we are not entering by experience into the richness of God's will. The commandment of God is exceeding broad. There is not a moment of life that the will of God does not command, no circumstance that it does not fill with meaning if we are responsive to the fulness of his revealed counsel for us.

The question arises: is this the will of determinate purpose or the will of commandment? That the term is used in the former sense is beyond question (*cf.* Matt. 18:14; John 1:13; Rom. 1:10; 15:32; I Cor. 1:1; II Cor. 1:1; Gal. 1:4; Eph. 1:5, 11; I Pet. 3:17; 4:19; II Pet. 1:21). But it is also used frequently in the latter sense (*cf.* Matt. 7:21; 12:50; 21:31; Luke 12:47; John 4:34; 7:17; 9:31; Acts 13:22; Rom. 2:18; Eph 5:17; 6:6; Col. 4:12; I Thess. 4:3; 5:18; Heb. 10:10; 13:21; I Pet. 4:2; I John 2:17; 5:14). In this instance it must be the latter. It is the will of God as it pertains to our responsible activity in progressive sanctification. The decretive will of God is not the norm according to which our life is to be patterned.

The will of God is regulative of the believer's life. When it is characterized as "good and acceptable and perfect", the construction indicates that these terms are not strictly adjectives describing the will of God. The thought is rather that the will of God is "the good, the acceptable, and the perfect".[3] In respect of that with which the apostle is now dealing the will of God is the good, the acceptable, and the perfect. The will of God is the law of God and the law is holy and just and good (*cf.* 7:12). We may never fear that the standard God has prescribed for us is only relatively good or acceptable or perfect, that it is an accommodated norm adapted to our present condition and not measuring up to the standard of God's perfection. The will of God is the transcript

---

[3] τὸ ἀγαθὸν καὶ εὐάρεστον καὶ τέλειον may be taken as examples of the substantival use of the adjective or as substantivized adjectives (*cf.* 1:19; 2:4; 7:18, 21; 8:3). The article τό can be taken as applying to εὐάρεστον and τέλειον though not repeated (*cf.* G. B. Winer: *op. cit.*, p. 127 and the examples cited by him: Mark 12:33; Luke 1:6; 14:23; Col. 2:22; Rev. 5:12).

of God's perfection and is the perfect reflection of his holiness, justice, and goodness. When we are commanded to be perfect as God is perfect (*cf.* Matt. 5:48), the will of God as revealed to us in his Word is in complete correspondence with the pattern prescribed, namely, "as your heavenly Father is perfect". Hence, when the believer will have attained to this perfection, the criterion will not differ from that now revealed as the will of God. Consummated perfection for the saints is continuous with and the completion of that which is now in process (*cf.* Col. 1:28; 4:12; Psalm 19:7–11).

12:3–8

3 For I say, through the grace that was given me, to every man that is among you, not to think of himself more highly than he ought to think; but so to think as to think soberly, according as God hath dealt to each man a measure of faith.
4 For even as we have many members in one body, and all the members have not the same office:
5 so we, who are many, are one body in Christ, and severally members one of another.
6 And having gifts differing according to the grace that was given to us, whether prophecy, *let us prophesy* according to the proportion of our faith;
7 or ministry, *let us give ourselves* to our ministry; or he that teacheth, to his teaching;
8 or he that exhorteth, to his exhorting: he that giveth, *let him do it* with liberality: he that ruleth, with diligence; he that showeth mercy, with cheerfulness.

3–5 In the two preceding verses the exhortations to sanctification have equal reference to all; there could not be any differentiation. But at verse 3 there is an obvious change. The change is not one that restricts the relevance to all of what Paul is going to say. It concerns every one: "I say ... to every man that is among you". The change is that the apostle has now in view the differences that exist among believers, differences which God in his sovereign providence and distributions of his grace has caused to exist. These differences are implicit in the various expressions—"according as God hath dealt to each a measure of faith" (vs. 3); "all the members have not the same office" (vs. 4); "having gifts differing according to the grace that was given to us" (vs. 6). So now what is in mind is the diversity in respect of endowment, grace, function, office, faith. We find now the directions pertaining to sanctification in the church of Christ as God's will takes account of this diversity.

At the outset the apostle refers to the grace given to himself— "I say through the grace that was given me". In thinking of the grace given him he could not be unmindful of the grace by which he was saved, the grace common to him and all believers (*cf.* Gal. 1:15; I Tim. 1:13–16). But he is thinking specifically of the grace bestowed upon him in his apostolic commission (*cf.* 1:5; 15:15, 16; I Cor. 3:10; 15:9, 10; Gal. 2:9; Eph. 3:7, 8; I Tim. 1:12). He properly assessed and exercised this grace and it was in pursuance of this office that he was bold to give these directions as they pertain to the recognition of diversity within the unity of the body of Christ and to the maintenance of the order and harmony so liable to be disrupted when the significance of this diversity is not appreciated.

One of the ways in which the design contemplated by the apostle is frustrated is by the sin of pride. Pride consists in coveting or exercising a prerogative that does not belong to us. The negative is here again to be noted and the liability to indulgence is marked by the necessity of directing the exhortation to all— "to every one that is among you". No one is immune to exaggerated self-esteem. In Meyer's words, "He, therefore, who covets a higher or another standpoint and sphere of activity in the community, and is not contented with that which corresponds to the measure of faith bestowed on him, evinces a wilful self-exaltation, which is without measure and not of God".[4]

But that which is commended must be observed no less than that which is forbidden. We are to "think so as to think soberly". Thus humble and sober assessment of what each person is by the grace of God is enjoined. If we consider ourselves to possess gifts we do not have, then we have an inflated notion of our place and function; we sin by esteeming ourselves beyond what we are. But if we underestimate, then we are refusing to acknowledge God's grace and we fail to exercise that which God has dispensed for our own sanctification and that of others. The positive injunction is the reproof of a false humility which equally with over self-

---

[4] *Op. cit., ad* 12:3.

esteem fails to assess the grace of God and the vocation which distinguishing distribution of grace assigns to each.

The criterion by which this sobriety of judgment is to be exercised is the "measure of faith" which God has imparted to each one. The meaning is not that the faith of each one determines the degree in which he will exercise sober judgment. It is not the character of the judgment that is reflected on here; the preceding clause takes care of that necessity. The "measure of faith" is that which sober judgment is to take into account in determining the assessment which each is to give of himself and therefore of the function or functions which he may properly perform in the church. The question that does arise is: to what does "faith" refer? Is it faith in the generic sense of faith in Christ by which we have been saved (*cf.* Eph. 2:8)? Or is faith used in a more specific sense of particular gifts which God has imparted to believers and of which there is great diversity?

The term "faith" is not to be understood here in the sense of that which is believed, the truth of the gospel (*cf.* Gal. 1:23; I Tim. 5:8; Jude 3). This could not be spoken of as distributed to each believer by measure, and "faith" must be understood as the faith exercised by the believer. Also, "measure of faith" is not to be understood as if faith were a quantity that could be divided into parts and thus measured out in portions. "Measure of faith" must reflect on the different respects in which faith is to be exercised in view of the diversity of functions existing in the church of Christ. The meaning is to be derived from the various expressions which follow—"but all the members do not have the same function" (vs. 4); "having gifts differing according to the grace that was given to us" (vs. 6), differing functions and gifts which are enumerated in verses 6–8. Each gift requires the grace necessary for its exercise and is itself the certification of this grace, for they are gifts given according to grace (*cf.* vs. 6). There are, therefore, distinct endowments variously distributed among the members of the Christian community and this is spoken of as dealing to each a measure of faith. Each receives what the apostle calls his own "measure". The only question then is: why is this distinguishing endowment, which implies the call to its exercise, spoken of as the "measure of faith"?

It should not be supposed that the strength of the faith that is unto salvation is here in view as if the possession and exercise of certain gifts imply a greater degree of saving faith or a richer exercise of those graces which are the evidence of that faith and which are called the fruit of the Spirit (Gal. 5:22–24). All believers without distinction are called upon to exemplify this faith and the fruit thereof. But that which is here implied in the measure of faith involves, as the succeeding context shows, limitation to the sphere of activity to which each particular gift assigns its possessor. It is called the measure of faith in the restricted sense of the faith that is suited to the exercise of this gift and this nomenclature is used to emphasize the cardinal place which faith occupies not only in our becoming members of this community but also in the specific functions performed as members of it. No gift is exercised apart from faith directed to God and more specifically faith directed to Christ in accordance with the apostle's word elsewhere, "I can do all things in him that strengtheneth me" (Phil. 4:13).

Commentators have properly called attention to the difference in respect of measure between Christ and the members of his body. He is "full of grace and truth" (John 1:14), it pleased the Father that "all the fulness should dwell in him" (Col. 1:19), "in him are hid all the treasures of wisdom and knowledge". There is no *measure* to his endowments. In the church there is distribution of gift and each member possesses his own measure for which there is the corresponding faith by which and within the limits of which the gift is to be exercised.[5]

The diversity of endowment and function referred to at the end of verse 3 is now illustrated and enforced in verse 4 by appeal to the human body. As the body has many members with their own particular function so is it in the church of Christ.[6] The significant feature of this appeal to the human body appears in verse 5: "so we, who are many, are one body in Christ, and severally members one of another". There are two considerations to be noted.

1. Here is expressed the concept of the church as "one body in Christ". This is the only instance of this designation in this epistle. The same thought appears in I Corinthians 10:17: "we, the many,

---

[5] Perhaps the most conspicuous use of the term "faith" in a specific sense is I Cor. 12:9. Here it is comparable to "the word of wisdom", "the word of knowledge", "gifts of healings" etc. (*cf.* also 14:22, 23; I Cor. 13:2).

[6] *Cf.* citations in Liddon: *op. cit.*, p. 233 for the use of this comparison in the ancient Roman world with reference to the body social or politic.

are one bread, one body". Although Paul does not in either passage call believers "the body of Christ", yet in I Corinthians 12:27 he says, "ye are the body of Christ, and severally members thereof" and here the thought is so similar that we cannot doubt that the concept of the church as the body of Christ was entertained when he penned the other passages (Rom. 12:5; I Cor. 10:17) although the reason did not arise for that particular form of statement. In the Epistles to the Ephesians and Colossians the doctrine of the church as the body of Christ is more fully unfolded.[7] In these Epistles this doctrine occupies a more prominent place because it is so pertinent to the themes being developed. But we are not to suppose that the doctrine of these later Epistles is not implicit in Romans and I Corinthians. The form of expression, "one body in Christ", is suited to the thought in this instance. The apostle's interest is now centred upon the necessity of carrying into effect in the community of believers that which is exemplified in the human body, namely, that although there are many members they do not all perform the same function. The governing thought of the whole passage, diversity of gift and office exercised according to the measure of faith in the harmony of mutual esteem and recognized interdependence, determines the mode of expression. And in this case there is no need to say more than "one body in Christ".

2. Believers are not only members of the one body but also of one another. This is an unusual way of expressing the corporate relationship (*cf.* Eph. 4:25). It is not, however, redundant. It points to what is not enunciated in the fact of unity, namely, community of possession, the communion which believers have with one another. They have property in one another and therefore in one another's gifts and graces. This is not the communism which destroys personal property; it is community that recognizes the distinguishing gifts which God has distributed and so individuality is jealously maintained. But the diversity enriches each member because they have communion in all the gifts of the Holy Spirit which God has dispensed according to his own will.

6–8 Verse 6 could be regarded as continuous with verse 5 and thus carrying on its thought: "we, the many, are one body in

---

[7] *Cf.* Eph. 1:23; 2:16; 4:4, 12, 16; 5:23; Col. 1:18, 24; 2:19; 3:15.

Christ, and severally members one of another, and having gifts differing according to the grace that was given to us". Thus the three clauses are coordinate, going with "the many" as the subject. It is smoother syntax and more in agreement with verses 6b, 7 and 8 to follow the construction underlying the version and regard verse 6 as introducing a new sentence. On this view we would have to supply a verb at the middle of the verse but this is no objection. This is not uncommon in the New Testament. The verb to be supplied would be the one most appropriate to the exercise of the prophetic gift, just as in verses 7 and 8 a verb appropriate to the exercise of ministry, teaching, exhortation, and the other gifts mentioned must likewise be supplied. In verse 6, as the version indicates, the verb "prophesy" is suitable.

In these verses seven distinct gifts are mentioned. In I Corinthians 12:8–10 nine are specified, in I Corinthians 12:28, 29 also nine, in Ephesians 4:11 either four or five according as we regard "pastors and teachers" as one office or as two. Some of the gifts mentioned in these lists are not given here in Romans 12. In I Corinthians 12:28 the order of rank is expressly stated, at least in respect of the order, apostles, prophets, teachers. This same order for apostles and prophets appears in Ephesians 2:20; 3:5; 4:11. In the last cited passage the office of evangelist appears as third and is nowhere else specified in these lists. In all cases where order is intimated apostles are first and prophets second. Hence in this passage (Rom. 12:6–8), since the gift of prophecy is listed and the apostolic office is not, prophecy is mentioned first.

The reasons why Paul does not refer to the apostolic office are apparent. There was no apostle at Rome (*cf.* 15:15–29, esp. vs. 20). He had alluded to his own apostolic commission in verse 3. It would scarcely be in accord with the pattern indicated in the New Testament for one apostle to give directions to another respecting the conduct of his office. The priority of the apostleship makes it thoroughly appropriate, on the other hand, for Paul to enjoin a prophet to exercise his gift "according to the proportion of faith".

As noted, not all the gifts referred to elsewhere are specified in this passage. It would not be proper to infer that only the gifts mentioned were present in the church at Rome. We may infer, however, that those dealt with and the corresponding directions were relevant and that the selection was sufficient to enforce concretely the regulative principles enjoined in verses 3—5.

Prophecy refers to the function of communicating revelations of truth from God. The prophet was an organ of revelation; he was God's spokesman. His office was not restricted to prediction of the future although this was likewise his prerogative when God was pleased to unveil future events to him (*cf.* Acts 21:10, 11). The gift of prophecy of which Paul here speaks is obviously one exercised in the apostolic church as distinct from the Old Testament. In the Old Testament the prophets occupied a position of priority that is not accorded to those of the New Testament (*cf.* Numb. 12:6-8; Deut. 18:15-19; Acts 3:21-24; Heb. 1:1; I Pet. 1:10-12). But the important place occupied by the gift of prophecy in the apostolic church is indicated by the prophecy of Joel fulfilled at Pentecost (Joel 2:28; Acts 2:16, 17), by the fact that prophets are next in rank to apostles, and that the church is built upon "the foundation of the apostles and prophets" (Eph. 2:20). The apostles possessed the prophetic gift; they also were organs of revelation. But the apostles had other qualifications which accorded them preeminence and "prophets" were not apostles.

The regulative principle prescribed for a prophet was that he exercise his gift "according to the proportion of faith".[8] This has been interpreted, as a literal rendering might suggest, "according to the analogy of the faith", faith being taken in the objective sense as the truth revealed and believed. This view would correspond to the expression, the analogy of Scripture, which means that Scripture is to be interpreted in accord with Scripture, that the infallible rule of the interpretation of Scripture is the Scripture itself.[9] Much can be said in support of this interpretation.

1. If the expression means "proportion of faith", it would have the same force as "measure of faith" (vs. 3), and, since every one is to judge himself and exercise his gift in accordance with the measure of faith given, why should this be repeated and directed to the prophet specifically?

2. There is good reason why a prophet should be reminded that the new revelations he has received are never in conflict with existing revelation. This is the mark of a true prophet (*cf.* Deut. 13:1-5; 18:20-22; I Cor. 14:37; I John 4:1-6).

---

[8] There is no possessive pronoun with "faith".
[9] *Cf.* Luther, possibly Calvin, Philippi, Hodge, Shedd and others.

3. The criterion by which men are to judge the claims of a prophet is the canon of revelation which they possess (*cf.* Acts 17:11).

4. There is warrant in classical Greek for the meaning "analogy" in the sense of that which is in agreement or correspondence with something else.[10]

On the other hand, there is not sufficient evidence to confirm this interpretation. The term in question occurs nowhere else in the New Testament. It is used elsewhere of mathematical proportion and progression, also in the sense of ratio and relation. The phrase "out of proportion" also occurs. The idea of proportion appears to be the preponderant one. This meaning, if applied here, is relevant. The prophet when he speaks God's word is not to go beyond that which God has given him to speak. As noted above, every gift must be exercised within the limits of faith and restricted to its own sphere and purpose. There is prime need that a prophet should give heed to this regulative principle because no peril could be greater than that an organ of revelation should presume to speak on his own authority. "The proportion of faith" points also in another direction. The prophet is to exercise his gift to the full extent of his prerogative; he is not to withhold the truth he is commissioned to disclose. Paul asserted his own faithfulness in this regard (Acts 20:20). Furthermore, this is not mere repetition of the "measure of faith" (vs. 3). In that case the accent falls on sober judgment. In verse 6 the emphasis is placed upon the proper discharge of the prophetic function and "proportion of faith" is by way of eminence the appropriate injunction.

The next gift mentioned is "ministry". The term is used of the ministry of the Word and even designates this ministry as performed by an apostle (cf. Acts 6:4; 20:24; 21:19; Rom. 11:13; II Cor. 4:1; 5:18; 6:3; Eph. 4:12; Col. 4:17; I Tim. 1:12; II Tim. 4:5, 11). As far as usage is concerned there is, therefore, abundant support for the view that the ministry of the Word is intended. In addition, this office follows prophecy and precedes that of teaching

---

[10] ἀναλογία occurs only here in the New Testament and rarely, if ever, in the LXX. In classical Greek it is used of mathematical proportion, with ὑπέρ in the sense of out of proportion, and also bears the sense of agreement or correspondence similar to ὁμοιότης.

in the apostle's enumeration. If an order of priority occurs here, then we would be compelled to regard the ministry as that of the Word, because no other phase of the church's ministration could have a higher place than that of teaching except the general ministry of the Word. On this assumption the first four functions would obviously be in the order of rank—prophecy, ministry of the Word, teaching, exhortation. However reasonable is this view we cannot be certain that this was the function in mind.

1. The term is also used in the more restricted sense of the ministry of mercy with reference to physical need (*cf.* Acts 6:1; 11:29; 12:25; II Cor. 8:4; 9:1, 12, 13). Furthermore, in this epistle (15:31) the term is used in this sense of Paul's own mission to Jerusalem, as is apparent from 15:25-27. The flexibility in the use of the term is apparent from I Corinthians 12:5 where Paul speaks of "diversities of ministrations".

2. It is not clear that in this passage the gifts enumerated are in the order of rank (*cf.* I Cor. 12:8–10). If the order of priority is not adhered to, there is no reason why the ministry of mercy should not be mentioned at this point.

3. Although this term is not used to denote the diaconate, yet the corresponding term "servant" is used in the sense of "deacon" and the verb in the sense of exercising the office of a deacon (Phil. 1:1; I Tim. 3:8, 10, 12, 13).

4. If the ministry of the Word is intended, it would be difficult to maintain the distinction of gift and function which in this context must be supposed. If ministry is understood in the broader sense the function would apply to the prophet, on the one hand, and to the teacher, on the other. Hence it would lack the distinguishing specificity which we would expect.

There does not, therefore, appear to be any conclusive reason for rejecting the view that this reference is to the diaconate. If this is the gift contemplated there is good reason why deacons should be exhorted to give themselves to this ministry. It is a ministry of mercy to the poor and infirm. In reference to this office there are two evils which the injunction serves to guard against. Since this office is concerned with material and physical benefits, it is liable to be underestimated and regarded as unspiritual. Hence the office is neglected. The other evil is that for this reason the deacon is liable to arrogate to himself other functions that appear to offer more profitable service. Both neglect and presumption are to be shunned; let the deacon devote himself to the ministration which his office involves. In the proper sense the work of this office is intensely spiritual and the evils arising from underesteem have wrought havoc in the witness of the church. On the contrary, "they that have served well as deacons gain to themselves a good standing, and great boldness in the faith which is in Christ Jesus" (I Tim. 3:13).

"He that teacheth, to his teaching." In dealing with the first two gifts the apostle used the terms "prophecy" and "ministry". Now he becomes more concrete and in the five functions that remain he speaks in terms of the *persons* exercising the gifts. The office of teaching differs from the prophetic. He who expounds the Word of God is not an organ of revelation. The prophet communicates truth and to that extent imparts teaching. But he is not a teacher in the specialized sense of him whose function it is to expound the meaning of that which has been revealed. His work is directed particularly to the understanding. He must devote himself to this task and be content with it.

"He that exhorteth, to his exhortation." As teaching is directed to the understanding, so is exhortation to the heart, conscience, and will. The conjunction of these two aspects of the ministry of the Word is imperative. They are sometimes combined in the ministry of the same person (*cf.* I Tim. 4:13; Tit. 1:9). Prophesying also is said to minister exhortation (I Cor. 14:3) as well as edification and comfort.

The terms used in this case could refer specifically to consolation; they are used in this sense in the New Testament. If thus interpreted the special gift refers to the aptitude to minister consolation, particularly to those in affliction. But even if exhortation is the meaning, the application of this to consolation is necessary. Exhortation needs to be directed to the cultivation of patience and perseverance and these are closely related to consolation.

The next gift mentioned is that of giving and the exhortation is that he do it with simplicity. The term sometimes means liberality (*cf.* II Cor. 8:2; 9:11, 13). But elsewhere it means simplicity, in the sense of singlemindedness of heart, of motive, and of purpose (*cf.* II Cor. 11:3; Eph. 6:5; Col. 3:22). It is not certain which of these meanings is here intended but there is much to be said in favour of simplicity. The giving in this instance is that of private means; it is not the giving from the treasury of the church. This latter is the responsibility of the diaconate and there is no evidence to think that this work of mercy is in view here.[11] Neither liberality nor sincerity of purpose appears to be the most appropriate injunction in reference to the distribution of funds from the treasury of the church. Whereas when one's own possessions are in view either of these virtues is particularly relevant. Besides, if the "ministry" (vs. 7) is that of the diaconate, as the evidence would seem to indicate, there would be duplication or at least additional specification which scarcely agrees with the interest of the apostle in this passage, namely, the exercise of the several gifts which God has distributed in the church. Since the giving is that of personal possession, the inculcation of sincerity of motive and purpose is most pertinent. Giving must not be with the ulterior motives of securing influence and advantage for oneself, a vice too frequently indulged by the affluent in their donations to the treasury of the church and to which those responsible for the direction of the affairs of the church are too liable to succumb.

"He that ruleth, with diligence."[12] There can be no question but those here referred to are those who exercise government and oversight in the church (cf. I Thess. 5:12; I Tim. 5:17). In the latter passage they are called "elders". In I Corinthians 12:28 this office is denoted by another term, namely, "governments". It would be absurd to suppose that there is any allusion here to government as exercised by one man. The other passages imply a plurality of elders (cf. also Acts 15:2, 4, 6, 22, 23; 16:4; 20:17, 28; Tit. 1:5; Heb. 13:7, 17). The apostle uses the singular in this case after the pattern followed in the other four instances without any reference to the number of those who might possess and exercise the several gifts. Hence no support could be derived from this text for the idea of one man as president in the government of the church nor of one man as chief over those who rule. The exhortation to diligence is a reminder of the vigilance that the rulers in the church need to observe. They are to shepherd the church of God and take heed to the flock over which the Holy Spirit has made them overseers (Acts 20:28). They are to watch for the souls of those under their care (Heb. 13:17). No con-

---

[11] The verb used is μεταδίδωμι, "give a share" (cf. Luke 3:11; Rom. 1:11; Eph. 4:28; I Thess. 2:8).
[12] For the verb προΐστημι in the sense of ruling cf. I Thess. 5:12; I Tim. 3:4, 5, 12; 5:17, in the sense of maintaining cf. Tit. 3:8, 14.

sideration adds more force to the apostle's charge than the fact that the church is the pillar and ground of the truth (I Tim. 3:15) and that every infraction upon or neglect of government directly prejudices the witness to the truth of which the church is the pillar.

"He that showeth mercy, with cheerfulness." There is a close relation of this gift to that of giving. But there is in the use of the word "mercy" the thought of more direct, personal ministry to those in need. The giving referred to earlier would not necessarily involve the individual and more intimate service which this ministry of mercy implies. The virtue enjoined in this case indicates this kind of care; it is to be performed with *cheerfulness*. Oftentimes the work of mercy is disagreeable and so it is liable to be done grudgingly and in a perfunctory way. This attitude defeats the main purpose of mercy. In Calvin's words, "For as nothing gives more solace to the sick or to any one otherwise distressed, than to see men cheerful and prompt in assisting them; so to observe sadness in the countenance of those by whom assistance is given makes them to feel themselves despised".[13]

In the case of the first four gifts the exhortation is concerned with the sphere in which the gift is to be exercised but in the case of the last three it is directed to the disposition of heart and will with which the service is to be rendered.[14]

12:9–21

9 Let love be without hypocrisy. Abhor that which is evil; cleave to that which is good.
10 In love of the brethren be tenderly affectioned one to another; in honor preferring one another;
11 in diligence not slothful; fervent in spirit; serving the Lord;
12 rejoicing in hope; patient in tribulation; continuing stedfastly in prayer;
13 communicating to the necessities of the saints; given to hospitality.
14 Bless them that persecute you; bless, and curse not.
15 Rejoice with them that rejoice; weep with them that weep.

---

[13] *Op. cit., ad loc.*
[14] *Cf.* Meyer: *op. cit., ad* 12:8.

16 Be of the same mind one toward another. Set not your mind on high things, but condescend to things that are lowly. Be not wise in your own conceits.
17 Render to no man evil for evil. Take thought for things honorable in the sight of all men.
18 If it be possible, as much as in you lieth, be at peace with all men.
19 Avenge not yourselves, beloved, but give place unto the wrath *of God*: for it is written, Vengeance belongeth unto me; I will recompense, saith the Lord.
20 But if thine enemy hunger, feed him; if he thirst, give him to drink: for in so doing thou shalt heap coals of fire upon his head.
21 Be not overcome of evil, but overcome evil with good.

In the six preceding verses the apostle had dealt with different offices and functions and gives in each case the appropriate exhortation. In verses 9-21 he enjoins those duties which all believers are to observe. The whole chapter is concerned with the concrete and practical aspects of sanctification and so the exhortations must cover the diverse situations of life. But verses 3–8 have in view duties which are not common to all; verses 9–21 deal with duties which no one can afford to neglect. It is easy to see the relevance to all of such virtues as love, brotherly kindness, zeal, hope, patience, prayer, hospitality, forbearance, fellow-sympathy, humility; it is with this gamut of graces the apostle proceeds to deal.

9, 10 "Let love be without hypocrisy." We might expect that the catalogue would begin with love (*cf.* Rom. 13:8–10; I Cor. 13:13; Gal. 5:22). In view of the primacy of love it is of particular interest to note how it is characterized. It is to be unfeigned. We find this emphasis elsewhere (II Cor. 6:6; I Pet. 1:22). No vice is more reprehensible than hypocrisy. No vice is more destructive of integrity because it is the contradiction of truth. Our Lord exposed its diabolical character when he said to Judas, "Betrayest thou the Son of man with a kiss?" (Luke 22:48). If love is the sum of virtue and hypocrisy the epitome of vice, what a contradiction to bring these together! Dissembling affection!

No criterion of our alignments is more searching than the antithesis instituted between the evil and the good. Our reaction to the former in all its forms is to be that of instant abhorrence; we must hate "even the garment spotted by the flesh" (Jude 23). Our attachment to the good is to be that of the devotion illustrated by the bond of marriage.[15] No terms could express the total difference in our attitude more than the recoil of abhorrence from that which belongs to the kingdom of darkness and our bonded allegiance to all that is good and well-pleasing to God (*cf.* I Thess. 5:22; Phil. 4:8, 9). When the good is the atmosphere of our life we suffocate in the paths of iniquity and the counsels of the ungodly (*cf.* Psalm 1:1, 2).

In the next series of injunctions there is a similarity of construction and this may be conveyed by the following rendering: "In brotherly love being kindly affectioned to one another, in honour preferring one another, in zeal not flagging, in spirit fervent, serving the Lord, in hope rejoicing, in affliction being patient, in prayer continuing instant, in the needs of the saints partaking, hospitality pursuing".

"In love of the brethren be tenderly affectioned one to another." The love of verse 9 is love to our fellowmen and in the context must refer particularly to the love exercised within the fellowship of the church. But here and in the verses that follow various expressions of that love are mentioned. It is plain that in the present instance the fellowship of the saints is viewed as a family relationship and as demanding therefore that which corresponds in the life of the church to the affection which the members of a family entertain for one another.[16] The particularity of the love believers bear to one another is hereby indicated and sanctioned. Even love on the highest level of exercise is discriminating in quality. This discrimination is exemplified in Paul's word elsewhere, "do good to all men, and especially to them who are of the household of faith" (Gal. 6:10).

"In honor preferring one another." The practical import of this is obvious. But there is a question whether the intent is the same as elsewhere when Paul says, "each counting other better than himself" (Phil. 2:3) or whether the idea is that we are to lead in bestowing honour. That is, the thought can well be that instead of looking and waiting for praise from others we should be foremost

---

[15] On κολλάω see this use in Matt. 19:5; I Cor. 6:16, 17.
[16] Φιλόστοργοι, though not occurring elsewhere in the New Testament, de suis to denote family affection in classical Greek.

in according them honour. We cannot be certain which thought is here present. In either case the exhortation is directed against the conceit by which we assert ourselves above others. The humility commended is not incompatible with the sober judgment commended in verse 3. We are to recognize the gifts God has bestowed upon us and exercise these in the awareness that others do not possess these same gifts and therefore are not qualified to assume the functions or prerogatives which the gifts involve. Humility does not overlook the differentiation that exists in the fellowship of faith nor can it be pleaded as an excuse for indolence. Paul considered himself "less than the least of all saints" (Eph. 3:8) but he did not allow this estimate of himself to keep him from asserting his high prerogatives as an apostle and minister of Christ. Among believers he is the noblest example of what he here commends and of the sobriety of judgment to be exercised "according as God hath dealt to each a measure of faith" (vs. 3).

11 The next three exhortations are closely related:[17] "in diligence not slothful; fervent in spirit; serving the Lord". The first is negative and is directed against weariness in well-doing (*cf.* Gal. 6:9).[18] The second is the positive counterpart and exhorts to the fervour with which our spirits are to be aglow. The "spirit" has been taken to refer to the Holy Spirit and so the thought would be "fervent in the Holy Spirit".[19] This meaning is appropriate, particularly in view of service to the Lord in the clause that follows. It is also true that only as our spirits are quickened by the Holy Spirit can we be fervent in our spirits. Although the term "spirit" is the personal name of the Holy Spirit and occurs frequently with this denotation, it also designates the human spirit and occurs often in Paul's epistles in this sense (*cf.* Rom. 1:9; I Cor. 2:11; 5:4; 7:34; II Cor. 7:1; Eph. 4:23; I Thess. 5:23). Since this reference to the human spirit is appropriate here, it is

---

[17] NEB puts the three in close relation by the rendering: "With unflagging energy, in ardour of spirit, serve the Lord".
[18] In Matt. 25:26 ὀκνηροί means "slothful", in Phil. 3:1 "irksome" or "troublesome". Here similar ideas are expressed: "be not indolent", "be not irked by the demands of". σπουδή sometimes means haste (Mark 6:25; Luke 1:39) and σπουδάζω *possibly* has this sense in II Tim. 4:9, 21; Tit. 3:12. But σπουδή more frequently means diligence or carefulness (*cf.* II Cor. 7:11, 12; 8:7, 8, 16; Heb. 6:11; II Pet. 1:5; Jude 3) and σπουδάζω has the same import in most cases if not in all.
[19] *Cf.* Barrett: *op. cit.*, *ad loc.*

not necessary to refer it to the Holy Spirit. The third defines the service in which sloth is to be shunned and fervour practised.[20] This reminder is the most effective antidote to weariness and incentive to ardour. When discouragement overtakes the Christian and fainting of spirit as its sequel, it is because the claims of the Lord's service have ceased to be uppermost in our thought. Although this exhortation is a general one and applies to every situation of life, it is not out of place in this series of particular exhortations;[21] it expresses that which is calculated to avert sloth, incite to constancy of devotion, and also guard against intrepid zeal which passes beyond the orbit of service to the Lord. "Serving the Lord" has this dual purpose of stirring up from sloth and regulating zeal.

12 The next three are also closely related: "rejoicing in hope; patient in tribulation; continuing stedfastly in prayer". Hope has reference to the future (*cf.* 8:24, 25). The believer must never have his horizon bounded by what is seen and temporal (*cf.* vs. 2). The salvation now in possession is so conditioned by hope that without hope its character is denied; "for in hope were we saved" (8:24). The hope is hope of the glory of God (5:2) and it is one of unalloyed, consummated bliss for the believer. Hope realized will be a morning without clouds; there will be no mixture of good and evil, joy and sorrow. Hence "rejoicing in hope" even now. Hope is not here, however, the object to which rejoicing is directed. In Philippi's words, "the summons meant is not to joy *at* hope ... but

---

[20] The reading καιρῷ in place of Κυρίῳ is weakly attested as far as external evidence is concerned. Against it are P46, א, A, B, L, the mass of the cursives, and other authorities. καιρῷ has been favoured by notable exegetes (*cf.* Meyer, Godet). The idea of serving the time in the sense of accommodating oneself to the circumstances of the time appears in Greek and Latin, and the thought of taking advantage of the opportunity appears in Paul (ἐξαγοραζόμενοι τὸν καιρόν, Eph. 5:16; Col. 4:5; *cf.* also Gal. 6:10). Hence the thought of serving the time is not alien to Paul's teaching nor inappropriate in this context. Furthermore, it is difficult to understand how καιρῷ could have been substituted for Κυρίῳ, whereas the reverse is easily understood. However, the confusion may have arisen from the similarity in writing and the external evidence is such that we may not adopt καιρῷ as the proper text. One cannot but detect the dialectic proclivity in Karl Barth's comment: "*serve the time*: plunge into the KRISIS of the present moment, for the decision is there" (*op. cit., ad loc.*).

[21] *Cf. contra* Godet who says: "The precept: *serve the Lord*, is too general to find a place in a series of recommendations so particular" (*op. cit., ad loc.*).

to joy *by means* or *in virtue of* hope".[22] The hope is the cause or ground of the joy. However tried by affliction the reaction appropriate in view of hope is rejoicing. There is no comfort in sorrow except as it is illumined by hope. How eloquent to this effect is Paul's word elsewhere to believers as they weep over the deceased, "ye sorrow not, even as others, who do not have hope" (I Thess. 4:13).

"Patient in tribulation." As Philippi again points out, this is not *enduring tribulation* but *stedfast in tribulation*.[23] Our attention had been already drawn to the tribulations characterizing the believer's pilgrimage and to his attitude toward them (5:3). Paul refers frequently to the affliction which he himself endured (*cf.* II Cor. 1:4, 8; 2:4; 6:4; 7:4; Eph. 3:13; I Thess. 3:7). It is also noteworthy how often with different aspects of life in view the apostle's teaching takes account of the believers' afflictions (*cf.* 8:35; II Cor. 1:4; 4:17; 8:2; I Thess. 1:6; 3:3; II Thess. 1:4). These often take the form of persecution and we are reminded that "all that would live godly in Christ Jesus shall suffer persucution" (II Tim. 3:12; *cf.* Rom. 8:35; II Cor. 12:10; II Thess. 1:4; II Tim. 3:11) and that "through many tribulations we must enter into the kingdom of God" (Acts 14:22; *cf.* Rev. 7:14). The exhortation of the present text evinces the need for constancy and perseverance in what is so pervasive in the life of faith.

The exacting demands involved in the preceding point up the relevance of the next injunction: "continuing stedfastly in prayer" (*cf.* Acts 1:14; 6:4; Col. 4:2). The measure of perseverance in the midst of tribulation is the measure of our diligence in prayer. Prayer is the means ordained of God for the supply of grace sufficient for every exigency and particularly against the faintheartedness to which affliction tempts us.

It is well to observe the interdependence of the virtues enjoined in this trilogy. How dismal would tribulation be without hope (*cf.* I Cor. 15:19) and how defeatist would we be in persecution without the resources of hope and patience conveyed to us through prayer. The sequence of David's thought reflects the apostle's exhortations: "Hear the voice of my supplications when I cry unto thee, when I lift up my hands towards thy holy oracle ...

---

[22] *Op. cit., ad loc.*
[23] *Ibid.*

12:1–21 MANIFOLD PRACTICAL DUTIES

Blessed be the Lord, because he hath heard the voice of my supplications. The Lord is my strength and shield; my heart trusted in him, and I am helped. Therefore my heart greatly rejoiceth and with my song will I praise him" (Psalm 28:2, 6, 7).

13 "Communicating to the necessities of the saints."[24] It is true that if we comply with this exhortation we shall distribute and impart our possessions to meet the needs of the saints. But though this is implied as a consequence the precise thought does not appear to be that of communicating but that of participating in or sharing the needs of the saints. The same term rendered here by "communicating" has clearly in other cases the sense of partaking (15:27; I Tim. 5:22; Heb. 2:14; I Pet. 4:13; II John 11) and probably also in Philippians 4:14. The corresponding noun means partaker (Matt. 23:30; I Cor. 10:18, 20; II Cor. 1:17; Phm. 17; Heb. 10:33; I Pet. 5:1; II Pet. 1:4; *cf.* also Luke 5:10; II Cor. 8:23 in the sense of partner and a compound form of the verb in Eph. 5:11; Phil. 4:14; Rev. 18:4).[25] The meaning, therefore, would be that we are to identify ourselves with the needs of the saints and make them our own. We are partakers of the gifts of others in the sense of verse 5 but we are also of their wants and needs.[26] The same identifying of ourselves with the lot of others, enjoined in verse 15, is here applied to the wants of the saints.

The next exhortation is closely related: "given to hospitality". The term translated "given" is one that means to follow after or pursue and implies that we are to be active in the pursuit of hospitality and not merely bestowing it, perhaps grudgingly (*cf.* I Pet. 4:9), when necessity makes it unavoidable. The same kind of activity is here enjoined as elsewhere in reference to love, peace, righteousness, the good, and the attainment of the prize of the high calling of God in Christ Jesus (*cf.* 14:19; I Cor. 14:1; Phil. 3:12, 14; I Thess. 5:15; I Tim. 6:11; Heb. 12:14; I Pet. 3:11). In apostolic times there was urgent need for the practice of this virtue. There were the persecutions by which Christians were

---

[24] The variant μνείαις (for the accepted reading χρείαις, "necessities") is not to be followed on any account, external or internal.
[25] Gal. 6:6 may be an instance of "communicate".
[26] Philippi's remark is to the effect that we do not communicate to the *needs* of the saints but to the saints themselves (*op. cit.*, *ad loc.*).

compelled to migrate. There were other reasons also for which they were moving from place to place. The messengers of the gospel were itinerating in the fulfilment of their commission. The world was inhospitable. Therefore hospitality was a prime example of the way in which believers were to be partakers in the needs of the saints. The conditions prevailing in apostolic times still obtain in various parts of the world and the need for this grace is as urgent as then. But even where economic and social conditions are more favourable, the practice of hospitality is not irrelevant. It is in these circumstances that the force of the verb "pursue" should be heeded. The occasions will present themselves if we are alert to the duty, privilege, and blessing (*cf.* Heb. 13:2; II Tim. 1:16–18).

14 No practical exhortation places greater demands upon our spirits than to "bless them that persecute" us. Implied in persecution is unjust and malicious maltreatment. It is provoked not by ill-doing on our part but by well-doing (*cf.* I Pet. 3:13–17). The reason for persecution is that "the mind of the flesh is enmity against God" (8:7) and is provoked to animosity against those who are God's witnesses to truth and godliness. It is the unreasonableness of this persecution that is liable to provoke resentment in the minds of believers and with resentment thoughts of vindictive retaliation. Herein lies the difficulty of compliance with the injunction. For if we refrain from retaliatory actions, how ready we are to indulge vindictive thoughts. It is not, however, mere abstinence that is here required nor is it simply endurance of the persecution (*cf.* I Pet. 2:20) but the entertainment of the kindly disposition expressed in blessing. To bless has different meanings. When we bless God we ascribe to him the praise that is his due (*cf.* Luke 1:64, 68; 2:28; 24:53; James 3:9). When God blesses us he bestows blessing upon us (*cf.* Matt. 25:34; Acts 3:26; Gal.3:9; Eph. 1:3). When we bless persons or things we invoke God's blessing upon them (*cf.* Luke 2:34; I Cor. 10:16; Heb. 11:20). It is this last meaning that applies to the exhortation of the text and in numerous other cases where the same duty is commended. The apostle's word is to the same effect as the teaching of our Lord (Matt. 5:44; Luke 6:27, 28). When Paul adds, "bless and curse not", he underlines the fact that our attitude is not to be a mixture of blessing and cursing but one of unadulterated blessing. The demand points up two considerations:

12:1–21 MANIFOLD PRACTICAL DUTIES

(1) that nothing less than the pattern of God's own lovingkindness and beneficence is the norm for us (*cf.* Matt. 5:45–48) and (2) that only the resources of omnipotent grace in Christ Jesus are equal to the demands of the believer's vocation.[27]

15, 16 We found above that the believer must identify himself with the needs of others (vs. 13).[28] In verse 15 we have another example of this sympathy. We might be ready to think that it is easy and natural to rejoice with those who rejoice. In mutual jollification it is natural to be joyful. But this is not the joy spoken of here. The rejoicing is that which arises from gratification before the Lord and in the Lord (*cf.* Phil. 4:4). In contrast with the weeping of the next clause there must be in view some particular occasion for special joy because of God's favour and blessing, some distinguishing manifestation of grace bestowed upon those who are designated as "them that rejoice". The point of the exhortation is that we are to enter into this rejoicing as if the occasion for it were our own. If we love our neighbour as ourselves, if we appreciate the community within the body of Christ, the joys of others will be ours (*cf.* I Cor. 12:26b). This mutuality is not native to us. Jealousy and envy, hatred and malice are our native bents (*cf.* Gal. 3:20, 21; Tit. 3:3) and this exhortation, as much as any in this catalogue of virtues, demonstrates the transformation (*cf.* vs. 2) that must be wrought in those who are "one body in Christ" (vs. 5).

"Weep with them that weep." This is also directed against a vice that is unspeakable in its meanness, to be glad at the calamities of others (*cf.* Prov. 17:5). Identification of ourselves with the lot of others is here again commended. Weeping means sorrow, pain, and grief of heart. It is not pleasant to weep; no one invites grief. But our love for others will constrain in us the sorrow of heart which the providence of God metes out to our brethren in Christ.

In these cases we are concerned with the emotions of joy and grief and are reminded again of the vicissitudes which belong to a believer's life. To each vicissitude there is the appropriate reaction and to these reactions, emotional or otherwise, fellow-believers must be sensitive and not ride ruthlessly athwart the psychology

---

[27] *Cf.* also I Cor. 4:12; I Pet. 3:9.
[28] χαίρειν and κλαίειν are imperatival infinitives (*cf.* στοιχεῖν in Phil. 3:16).

which the situations of others create. We remember another word in the New Testament. "Is any among you afflicted? let him pray. Is any cheerful? let him sing psalms" (James 5:13), and we appreciate the wisdom of Solomon: "As he that taketh away a garment in cold weather, and as vinegar upon nitre, so is he that singeth songs to an heavy heart" (Prov. 25:20).

"Be of the same mind one toward another."[29] Exhortation to unity of mind and spirit in the Lord is frequent (*cf.* 15:5; II Cor. 13:11; Phil. 2:2; 4:2). It is possible that the apostle intended to relate this exhortation to the preceding verse and would mean that we are to have so much fellow-feeling towards one another that we shall rejoice with those who rejoice and weep with those who weep (*cf.* Phil. 2:4). But there is no need to posit this kind of dependence. As in these instances cited above there is sufficient reason for inculcating harmony that will have broader reference than the sympathy contemplated in the preceding verse. There is a difference between being of "the same mind one with another" (15:5) and being of "the same mind one toward another". The latter indicates the thought which each person is to entertain with respect to the other and requires that there be concord in this mutual interplay of thought regarding one another. Let no discordant sentiments be entertained in these reciprocal relations.

The next two clauses are directed against the high-mindedness of vain ambition, the grasping for position and honour. High things are contrasted with the lowly and humble. There is a question whether "the lowly" refer to things or persons; expositors are divided. It is more likely that the former is correct because of the contrast with "high things". If this is the intent then the thought is that we are to be content with a lowly estate and with humble tasks (*cf.* Phil. 4:11; I Tim. 6:8, 9; Heb. 13:5). The term rendered "condescend" means to be carried away with (*cf.* Gal. 2:13; II Pet. 3:17) and indicates that our feelings and attitudes are to be so much in line with lowly things that we shall be perfectly at home with these circumstances. If "the lowly" refer

---

[29] There is no need to take the participle φρονοῦντες as dependent upon the preceding infinitives. In the preceding context there are numerous participles with imperative force and later in vss. 17, 18. If we were to insist on dependence of this sort, the same would apply to the next two participles and they will not fit such a construction. Neither are we to construe them with μὴ γίνεσθε (vs. 16b).

to persons,[30] then the thought is that we are to be at home with humble folk. Whatever the denotation of "lowly" may be, the practical import would include both lines of thought, for the one would imply the other. The vice against which the exhortations are directed is a common one and gnaws at the root of that community in the church of Christ on which the apostle lays so much emphasis. There is to be no aristocracy in the church, no cliques of the wealthy as over against the poor, no pedestals of unapproachable dignity for those on the higher social and economic strata or for those who are in office in the church (*cf.* I Pet. 5:3). How contradictory to all such pretension is the character of the church's head: "I am meek and lowly in heart" (Matt. 11:29).

"Be not wise in your own conceits."[31] Literally rendered it is: "be not wise in your own eyes" (*cf.* 11:25; Prov. 3:7). Apparently the conceit in view is that self-sufficiency by which our own judgment is so highly esteemed that we will not have regard to wisdom that comes from any other source. It strikes at the opinionated person who has no regard for any one else's judgment. "The wisdom that is from above is first pure, then peaceable, gentle, easy to be entreated" (James 3:17). The opinionated person is intractable and impervious to any advice but his own. Just as there is to be no social aristocracy in the church, so there is to be no intellectual autocrat.

17-21 Misunderstanding of these admonitions arises from failure to see that they are concerned with our private, individual, personal relations to one another and not with magisterial and judicial administration. It is noteworthy that the apostle proceeds immediately after these admonitions to deal with the prerogatives and functions of the magistrate and therefore with the civil, judicial, and penal institution. To the magistrate is given the power of the sword to avenge the evil-doer (*cf.* 13:4). If he avenges wrongdoing he inflicts the evil of penalty. So for the governing authorities not to render evil for evil and not execute wrath (*cf.* 13:2, 5, 6) would mean abdication of the prerogative and obligation devolving upon them by God's appointment. It is necessary,

---

[30] In all other instances ταπεινός refers to persons (Matt. 11:29; Luke 1:52; II Cor. 7:6; 10:1; James 1:9; 4:6; I Pet. 5:5).
[31] παρ' ἑαυτοῖς has the force of "in the sight of yourselves", "in the judgment of yourselves" (*cf.* Arndt and Gingrich: *op. cit.*, *ad* παρά, II, 2, b).

therefore, to appreciate the difference between what belongs to political jurisprudence and that which is proper in private relationships with our fellow-men. To transfer the prohibitions and injunctions of the respective spheres would be not only distortion but perversion and would lead to the gravest travesties. Here is an appropriate example of the need of observing the universe of discourse in the interpretation and application of each part of Scripture.

"Render to no man evil for evil." This is the negative complement of what we found positively in verse 14. It serves to point up the relevance of this admonition to observe that it applies in our individual relations even to the crimes which are subject to penalty by the civil magistrate; we may not as private citizens take upon ourselves the execution of the demands of justice in the sphere of government. "Avenge not yourselves, beloved" (vs. 19). The essence of the exhortation is, however, that we may never indulge in vindictive retaliation (*cf.* I Thess. 5:15; I Pet. 3:9).

The next appeal does not, as the A.V. might suggest, refer to honesty in our relations with men, though this is an important ingredient in what is commended.[32] The appeal is to "take thought for things honorable in the sight of all men". For the first time in this chapter[33] this type of consideration appears, namely, the need for maintaining a deportment that approves itself to men. The close parallel, "We take thought for things honorable not only in the sight of the Lord but also in the sight of men" (II Cor. 8:21), points up this consideration because emphasis falls upon the necessity of taking care for what is honourable in the sight of men in addition to the Lord's approbation. Elsewhere Paul speaks of commending himself to "every conscience of men in the sight of God" (II Cor. 4:2). He also requires that a bishop "must have a good report from those who are without" (I Tim. 3:7). "All men" in our text must include, therefore, those outside the church. This reminds us that the norms of behaviour governing Christian conduct are norms that even unbelievers recognize as worthy of approval and that when Christians violate these canons they bring reproach upon the name of Christ and upon their own profession. This does not mean that the unbelieving world

---

[32] For similar use of προνοέω *cf.* I Tim. 5:8.
[33] *Cf.* 2:24.

prescribes norms of conduct for the Christian but only that the Christian in proving what is the good, and acceptable, and perfect will of God must have regard to what can be vindicated as honourable in the forum of men's judgment. We may never overlook the effect of the work of the law written on the hearts of all men (*cf.* 2:15) as also how alert the unbelieving are to inconsistency in the witness of believers.

"If it be possible, as much as in you lieth, be at peace with all men."[34] This must be as inclusive in its scope as the preceding clause; there is no restrictive use of the expression "all men". It is obvious, however, that a reservation is made in this instance respecting the obligation to be at peace. "If it be possible" indicates that it may not always be possible. We may not suppose that the implied impossibility has in view any inability arising from our weakness as, for example, inability to restrain our own impulses of anger or resentment. The impossibility is that of another character; it is "a case of the *objective* impossibility ... chiefly where truth, right, and duty command resistance".[35] It would violate the witness of Jesus to demand peace at the expense of these priorities (*cf.* Matt. 10:34–36; Luke 12:51–53). "The wisdom that is from above is first pure, then peaceable" (James 3:17) and we are to follow peace and holiness (*cf.* Heb. 12:14). As Philippi again observes, "by the side of speaking the truth in love must ever stand loving in truth".[36]

"As much as in you lieth." If the preceding clause alludes to the impossibility proceeding from considerations objective to ourselves, this bears upon the exercise of every means within our power to maintain peace with our fellow-men. The responsibility for discord must to no extent be traceable to failure on our part to do all that is compatible with holiness, truth, and right.

This exhortation as a whole underlines the evil of indulging discord for its own sake or when necessity does not demand it. Peaceableness of disposition and behaviour is a virtue to be cultivated in our relations with all men; there is no circumstance in which our efforts to preserve and promote peace may be suspended.

---

[34] To take εἰ δυνατόν with what precedes would be not only indefensible, it would be perverse. There is no qualification applicable to what precedes. It is necessary in what follows.
[35] Philippi: *op. cit., ad loc.*
[36] *Ibid.*

This is the force of "as much as in you lieth". On the other hand, we may never be at peace with sin and error. If peace means complicity with sin or error or if it encourages these, then peace must be sacrificed. We are to love our neighbour as ourselves and we may not refrain from the rebuke and dissent which may evoke his displeasure but which his highest interest requires.

In verse 19 the tenderness of the appeal with which the chapter begins is here introduced in another form. In verse 1 the entreaty was enforced by appeal to the mercies of God. Now the apostle addresses his readers in terms of the bond of affection that unites him to them; he calls them "beloved". No form of address could bespeak greater love and esteem (*cf.* 16:5, 9, 12; Eph. 6:21; Col. 1:7; 4:7, 9, 14; II Tim. 1:2; Phm. 1). It underlines the solicitude Paul entertained that believers should not give way to avenging retaliation. There is a close relation between this prohibition and that of verse 17, not to render evil for evil. But there must be some difference. This probably resides, as Calvin suggests, in the more serious kind of injury inflicted and of recompense contemplated in this instance. The fact that in conjunction with the restraint here enjoined there is the imperative added, "give place to the wrath", indicates that it is proper to reckon with the retribution due though we ourselves are not to execute the same. In verse 17 no such retribution necessarily comes into the purview.

What is the wrath to which we are to give place? Various interpretations have been proposed. One is that it is the wrath of our adversary. Give way to his wrath. If wrath is to have a place, if it is to be allowed scope, let it be that of your adversary, not yours. Hence let there be no place for your wrath. This view could derive some support from Luke 14:9: "give this one place". Another view is that we are to give place to our own wrath. Give it time to spend itself, give it a wide berth so that it may be dissipated. Pent-up resentment is always liable to explode. A third view that might be entertained is that the wrath is that referred to in 13:4, 5, namely, the judicial penalty exacted by the civil magistrate in the execution of justice for wrongdoing (*cf.* 13:2). The fourth view is that the wrath is the wrath of God.

The most conclusive argument against the first view is that the wrath of an adversary is not necessarily contemplated. This is an importation. There could be numerous situations prompting us to vengeful retaliation in which the wrath of the person inflicting injury would not be a factor. Hence to adopt an interpretation that is premised on an arbitrary supposition is without warrant. The second view has little to commend it on the basis of usage.[37] It is apparent that our vindictive anger is not to be vented; this is the force of the prohibition. But if our anger is to be curbed, if it is not to be given entertainment, then, according to the analogy of Ephesians 4:27, we are not to give it place. It would be contrary to the pattern of this latter passage to suppose that the same thought could be expressed by saying "give it place". These foregoing objections do not apply to the third view. And since Paul proceeds to deal immediately with the office of the magistrate as "the servant of God, an avenger unto wrath to him that doeth evil", there is much to commend this interpretation. Vindicatory retribution is the prerogative of the magistrate and the effect of the exhortation would be "Let the place of vengeance be occupied by the magistrate and do not you presume to occupy it". The fourth view, however, has the most to commend it.

1. In Paul's usage "the wrath" and also "wrath" without the article is pervasively the wrath of God (*cf.* 2:5, 8; 3:5; 5:9; 9:22; Eph. 2:3; I Thess. 1:10; 2:16; 5:9). In every instance, with the possible exception of 13:5, where "the wrath" is spoken of without any further specification (3:5; 5:9; 9:22; I Thess. 2:16) it is the wrath of God. No argument so far adduced bears the weight of this consideration.

2. The admonition to "give place to the wrath" is supported by appeal to Scripture. But the Scripture quoted (Deut. 32:35) is the assertion of the divine prerogative: "Vengeance belongeth to me; I will recompense, saith the Lord". This defines the wrath, and only the most conclusive counter-argument could remove the specification which this quotation provides. Suffice it to ask: what wrath other than the wrath of God could be supported by appeal to God's unique prerogative of executing retribution?

Here we have what belongs to the essence of piety. The essence of ungodliness is that we presume to take the place of God, to take everything into our own hands. It is faith to commit ourselves to God, to cast all our care upon him and to vest all our interests in him. In reference to the matter in hand, the wrongdoing of which

---

[37] The Latin *dare irae spatium* has temporal meaning. But τόπος does not lend itself to the temporal idea.

we are the victims, the way of faith is to recognize that God is judge and to leave the execution of vengeance and retribution to him. Never may we in our private personal relations execute the vengeance which wrongdoing merits. We see how the practical details of the Christian ethic reveal the soul of piety itself. How appropriate likewise is the word of Peter in pleading the example of Christ: "who, when he was reviled, reviled not again; when he suffered, threatened not; but committed himself to him that judgeth righteously" (I Pet. 2:23; *cf.* Psalm 37:5–13).

The foregoing commitment of judgment to God might appear to leave room for the harbouring of desires for the execution of judgment on God's part upon those who make us the victims of their wrongdoing. This would be inconsistent with verse 14. But it is also countered by verse 20.

It is noteworthy how often the apostle quotes from the book of Proverbs in this chapter (at vs. 16 from Prov. 3:7, at vs. 17 from Prov. 3:4, and here in vs. 20 from Prov. 25:21, 22). The kindness enjoined is a practical and concrete way of exemplifying the disposition to which we are exhorted in verse 14. In the latter text, however, much more is in view than that of supplying physical needs. But if practical generosity is absent the presence of the disposition is suspect (*cf.* James 2:15, 16). The only question in this verse is the meaning of the last clause, "thou shalt heap coals of fire upon his head".

One interpretation relates the coals of fire to the execution of God's vengeance and recompense (vs. 19b).[38] This would require the thought that our deeds of kindness minister to this end and that, instead of being the executioners of vengeance, we are to be consoled by the fact that kindness only promotes that result. There are two objections to this view. (1) No warrant can be elicited from Scripture by which the execution of God's vengeance could be pleaded as the reason for bestowing kindness upon our enemies. That vengeance belongs to God is the reason why we are not to mete out vengeance but not the reason for acts of benefi-

---

[38] *Cf.* Psalm 11:6; 140:10; Ezek. 10:2. II Esdras 16:53 is sometimes adduced to support this interpretation. But the section in which this verse occurs is believed to be late. With respect to chapters 15 and 16 W. O. E. Oesterley says: "These chapters may, with some confidence, be assigned to a time between 240 A.D. and 270 A.D." (*An Introduction to the Books of the Apocrypha*, pp. 155f.); *cf.* also C. C. Torrey: *The Apocryphal Literature* (New Haven, 1945), pp. 116f.; Bruce M. Metzger: *An Introduction to the Apocrypha* (New York, 1957), p. 22.

cence. (2) Verse 21 is closely related to verse 20 and points to the result of our acts of mercy: it is that evil may be overcome. As will be observed, this envisions a saving effect on the perpetrators of the evil which verse 20 has in mind.

A second view, with slight variations respecting the state of mind induced in the enemy,[39] is the one most widely held. It is, that heaping coals of fire on the head refers to the burning sense of shame and remorse constrained in our enemy by the kindness we shower upon him. If the first view mentioned is not acceptable, then this must be the direction in which the interpretation must be sought. Whatever may be the state of mind induced in our enemy, whether that of burning shame or the softening of penitence, it is one that ameliorates his enmity, and the action of heaping coals of fire on his head is for the purpose of constraining that effect.

As indicated above, verse 21 is closely related to verse 20. There is a question whether "the evil" is the wrong perpetrated by our enemy or the wrong to which we may be tempted, namely, that of vindictive retaliation (vs. 19a). If the latter is in view then the thought is that we are not to be overcome by this evil of retaliation but that by resisting the impulse and bestowing kindness upon our enemy rather than vengeance we thereby overcome temptation and promote our sanctification. We achieve victory in the conflict that goes in on our own souls by doing the good of beneficence toward our enemy. This interpretation does not dissolve the connection with the preceding context. "The evil" would hark back to "avenge not yourselves" (vs. 19) and "the good" to the kindness extended to our enemy (vs. 20).

The first view mentioned is more generally accepted and is to be preferred for the following reasons. (1) The evil of the impulse to

---

[39] "Either our enemy will be softened by kindness, or, if he is so ferocious that nothing may assuage him, he will be stung and tormented by the testimony of his conscience, which will feel itself overwhelmed by our kindness" (Calvin: *op. cit., ad loc.*). "The true and Christian method, therefore, to subdue an enemy is, to 'overcome evil with good.' This interpretation, which suits so well the whole context, seems to be rendered necessary by the following verse" (Hodge: *op. cit., ad loc.*). For a more recent illuminating and discriminating study *cf.* William Klassen: "Coals of Fire: Sign of Repentance or Revenge?" in *New Testament Studies*, 9, pp. 337–350. The various views are set forth and examined. Klassen's conclusion is that "the interpretation so widely accepted by interpreters that the coals of fire refer to shame, remorse or punishment lacks all support in the text. In the Egyptian literature and in Proverbs the 'coals of fire' is a dynamic symbol of change of mind which takes place as a result of a deed of love" (p. 349).

retaliation is not in the forefront at this point. It is at verses 17 and 19. But at this stage the thought is concentrated on the well-doing of the believer in contrast with ill-doing on the part of his enemy. The hostility of the latter is in the forefront. (2) This view is a more fitting conclusion to verse 20. If heaping coals of fire refers to a beneficent result, then verse 21b alludes to this beneficent result and the good which overcomes is that of verse 20a. It is a fitting commendation of that enjoined in verse 20. (3) The idea of overcoming is more in accord with an assault that comes from without than with an inward impulse. (4) This section begins with verse 17a. The implication is that we are to render good for evil. If we apply this assumed antithesis, then the evil in mind in verse 21, as in 17a, is the evil perpetrated by another and therefore the evil to be overcome.

The meaning then would be that we are not to be vanquished ethically by the evil heaped upon us. On the contrary, by well-doing we are to be the instruments of quenching the animosity and the ill-doing of those who persecute and maltreat us. How relevant to the believer's high and holy calling! Vengeance, retaliation foments strife and fans the flames of resentment. How noble the aim that our enemy should be brought to repentance, at any rate to the shame that will restrain and perhaps remove the ill-doing which hostility prompts.

ROMANS XIII

B. THE CIVIL MAGISTRATE
(13:1–7)

13:1–7

1 Let every soul be in subjection to the higher powers: for there is no power but of God; and the *powers* that be are ordained of God,
2 Therefore he that resisteth the power, withstandeth the ordinance of God: and they that withstand shall receive to themselves judgment.
3 For rulers are not a terror to the good work, but to the evil. And wouldest thou have no fear of the power? do that which is good, and thou shalt have praise from the same:
4 for he is a minister of God to thee for good. But if thou do that which is evil, be afraid; for he beareth not the sword in vain: for he is a minister of God, an avenger for wrath to him that doeth evil.
5 Wherefore *ye* must needs be in subjection, not only because of the wrath, but also for conscience' sake.
6 For for this cause ye pay tribute also; for they are ministers of God's service, attending continually upon this very thing.
7 Render to all their dues: tribute to whom tribute *is due*; custom to whom custom; fear to whom fear; honor to whom honor.

This section is not a parenthesis in this part of the epistle extending from 12:1 through 15:13. The obligations incident to our subjection to civil authorities belong to "the good and acceptable and perfect will of God" (12:2). The reason for dealing with this topic at this point should not be artificially sought in some kind of connection with what immediately precedes as, for example, that in 12:19–21 Paul is dealing with the injustices Christians may suffer at the hands of their personal enemies and in 13:1–7 with the injustices which they may suffer at the hands of magistrates or which are properly avenged by the magistrate. It is true that the juxtaposition of 12:17–21 and 13:1–7 is most significant for the avoidance and correction of erroneous applications of the teaching in 12:17–21, as was noted earlier.[1] But we may not say that this was the reason for the sequence which Paul follows. It is apparent how diverse are the concrete aspects of the believer's life dealt with in 12:3–21 and particularly how many of the circumstances in his social life come within the apostle's purview. In 13:1–7 we have an all-important relationship affecting the life and witness of a believer and there is good reason why Paul should treat of it, as he does, in this portion of the epistle. There is also sufficient ground for thinking that there was some urgent need for pressing home upon the believers at Rome the teaching which is given here respecting the prerogatives of magistrates and the obligations of subjects in relation thereto.

We know from the New Testament itself that the Jews had questions regarding the rights of the Roman government (*cf.* Matt. 22:16, 17; Mark 12:14; Luke 20:21, 22). We also know that the Jews were disposed to pride themselves on their independence (*cf.* John 8:33). We read also of seditious movements (Acts 5:36, 37). There is also the evidence from other sources respecting the restlessness of the Jews under the Roman yoke.[2] We are told that Claudius "had commanded all the Jews to depart from Rome" (Acts 18:2). This expulsion must have been occasioned by the belief that Jews were inimical to the imperial interests if not the aftermath of Jewish insurrection. In the mind of the authorities Christianity was associated with Judaism and any seditious temper attributed to Judaism would likewise be charged to Christians. This created a situation in which it was necessary for Christians to avoid all revolutionary aspirations or actions as well as insubordination to magistrates in the rightful exercise of their authority.

Not only was there this danger arising from association with Judaism, there was also within the Christian community the danger of perverted notions of freedom, especially in view of the kingship and lordship of Christ. The fact that Paul on three occasions[3] in his epistles found it necessary to reflect on our duties in reference to magistrates and Peter likewise to the same effect in

---

[1] *Cf.* comments *ad* 12:19.
[2] *Cf.* citations in Liddon: *op. cit.*, p. 246.
[3] In addition to Rom. 13:1–7 *cf.* I Tim. 2:1–3; Tit. 3:1.

13:1-7 THE CIVIL MAGISTRATE

his first epistle[4] shows that there was a reason for reminding believers of the necessity to be subject to the magisterial authorities.

Furthermore, Christians often suffered at the hands of these authorities and there was greater reason to draw the line between the disobedience which loyalty to Christ demanded (*cf.* Acts 4:19, 20; 5:29) and the obedience which the same loyalty required.

1, 2 "The higher powers" refer without question to the governing authorities in the commonwealth. The term "authorities" is the more literal rendering and points to the right to rule belonging to the persons involved and to the subjection required on the part of the subjects. At the time when Paul wrote civil magistracy was exercised by the Roman government and the direct reference is to the executors of this government. The only question that arises is whether "authorities" denote also invisible angelic powers standing behind the human governors. This question would not arise were it not that in the New Testament and especially in Paul's epistles this same term "authorities" is used to denote suprahuman beings, and Oscar Cullmann has vigorously contended that in this instance the term has a dual reference, to the angelic powers and to the human executive agents.[5] The governing authorities are those in whom are vested the right and the power of ruling in the commonwealth and the evidence does not indicate that any other than human agents are in view.

"Every soul" is to be in subjection. Every soul means every person and does not reflect on the soul in man as distinguished from the body. Frequently in Scripture the word "soul" is used in this sense as synonymous with the whole person and sometimes as equivalent to the personal pronoun (*cf.* Matt. 12:18; Luke 12:19; Acts 2:27, 41, 43; 3:23; 7:14; Rom. 2:9; Heb. 10:38, 39; James 1:21; 5:20; I Pet. 1:9; 3:20; Rev. 16:3). The implication is that no person is exempt from this subjection; no person enjoys special privileges by which he may ignore or feel himself free to violate the ordinances of magisterial authority. Neither infidelity nor faith offers immunity. It is of particular significance that it is to the church Paul is writing. The Westminster Confession of Faith states the case well when it says: "Infidelity, or difference

---

[4] I Pet. 2:13-17.
[5] See Appendix C (pp. 252 ff.) for presentation and criticism of this thesis.

in religion, doth not make void the magistrates' just and legal authority, nor free the people from their due obedience to them: from which ecclesiastical persons are not exempted, much less hath the Pope any power and jurisdiction over them in their dominions, or lives, if he shall judge them to be heretics, or upon any other pretence whatsoever".[6]

The term for "subjection" is one more inclusive than that for obedience. It implies obedience when ordinances to be obeyed are in view, but there is more involved. Subjection indicates the recognition of our subordination in the whole realm of the magistrates' jurisdiction and willing subservience to their authority. This is enforced still more if the rendering of the whole clause is given the reflexive form: "Let every soul subject himself to the governing authorities". This rendering, for which much can be said, stresses active participation in the duty of subjection.

The next two clauses give the reason for this subjection.[7] They are explanatory the one of the other. They point to the source whence civil government proceeds and to the sanction by which subjection is demanded. Certain observations will bring out the meaning. (1) Paul is dealing with existing governmental agents. This is the force of "the *powers* that be". He is not now treating of government in the abstract nor entering into the question of the different forms of government. He is making categorical statements regarding the authorities in actual existence. (2) When he says they are "of God", he means that they derive their origin, right, and power from God. This is borne out by several considerations urged later in this passage but here it is expressly stated and excludes from the outset every notion to the effect that authority in the state rests upon agreement on the part of the governed or upon the consent of the governed. Authority to govern and the subjection demanded of the governed reside wholly in the fact of divine institution. (3) The propositions that the authorities are of God and ordained of God are not to be understood as referring merely to God's decretive will. The terms could be used to express God's decretive ordination but this is not their

---

[6] Chapter XXIII, Section IV.
[7] In the first clause ὑπό is more strongly attested. ἀπό is the preposition we might expect and probably explains its occurrence in D, G, and other authorities. In the second clause the addition of ἐξουσίαι after οὖσαι has much authority against it and should not be adopted.

precise import here. The context shows that the ordination of which the apostle now speaks is that of institution which is obliged to perform the appointed functions. The civil magistrate is not only the means decreed in God's providence for the punishment of evildoers but God's instituted, authorized, and prescribed instrument for the maintenance of order and the punishing of criminals who violate that order. When the civil magistrate through his agents executes just judgment upon crime, he is executing not simply God's decretive will but he is also fulfilling God's preceptive will, and it would be sinful for him to refrain from so doing.[8]

For these reasons subjection is required and resistance is a violation of God's law and meets with judgment. Since verse 3 speaks of the "terror" which rulers are to the evil work there must be some reference to the penal judgment which magistrates inflict upon evil-doers. But since all that precedes stresses the ordinance of God there must also be reflection upon the divine sanction by which this penal judgment is executed and therefore upon the judgment of God of which the magistrate's retribution is an expression. We have here in this term "judgment" the twofold aspect from which it is to be viewed. It is punishment dispensed by the governing authorities. But it is also an expression of God's own wrath and it is for this reason that it carries the sanction of God and its propriety is certified.[9]

There are many questions which arise in actual practice with which Paul does not deal. In these verses there are no expressed qualifications or reservations to the duty of subjection. It is, however, characteristic of the apostle to be absolute in his terms when dealing with a particular obligation. At the same time, on the analogy of his own teaching elsewhere or on the analogy of Scripture, we are compelled to take account of exceptions to the absolute terms in which an obligation is affirmed. It must be so in this instance. We cannot but believe that he would have endorsed and practised the word of Peter and other apostles: "We must obey God rather than men" (Acts 5:29; *cf.* 4:19, 20). The

---

[8] *Cf.* review by the present writer in *The Westminster Theological Journal*, VII, 2, May 1945, pp. 188ff.
[9] ἑαυτοῖς λήμψονται may express the thought of bringing upon themselves and in that event the responsibility for the penal judgment inflicted would be expressed.

magistrate is not infallible nor is he the agent of perfect rectitude. When there is conflict between the requirements of men and the commands of God, then the word of Peter must take effect.

Again Paul does not deal with the questions that arise in connection with revolution. Without question in these two verses we are not without an index to what we ought to do when revolution has taken place. "The *powers* that be" refer to the *de facto* magistrates. And in this passage as a whole there are principles which bear upon the right or wrong of revolution. But these matters which become acute difficulties for conscientious Christians are not introduced in this passage. The reason lies on the surface. The apostle is not writing an essay on casuistical theology but setting forth the cardinal principles pertaining to the institution of government and regulating the behaviour of Christians.[10]

3, 4 While the first clause of verse 3 attaches itself to the last clause of verse 2, it is scarcely proper to say that it assigns the ground why rebels will bring upon themselves penal judgment.[11] It is preferably taken as enunciating the prerogative of the rulers, arising from the appointment or ordinance of God, and therefore as validating the penal judgment which these rulers administer. It should be observed that in this clause we have an express intimation of the magistrate's function and it is because he exercises this office that he has the authority to inflict punishment.

The "terror" which rulers are to the evil work is the fear of punishment evoked in the hearts of men by reason of the authority vested in rulers to execute this punishment. This fear can be of two kinds, the fear that inhibits wrongdoing and the fear that results when wrong has been committed. It would appear that the latter is particularly in view. In the next clause the question, "wouldest thou have no fear of the power?" enjoins the absence of the fear that is the result of wrongdoing. This is confirmed by verse 4 when it says, "But if thou do that which is evil, be afraid"; it is the fear of the penalty which the magistrate executes as the bearer of

---

[10] "With the origin of a government, or its political form the Apostle does not concern himself: nor does he enter upon the question at what point during a period of revolutionary change a given government is to be considered as οὖσα, or as non-existent; and when a government, originally illegitimate, acquires a prescriptive right. The imperial authority was too old, and too firm to make these questions practical" (Liddon: *op. cit.*, pp. 247f.).

[11] *Cf.* Liddon and Meyer.

the sword. However, there could also be reference to the fear that inhibits wrongdoing. If we are minded only to do that which is good, then we have no reason to be actuated by the fear that restrains wrongdoing.

When it is said that "rulers are not a terror to the good work but to the evil" the good work and the evil are personified. For what is meant is terror to the person performing evil. There are two observations respecting this clause. (1) The thought is focused upon the punishment of evil-doing. It is significant that the apostle mentions this first of all in dealing with the specific functions assigned to the civil magistrate. There is the tendency in present-day thinking to underestimate the punitive in the execution of government and to suppress this all-important aspect of the magistrate's authority. It is not so in apostolic teaching. (2) It is with the *deed* that the magistrate is concerned. Paul speaks of the good and evil *work*. It is not the prerogative of the ruler to deal with all sin but only with sin registered in the action which violates the order that the magistrate is appointed to maintain and promote.

The next clause can be interpreted either as a question or as a statement. In the latter case the rendering would be: "Thou wouldest then have no fear of the power" and means "if thou wouldest have no fear of the power, do that which is good". But it is preferable, with the version quoted, to regard it as a question. The sense is to the same effect. But the question expresses the thought more forcefully. If we do that which is good, then we shall have no reason to fear the ruling authority.

"Thou shalt have praise from the same." The praise given by the magistrate is not reward in the proper sense of the term. Evil-doers receive their punitive reward but those who do well do not receive any meritorious award. The term used for "praise" does not bear this signification but rather that of approval (*cf.* I Cor. 4:5; II Cor. 8:18; Phil. 4:8; I Pet. 2:14) and is used of the praise that redounds to God for the riches of his grace (*cf.* Eph. 1:6, 12, 14; Phil. 1:11). This praise may be followed by reward in certain instances but the idea of reward is not implicit in the term. The praise could be expressed by saying that good behaviour secures good standing in the state, a status to be cherished and cultivated.

The first clause in verse 4 states what is, positively, the chief purpose of magisterial authority. The ruler is the minister of God for good. The term "minister of God" harks back to verses 1 and 2 where the "authority" is said to be of God, ordained of God, and the ordinance of God. But now there is intimated the specific capacity in which this ordination consists. This designation removes every supposition to the effect that magistracy is *per se* evil and serves good only in the sense that as a lesser evil it restrains and counteracts greater evils. The title here accorded the civil ruler shows that he is invested with all the dignity and sanction belonging to God's servant within the sphere of government. This is borne out still further by the purpose for which he is God's servant; he is the minister of God for that which is *good*. And we may not tone down the import of the term "good" in this instance. Paul provides us with a virtual definition of the good we derive from the service of the civil authority when he requires that we pray for kings and all who are in authority "that we may lead a tranquil and quiet life in all godliness and gravity" (I Tim. 2:2). The good the magistrate promotes is that which subserves the interests of piety.

There is a direct, personal address in this clause, expressed in the words "to thee", showing the relevance for the well-being of the individual believer of that service which the magistrate renders.

The second clause, as has been observed above, points to the kind of fear particularly in view in verse 3 and the third clause gives the reason why this fear is to be entertained. This reason is that the magistrate "bears not the sword in vain". The sword which the magistrate carries[12] as the most significant part of his equipment is not merely the sign of his authority but of his right to wield it in the infliction of that which a sword does. It would not be necessary to suppose that the wielding of the sword contemplates the infliction of the death penalty exclusively. It can be wielded to instil the terror of that punishment which it can inflict. It can be wielded to execute punishment that falls short of death. But to exclude the right of the death penalty when the nature of the crime calls for such is totally contrary to that which the sword signifies and executes. We need appeal to no more than New Testament usage to establish this reference. The sword is so frequently associated with death as the instrument of execution

---

[12] The verb is φορέω and is more expressive in this connection than φέρω.

13:1–7 THE CIVIL MAGISTRATE

(*cf.* Matt. 26:52; Luke 21:24; Acts 12:2; 16:27; Heb. 11:34, 37; Rev. 13:10) that to exclude its use for this purpose in this instance would be so arbitrary as to bear upon its face prejudice contrary to the evidence.[13] "In vain" means to no purpose.

"For he is a minister of God, an avenger for wrath to him that doeth evil." In the first clause the ruler is said to be the minister of God for good. Now the same office is accorded to him for avenging evil. The parallelism is noteworthy—the same dignity and investiture belong to the ruler's penal prerogative as to his function in promoting good. This penal function is said to consist in being "an avenger unto wrath" to the evil-doer. This is the first time that the term "wrath" is used in reference to the civil magistrate. In verse 2 we found that the "judgment" alludes to the judgment of God of which the retribution executed by the civil magistrate is the expression and from which this retribution derives its sanction. The question would arise here: whose "wrath" is in view, that of God, or that of the magistrate, or that of both? In 12:19, as demonstrated above, "the wrath" is the wrath of God and the usage would point to the same conclusion in this instance. Furthermore, there is not warrant for thinking that the magistrate's reaction to crime is to be construed in terms of wrath. Hence "wrath" should be regarded as the wrath of God. Thus the magistrate is the avenger in executing the judgment that accrues to the evil-doer from the wrath of God. Again we discover the sanction belonging to the ruler's function; he is the agent in executing God's wrath. And we also see how divergent from biblical teaching is the sentimentality that substitutes the interests of the offender for the satisfaction of justice as the basis of criminal retribution.

5 Commentators are divided on the question whether the necessity enunciated here arises from what is stated in verse 4 or harks back to the whole of the preceding context. It makes little difference to the force of the conclusion drawn in this verse and indicated by "wherefore". In the latter part of verse 4 enough is stated to ground the conclusion of verse 5; the designation "minister of God" as well as the allusion to the ruler as agent in executing God's wrath point to an investiture that *demands* subjection. But

---

[13] The sword is the *insignium juris vitae et necis.*

even if we find the immediate grounding of verse 5 in the last clause of verse 4, we cannot dissociate verse 4b from all that had been stated previously respecting the prerogatives of magistrates as proceeding from the ordinance of God. In any case, no proposition in this passage expresses the divine sanction of civil government more than this one, namely, that we must be subject "for conscience' sake". Paul uses this word "conscience" frequently and it is apparent that the meaning is conscience toward God (*cf.* Acts 23:1; 24:16; II Cor. 1:12; 4:2; 5:11; I Tim. 1:5; 3:9; II Tim. 1:3). The meaning here must be that we are to subject ourselves out of a sense of obligation to God. The thought then is that we are not only to be subject because insubjection brings upon us penal judgment but also because there is the obligation intrinsic to God's will irrespective of the liability which evil-doing may entail. God alone is Lord of the conscience and therefore to do anything out of conscience or for conscience' sake is to do it from a sense of obligation to God. This is stated expressly in I Peter 2:13: "be subject to every ordinance of man for the Lord's sake". The necessity, therefore, is not that of inevitable outcome (*cf.* Matt. 18:7; Luke 21:23; I Cor. 7:26) but that of ethical demand (*cf.* I Cor. 9:16).

6 In view of all that is involved in verse 5 regarding the divine sanction by which the magistrate discharges his functions there is no need to seek any remoter basis for the terms with which verse 6 begins, "for for this cause". If the magistrate is to perform the ministry which is given him of God, he must have the material means for the discharge of his labours. Hence the payment[14] of tribute is not a tyrannical imposition but the necessary and proper participation on the part of subjects in the support of government. This reason for the payment of taxes is stated in the latter part of the verse: "for they are ministers of God's service, attending continually upon this very thing".

The term for "ministers" in this instance is different from that used on two occasions in verse 4. But it does not denote a less dignified kind of ministry as if the collection of taxes, since it is a monetary affair, called for the use of a term of inferior signification. This term and its cognates are used in the New Testament, with

---

[14] There is no reason for taking τελεῖτε as imperative.

13:1-7 THE CIVIL MAGISTRATE

one possible exception,[15] with reference to the service of God and sometimes of the highest forms of ministry in the worship of God (*cf.* Luke 1:23; Acts 13:2; Rom. 15:16, 27; II Cor. 9:12; Phil. 2:17; Heb. 1:7, 14; 8:2; 10:11). Hence, if anything, this designation enhances the dignity attaching to the ministry of rulers. In the administration associated with taxes and customs there is to be no depreciation of their office. In the version this thought is properly expressed by saying that they are "ministers of God's service", although in the Greek they are simply called "ministers of God".

The "very thing" upon which the rulers are said to attend continually must in the context refer to the taxes. It would not be reasonable to regard the antecedent as the more general functions specified in the earlier verses. The thought is now focused on the payment of taxes and this is the "very thing" in view. The verb used in this clause adds likewise to the emphasis that falls in this verse upon the propriety and dignity of this phase of the magistrate's administration (*cf.* Acts 1:14; 2:42; 6:4; Rom. 12:12; Col. 4:2).[16]

By implication this verse also reflects on the purposes for which taxes are collected and on the uses which they serve. They subserve the ends for which rulers are appointed and not the abuses which are so frequently attendant upon the expenditure of them. In the words of Calvin, rulers "should remember that all that they receive from the people is public property, and not a means of satisfying private lust and luxury".[17]

7 "Render to all their dues." This should not be taken as a general exhortation that we are to discharge our obligations to all men. It is to be understood of the obligations we owe to those in authority in the state. This limitation is required by the context. With our all-inclusive obligations verses 8-10 deal. But within this sphere of obligation to magistrates the exhortation embraces every kind of debt owing. The "dues" are not merely those pertaining to taxes but, as the remaining part of the verse indicates,

---

[15] Phil. 2:25; *cf.* also Phil. 2:30. The Greek word is λειτουργός (as distinct from διάκονος in vs. 4).
[16] προσκαρτερέω. *Cf.* Jesus' own endorsement of custom and tribute in Luke 20:22-25 and the false charge in Luke 23:2.
[17] *Op. cit., ad loc.*

155

include the debts of veneration and honour. Hence this summary imperative is inclusive of all the obligations to be fulfilled within the sphere of civil government. The form of the imperative underlines the strength accorded to it.

The "tribute" corresponds to our term "tax", levied on persons and property (*cf.* Luke 20:22; 23:2), "custom" refers to the tax levied on goods and corresponds to customs payments.

"Fear to whom fear." The word used here for fear is the same as that rendered "terror" in verse 3. But in the latter verse the behaviour enjoined is that which will obviate the necessity of fear and therefore the absence of fear is commended, at least the absence of that which will be the occasion for fear. Fear is the accompaniment of wrongdoing. For this reason it might be thought that the magistrate is not in view in this present exhortation: two opposing attitudes would not be commended. Hence, it is thought, God is the person to whom fear is to be accorded as in I Peter 2:17: "Fear God. Honor the king". This interpretation is neither necessary nor feasible. (1) The kind of fear contemplated in verse 3, namely, the fear of the punishment executed for wrongdoing, should be absent in reference to God as well as to the magistrate: we are under an even greater obligation to avoid the conduct that will make us liable to divine retribution. Thus to make God the object does not relieve the apparent discrepancy between the two verses. (2) The apostle is dealing with our obligations to the civil authorities and it would be alien to the coordination and sequence to introduce a reference to the fear we owe to God. The identical form of statement in all four imperatives requires us to believe that they all belong to the same sphere. If the fear of God were meant the name of God would have to be mentioned in order to indicate the break in the sequence.

The solution lies in the different connotations. In verse 3 the fear is that of the punishment to be inflicted; in verse 7 it is the fear of veneration and respect. In reference to God this is the fear of reverential awe (*cf.* Acts 9:31; Rom. 3:18; II Cor. 7:1; Eph. 5:21), in reference to men the veneration due on account of their station (*cf.* Eph. 6:5; I Pet. 2:18). It is possible that difference of rank among officers of state is indicated by the terms "fear" and "honor", that the former has in view the respect paid to those on the highest level of authority and the latter that paid to those of lower rank. But there is not sufficient evidence to insist on this distinction. Both

13:1–7 THE CIVIL MAGISTRATE

terms could be used for the purpose of emphasizing the obligation to exercise not only the subjection due to rulers but also the veneration that belongs to them as ministers of God.

C. THE PRIMACY OF LOVE
(13:8–10)

13:8–10

8 Owe no man anything, save to love one another: for he that loveth his neighbor hath fulfilled the law.
9 For this, Thou shalt not commit adultery, Thou shalt not kill, Thou shalt not steal, Thou shalt not covet, and if there be any other commandment, it is summed up in this word, namely, Thou shalt love thy neighbor as thyself.
10 Love worketh no ill to his neighbor: love therefore is the fulfilment of the law.

8–10

There is transition at this point. Verses 1–7 are strictly concerned with the state and our relations to it. Verses 8–10 are not restricted to this sphere. Just as the imperative with which verse 7 begins is to be understood of the dues rendered to magistrates and their agents, so the imperative of verse 8 applies to every relationship. However, the transition is not an abrupt one. The apostle easily and appropriately passes from the subject of debts paid to rulers in the state to the subject of our obligations to all men. So he proceeds: "owe no man anything". It is necessary to take this as imperative. It could be regarded as indicative. But then the sentence would have to read: "ye owe no man anything but to love one another". The purpose would be to stress the primacy of love. But exegetically this construction is out of the question. It would be strange indeed for Paul to say this after having insisted that we are to pay our debts to the civil authorities. Besides, he does not proceed to say that the only debt we owe to men is love. He goes on to say that love enables us to fulfil our obligations to men but not to teach that love displaces all other commandments.

The force of the imperative is that we are to have no unpaid debts; that we are not to be in debt to any. In accord with the analogy of Scripture this cannot be taken to mean that we may never incur financial obligations, that we may not borrow from others in case of need (*cf.* Exod. 22:25; Psalm 37:26; Matt. 5:42;

13:8-10 THE PRIMACY OF LOVE

Luke 6:35). But it does condemn the looseness with which we contract debts and particularly the indifference so often displayed in the discharging of them. "The wicked borroweth, and payeth not again" (Psalm 37:21). Few things bring greater reproach upon the Christian profession than the accumulation of debts and refusal to pay them.

"Save to love one another." This has frequently, if not generally, been regarded as the one exception to what precedes and would mean that the only unpaid debt is that of love, that love to our neighbour is a debt that can never be discharged. It is true that love is inexhaustible; it is a duty from which we are never relieved. In Philippi's words, "By its very nature, love is a duty which, when discharged, is never discharged, since he loves not truly who loves for the purpose of ceasing from loving . . . by loving love is intensified, the more it is exercised the less can it be satisfied".[18] But it appears rather incongruous for the apostle, in a passage which enjoins love and asserts its primacy, to say or imply that love is an unpaid debt. There is, therefore, another way of taking the Greek terms rendered by the word "save". These terms frequently mean "except" and state an exception to that which has been asserted. But they also are used in the sense of "but" or "only" (*cf.* Matt. 12:4; John 17:12; Rom. 14:14; Gal. 1:19) and do not state an express exception to what precedes but only another consideration or reservation relevant to what has been stated. It would seem preferable to follow this usage here. So the thought would be: "Owe no man anything; only do love one another". This is to say, love is not regarded as a debt unpaid, nor is there any reflection upon the inexhaustible debt which love involves, but the apostle is simply reminding us of what we owe in the matter of love. We are to remember that love is a perpetual obligation.[19]

The question arises: what is the love here spoken of? Is it the love believers exercise towards one another within the fellowship of faith or is it the more embracive love to all men? It cannot be doubted that a distinct quality belongs to the mutual love operative among believers. It is of this love Paul speaks in 12:9, 10. And the expression "one another" in the present case would suggest the same. The solution to the question would appear to be as follows.

---

[18] *Op. cit., ad loc.*
[19] *Cf.* Barrett: *op. cit., ad loc.*

In enunciating the primacy of love and writing to the church as Paul now is it would not be possible to think of love on any lower plane than that of love in its highest exercise, love as exercised within the fellowship of the saints. And so Paul says "one another", thus focusing attention upon that circle to which the epistle is addressed. But it is likewise not feasible to restrict the love enjoined to the circle of believers. For the apostle proceeds immediately to show the relation of love to the law of God and the law of God of which he speaks is the law regulative of behaviour in our social relationships with all men. If the love of which he speaks is the fulfilment of the law, then the love must be as broad as the law itself and the law has respect to our relations to all men. This is indicated in the next clause: "for he that loveth the other hath fulfilled the law".[20] "The other" is the person other than oneself and cannot be restricted in this case to believers.[21]

It is apparent that in this passage the apostle is not dealing with love to God. He is dealing exclusively with love to our fellowmen, as the commandments quoted later show. It is just as true that love to God is the fulfilment of the law that pertains to our relation to God (*cf.* Matt. 22:37, 38; Mark 12:29, 30; Luke 10:27). But here it is love in inter-human relations that is in view (*cf.* Matt. 22:39; Mark 12:31; Luke 10:29–37). So in this instance the law that love is said to fulfil is the law pertaining to mutual relations among men.

"Hath fulfilled the law" is the perfect of completed action. "Fulfil" is a richer term than "obey". It means that the law has received the full measure of that which it requires. The completeness of conformity is thereby expressed (*cf.* Gal. 5:14).[22]

We are not to regard love as dispensing with law or as displacing law as if what has misleadingly been called "the law of love" has been substituted under the gospel for the law of commandments or precepts. Paul does not say that the law is love but that love fulfils the law and law has not in the least degree been depreciated or deprived of its sanction. It is because love is accorded this

---

[20] This is the literal rendering. "Neighbor" occurs in verse 9 but not in verse 8.
[21] There is no reason to suppose that "the other" is the other law, that is the rest of the law. The other commandments are not "other"; they are the commandments that love fulfils.
[22] *Cf.* Arndt and Gingrich: *op. cit.*, ad πληρόω, 3.

13:8–10 THE PRIMACY OF LOVE

quality and function that the law as correlative is confirmed in its relevance and dignity. It is the law that love fulfils.

Love is emotive, motive, and expulsive. It is emotive and therefore creates affinity with and affection for the object. It is motive in that it impels to action. It is expulsive because it expels what is alien to the interests which love seeks to promote.

If love is the fulfilment of the law this means that no law is fulfilled apart from love. This must apply, therefore, to the law that governs our conduct in the state (vss. 1–7). It is a great fallacy to suppose that in the state we have simply the order of justice but that in other spheres, particularly in the church, we have the order of love. There is no such distinction; far less is there antithesis. It is only through love that we can fulfil the demands of justice. The magistrate cannot properly exercise his authority except as he is animated by love to God and to the subjects of his realm. The subjects cannot render to him the veneration that is his due and be law-abiding for conscience' sake save as they recognize God's institution and with godly fear subject themselves to it. "Fear God. Honor the king" (I Pet. 2:17).[23]

Verse 9 corroborates and expands what is affirmed in verse 8. In the latter verse Paul had referred to the law. Now he gives examples of what the law is. He enumerates four[24] of the ten commandments. The order followed represents the order in which they appear in the Greek version of the Old Testament (*cf.* Deut. 5:17–21). The command respecting adultery precedes that respecting murder elsewhere in the New Testament (Luke 18:20; James 2:11). This enumeration from the decalogue indicates that, in Paul's esteem, the law which love fulfils finds its epitome in the ten commandments. That the precepts mentioned do not comprise the whole law is expressed by the words, "if there be any other commandment". This appeal to the decalogue demonstrates the following propositions. (1) The decalogue is of permanent and

---

[23] "It is as though he had said, 'When I request you to obey rulers, I require only what all believers ought to perform by the law of love. If you wish the good to prosper... you ought to strive to make the laws and judgments prevail, in order that the people may be obedient to the defenders of the laws, for these men enable us to enjoy peace.' To introduce anarchy, therefore, is to violate charity" (Calvin: *op. cit., ad loc.*)

[24] οὐ ψευδομαρτυρήσεις appears after οὐ κλέψεις in ℵ, the mass of the cursives, and some versions but is omitted in P⁴⁶, A, B, D, G, L, and some versions.

abiding relevance. (2) It exemplifies the *law* that love fulfils and is therefore correlative with love. (3) The commandments and their binding obligation do not interfere with the exercise of love; there is no incompatibility. (4) The commandments are the norms in accordance with which love operates.

It should be noted that the commandments mentioned are all negative in form. It is often pleaded that ethics should not be negative but positive. The fallacy here is that the plea is unrealistic; it overlooks the fact of sin. If there were no liability to sin and no fact of sin there would be no need of prohibition. It is because God's law is realistic that eight of the ten commandments are negative and one other has a negative element. God's law must be negative of sin. The one absolute prohibition in Paul's teaching to which there is no reservation is, "abstain from every form of evil" (I Thess. 5:22). Truth is negative of error, right of wrong, righteousness of iniquity. The gospel is good news because it is first of all salvation from sin (*cf.* Matt. 1:21). Even love itself is negative: it "worketh no ill to his neighbor" (vs. 10). And here in verse 9 we have examples of the ills it does not perpetrate: adultery, murder, theft, coveting. The commandment to love is positive and Paul elsewhere gives us a catalogue of its positive qualities. "Love suffereth long and is kind . . . rejoiceth with the truth; beareth all things, believeth all things, hopeth all things, endureth all things" (I Cor. 13:4, 6, 7). But even in this passage we also have negations: "love envieth not; love vaunteth not itself, is not puffed up, doth not behave itself unseemly, seeketh not its own, is not provoked, taketh not account of evil; rejoiceth not in unrighteousness" (I Cor. 13:4, 5, 6). When we translate these into imperatives directed to love they become negatives. Who is to say that the demands of love, both positive and negative, are not to be directed to love and its proper exercise commanded?

"Thou shalt love thy neighbor as thyself." This is an exact quotation from Leviticus 19:18. In the Old Testament passage it comes at the end of a lengthy series of commandments most of which are in prohibitory form (vss. 9–18). When Paul says that all the commandments are "summed up in this word", it is not certain whether he means that they are summarily *repeated*, that is recapitulated, or whether he means simply summed up in the sense of condensed. In any case the main thought is that when love is in exercise, then all the commandments receive their fulfilment and so they can all be reduced to this demand. The person who loves his neighbour as himself will not work towards him the ills prohibited and will, on the contrary, discharge the positive counterpart.

Something frequently overlooked deserves comment. It is the expression "as thyself". This implies that we do love our own selves. Love of oneself is not to be equated with selfishness or egotism. We are selfish when we do not love our neighbours as ourselves, when we are so absorbed with our own selves that we have no regard for others. Unselfish concern for others fulfils the injunction: "not looking each of you to his own things, but each of you also to the things of others" (Phil. 2:4). But this does not say or imply that we may be oblivious of our own things and, particularly, not oblivious of our own persons. It is unnatural and impossible for us not to love ourselves. "No man ever hated his own flesh" (Eph. 5:29) and in accord with this Paul says: "He that loveth his wife loveth himself" (Eph. 5:28). The various injunctions which might appear to contradict this love for oneself are not incompatible (*cf.* 12:10; Phil. 2:3). When we esteem others better than ourselves or when we sacrifice ourselves for the good of others (*cf.* John 15:13; Rom. 5:7), we do not thereby cease to love ourselves. The love of God is supreme and incomparable. We are never asked to love God as we love ourselves or our neighbour as we love God. To God our whole being in all relationships must be captive in love, devotion, and service. To conceive of such captivity to our own selves or to any creature would be the essence of ungodliness. Of this distinction our Lord's words are eloquent: "Thou shalt love the Lord thy God with all thy heart, and with all thy soul, and with all thy mind, and with all thy strength ... Thou shalt love thy neighbor as thyself" (Mark 12:30, 31).

"Love therefore is the fulfilment of the law." The version has advisedly chosen the term "fulfilment" rather than "fulfilling". The latter term suggests process but this is not the force here. In verse 8 the tense of the verb points to the perfect of completed action. So here the noun denotes the full measure. It is common for commentators to regard the use of the noun in this instance as serving the same purpose and expressing the same meaning as the perfect tense of the verb in verse 8. This is questionable. The verb has frequently the sense of "fulfil"[25] and so it is proper to render the

---

[25] *Cf.* Matt. 1:22; 3:5; Luke 1:20; 4:21; John 12:38; Acts 1:16; Rom. 8:4.

clause in question, "he that loveth the other hath fulfilled the law". But it is doubtful if the noun ever bears the signification expressed by "fulfil".[26] Pervasively, if not uniformly, it has the meaning of that which "fills" or that which is "filled" and frequently the proper rendering is "fulness" (*cf.* John 1:16; Rom. 15:29; I Cor. 10:26; Gal. 4:4; Eph. 1:10; 3:19; 4:13; Col. 1:19; 2:9). Sometimes it means that which is filled in to make something complete (*cf.* Matt. 9:16; Mark 2:21).[27] It could mean complement in Ephesians 1:23.[28] Hence usage would suggest that the precise meaning is that of "fulness" and that the apostle has enriched and added to the notion of fulfilment expressed in verse 8 by indicating through the use of the noun in verse 10 that love gives to the law the full measure of its demand. The law looked upon as something to be filled is filled to the brim by love. It is not as if something other than love does part of the filling up and then love enters to complete the process but that love does all of the filling. From beginning to end it is love that fills and so in this sense it is with or by love that the law is filled.

---

[26] Rom. 11:12 has been taken in this sense by some. The noun is $πλήρωμα$.
[27] In these instances it is that which is filled in to make the garment complete and the thought is that the patch of new cloth on the old garment, intended to complete the garment, only takes away from the completeness which the garment should have.
[28] But, exegetically speaking, this is not to be preferred in the light of Eph. 3:19; 4:13.

D. THE APPROACHING CONSUMMATION
   (13:11-14)

13:11-14

11 And this, knowing the season, that already it is time for you to awake out of sleep: for now is salvation nearer to us than when we *first* believed.
12 The night is far spent, and the day is at hand: let us therefore cast off the works of darkness, and let us put on the armor of light.
13 Let us walk becomingly, as in the day; not in revelling and drunkenness, not in chambering and wantonness, not in strife and jealousy.
14 But put ye on the Lord Jesus Christ, and make not provision for the flesh, to *fulfil* the lusts *thereof*.

11, 12 "And this" means "and indeed" or "and the more" (*cf.* Eph. 2:8; Phil. 1:28). This introduction therefore indicates another reason why the readers are to fulfil the royal law, "Thou shalt love thy neighbor as thyself". The reason is immediately appended: "knowing the time". "Time" (season) here is not time in general but a time with distinct significance, a time charged with issues of practical moment so that it is now high time to awake out of sleep. How we may further characterize this "time" depends upon the interpretation of the "salvation" which is said to be nearer than when we first believed.

The term "salvation" could be used in the sense of deliverance from some temporal oppression or affliction (*cf.* Phil. 1:19). It might be supposed, therefore, that the apostle is thinking of some present distress afflicting the church from which he hopes there will soon be deliverance. The usage of the New Testament, however, would point to the conclusion that when this term is used with reference to the future it denotes the consummation of salvation to be realized at the advent of Christ (*cf.* Phil. 2:12; I Thess. 5:8, 9; Heb. 1:14; 9:28; I Pet. 1:5; 2:2). Hence it is the completion of the salvation process that is said to be nearer than when we believed. Since this completion is consummatory and is bound up with what is central in the eschatological hope, we would have to regard this passage as having a distinctly eschatological emphasis. The term "season" or "time" should thus be taken in a sense that is relevant to this emphasis. The term does not of itself have eschatological reference.[29] It may denote any particular season or period (*cf.* Matt. 11:25; 12:1; Luke 4:13; 8:13; 21:36; Acts 7:20; 12:1; 14:17; I Cor. 7:5; Gal. 4:10; Eph. 2:12; II Tim. 4:6). Frequently the word is used with reference to an appointed time and therefore to the time fixed for and appropriate to certain events or even duties (*cf.* Matt. 26:18; Luke 19:44; John 7:6, 8; Acts 17:26; Rom. 5:6; 9:9; II Cor. 6:2; Gal. 6:9, 10; II Thess. 2:6; I Tim. 2:6; 6:15; Tit. 1:3; I Pet. 5:6). It is sometimes used to denote a definite period of climactic significance in the unfolding of God's redemptive plan (*cf.* Matt. 26:18; Mark 1:15; Rom. 3:26; Rev. 1:3). The plural is also used with similar signification (*cf.* I Tim. 2:6; Tit. 1:3). But the term has also expressly eschatological application (*cf.* Mark 13:33; Luke 21:8; I Pet. 1:5; Rev. 11:18). A distinctly eschatological aspect appears also in the use of the plural in such passages as Luke 21:24; Acts 3:20; I Timothy 4:1; 6:15. With these diverse uses of the term in view the application in the passage before us would appear to be that the apostle is thinking of the present time in which he is writing as the period that has its terminus in the consummation. It is the last epoch in this world's history, the time in which the complex of consummating events is impending. These are the last days (*cf.* Acts 2:17; II Tim. 3:1; Heb. 1:2; James 5:3; I Pet. 1:20; II Pet. 3:3; I John 2:18). With this perspective in reference to the readers' place in history Paul assumes they are familiar and he is reminding them of its meaning for practical godliness. They have their place in "the fulness of the time" (Gal. 4:4), in the "dispensation of the fulness of the times" (Eph. 1:10), in "the ends of the ages" (I Cor. 10:11), in "the consummation of the ages" (Heb. 9:26). The exhortation is, therefore, to much the same effect as that of Paul elsewhere (Tit. 2:12, 13) and of Peter (II Pet. 3:14). The "season" is that

---

[29] For a recent study of καιρός and for a discriminating and searching criticism of the viewpoint whereby χρόνος and καιρός are sharply distinguished and the latter regarded as time considered in relation to personal action *cf.* James Barr: *Biblical Words for Time*, Studies in Biblical Theology No. 33 (Naperville, 1962); *cf.* also by the same author *The Semantics of Biblical Language* (London, 1961).

which derives its character from the consummating events towards which the present age is hastening, events which have their focus in "the appearing of the glory of the great God and our Saviour Jesus Christ" (Tit. 2:13). The foregoing interpretation of the "salvation" and "season" would give the direction for the understanding of other details in verses 11, 12.

"The night is far spent, the day is at hand." "The day", without further characterization or specification, is used by Paul and other New Testament writers as an eschatological designation (*cf.* I Cor. 3:13; I Thess. 5:4; Heb. 10:25; II Pet. 1:19). This use of the simple expression "the day" is defined by closely related expressions such as "that day" and "the great day" (*cf.* Matt. 7:22; 24:36; II Thess. 1:10; II Tim. 1:12, 18; 4:8; Jude 6). That "the day" and "that day" could be used to denote the eschatological day without further specification arises, no doubt, from the frequency with which the word "day" is used in various combinations to designate what is strictly eschatological—"the day of judgment", "the last day", "the day of wrath", "the day of the Lord", "the day of God", "the day when the Son of man is revealed", "the day of Christ" (*cf.* Matt. 10:15; 12:36; Luke 17:24, 30; John 6:39; 14:48; Acts 17:31; Rom. 2:15, 16; I Cor. 1:8; 5:5; Eph. 4:30; Phil. 1:6, 10; I Thess. 5:2; II Thess. 2:2; II Pet. 3:7, 10; I John 4:17). With this copious use of the term "day" in mind, no other interpretation could begin to gather to itself as much support as that which interprets "the day" in the present text as referring to the day when Christ will come with salvation for his people (*cf.* Heb. 9:28). How then could the apostle have said that the day of Christ was at hand?

It is often claimed that the apostle, like other New Testament writers, expected the advent of Christ within a short time and that this expectation was reproduced in his teaching in the form of affirmation to that effect (*cf.* I Cor. 7:29–31).[30] Would not the

---

[30] "Paul's earliest extant epistles, those to the Thessalonians, suggest that at that time he thought that the Advent of the Lord might come within a few months: it would certainly come within the lifetime of most present members of the Church. The same thought is present in I Corinthians, and it affects his judgment on ethical problems (see chap. vii). It is all the more striking that in this epistle there is no mention of the imminence of the Advent, apart from these few verses. The whole argument stands independently of any such expectation... Only in the present passage the old idea of the nearness of the Day of the Lord survives to give point to his moral exhortations" (Dodd: *op. cit.*, p. 209). *Cf.* also Leenhardt: *op. cit.*, p. 339.

events then prove that the apostle was mistaken not simply in his expectation but also in his teaching?

The answer to this question would appear to reside in two considerations. (1) The New Testament does teach that the day of the Lord is at hand (*cf.* Phil. 4:5; James 5:8; I Pet. 4:7; Rev. 22:10–12, 20). This is not to be interpreted, however, in the sense of imminence in our sense of that word. Paul himself who gives expression to this thought of nearness found occasion to warn against the supposition of imminence (II Thess. 2:1–12). And in this epistle he teaches the restoration of Israel, even though at the time of writing there were no apparent signs of Israel's conversion satisfying the terms of his prediction (*cf.* 11:12, 15, 26). And Peter, though he had written that "the end of all things is at hand" (I Pet. 4:7), had occasion to deal with the objections proceeding from the lapse of time. He reminded his readers that "one day is with the Lord as a thousand years and a thousand years as one day" (II Pet. 3:8) and, therefore, that the lapse of a thousand years no more interfered with the fulfilment of the promise nor with the certainty of the Lord's coming than the passage of a single day. It is necessary, therefore, to gain this perspective with reference to the New Testament concept of the nearness of the advent. It is the nearness of prophetic perspective and not that of our chronological calculations. In the unfolding of God's redemptive purpose the next great epochal event, correlative with the death of Christ, his resurrection and ascension, and the outpouring of the Holy Spirit at Pentecost, is Jesus' advent in glory. This is the event that looms on the horizon of faith. There is nothing of similar character between the present and this epochal redemptive event. In this sense it is nigh. And this was as true when the apostle wrote as it is today. (2) Correlative with the nearness of "the day" is the other statement, "the night is far spent". Obviously "the day" and "the night" are contrasted and as "the day" is characterized by light so is the night by darkness. "The day" makes manifest (*cf.* I Cor. 3:13), the night conceals. The Lord's coming is represented as bringing to "light the hidden things of darkness" (I Cor. 4:5) and is associated with light because then the whole panorama of history will be placed in the pure light of God's judgment (*cf.* Rom. 14:10; II Cor. 5:10). In respect of the splendour of this light all that precedes Christ's advent in glory is *relatively* darkness and is thus called "the night". Furthermore,

13:11-14 THE APPROACHING CONSUMMATION

that which precedes Christ's coming is "this age" in contrast with "the age to come" and "this age" is evil (*cf.* Luke 16:8; Rom. 12:2; I Cor. 1:20; 2:6-8; II Cor. 4:4; Gal. 1:4; II Tim. 4:10). This indicates another reason why that which antedates Christ's advent should be called "the night" and associated with darkness. We are also provided with a perspective that throws light upon the statement that "the night is far spent". For "the night" would have to be identified with "this age" and therefore with the whole period of this world's history prior to the advent. And we have good reason to infer that the apostle is reflecting upon the relative brevity of what is yet to run its course of the history of this world, that history is hastening to its terminus. Paul elsewhere speaks of what is past as "the ages and the generations" (Col. 1:26). He identifies the present as "the ends of the ages" (I Cor. 10:11) and in Hebrews 9:26 it is called "the consummation of the ages". In this light not only is it appropriate to say "the night is far spent"; it is also necessary, and it is the bearing of this truth upon practical godliness that the apostle is now stressing. "Let us therefore cast off the works of darkness, and let us put on the armor of light."

Sleep, night, darkness are all co-related in our ordinary experience. The same is true in the moral and religious realm. And what the apostle is pressing home is the incompatibility of moral and religious slumbers with the position which believers now occupy in the great drama of redemption. The basic sanction of love to our neighbour as ourselves applied to the Old Testament as well as to the New (vss. 8-10). But the consideration Paul is now pleading is one that could apply only to the particular "season" contemplated in the present passage and urged as the reason for godly living. The day of Christ, though not yet come, is nevertheless throwing its light backward upon the present. In that light believers must now live; it is the dawning of the day of unprecedented splendour. It is high time to awake to the realization of this fact, to be aroused from spiritual torpor, to throw off the garments of slumber, and to put on the weapons that befit the tasks of such a "season" in redemptive history. Each calendar day brings nearer to us the day of final salvation, and, since it is life in the body that is decisive for eternal issues, the event of death points up for each person how short is "the season" prior to Christ's advent. As "we must all be made manifest before the judgment-seat of Christ" (II Cor. 5:10; *cf.* Rom. 14:10) and Christ is ready to "judge living and dead" (II Tim. 4:1; *cf.* I Pet. 4:5; James 5:9), indulgence of the works of the flesh is contradiction of the believer's faith and hope.

"The works of darkness" are the works belonging to and characteristic of darkness and darkness is to be understood in the ethical sense (*cf.* I Cor. 4:5; 6:14; Eph. 5:8, 11; Col. 1:13). "The armor of light" is likewise to be understood ethically and religiously and suggests by the terms used that the life of the believer is the good fight of faith (*cf.* II Cor. 6:7; Eph. 6:10–18).

13, 14 The excesses which the apostle enumerates in verse 13 were common in the empire at this time and particularly at Corinth from which the epistle was written. The terms indicate abandonment to debauchery and the quarrels which are the sequel. The positive exhortation in verse 14 points up the contrast which the lordship of Christ creates and demands. The figure is that of putting on Christ. Elsewhere Paul speaks of putting on the new man (Eph. 4:24; Col. 3:10), of putting on the armour of God (Eph. 6:11) and the weapons of light (vs. 12), of putting on the breastplate of righteousness, of faith, and bowels of compassion (Eph. 6:14; Col. 3:12; I Thess. 5:8). But none of these measure up to the significance of the present formula. It is used once elsewhere (Gal. 3:27). This latter text is to be interpreted in the light of Romans 6:1–10. To put on Christ is to be identified with him not only in his death but also in his resurrection. It is to be united to him in the likeness of his resurrection life. The full title "the Lord Jesus Christ" underlines the inclusiveness involved in the exhortation. Nothing less than the complete negation of vice and the perfection of purity and virtue exemplified in Christ make up the habitude required of a believer. When we think of Christ as holy, harmless, undefiled, and separate from sinners, we see the total contrast between the vices described in verse 13 and the pattern of verse 14. The negative is as exclusive as the positive is inclusive. We are not to make any provision for the fulfilment of the lusts of the flesh. The flesh is not to be equated with the body but includes all sinful propensions (*cf.* 7:5; 8:5–8; Gal. 5:19–21; 6:8; Eph. 2:3).

Romans xiv

E. THE WEAK AND THE STRONG
(14:1–23)

14:1-12

1 But him that is weak in faith receive ye, *yet* not for decision of scruples.
2 One man hath faith to eat all things: but he that is weak eateth herbs.
3 Let not him that eateth set at nought him that eateth not; and let not him that eateth not judge him that eateth: for God hath received him.
4 Who art thou that judgest the servant of another? to his own lord he standeth or falleth. Yea, he shall be made to stand; for the Lord hath power to make him stand.
5 One man esteemeth one day above another: another esteemeth every day *alike*. Let each man be fully assured in his own mind.
6 He that regardeth the day, regardeth it unto the Lord: and he that eateth, eateth unto the Lord, for he giveth God thanks; and he that eateth not, unto the Lord he eateth not, and giveth God thanks.
7 For none of us liveth to himself, and none dieth to himself.
8 For whether we live, we live unto the Lord; or whether we die, we die unto the Lord: whether we live therefore, or die, we are the Lord's.
9 For to this end Christ died and lived *again*, that he might be Lord of both the dead and the living.
10 But thou, why dost thou judge thy brother? or thou again, why dost thou set at nought thy brother? for we shall all stand before the judgment-seat of God.
11 For it is written,
As I live, saith the Lord, to me every knee shall bow, And every tongue shall confess to God.
12 So then each one of us shall give account of himself to God.

What extends from 14:1 to 15:13 is another well-defined section of the epistle. This section is coordinate with what precedes in chapters 12 and 13 in that it deals with what is concrete and practical in the life of the believer and, more particularly, with his life in the fellowship of the church. But this section is concerned specifically with the weak and the strong and with the attitudes they are to entertain in reference to one another.

There is a similarity between the subject dealt with and what we find in other epistles of Paul. Most patent is the similarity to situations of which Paul treats in I Corinthians 8:1–13; 10:23–33. But also in the epistles to the Galatians and Colossians there appear to be points of contact. In Romans 14:5 reference is made to distinctions of days and in Galatians 4:10 we read: "Ye observe days, and months, and seasons, and years". In Colossians 2:16, 17 we have reference to feast days, new moons, and sabbath days as a shadow of things to come. Furthermore, in Colossians 2:16, 20–23 we have allusions to a religious scrupulosity concerned with food and drink, and the slogan of the proponents was "handle not, nor taste, nor touch" (Col. 2:21). In the case of these two latter epistles it is not, however, the similarity that is most striking; it is the totally different attitude on the part of the apostle. In these two epistles there is a severely polemic and denunciatory note in reference to these same matters. In Galatians the observance of days and seasons is viewed with grave apprehensions. "I am afraid of you, lest by any means I have bestowed labor upon you in vain" (Gal. 4:11). In Colossians likewise the reproof directed at the ascetics is of the severest character: "If ye died with Christ from the rudiments of the world, why, as though living in the world, do ye subject yourselves to ordinances...? Which things have indeed a show of wisdom... but are not of any value against the indulgence of the flesh" (Col. 2:20, 23). This polemic severity we do not find in the section with which we are now concerned in Romans. Here there is a tenderness and tolerance that reflect a radically different attitude. "But him that is weak in faith receive ye" (14:1). "One man esteemeth one day above another: another esteemeth every day *alike*. Let each man be fully assured in his own mind" (14:5). Why this difference? The reason is clear. In Galatians Paul is dealing with the Judaizers who were perverting the gospel at its centre. They were the propagandists of a legalism which maintained that the observance of

14:1-23 THE WEAK AND THE STRONG

days and seasons was necessary to justification and acceptance with God. This meant a turning back again "to the weak and beggarly rudiments" (Gal. 4:9); it was "a different gospel which is not another", and worthy of the apostle's anathemas (*cf.* Gal. 1:8, 9). In Romans 14 there is no evidence that those esteeming one day above another were involved in any respect in this fatal error. They were not propagandists for a ceremonialism that was aimed at the heart of the gospel. Hence Paul's tolerance and restraint. The Colossian heresy was more complicated than the Galatian. At Colossae the error which Paul controverts was basically gnostic and posited, as F. F. Bruce observes, "a clear-cut dualism between the spiritual and material realms" and regarded salvation as consisting in the liberation of the spiritual from the material. Thus "asceticism was commonly regarded as an important element in the process of this liberation".[1] There was also the worship of angelic beings (*cf.* Col. 2:18) who were conceived of as the media of revelation from God and the mediators through whom "all prayer and worship from man to God could reach its goal".[2] Asceticism was also part of the ritual by which the favour of these angelic powers was to be gained. This heresy struck at the heart of the gospel and its peculiar gravity rested in the denial of Christ's preeminence as the one in whom dwelt the fulness of Godhood (*cf.* Col. 2:9) and as the only mediator between God and man. Hence the vigour of Paul's denunciations. There is not the slightest evidence that the asceticism of the weak in Romans 14 was bound up with the heretical speculations of the Colossian heresy. The climate is, therefore, radically different.

It could be argued with a good deal of plausibility that the weakness contemplated in Romans 14 is identical with that of I Corinthians 8. The latter consists clearly in the conviction entertained by some that food offered to idols had been so contaminated by this idolatrous worship that it was not proper for a Christian to partake of it. The whole question in the Corinthian epistle is focused in food or drink offered to idols. It might seem that the similarity of attitude and injunction in Romans 14 would indicate the same issue. This inference is not established and the evidence would point to the conclusion that the weakness in view

---

[1] F. F. Bruce: *Commentary on the Epistle to the Colossians* (Grand Rapids, 1957), p. 166, n. 10.
[2] *Ibid.*, p. 167.

in Romans 14 is more diversified. This is not to say that weakness of faith respecting meat offered to idols did not come into view in the Roman epistle. The case is simply that more has to be taken into account. The reasons for this conclusion are as follows. (1) In Romans 14 there is no mention of food or wine offered to idols. If this were exclusively the question we would expect an explicit reference as in I Corinthians 8 and 10. (2) Distinction of days comes into view in Romans 14. This is not reflected on in the Corinthian passages. It is very difficult to trace a relationship between scrupulosity respecting days and that concerned with food offered to idols. (3) The weakness of Romans 14 involved a vegetarian diet (*cf.* vs. 2). There is no evidence that the weak in reference to food offered to idols scrupled in the matter of flesh-meat if it had not been offered to idols. For these reasons we shall have to conclude that the weakness in Romans 14 was more generic in character.

There has been much difference of opinion as to the source whence this weakness came and the background that gave to it its precise complexion. To be less positive than some exegetes have been would appear to be necessary. Rome was cosmopolitan and so was the church there. It may have been, and the evidence offers much to favour the thesis, that various types of weakness proceeding from different backgrounds and influences were represented in that situation which the apostle envisaged. It is not necessary to suppose that all within the category of the weak were characterized by the same kind of weakness. Some who were weak in one respect may have been strong in a particular in respect of which others were weak. The diversity may be the explanation of Paul's treatment. This passage deals with the question of the weak and the strong in a way that applies to every instance in which religious scrupulosity arises in connection with such things as those exemplified in this chapter.

1–3 "Receive ye." This exhortation is directed to those who are not themselves in the category of the weak and therefore to those who were strong in faith and did not entertain these scruples. Since it is not in the form, "ye who are strong receive the weak" (*cf.* 15:1), the implication appears to be that the church at Rome was not as a whole characterized by this weakness but that the weak were a minority. This would gather support from the consideration that in this section of the epistle the exhortations are preponderantly directed to the strong. "Receive ye" means that there is to be no discrimination in respect of confidence, esteem, and affection. The strength of the plea is indicated by the use of the same term in verse 3 for God's reception of us and in 15:7 for Christ's reception. The latter text enforces the unrestrained character of this mutual acceptance by enjoining that it is to be patterned after the grace of Christ in receiving us to the glory of God. Nothing exposes the meanness of the discrimination against which the entreaty is directed more than the contradiction it offers to the attitude of the Saviour himself.

"Not for decision of scruples." The general thought expressed is rather clear. It is that the acceptance of the weak is not to be for the purpose of fanning the flames of dissension respecting differences of conviction on the matters in question, namely, eating and drinking, observance or non-observance of days. But what the precise thought is it is difficult to determine. The word rendered "scruples" means "thoughts" and is sometimes used with depreciatory reflection so that it virtually means "evil thoughts" (*cf.* Luke 5:22; 6:8; 9:46, 47; 24:38; Rom. 1:21; I Cor. 3:20; Phil. 2:14; I Tim. 2:8). The other word rendered "decision" is a plural form and refers most probably to the act of distinguishing (*cf.* I Cor. 12:10; Heb. 5:14). Hence the thought would appear to be "not to distinguishing of thoughts". This is to say "nor for the purpose of subjecting the convictions and thoughts of one another to censorious scrutiny". Since this is contrasted with "receive ye" and the latter is directed to the strong, the accent falls upon the necessity of avoiding the provocations which would befall the weak if their scruples were made the subject of analysis and dispute.

In verse 2 one form of the distinction between the strong and the weak is instanced. The weak are vegetarians; the strong are able to eat all kinds of food. In verse 3 the apostle places his finger on the vice so liable to be indulged by the respective groups. That of the strong is the disposition to despise or treat with contempt the weak and that of the weak to judge the strong. Both are condemned with equal vigour. In actual practice these vices appear respectively in the smile of disdainful contempt and in the frown of condemnatory judgment. These exemplify the attitudes which the apostle condemns and they point up their disruptive tendency within the fellowship which "receive ye" contemplates.

The concluding clause of verse 3, "for God hath received him" has been taken as referring both to him who does not eat and to him who eats. No doubt it is true that God has received the weak as well as the strong and his reception of the weak provides the reason for the exhortation to the strong stated in verse 1. But in this instance proximity to the exhortation directed to the weak and the more direct relevance of this consideration to the condemnatory judgment in which the weak are disposed to indulge favour the view that the reference is to God's reception of the strong. The wrong of censorious judgment is rebuked by the reminder that if God has received a person into the bond of his love and fellowship and if the conduct in question is no bar to God's acceptance, it is iniquity for us to condemn that which God approves. By so doing we presume to be holier than God. Furthermore, the next verse is directed against the vice of the weak and asserts with reference to the strong something coordinate with God's reception of him, namely, that "he shall be made to stand; for the Lord hath power to make him stand".

4 In this verse the wrong of censorious judgment on the part of the weak is exposed by showing the intrusive presumption that it involves. It is the impropriety of intermeddling in the domestic affairs of other people that is expressed in the question. This is then applied to the relation of a believer to Christ's lordship. It is doubtful whether the next clause, "to his own lord he standeth or falleth" carries on the thought of the question and refers simply to the master of a house or whether the Lord Christ is contemplated.[3] But even if it is the master of the house that is in view, the figure is immediately applied in the succeeding clause to the lordship of Christ over the believer. "Yea, he shall be made to stand; for the Lord[4] hath power to make him stand". The Lord in this case is the Lord Christ and what is affirmed is the certitude of the believer's standing firm in the service of Christ. It has been maintained that the standing firm in this case refers to the final judgment. It is true that the thought of judgment is present in this verse. In the sphere of ordinary domestic relations the servant of

---

[3] It is more likely that κυρίῳ refers to the master in the human household. In Christ's household, as the clauses which follow show, the alternatives of standing or falling are not in view.

[4] Κύριος is supported by P⁴⁶, ℵ, A, B, C, and P.

another is not to be judged by our norms but by those of his own master. He stands well or ill according to the judgment of his master. Likewise in the believer's relation to Christ it is Christ's judgment that is paramount, not ours. But there is no warrant for supposing that the judgment in view is specifically that of the last judgment. The "standing" is that which is directly pertinent by way of rebuke to the censorious judgment on the part of the weak here and now. The weak tended to regard the exercise of liberty on the part of the strong as a falling down in their devotion to Christ and as therefore subjecting them to the Lord's disapproval. The apostle's assurance is to the contrary effect and should, therefore, be regarded as having reference to the standing of the strong believer and of his conduct in the approbation of the Lord Christ. He will stand firm and the reason is given: the power of the Saviour is the guarantee of his stedfastness. This appeal to the power of Christ offers poignant reproof to the sin of censorious judgment. The suspicion which the latter involves is a reflection upon the sustaining power of Christ and overlooks the fact that the conduct which meets with the Lord's approval cannot imperil the stedfastness of the person concerned.

5, 6 In these verses another form of scrupulosity is introduced and is concerned with the sanctity which some believers attached to certain days. The difference resided in the fact that other believers attached no distinguishing religious significance to these particular days. "One man esteemeth[5] one day above another: another esteemeth every day *alike*". That this divergence of opinion is in the same category as that concerned with certain kinds of food appears from the fact that in verse 6 the apostle returns to the subject of eating and not eating and gives the esteeming of a day as an example of the conscientious devotion to the Lord which eating and not eating exemplify.

As will be argued later, the most reasonable, if not the only feasible, view of this scrupulosity on the part of some is that they regarded the holy days of the ceremonial economy as having

---

[5] Here we have a good example of the way in which the apostle can change from one shade of meaning to another in the use of the same term. In verses 3 and 4 κρίνω is used in the depreciatory sense of censorious judgment. In verse 5 it is used in the sense of "esteem" to which no criticism belongs.

abiding sanctity.[6] Others recognized that these ritual observances were abrogated with the passing away of the ceremonial institution.

Since this difference of conviction among believers is in the same category as the difference respecting the use of certain kinds of food, we must conclude that the observance of the days in question did not proceed from any continuing divine obligation. The person who esteems every day alike, that is, does not regard particular days as having peculiar religious significance, is recognized by the apostle as rightfully entertaining this position. This could not be the case if the distinction of days were a matter of divine obligation. Hence it is the person esteeming one day above another who is weak in faith: he has not yet understood the implications of the transition from the old economy to the new. Again, however, we must note the apostle's forbearance and the demand that those who are characterized by this weakness be received into the confidence and fellowship of the church. The diversity of approved conviction is illustrated by the injunction, "Let each man be fully assured in his own mind". This points to the personal persuasion indispensable, in these matters of conduct, to the sense of devotion to the Lord, expressly referred to in the succeeding verses as that by which the believer's life is to be regulated. Whether he eats or does not eat, esteems the day or does not, it is to the Lord (vss. 6–8). The injunction to be fully assured in one's own mind refers not simply to the *right* of private judgment but to the *demand*. This insistence is germane to the whole subject of this chapter. The plea is for acceptance of one another despite diversity of attitude regarding certain things. Compelled conformity or pressure exerted to the end of securing conformity defeats the aims to which all the exhortations and reproofs are directed.

The coordination in verse 6 might lend itself to the view that it is the strong believer who esteems one day above another because the reference to such observance is immediately followed by reference to the strong believer's eating practices. For the reasons already adduced this cannot be the case. Besides, in the other epistles (Gal. 4:10, 11; Col. 2:16, 17) the observance of days, because of its association with the heresies prevalent in the Galatian and Colossian churches, is unsparingly condemned. The observance in the church at Rome is tolerated because it was not

---

[6] See Appendix D (pp. 257ff.) for fuller discussion.

bound up with heresy. But for this reason those observing the days must have been the weak in faith.

The threefold repetition of the words "unto the Lord" in verse 6 expresses the religious conviction, namely, conscience toward the Lord, out of regard for which the diverse practices are followed. This is the vindication in the respective cases. In the realm of liberty a believer's conduct is not unreligious. Whatever he does or refrains from doing is "unto the Lord" and so he may never be destitute of the consciousness that he is serving the Lord Christ (*cf.* I Cor. 10:31). This expression "unto the Lord" anticipates what is unfolded in verses 7, 8.

Proof that the strong believer eats to the Lord is derived from the fact that he gives God thanks. The thought is that thanksgiving implies gratitude to God and the awareness that what he eats is the gift of God to be enjoyed. This state of mind carries with it the conviction that he eats to the Lord. Elsewhere thanksgiving is represented as that which sanctifies food. "For every creature of God is good, and nothing is to be rejected, if it be received with thanksgiving: for it is sanctified through the word of God and prayer" (I Tim. 4:4, 5). This thanksgiving is exemplified in the blessing pronounced before meals (*cf.* Matt. 15:36; Acts 27:35; I Cor. 10:30), though not to be restricted to it.

The consciousness of devotion to the Lord is also true of the weak believer in his abstinence from certain foods: "he that eateth not, unto the Lord he eateth not". There is, therefore, no undervaluation of the weak believer. He is credited with an equal sense of devotion to Christ, and he likewise gives thanks. This is not to be understood as meaning that he gives thanks for what he does not eat nor that he gives thanks to God because he abstains from that of which the strong believer partakes. The words "and giveth God thanks" should be taken as referring to the thanks he offers for that of which he does partake. [7] And this thanksgiving is likewise in his case a manifestation of his sense of indebtedness to God and devotion to Christ. The change from "for he giveth God thanks" to "and giveth God thanks" is striking. The former states a reason, the latter is a statement of fact. The distinction is not, however, to be loaded with the meaning that although the weak does not eat

---

[7] "But the thanks are given neither for *what* he eats not, which were absurd, nor *that* he eats not, which were Pharisaic (Luke xviii. 11), but for what he eats, namely vegetable food" (Philippi: *op. cit., ad loc.*).

nevertheless he gives thanks. If stress is to be laid on the distinction it should not be given more significance than that in the one case giving thanks is adduced as the reason, in the other case it is stated as an all-important and necessary condition.

7, 8 Verse 7 does not mean, as sometimes popularly understood and quoted, that a man is not sufficient to himself in the social and economic spheres. It is not directed against selfish and self-assertive independence in the order of society. In this passage as a whole this attitude is condemned and the demand of considerateness for others is inculcated. But in this verse, as verse 8 clearly shows, what is being asserted is that the believer lives *to the Lord*, not to himself. It is a negative way of expressing what is involved in the thrice repeated "unto the Lord" of verse 6 and the living and dying "unto the Lord" of verse 8. In these two verses it is the principle regulating and controlling the believer's subjective attitude that is in view, the disposition of subservience, obedience, devotion to the Lord, and it indicates, as noted earlier (*cf.* 12:2), that the guiding aim of the believer is to be well-pleasing to the Lord. In 12:2 this is stated in terms of pleasing God, now it is the Lord Christ who is contemplated. There is no conflict. If we discover by experience what the will of God is as the good and well-pleasing and perfect, it is because we have come to the recognition of the lordship of Christ in all of our life. The lordship of Christ in his mediatorial capacity is as inclusive and pervasive as is the sovereignty of God (*cf.* Matt. 11:27; 28:18; John 3:35; 5:23; Acts 2:36; Eph. 1:20–22; Phil. 2:9–11; I Pet. 3:22). It is only in the faith of Jesus and obedience to him that we can discover what the will of God is.

It might appear that in verses 7, 8 the thought is no longer that of conscious devotion to the Lord but that of the objective relation which Christ sustains to the believer. For how could our dying be regarded as taking place in the exercise of consecration to the Lord? There are two reasons for rejecting this supposition. (1) The import of the expression "unto the Lord", repeated three times in verse 6, must be carried over to the same expression in verse 8. This appears particularly in the words "whether we live, we live unto the Lord". Verse 7 gives the reason why it is to the Lord we eat or eat not, and verse 8 is the positive counterpart to what is denied in verse 7. So the sequence and close connection of the three verses would require that the conscious service of the Lord, so clearly in view in verses 6, 7, must govern the sense of "unto the Lord" in verse 8. (2) It is true that the event of death is not something *wrought* by our volition. But the same is true of what is here contrasted with it, namely, life. It is not by our will that the tenure of life is determined. There is, therefore, to this extent a parallel between life and death. The thought would thus appear to be that as the believer contemplates death, as well as in all the details of behaviour in this life, he is conscious of the Lord's will and in the act of dying his sense of devotion to the Lord is not suspended. No doubt, as far as the latter is concerned, it is the consciousness of being the Lord's that is uppermost but the accent still falls on what is true in the consciousness of the believer (*cf*. II Cor. 5:8, 9; Phil. 1:20–25). And this conscious resignation to and acceptance of death find their support in the assurance mentioned in the latter part of verse 8 that "whether we live therefore, or die, we are the Lord's".

This assurance, though it is entertained by the believer and is indispensable to his consecration to the Lord in living and dying, refers not to the faith which is consciously exercised by the believer but to the relation which Christ sustains to him, namely, that of possession.[8] It prepares for the assertion of Christ's all-embracive lordship in verse 9.

In these two verses we have witness borne to the transformation wrought in the life of a believer in the attitude to death. It is not because death itself has lost its character as the wages of sin or that it has ceased to be the last enemy. Death does not become good; it is an evil, the abnormality which sin brought into the world. We have in Paul the recognition of this in his own case when he says, "not for that we would be unclothed, but that we would be clothed upon "(II Cor. 5:4). We are also reminded that only in the resurrection will death be swallowed up in victory (I Cor. 15:54). The transformed attitude to death (*cf*. Heb. 2:14, 15) springs not from any change in the character of death but from the faith of what Christ has done to death and from the living hope of what he will do in the consummation of his conquest. It is the

---

[8] "Hence it follows... that he remains in every state of the case the Lord's *property*. As the dative τῷ κυρίῳ, *to the Lord*, in the first part of the verse, expressed consecration; so the genitive τοῦ κυρίου, *of the Lord*, in the last proposition, expresses possession" (Godet: *op. cit., ad loc.*).

resurrection of Christ, the hope of resurrection after the pattern of his, and the removal of sin which is the sting of death that transform the *relation* of the believer to death. So radical is this change that in the faith of it the apostle could "desire to depart and to be with Christ; for it is very far better" (Phil. 1:23).

9 This verse harks back to the latter part of verse 8 and states the ground upon which rests the lordship of possession just enunciated. This ground is stated, however, in terms of the way in which Christ secured this lordship and, more particularly, in terms of the purpose Christ had in view in dying and rising again, namely, that he might secure this lordship. There are several observations respecting this text.

(1) The lordship of Christ here dealt with did not belong to Christ by native right as the Son of God; it had to be secured. It is the lordship of redemptive relationship and such did not inhere in the sovereignty that belongs to him in virtue of his creatorhood. It is achieved by mediatorial accomplishment and is the reward of his humiliation (*cf.* Acts 2:36; Rom. 8:34; Phil. 2:9–11).

(2) It is to the end of securing and exercising this lordship that he "died and lived".[9] The latter does not refer to his life on earth prior to his death but to his resurrection.[10] The sequence indicates this. If the life on earth were in view the order would have been "lived and died". Besides, Paul uses the corresponding noun "life" with reference to the resurrection (5:10; II Cor. 4:10),[11] and mention of the resurrection is demanded here as an integral event of the process by which the lordship was achieved. It is appropriate that this term should have been used rather than other terms denoting resurrection because this same word is used in verses 7, 8 and, more particularly, because "died and

---

[9] ἀπέθανεν καὶ ἔζησεν supported by ℵ*, A, B, C and several versions is to be preferred to ἀπέθανεν καὶ ἀνέστη supported by G and the Vulgate and to various forms of a longer reading the most important of which is ἀπέθανεν καὶ ἀνέστη καὶ ἔζησεν supported by L, P, and the mass of the cursives.

[10] The aorist is adapted to express his becoming alive from the dead. It is inceptive aorist. Most frequently the resurrection of Christ is represented as the action of God the Father. This instance could be taken as referring to the action of Jesus himself after the analogy of John 2:19; 10:17, 18. But it is more likely that there is no reflection on agency. The thought is focused on the fact of his having lived again.

[11] Rev. 1:18; 2:9 are important parallels in which ζάω is used with reference to the resurrection.

14:1-23 THE WEAK AND THE STRONG

lived" is parallel to "the dead and the living" in the latter part of the text. It is by the life which Jesus lives in his resurrection power that believers live unto the Lord. Thus there is a correspondence between Jesus' resurrection viewed as "living" and the life of devotion to Christ, so much in the forefront in this passage (*cf.* 6:4, 5; II Cor. 4:10–12; Col. 3:1–3).

(3) Christ is represented as achieving dominion over "both the dead and the living". The order here is determined by correspondence with what is said of Christ that he "died and lived". The form "both the dead and the living" emphasizes the sovereignty which Christ exercises equally over both spheres. He has achieved this dominion because he himself entered the realm of death, conquered death, and rose triumphant as the Lord of life. He established his supremacy in both domains and therefore in whatever realm believers have their abode they are embraced in his lordly possession as those for whom he died and rose again. The idea of this lordship is amplified in Ephesians 4:9, 10 where Christ is said to fill all things and the process by which the same is secured is descent into the lower parts of the earth and ascent above all the heavens.[12]

(4) Although it is proper to think of Christ's dominion as embracing unbelieving dead and living (*cf.* John 5:26–29), yet because of the context it would not be feasible to understand this text as having all-inclusive reference. We cannot interpret the last clause in verse 8 inclusively and verse 9, it must be remembered, sets forth the basis of the assurance "we are the Lord's", an assurance belonging only to believers.

10-12 Here the apostle returns to the thought of verse 3 that the weak are not to *judge* the strong nor the strong to *set at nought* the weak. But the difference of form adds strength to the indictment of the respective vices. In verse 3 there is exhortation to abstain from these attitudes. Now we have the interrogative address (*cf.* vs. 4a) which points up the presumption of judging or despising a brother. The emphasis may be expressed by saying: "Who are *you* to judge your brother? or who are *you* to despise your brother?" The arraignment derives its warrant both from

---

[12] *Cf.* E. K. Simpson: *Commentary on the Epistle to the Ephesians* (Grand Rapids, 1957), p. 91, n. 17.

what precedes, namely, that Christ is Lord, and from what follows, namely, that it is before God's judgment-seat we all must appear. The sin in each case, therefore, resides in the assumption to ourselves of prerogatives that belong only to Christ and to God.

The reproofs of verse 10 draw their force particularly from the appeal to God's judgment-seat at the end of the verse.[13] We are not to suppose that the appeal to God's judgment has relevance as reproof only to the "judging" on the part of the weak or even that it has more relevance to them. The vice of the strong is equally incompatible with the restraint which the future judgment requires. That all will stand before God's judgment-seat offers the severest kind of rebuke to the impiety of our sitting in judgment upon others whether it be in the form of censorious condemnation or haughty contempt.

The universality of the final judgment for just and unjust the apostle had unfolded earlier in this epistle (2:5–16). In the present text he is addressing believers and therefore of believers it is said "we shall all stand before the judgment-seat of God". In II Corinthians 5:10 it is to believers likewise he speaks when he says, "We must all be made manifest before the judgment-seat of Christ". These two texts therefore place beyond all dispute the certainty of future judgment for believers. It is only by deflection from biblical patterns of thought that doubt could be entertained or the consciousness of the believer fail to be conditioned by it. Furthermore, this judgment is not merely of persons. It is of the behaviour of believers Paul is here speaking and it is for the correction of wrong behaviour that the fact of God's future judgment is adduced. Conduct is to be judged. The other passage puts this beyond question: each one will "receive the things *done* in the body, according to what he hath done, whether it be good or bad" (II Cor. 5:10; *cf.* I Cor. 3:8–15; 4:5; Eccl. 12:14). The judgment embraces not only all persons but also all deeds.

The support from Scripture is derived from Isaiah 45:23. In the part of the verse quoted the only significant change from the Hebrew and Greek is that instead of using the formula, "By myself I have sworn" the apostle uses another Old Testament formula

---

[13] The reading θεοῦ is supported by such uncials that the other reading Χριστοῦ could scarcely be adopted. It may well be that Χριστοῦ in II Cor. 5:10 influenced the text in Rom. 14:10 and this would be another reason for regarding θεοῦ as the proper variant in the latter case.

14:1-23 THE WEAK AND THE STRONG

which has the same effect: "As I live, saith the Lord" (*cf.* Numb. 14:28; Deut. 32:40; Isa. 49:18; Ezek. 33:11). The remainder as quoted corresponds with the Greek version except for a slight alteration in the order of words. The refrain of this chapter in Isaiah is that the Lord is God and there is none else (*cf.* vss. 5-7, 14, 18, 21, 22). This is directly germane to the fact of judgment. It is because God is God and there is none else that he must bring the whole panorama of history before him for final adjudication. Everything must be adjudged with equity. "He will judge the world with righteousness, and the peoples with his truth" (Psalm 96:13; *cf.* 98:9). Reluctance to entertain the reality of this universal and all-inclusive judgment springs from preoccupation with what is conceived to be the comfort and joy of believers at the coming of Christ rather than with the interests and demands of God's glory. The latter should always be paramount in the outlook of the believer. And it should not be forgotten that, although God will bring evil as well as good into judgment, there will be no abatement of the believer's joy, because it is in the perspective of this full disclosure that the vindication of God's glory in his salvation will be fully manifest. It is only in the light of this manifestation that the believer's joy could be complete. Judgment involves severity and by this consideration the believer should always be actuated in the life of faith. But it also is filled with grandeur and a grandeur indispensable to the consummation of redemption as well as to the consummation of all things.[14]

Verse 12 completes the appeal to the fact of judgment by the reminder that implied in the same is the account which each person for himself will render to God. It is to God each will render account, not to men. It is concerning himself he will give account, not on behalf of another. So the thought is focused upon the necessity of judging *ourselves now* in the light of the account which will be given ultimately to God.[15] We are to judge ourselves rather than sit in judgment upon others.

14:13-23

13 Let us not therefore judge one another any more: but judge ye this rather, that no man put a stumblingblock in his brother's way, or an occasion of falling.

---

[14] *Cf.* Phil. 2:10, 11 for another instance of quotation from Isa. 45:23.
[15] There is not good warrant for the omission of τῷ θεῷ at the end o verse 12.

14 I know, and am persuaded in the Lord Jesus, that nothing is unclean of itself: save that to him who accounteth anything to be unclean, to him it is unclean.
15 For if because of meat thy brother is grieved, thou walkest no longer in love. Destroy not with thy meat him for whom Christ died.
16 Let not then your good be evil spoken of:
17 for the kingdom of God is not eating and drinking, but righteousness and peace and joy in the Holy Spirit.
18 For he that herein serveth Christ is well-pleasing to God, and approved of men.
19 So then let us follow after things which make for peace, and things whereby we may edify one another.
20 Overthrow not for meat's sake the work of God. All things indeed are clean; howbeit it is evil for that man who eateth with offence.
21 It is good not to eat flesh, nor to drink wine, nor *to do anything* whereby thy brother stumbleth.
22 The faith which thou hast, have thou to thyself before God. Happy is he that judgeth not himself in that which he approveth.
23 But he that doubteth is condemned if he eat, because *he eateth* not of faith; and whatsoever is not of faith is sin.

This section is directed largely to the strong and enjoins upon them the action which love for the weak requires. In this part of the epistle it has been already noted how much emphasis falls upon love (*cf.* 12:9; 13:8–10). The necessity of walking according to love (vs. 15) is in this section applied to the behaviour which consideration for the well-being of weaker brethren must constrain on the part of the strong.

13, 14 It is not possible in simple translation to bring out the force of the two distinct senses in which the word "judge" is used in verse 13 nor the effect of the different tenses. In the first instance "judge" is used in the sense of censorious judgment, in the second it is used in the good sense to "determine" (*cf.* II Cor. 2:1). We found a similar distinction in verses 4 and 5. Thus we have another example of the way in which the apostle can use the same term with different meaning in successive clauses. The effect of the different tenses may be thus expressed: "do not continue to judge one another any more but come to determine this rather". The coming to be of the right kind of judgment is contrasted with the existing wrong kind of judgment.[16]

Since censorious judgment was the vice of the weak (*cf*. vss. 3, 4, 10), it might be thought that this exhortation is addressed to them. In that event the latter part of verse 13 would have to be applied to the weak and construed as meaning that they could place a stumblingblock in the way of the strong. It is not impossible to think of such an eventuality. A weak person in pressing his pleas for abstinence may cause doubts to arise in the mind of the strong and the strong is thus weakened in his faith and caused to stumble. Questionings are aroused where they ought not to exist and the perplexity resulting is an impediment rather than a help.

It is, however, impossible to carry over this interpretation to verses 14, 15. In these verses it is the weak person who is represented as stumbling and thereby grieved. Verses 14, 15 are so closely related to verse 13 that the latter part of verse 13 must be regarded as referring to the stumbling of the weak and the exhortation, therefore, as directed to the strong. It should be remembered that verses 10–12 contemplate both classes and the vice of both is that of presuming to take upon themselves the prerogative that belongs only to God, namely, that of judgment. In this way even the vice of the strong is regarded as a "judging". In view of this broader implication found in verses 10–12 it is proper to apply the exhortations of verse 13 to the strong and even regard them exclusively as those addressed. It is not out of the question to regard the prohibitive part of verse 13 as directed to both classes. But the positive clause must apply to the strong and, since the negative and positive are interdependent, it is better to take the whole as exhortations addressed to the strong.[17] They are not to place a "stumblingblock" or "occasion of falling" in the way of a weak brother.

A stumblingblock is an impediment in the way over which a person may stumble. An occasion of falling refers literally to a trap. Here these terms are used metaphorically and convey the

---

[16] On the distinction between the present subjunctive with imperative force in κρίνωμεν and the aorist imperative κρίνατε *cf.* Blass and Debrunner: *op. cit.*, pp. 172f.

[17] It is possible that the first exhortation of verse 13 is directed to both parties and then restriction to the strong in the second clause. But for the reasons stated it appears more reasonable to regard both clauses as having the same reference.

same thought, namely, that which becomes the occasion of falling into sin. In the most aggravated sense an occasion of falling is placed before a person when the intention is that of seduction; there is deliberate intent that the person may fall. We are not to suppose that the strong in this case are conceived of as actuated by that express intent. But this only accentuates the care that must be taken by the strong in the circumstance of weakness on the side of their brethren. The strong are regarded as placing a stumblingblock when they do not desist from what becomes an occasion of stumbling for the weak brother. What is condemned is the inconsiderateness that discards the religious interests of the weak.

The conviction underlying abstinence from certain foods and drinks was that these things were intrinsically evil and that the use of them for these purposes was defiling and contrary to the morals which should govern the Christian. The apostle sets forth the biblical principle that nothing is unclean of itself, that, as he says elsewhere, "every creature of God is good and nothing is to be rejected, if it be received with thanksgiving" (I Tim. 4:4). It is the truth affirmed by our Lord (*cf.* Mark 7:15). What is significant about Paul's enunciation of this principle is the way in which he expresses it: "I know, and am persuaded in the Lord Jesus". No form of words could express more fully the certitude of his conviction than "I know, and am persuaded" and no sanction could certify the rightness of this conviction more than to add, "in the Lord Jesus". The latter formula should not be taken as a mere appeal to the teaching of Christ in the days of his flesh (*cf.* Mark 7:19), although this teaching is relevant. Paul refers here to union and fellowship with Christ, and "in Christ Jesus" means that the conviction springs from, is consistent with, and is certified by the union and communion with Christ which, for the apostle, is the most characteristic way of defining his relation to the Saviour.

The word "unclean" is a term that originally means common and then came to mean defiled or impure (*cf.* Mark 7:2, 5; Acts 10:14; Heb. 10:29; Rev. 21:27). That "nothing is unclean of itself" is the justification of the belief entertained by the strong that he may eat all things (vs. 2) and is the reason why abstinence on the part of some is due to weakness of faith. This principle is the refutation of all prohibitionism which lays the responsibility for

14:1–23 THE WEAK AND THE STRONG

wrong at the door of things rather than at man's heart. The basic evil of this ethic is that it makes God the Creator responsible and involves both blasphemy and the attempt to alleviate human responsibility for wrong. It was necessary for the apostle to preface his plea to the strong with the insistence that nothing is unclean of itself. Otherwise the plea would lose its character as one based entirely upon consideration for the religious interests of the weak. If certain things were intrinsically evil, then the strong would be required to abstain from their use out of regard to their own religious interests.

Though nothing is unclean of itself, it does not follow that every thing is clean for every one. This is the force of the latter part of verse 14. The conviction of each person must be taken into account. The situation dealt with here is similar to that with which the apostle deals in I Corinthians 8:4, 7. "We know", Paul says, "that no idol is *anything* in the world, and that there is no God but one." However, account must be taken of the fact that "there is not in all men that knowledge". So, in our present text, "nothing is unclean of itself" but not all men have that knowledge or conviction. It is apparent that the distinction is between what is true objectively and what is recognized as true subjectively.

The conjunction rendered "save" does not state an exception to what had been asserted in the first part of the verse. It simply introduces a consideration that belongs to the situation. "There is nothing unclean of itself"; this is a proposition that is absolutely and universally true and there is no exception. But it is also true that not all have sufficient faith to know this.[18]

15 As noted above, the appeal to the strong is not based upon consideration for their own religious interests but upon regard for the religious interests of the weak. They are not to place a stumblingblock in the way of a weak brother, and the latter is weak because he esteems something to be unclean. These considerations explain the words "for if" with which verse 15 begins. They point back to verses 13 and 14 and introduce the reason why the strong believer is to abstain from the use of certain foods. If he discards the scruples of the weak and does not have concern for his religious interests, then he violates the dictates of love.

---

[18] *Cf.* comments at 13:8 for this use of εἰ μή.

The main question in the early part of this verse is the meaning of "thy brother is grieved". It might appear that the grief is the pain of annoyance and displeasure experienced when he sees the strong believer partake of food which he, the weak brother, esteems to be forbidden. He takes offense at the liberty which the strong believer exercises. This interpretation might seem to be supported by 15:1, 2: "Now we that are strong ought to bear the infirmities of the weak, and not to please ourselves. Let each one of us please his neighbor for that which is good, unto edifying". So it could be said: "avoid what is displeasing to others; defer to their wishes and pleasures". It must be admitted that weak believers do often experience acute pain of heart when they observe others exercise liberties that in their esteem are improper, and a strong believer actuated by love will seek to spare his fellow-believer this pain. There are, however, good reasons for rejecting this view of the grief in question.

1. This interpretation will not satisfy what is involved in the terms "stumblingblock" and "occasion of falling" in verse 13. They imply that the weak believer falls into sin. If the grief were merely the painful displeasure in the mind of the weak, this could not be construed as a fall. It is true that his displeasure arises from the censorious judgment in which he indulges, a judgment which is wrong and which Paul condemns (vss. 3, 4, 10). But at verse 13, in the use of the terms "stumblingblock" and "occasion of falling", the apostle introduces something new in the conduct liable to befall the weak and something not reflected on in the preceding verses. It is this new ingredient that is not accounted for by the mere notion of displeasure. The sin on the part of the weak implied in the fall which the stumblingblock occasions is the violation of conscience entailed for the weak when he is induced by the example of the strong to do that which he esteems wrong. He violates his religious scruples; this is the stumbling and falling envisioned in verse 13.

2. Verse 15 indicates the gravity of what is involved in the grief, a gravity that could not apply to mere displeasure at the conduct of the strong. The exhortation "Destroy not by thy food that one on whose behalf Christ died" implies that the grief befalling the weak is morally and religiously destructive. The sin committed, therefore, is of a grievous character and the grief can be nothing less than the vexation of conscience that afflicts a

believer when he violates conscience and does what he esteems to be disloyalty to Christ.

3. Verses 20–23 confirm this same conclusion. Here again the thought of stumbling is introduced and this is clearly indicated to be eating or drinking when, in the place of faith, there is doubt. "Whatsoever is not of faith is sin" (vs. 23).[19]

Hence a weak believer "is grieved" when he has violated his religious convictions and is afflicted with the vexation of conscience which the consequent sense of guilt involves. It is this tragic result for the weak believer that the strong believer must take into account. When the exercise of his liberty emboldens the weak to violate his conscience, then, out of deference to the religious interests of the weak, he is to refrain from the exercise of what are intrinsically his rights. No charge could be weighted with greater appeal than "Destroy not by thy food that one on whose behalf Christ died" (*cf.* I Cor. 8:11).

When the apostle bases his plea upon the vicarious death of Christ, he is reminding the strong believer of two things: (1) the extent of Christ's love for the weak believer; (2) the death of Christ as the bond of fellowship among believers. If Christ loved the weak believer to the extent of laying down his life for his salvation, how alien to the demands of this love is the refusal on the part of the strong to forego the use of a certain article of food when the religious interests of the one for whom Christ died are thereby imperilled! It is the contrast between what the extreme sacrifice of Christ exemplified and the paltry demand devolving upon us that accentuates the meanness of our attitude when we discard the interests of a weak brother. And since the death of Christ as the price of redemption for all believers is the bond uniting them in fellowship, how contradictory is any behaviour that is not patterned after the love which Christ's death exhibited! "If because of food thy brother is grieved, thou walkest no longer in love."

The imperative "destroy not" is one that implies grave consequences for the weak when he is emboldened to violate his conscience. The accent falls, however, upon the responsibility of

---

[19] The more accentuated would be the adverse judgment of the strong on the part of the weak the more would be excluded the liability to stumble; the greater the grief at the conduct of the strong the less liable would the weak be to follow his example. *Cf.* the pertinent remarks of Philippi: *op. cit., ad loc.*

the strong for the detriment that befalls the weak. In the event that the strong does not refrain from placing a stumblingblock he is charged with this offense. "Destroy" is a strong word (*cf.* Matt. 10:28; 18:14; Luke 9:25; 13:3; John 3:16; 10:28; Rom. 2:12; I Cor. 8:11; 15:18; II Cor. 4:3; II Pet. 3:9) and enforces the responsibility of the strong and the seriousness of the offense in which his failure to respect the infirmity of the weak involves both himself and the weak brother. The strong is not said to be destroyed. In accord with the emphasis of the passage his sin resides entirely in the violation of the demands of love to his brother and in his failure to entertain and exercise concern for the religious well-being of the brother. He has not loved his neighbour as himself (*cf.* 13:8). So both the indictment of the strong (vs. 15a) and the imperative (vs. 15b) show how jealously the requirements of love must be observed even in the realm of what has been called the *adiaphora* or, more properly, in the use of those things that are intrinsically right and good.

The strength of the word "destroy" underlines the serious nature of the stumbling that overtakes the weak brother. Are we to suppose that he is viewed as finally perishing? However grave the sin he commits it would be beyond all warrant to regard it as amounting to apostasy. The exhortation "destroy not" is directed to the strong. In a similar situation the weak person is represented as perishing (I Cor. 8:11). But here likewise it would be beyond warrant to think of apostasy.[20] Furthermore, the destruction contemplated as befalling the weak should not be construed as eternal perdition. All sin is destructive and the sin of the weak in this instance is a serious breach of fidelity which, if not repaired, would lead to perdition. It is upon the character of the sin and its consequence that the emphasis is placed in order to impress upon the strong the gravity of his offense in becoming the occasion of stumbling. It would load the exhortation with implications beyond this intent to suppose that the weak believer by his sin is an heir of eternal destruction. It is a warning, however, to the strong believer that what he must consider is the nature and tendency of sin and not take refuge behind the security of the believer and the final perseverance of the saints.

---

[20] *Cf. contra* Philippi (*ibid.*), who says that this is "a *dictum probans* for the possibility of apostasy".

14:1-23 THE WEAK AND THE STRONG

16, 17 The question in verse 17 is the reference in "your good". Various views have been held—the gospel, the Christian profession, the kingdom of God. But no view suits the context better than the liberty which the strong believer enjoys in regard to eating and drinking. It has been objected that this is too restrictive because it would then be the exclusive property of the strong. This objection, however, has no validity. The strong is being addressed in this context (*cf.* vss. 13, 15, 19-21) and there is no need to broaden the application. Why should not the strong be exhorted here to avoid the consequences of undue exercise of his liberty? In another context Paul protests: "why am I evil spoken of for that for which I give thanks?" (I Cor. 10:30). That for which a strong believer gives thanks (*cf.* vs. 6) may properly be regarded as his "good"; it is his liberty in Christ to enjoy what God has created to be received with thanksgiving. However, when the damage to the weak, mentioned in verse 15, results, then this liberty comes into disrepute and it is this evil the exhortation of verse 16 seeks to prevent.

In verse 17 a reason is given for the exercise of restraint on the part of the strong. No consideration could have greater relevance or force than to be reminded negatively and positively of that in which the kingdom of God consists. The kingdom of God is that realm to which believers belong. Nothing defines their identity more characteristically than that they are members of it (*cf.* John 3:3-8; I Thess. 2:12). It should not be forgotten that the emphasis falls upon the rule of God. It is the sphere in which God's sovereignty is recognized and his will is supreme. Thus the mention of God's kingdom should always have the effect of summoning believers to that frame of mind that will make them amenable to the paramount demand of their calling, the will of God. It is in this perspective that the negation appears in its true light—it "is not eating and drinking".[21] When questions of food and drink become our chief concern, then it is apparent how far removed from the interests of God's kingdom our thinking and conduct have strayed (*cf.* Matt. 6:31-33).[22]

Difference exists among expositors as to the import of "righteousness and peace". Some maintain that these terms are forensic,

---

[21] Note βρῶσις and πόσις, not βρῶμα and πόμα.
[22] *Cf.* I Cor. 8:8 which is Paul's own comment on the negative of the present text.

righteousness referring to the righteousness of justification (*cf.* 1:17; 3:21, 22; 10:3, 6) and peace to peace with God (*cf.* 5:1).[23] Others maintain that these terms are to be understood ethically and therefore refer to righteousness as fulfilled and peace promoted and preserved by believers.[24] While it is true that all uprightness and concord as observed by the believer rest upon justification and peace with God, there is much more to be said in favour of the second view. (1) "Joy in the Holy Spirit" is subjective; it is joy in the believer's heart. Since this joy is coordinated with righteousness and peace we would expect the two latter to be in the same category. (2) Verse 18 points back to verse 17. "Herein" refers to the elements specified in verse 17. In these elements the believer is said to serve Christ, be well-pleasing to God, and approved of men. The service of Christ is, without question, an obligation devolving upon us and the discharge is said to make us well-pleasing to God. These ideas do not accord with forensic righteousness and peace. (3) Likewise in verse 19 we have hortatory terms directed to our responsibility. Of particular relevance are the words, "follow after things which make for peace". This enjoins upon us the promotion of concord in the church and is an index to what is meant by "peace" in verse 17. Furthermore, the demand to follow things that are unto edification points in the same direction. For these reasons "righteousness" and "peace" should be taken as the rectitude and harmony that must govern the attitude and behaviour of the believer within the fellowship of the church. There is, however, a parallel between what obtains in the subjective realm of attitude and conduct and what is true in the sphere of the forensic. This can be seen by comparing 5:1, 2 with 14:17. Justification, peace with God, and rejoicing in hope of the glory of God correspond to righteousness, peace, and joy in the Holy Spirit. The Godward reference of all grace in us is likewise patent. It is joy in *the Holy Spirit*, and the norm by which righteousness is directed and peace cultivated is the will of God.

18 Here again the principle set forth in verses 6–8 is reaffirmed and the same guiding principle of the believer's life as in 12:2. "Approved of men" is the opposite of the disrepute referred to in

---

[23] *Cf.* Calvin, Philippi, Hodge: *op. cit., ad loc.*
[24] *Cf.* Meyer, Godet, Sanday and Headlam, Barrett: *op. cit., ad loc.*

14:1–23 THE WEAK AND THE STRONG

verse 16. We may not rigidly restrict the approval in view to those who are of the household of faith. The damage which befalls the church by inconsiderate conduct on the part of strong believers has its repercussions in the judgments of those outside and the good name of the church as the community of love and concord should be maintained so that adversaries may not have occasion to speak reproachfully (*cf.* 2:24; I Tim. 3:7; 6:1).

19 The preceding verses make clear the import of this exhortation. It is the strong who are being exhorted, as in the preceding verses and in verses 20–22.

20 Verse 20a is to the same effect as verse 15b. "Overthrow" is the opposite of the building up involved in the word "edify" of verse 19. "The work of God" may most properly be understood as referring to the weak believer who, though weak, is still God's workmanship (*cf.* Eph. 2:10). God is building up. Loveless brandishing of liberty breaks down. How antithetical! Verse 20b is a reiteration in more summary form of verse 14. It is more likely that the "man who eateth with offence" is the weak believer. He stumbles when he eats because it is not of faith and with a clear conscience. This corresponds with verse 14b, and the express mention of the brother who stumbles in verse 21 would support this view.[25] He eats with offence because he violates conscience in so doing.

21 This is also directed to the strong. For the first time we are informed that the drinking of wine was involved in the scruples of the weak.[26]

22 Verse 22a is another exhortation to the strong and means that they are not to parade and protest their rights and liberties to the detriment of the weak and with the evil consequences delineated in the preceding verses. The words "have to thyself before God" is another way of vindicating the strong in the possession and

---

[25] διὰ προσκόμματος is the genitive of attendant circumstance as διὰ γράμματος καὶ περιτομῆς in 2:27.
[26] κρέα is flesh-meat and is more specific than βρῶμα in verse 20. Of course a vegetarian diet is expressly referred to in verse 2. There are variants in verse 21. At the end ἢ σκανδαλίζεται ἢ ἀσθενεῖ is added by B, D, G, the mass of the cursives, and some versions. See also Appendix E (pp. 260ff.) on the application of the principle here enunciated.

conviction of their liberty (*cf.* vss. 14a, 20b). They have this conviction in the presence of God and may not surrender it. But they are not to brandish it to the destruction of others. Verse 22b is a further corroboration of what is implicit in the preceding clause, as just noted. It is a particularly forceful way of commending the intelligent and mature faith whereby a Christian entertains no scruples in eating and drinking. It is not a future blessedness that is reflected on but, as Gifford says, "the present blessedness of a clear and undoubting conscience".[27] In pronouncing the strong believer "blessed" there is, however, no retraction of the leading plea of the passage. It is, rather, the blessedness of this state of mind and conscience that underscores the necessity of exercising the restraint which the weakness of others constrains.

23 This verse is concerned with the weak and "the danger of the weak brother is now brought into striking contrast with the happy condition of him who is strong in faith, and so supplies a further motive to the charitable restraint of freedom".[28] We may not tone down the condemnation to which the weak believer is subjected when he eats without clear conscience. It is not merely the condemnation of his own conscience; it is condemnation before God. This is proven by the last clause that "whatsoever is not of faith is sin". Just as the strong believer entertains his conviction of liberty before God (vs. 22a) and is blessed before God (vs. 22b), so the weak is condemned before God when he violates conviction (*cf.* vss. 14b, 15). The concluding clause is to be understood as applying to the subject in hand. It is true that without faith it is impossible to please God (*cf.* 8:7, 8; Heb. 11:6) and thus unbelievers can do nothing that is well-pleasing to God in terms of the criteria of holiness and rectitude. But we may not regard the apostle as stating this general principle in this instance but as reaffirming that a *believer* sins when he does what is not approved in his conviction and faith.[29]

---

[27] *Op. cit., ad loc.* μακάριος is a particularly commendatory term and finds its basis in the principle stated in verse 14a.
[28] Gifford: *op. cit., ad loc.*
[29] On the occurrence of the doxology found in some manuscripts at the end of this chapter see the discussion in Appendix F (pp. 262 ff.).

Romans xv

F. CHRIST'S EXAMPLE
(15:1–6)

15:1–6

1 Now we that are strong ought to bear the infirmities of the weak, and not to please ourselves.
2 Let each one of us please his neighbor for that which is good, unto edifying.
3 For Christ also pleased not himself; but, as it is written, The reproaches of them that reproached thee fell upon me.
4 For whatsoever things were written aforetime were written for our learning, that through patience and through comfort of the scriptures we might have hope.
5 Now the God of patience and of comfort grant you to be of the same mind one with another according to Christ Jesus:
6 that with one accord ye may with one mouth glorify the God and Father of our Lord Jesus Christ.

1, 2 Continuing the same theme as in chapter 14 the obligation of the strong in relation to the weak is developed still further. This is the only instance in which the term used for "strong" appears in the restricted sense applicable in this passage, though the general sense is the same as elsewhere (*cf.* II Cor. 12:10; 13:9). "Bear" is not to be understood in the sense of "bear with" frequent in our common speech but in the sense of "bear up" or "carry" (*cf.* 11:18; Gal. 5:10; 6:2, 5)[1]. The strong are to help the weak and promote their good to edification (vs. 2). Besides, the weak are represented as having "infirmities" and the exhortation of Galatians 6:2 must surely apply. "Let each one please his neighbour", as also the negative "not to please ourselves", must not be interpreted to mean that we are always to defer to the whims and

---

[1] In Rev. 2:2 βαστάζω has the sense of "put up with". It is questionable if it has this meaning anywhere else in the New Testament.

wishes of others, not even those of fellow-believers and thus always follow the course of action that pleases them. To please men is not a principle of the believer's life (*cf.* Gal. 1:10). Paul provides us with an example of the pleasing that he has in mind (I Cor. 10:33) and in the present passage is to be restricted to that situation dealt with. The strong are not to indulge their own liberties so as to be an occasion of stumbling to the weak and thus induce in them the grief and in that sense the displeasure reflected on in 14:15. It is the pleasing that will maintain in the weak the peace of conscience which emulation of the conduct of the strong will disturb and destroy (*cf.* also I Cor. 8:12). The aim specified in this pleasing of the weak, "for that which is good, unto edifying", indicates the considerations by which the strong are to be governed.[2] Disregard for the scruples of the weak breaks down the work of God (*cf.* 14:15, 20) and is fraught with *evil* consequences. Considerateness promotes what, in contrast, is *good* and builds up not only the weak themselves but the whole fellowship (*cf* 14:19).

3 Here is appeal to the supreme example in order to enforce the obligation enjoined in the two preceding verses. It is noteworthy how the apostle adduces the example of Christ in his most transcendent accomplishments in order to commend the most practical duties (*cf.* II Cor. 8:9; Phil. 2:5–8). The thought is focused in this case upon the disinterestedness of Christ. He did not look upon his own things but upon those of others. He identified himself with the supreme interests of those whom he came to save and thus bore the utmost of reproach and shame by commitment to that end in fulfilment of the Father's will. The quotation from Psalm 69:9 specifies the particular aspect of Christ's not pleasing himself which the apostle deems most relevant to the duty being enjoined. This scripture he regards as a forecast of Christ's self-humiliation. The frequency with which this Psalm is alluded to in the New Testament and its details represented as fulfilled in Christ marks it as distinctly messianic.[3] The part quoted must be understood in the light of what immediately precedes in the Psalm: "the zeal of thy house hath eaten me up". It is not our reproaches that are in view but the reproaches of dishonour

---

[2] The distinction drawn by Gifford: *op. cit.*, *ad loc.* between εἰς as marking the aim and πρός the standard of judgment can hardly be maintained.

[3] *Cf.*, for the listing and comparison of passages, Liddon: *op. cit.*, p. 274.

levelled against God.[4] These reproaches vented against God by the ungodly fell upon Christ. This is to say that all the enmity of men against God was directed to Christ; he was the victim of this assault. It is to this Paul appeals as exemplifying the assertion that Christ "pleased not himself". We may well ask then: how does this feature of our Lord's humiliation bear upon the duty of pleasing our neighbour in the situation which Paul has in view? It is the apparent dissimilarity that points up the force of Jesus' example. There is a profound discrepancy between what Christ did and what the strong are urged to do. He "pleased not himself" to the incomparable extent of bearing the enmity of men against God and he bore this reproach because he was jealous for God's honour. He did not by flinching evade any of the stroke. Shall we, the strong, insist on pleasing ourselves in the matter of food and drink to the detriment of God's saints and the edification of Christ's body? It is the complete contrast between Christ's situation and ours that enhances the force of the appeal.[5] The same applies to all the passages in which Christ's example is urged and with the particularity relevant in each case.

4 The "for" at the beginning of this verse intimates the reason for the propriety of appeal to Scripture for support. Paul vindicates the use of Psalm 69:9 in verse 3 by the purpose which Scripture is intended by God to subserve: "whatsoever things were written aforetime were written for our learning" (*cf.* I Cor. 10:6, 10; II Tim. 3:16, 17). The extent to which Paul's thought was governed by this truth is evident from the frequency of appeal to Scripture in this epistle. The form of statement here and in the parallels cited above shows that in Paul's esteem Scripture in all its parts is for our instruction, that the Old Testament was designed to furnish us in these last days with the instruction necessary for the fulfilment of our vocation to the end, and that it is as *written* it promotes this purpose. The instruction which the Scriptures impart is directed to patience and comfort. Patience is endurance and stedfastness.

---

[4] *Cf. contra* Sanday and Headlam: *op. cit., ad loc.*
[5] It may be that the reproaches cast at the strong by weak brethren are in view and thus some parallel between Christ and the strong would be intimated. This, however, seems remote from the thought at this point. But, even if granted, the contrast between Christ and the strong believer would not be eliminated. How incomparably more shameful were the reproaches cast upon Christ!

Both the stedfastness and the comfort[6] are derived from the Scriptures and are, therefore, dependent upon these Scriptures and draw their character and value from them. These are generated by Scripture and their quality is determined by Scripture. However, the stedfastness and consolation are said to be the means of something more ultimate, namely, hope. Hope in this case is to be understood of that which the believer entertains, the state of mind. There cannot be the exercise of hope except as it is directed to an object, that hoped for. But to "have hope" is to exercise hope (*cf.* Acts 24:15; I Cor. 3:12; 10:15; Eph. 2:12, I Thess. 4:13; I John 3:3). In this text the instruction, stedfastness, and consolation derived from Scripture are all represented as contributing to this exercise of hope and thereby is demonstrated the significance for the believer and for the fellowship of the saints of the prospective outreach which hope implies (*cf.* 8:23–25 and vs. 13).

5, 6 These verses are not directly in the form of prayer addressed to God. They are in the form of a wish addressed to men that God would accomplish in them the implied exhortation, an eloquent way of doing two things at the same time, exhortation to men and prayer to God. Without the enabling grace of God exhortation will not bear fruit. Hence the combination. No form of exhortation is more effective in address to men than this. The following considerations respecting these verses should be noted. (1) The titles—"God of patience and of comfort" point back to the terms "patience" and "comfort" in verse 4 and mean that God is the source and author of these (*cf.* II Cor. 1:3).[7] God is characterized and recognized by the grace he imparts to us in the life and fellowship of faith. (2) The close relation of God to the Scriptures is clearly indicated. Patience and comfort are derived from the Scriptures (vs. 4) and they are also derived from God. There is no disjunction. The Scriptures are the abiding Word of God and therefore the living Word. It is through their means that God imparts to us the patience and comfort that are his. Paul's thought cannot be adjusted to any other view than that the

---

[6] παράκλησις is consolation and it is not necessary to adopt the meaning "exhortation".

[7] *Cf.* "God of peace" (15:33; 16:20; II Cor. 13:11; Phil. 4:9; I Thess. 5:23; Heb. 13:20) and "God of hope" (15:13).

15:1-6 CHRIST'S EXAMPLE

Scriptures sustain to God that abiding relation that they themselves are his Word (*cf.* 3:1, 2). (3) "To be of the same mind one with another" (*cf.* Phil. 2:2, 5)[8] is a plea for the mutual esteem and forbearance which have been the plea from the beginning of this section (14:1) and is addressed to both weak and strong. "According to Christ Jesus" could mean in accordance with the will of Christ. In that event the harmony enjoined is qualified as consonant with Christ's revealed will and is not harmony irrespective of such conformity. In view of the appeal to Christ's example in verse 3 it is more likely that the meaning is "according to Christ's example" though not by any means limiting the thought to the specific particular mentioned in verse 3 (*cf.* Phil. 2:5). But even in this case the implications of the other meaning would be present. What is after Christ's example must always accord with his will. (4) The end to which this harmony is directed is the distinctive feature of these two verses. It is that in unison and unity they might glorify God the Father. The terms "with one accord ... with one mouth" (*cf.* Acts 1:14; 2:46) express the unity with which inwardly and outwardly the glorifying of God is to take place. To glorify God is to exhibit his praise and honour. In the background lurks the thought of the prejudice incurred for the final end to be promoted by the church when the fellowship of the saints is marred by suspicions and dissensions and in this case particularly by the arrogance of the strong and the stumblings of the weak. No consideration could enforce the exhortation more strongly than to be reminded of the glory of God as the controlling purpose of all our attitudes and actions. The form of the title by which the Father is designated could be rendered "God even the Father of our Lord Jesus Christ" or "God and the Father of our Lord Jesus Christ". There is not sufficient reason to insist upon this rendering. The Father is not represented merely as the *Father* of Christ but also as the *God* of our Lord Jesus Christ (*cf.* Matt. 27:46; John 20:17; Eph. 1:17; Heb. 1:9).[9] Hence the rendering of the version is in accord with the New Testament pattern of thought and its propriety should not be contested. In either case, however, our attention is

---

[8] The Greek is ἐν ἀλλήλοις.
[9] *Cf.* for defence of this rendering Sanday and Headlam: *op. cit., ad loc.*

here drawn to what is ultimate in our glorifying of God, the glory of God the Father.[10]

---

[10] This ultimacy is exemplified in other cases as, for example, in the love of God. The love of the Father is ultimate and fontal (*cf.* John 3:16; Rom. 5:8; 8:29; Eph. 1:4, 5; I John 4:9, 10).

G. JEWS AND GENTILES ONE
(15:7-13)

15:7-13

7 Wherefore receive ye one another, even as Christ also received you, to the glory of God.
8 For I say that Christ hath been made a minister of the circumcision for the truth of God, that he might confirm the promises *given* unto the fathers,
9 and that the Gentiles might glorify God for his mercy; as it is written,
    Therefore will I give praise unto thee among the Gentiles,
    And sing unto thy name.
10 And again he saith,
    Rejoice, ye Gentiles, with his people.
11 And again,
    Praise the Lord, all ye Gentiles;
    And let all the peoples praise him.
12 And again, Isaiah saith,
    There shall be the root of Jesse,
    And he that ariseth to rule over the Gentiles;
    On him shall the Gentiles hope.
13 Now the God of hope fill you with all joy and peace in believing, that ye may abound in hope, in the power of the Holy Spirit.

7 As in verses 5, 6 both weak and strong are in view, so here. In 14:1 the same exhortation is addressed to the strong in reference to the weak but now both classes are exhorted to mutual embrace in confidence and love. The necessity is underlined by what Christ has done. If Christ has received us,[11] are we to refuse fellowship to those whom Christ has received? If we place restraints upon our acceptance of believers, we are violating the example of

---

[11] ὑμᾶς rather than ἡμᾶς is the more strongly attested variant. The former is supported bij ℵ, A, C, G, the mass of the cursives, and several versions. In view of the textual patterns which appear in this epistle it is difficult to defend ἡμᾶς. Internal evidence would not be a factor in this case.

that redemptive action upon which all fellowship in the church rests. In 14:3 the fact that God has received the strong believer is urged as the reason why the weak should receive him. Christ's reception of all without distinction is the ground upon which fellowship is to be unrestrained. "To the glory of God" should be taken in conjunction with Christ's action in receiving us.[12] In verses 8 and 9 two respects are mentioned in which the glory of God is exhibited in Christ's being made a minister of the circumcision. But we may not limit the glory of God in verse 7. There is a close connection between "to the glory of God" (vs. 7) and the glorifying of the Father (vs. 6). The harmony enjoined is for the glory of God the Father. This, as well as the harmony, is patterned after Christ's example; his receiving of us is to the glory of God and no consideration could enforce the necessity of mutual confidence and love more than that Christ's receiving of all, weak and strong, was not only in perfect accord with God's glory but was directed specifically to that end. The ultimate goal of Christ's action was likewise the glory of the Father (*cf.* John 17:4). We are reminded of the coalescence of supreme grace to us and the promotion of God's glory (*cf.* Eph. 1:14; Phil. 2:11).

8, 9a   These two verses appear to be not so much proof that Christ received all without distinction as additional argument to support the obligation to harmony and fellowship enjoined in the preceding verses. We are here introduced to a distinction not overtly mentioned in this section of the epistle, that between Jews and Gentiles. We may not infer from this that the weak were Jews and the strong Gentiles.[13] The respective parties may well have been drawn from both racial groups. But this reference to Jews and Gentiles does suggest, if it does not show, that the exhortation to mutual acceptance had in view the need to overcome all racial prejudice and discrimination in the communion of the saints at Rome. The stress upon the Gentiles in the succeeding verses makes evident the emphasis which the apostle felt called upon to place upon the world-wide redemptive purpose which Christ fulfilled in his very capacity as "minister of the circumcision". Any

---

[12] The punctuation in the version quoted is based on the assumption that to "the glory of God" goes with "receive ye one another". This construction is not to be followed. *Cf.* A.V.
[13] *Cf. contra* Gifford: *op. cit., ad loc.*

tendency to limit to Israel the relevance of this ministry is plainly excluded. The following considerations should be noted. (1) "The circumcision" stands for those of the circumcision, namely, Israel after the flesh (*cf.* 3:1, 30; 4:12; Gal. 2:7–9). The reference to "the fathers" (vs. 8) and to "the Gentiles" (vs. 9) by way of distinction demonstrates this. That Christ has become[14] a minister of the circumcision accentuates again the way in which Israel comes within the purview of Christ's mission (*cf.* Matt. 15:24; John 4:22). (2) It is necessary, however, to find a more significant allusion in the term "circumcision". This was the sign and seal of the covenant with Abraham (Gen. 17:1–21; *cf.* 4:11). Christ is therefore the minister of the covenant of which circumcision was the seal and it is in pursuance of that covenant that he came and fulfilled the office here mentioned (*cf.* Gal. 3:16). (3) The design of his being made a minister of the circumcision was to confirm the promises made unto the fathers.[15] The force of "confirm" is to establish and bring to realization. This is equivalent to bringing the covenant sealed by circumcision to fruition. For the covenant is the certification of promise and to fulfil the covenant is to fulfil its promises. It is in this light that the expression "for the truth of God" is to be understood. The oath-certified promises are God's promises and to their fulfilment his truth is pledged. God's faithfulness cannot fail and so Christ came to vindicate and bring to effect God's faithfulness (*cf.* Matt. 26:54). (4) The relation of verse 9 to verse 8 concerns the question: what is the design for the Gentiles of Christ's office as minister of the circumcision? It might be supposed that his ministry to the Gentiles would be independent and follow a different though parallel line. Such a construction would run counter to all that the apostle had argued in the earlier portions of the epistle (*cf.* 4:11, 12, 16, 17, 23–25; 11:11–32). But not only so. The syntax of these verses is eloquent of the fact that mercy to the Gentiles is likewise the design of Christ's being made a minister of the circumcision. The latter is not only that he might confirm the promises but also that "the Gentiles might glorify God for his mercy". This implies that the Gentiles are partakers of God's mercy. However, in accord with the emphasis upon glorifying God in verses 6 and 7 and in order to provide a more

---

[14] The perfect tense should be noted—γεγενῆσθαι.
[15] The τῶν πατέρων has the force of the promises belonging to the fathers and is properly understood as the promises given to them.

suitable parallel to "confirm" in the preceding clause as well as to enhance the beneficent result, the apostle expresses the thought by saying "glorify God for his mercy". This Paul then proceeds to demonstrate by a series of quotations from the Old Testament.

9b–12 The first quotation is derived from II Samuel 22:50; Psalm 18:49 and, apart from the omission of the vocative "Lord", is a verbatim quotation of the Greek version of Psalm 18:49 (Heb. 18:50; LXX 17:50) which, in turn, adheres closely to the Hebrew. Verse 10 is taken from Deuteronomy 32:43 and follows the Hebrew rather than the Greek version, verse 11 from Psalm 117:1 and the variation from the Hebrew and the Greek version consists only in the change of person in the second clause, verse 12 from Isaiah 11:10 and with slight abridgement follows the Greek version. Common to all of these quotations in the form quoted by the apostle is the reference to the Gentiles. As is apparent from verse 9 this is the interest that guided the selection of these passages. They all are adduced to support the proposition that one of the designs in Christ's being made a minister of the circumcision was the salvation of the Gentiles and they show the extent to which in the apostle's esteem the Old Testament had envisioned the outreach to all nations of that blessing which lay at the centre of the Abrahamic covenant. These texts quoted by Paul here and numerous others all bear witness to the way in which the outlook of the Old Testament had been regulated and inspired by the promises to Abraham (Gen. 12:3; 22:18). Although the first three quotations do not expressly state that the Gentiles will respond to the witness borne (vs. 9) or to the imperatives addressed (vss. 10, 11) to them, yet they must be understood as implying the subjection to the root of Jesse indicated in the last quotation (vs. 12).[16] Even if this inference were not made, they would still involve on the part of the inspired writers and in Paul's esteem the relevance to the Gentiles of that obligation to praise the Lord and rejoice in him which only covenant relationship could secure.

13 This verse may well be regarded as bringing this section of the epistle to a close. In accordance with the last quoted word

---

[16] This is particularly true in verse 10 in view of the way in which the Hebrew of Deut. 32:43 is rendered.

(vs. 12) the emphasis falls clearly on hope. The clause to which all else is subordinate is the final one, "that ye may abound in hope, in the power of the Holy Spirit". The form of this verse is the same as that of verse 5; it is indirectly prayer to God and combines invocation and exhortation. The title "God of hope" is to be construed after the same pattern as the titles in verse 5 and "the God of peace" (vs. 33; *cf.* I Thess. 5:23; Heb. 13:20). God is the God of hope because he generates hope in us. It is, however, difficult to suppress the thought in this instance that the title points also to God as the object of hope. God himself is the ultimate hope of the people of God because he is their portion, their inheritance, and their dwelling-place (*cf.* Psalms 73:24–26; 90:1; Eph. 3:19; Rev. 21:3).

The fulness of joy and peace which the apostle invokes for his readers is based upon what is implied in the title "God of hope". Only the hope created by God gives warrant for joy and peace and when this hope is present joy and peace should be full. The joy is joy in the Lord (*cf.* Gal. 5:22; Phil. 4:4; I John 1:4) and the peace is the peace of God (*cf.* Phil. 4:7).[17] As joy and peace are conditioned by hope, so they are produced by faith and they promote hope. The fulness of joy and peace invoked is to the end that hope may abound more and more in the hearts of those who entertain it. The graces in exercise in believers never reach the point of fulness to which no more can be added. Joy and peace emanate from hope and they contribute to the abounding of the same. The object contemplated in hope far transcends human conception and the discrepancy between what believers are now and what they will be (*cf.* I John 3:2) makes the entertainment of hope presumption except as it is generated and sealed by the Holy Spirit. This is the significance of the concluding words of the invocation, "in the power of the Holy Spirit". The prayer begins and ends with the accent upon divine agency and resource. Within this sphere alone can the grandeur of hope be contemplated and within it hope has the certification which the earnest of the Spirit accords to it (*cf.* Eph. 1:13, 14).

---

[17] It is not peace with God (5:1). We could not suitably be regarded as filled with peace with God and, besides, peace is coordinate with joy.

XIX. PAUL'S GENTILE MINISTRY, POLICY, AND PLANS (15:14-33)

15:14-21

14 And I myself also am persuaded of you, my brethren, that ye yourselves are full of goodness, filled with all knowledge, able also to admonish one another.
15 But I write the more boldly unto you in some measure, as putting you again in remembrance, because of the grace that was given me of God,
16 that I should be a minister of Christ Jesus unto the Gentiles, ministering the gospel of God, that the offering up of the Gentiles might be made acceptable, being sanctified by the Holy Spirit.
17 I have therefore my glorying in Christ Jesus in things pertaining to God.
18 For I will not dare to speak of any things save those which Christ wrought through me, for the obedience of the Gentiles, by word and deed,
19 in the power of signs and wonders, in the power of the Holy Spirit; so that from Jerusalem, and round about even unto Illyricum, I have fully preached the gospel of Christ;
20 yea, making it my aim so to preach the gospel, not where Christ was *already* named, that I might not build upon another man's foundation;
21 but, as it is written,
They shall see, to whom no tidings of him came,
And they who have not heard shall understand.

14 At this point begins the concluding part of this epistle, devoted to encouragement, explanation, greeting, and final doxology. In earlier portions there is oftentimes the severity of rebuke, correction, and warning. But the apostle would not have this feature to be interpreted as implying a low estimate of the attainments of the church at Rome. At the outset he had paid his compliment to the believers there for their faith and for the encouragement which they would impart to him when he would

15:14–33 PAUL'S GENTILE MINISTRY, POLICY, AND PLANS

achieve his desire to visit them (1:8, 12). But now again in stronger terms he gives his assessment of their virtues. The bond of fellowship is expressed in the address "my brethren" and he could scarcely have devised a combination of words that would more effectively convey to them his own personal conviction of the fruit of the gospel in their midst: "I myself also am persuaded of you".[18] They were, he believed, "full of goodness" and "filled with all knowledge". This complementation and the fulness in each case show the maturity which characterized the Roman community of believers. "Goodness" (*cf.* Gal. 5:22; Eph. 5:9; II Thess. 1:11) is that virtue opposed to all that is mean and evil and includes uprightness, kindness, and beneficence of heart and life. The "knowledge" is the understanding of the Christian faith and is particularly related to the capacity for instruction reflected on in the next clause. It may not be extraneous to suggest that the reference to these two qualities in particular may have been dictated by their relevance to the subject dealt with in the preceding section (14:1–15:13). Goodness is the quality which will constrain the strong to refrain from what will injure the weak and knowledge is the attainment that will correct weakness of faith. The treatment of differences in 14:1–15:13 was not hypothetical; there must have been a situation requiring it. But we must not exaggerate the situation; the church was "full of goodness, filled with all knowledge". Thus the believers there were themselves able to instruct and admonish one another.

15 Having given the commendation of verse 14 the apostle now proceeds to explain the boldness with which he had written. He is careful, however, to state the true measure of this boldness. He does not say "boldly" but "more boldly" which in this case does not mean "more than boldly" but somewhat or rather boldly and he modifies this still further by saying "in some measure".[19] All of this indicates his concern that the believers would properly evaluate the degree of boldness he exercised. The reason for it was to put them in remembrance and here again there is the

---

[18] There is the assumption that others entertained this esteem. Paul was not behind others in this respect.
[19] ἀπὸ μέρους surely means "partly" and is properly rendered "in some measure". To take it as referring to "parts" of the epistle is scarcely warranted, even though it is true that the apostle's boldness is apparent at points where he writes in tones of severity.

209

softening appropriate to the goodness and knowledge already credited to them. It is all-important to note that the main apology resides in the next clause and in what follows in verse 16. It is only because of the grace given him of God that he could dare to write as he did. This is characteristic of Paul. It is in pursuance of divine commission and the enduement with grace which belongs to it that he exercises his ministry (*cf.* I Cor. 9:16; Eph. 3:7–9).

16 We are now informed of the office alluded to in the last clause of verse 15. Grace was given to the end that he might be the minister of Christ to the Gentiles. Paul had repeatedly referred to this office (1:5; 11:13; 12:3). But in this verse there are distinctive features which ought to be marked. (1) When he calls himself a "minister" of Christ he uses a term which in its various forms is often charged with the sacredness belonging to worship (*cf.* Luke 1:23; Acts 13:2; Rom. 15:27; II Cor. 9:12; Phil. 2:17; Heb. 1:7, 14; 8:2, 6; 9:21; 10:11). It should be understood with these associations, for this is in accord with and anticipates the ideas expressed later respecting the character of his ministry. (2) When he defines his ministry as "ministering the gospel of God" the apostle uses a word occurring nowhere else in the New Testament which may properly be rendered "acting as a priest". So the ministry of the gospel is conceived of after the pattern of priestly offering. It is not to be supposed that the gospel itself is regarded as the offering. The offering is specified in the next clause. The dignity belonging to this office of preaching the gospel is, however, hereby underlined and the kind of priestly action performed in the exercise of the apostolic office is thus shown to be of an entirely different character from that of the Levitical priesthood and also from that of Christ himself. (3) The expression "the offering up of the Gentiles" is without precise parallel in the New Testament. But it has its parallel in Isaiah 66:20: "And they shall bring all your brethren out of all the nations for an offering unto the Lord".[20] It may be that Paul derived this concept from the Isaianic passage which appears in a context of blessing to all nations and tongues (*cf.* Isa. 66:18). This then is the offering which Paul as apostle of the Gentiles offers to God in the exercise

---

[20] The Hebrew is מנחה and the LXX $\delta\tilde{\omega}\rho o\nu$. But the word used by Paul, $\pi\rho o\sigma\varphi o\rho\acute{a}$, would be the more appropriate.

15:14-33 PAUL'S GENTILE MINISTRY, POLICY, AND PLANS

of priestly activity. The Gentiles as converted to the faith of the gospel are regarded as presented holy unto God. Again we see how extraneous to the Levitical pattern is the priestly function exercised by the ministers of the new covenant. (4) Carrying on the ideas associated with priestly activity Paul adds "acceptable" (*cf.* I Pet. 2:5). An offering to be acceptable to God must conform to conditions of purity. So in this case. The conditions of holiness are created by the Holy Spirit. Hence the clause, "sanctified by the Holy Spirit", stands in apposition to "acceptable". The apostle thinks of his function in the priestly action as ministering that gospel which is efficacious through the grace of the Holy Spirit. Thus the Gentiles become an offering acceptable to God. This is his apology for the boldness he exercised in putting his readers in remembrance. He has said enough to vindicate the epistle and to remove any accusation which his severity might provoke.

17-19a The result specified in the preceding verse, the acceptable offering up of the Gentiles, and the ministration of the gospel contributing by God's grace to that end gave the apostle abundant ground for glorying and he says "I have therefore my glorying".[21] He is referring to the *act* of glorying. The ground is implicit in the "therefore" which points back to verses 15b, 16. He is careful to add, however, "in Christ Jesus". Boasting is excluded except as it is in the Lord (*cf.* I Cor. 1:29-31; II Cor. 10:17). And he makes a further qualification; his glorying is "in things pertaining to God". This should not be understood in the sense of his personal relation to God but, as the preceding verse and especially the succeeding indicate, of the things pertaining to the gospel and kingdom of God. There is nothing of egoism in his glorying; it is glorying in God's grace and when thus conditioned it cannot be too exuberant.

That Paul is thinking of the gospel triumphs (*cf.* II Cor. 2:14) wrought through his instrumentality in verse 17 is demonstrated by verse 18. For here he protests that only of the things which Christ wrought through him would he dare to speak. But he does dare to speak of these. He does not say "the things I have wrought through

---

[21] In the Greek there is no possessive pronoun answering to "my". It is τὴν καύχησιν and the article is omitted in P⁴⁶, ℵ, A, and the mass of the cursives. The sense is not materially affected by the omission or insertion of the article in view of the distinct specification given in the words that follow.

211

Christ". It is Christ's action through the apostle and this action was in both "word and deed". The things of which he dares to speak in the glorying concerned are, however, only those things which had been wrought through the apostle himself rather than through others. C. K. Barrett has expressed both thoughts succinctly: "(i) I would not dare to speak of this if it were not Christ's work (rather than mine); (ii) I would not dare to speak of this if it were not Christ's work through me (rather than any one else)".[22] "Word and deed" are to be construed with "Christ wrought through me" rather than "obedience". This conjunction is eloquent witness to the coordination of word and deed in that which Christ does from his exalted glory. The same applies to what he had done during the days of his flesh upon earth. It also certifies to us that behind Paul's words as well as deeds were the activity and authority of Christ.

Verse 19a is a further specification of things Christ wrought through Paul and is obviously continuous with "by word and deed" of verse 18. This could be taken as specifying the way in which Christ wrought through the apostle in the accomplishment of the things mentioned in verse 18; Christ wrought by the power of signs and wonders. But it is preferable to regard the statement as an additional particularizing of the things Christ wrought through the apostle and we may not even equate the signs and wonders with "deed" in verse 18. The signs and wonders were deeds but not all deeds are in this category. The word "power" in this instance is regarded by commentators as the power derived from signs and wonders. "The power of the Holy Spirit" later is certainly the power derived from the Holy Spirit, more accurately expressed as the power *exercised* by the Spirit. But it may not be out of place to suggest that "power" in the first instance is rather the power *exemplified* in signs and wonders.

The three standard terms for miracles in the New Testament are powers, signs, and wonders. Only two of these are used here; the word "power" is used in construction with signs and wonders for the reason indicated. Signs and wonders do not refer to two different sets of events. They refer to the same events viewed from different aspects. A miracle is both a sign and a wonder. As a sign it points to the agency by which it occurs and has thus certificatory

---

[22] *Op. cit., ad loc.*

15:14-33 PAUL'S GENTILE MINISTRY, POLICY, AND PLANS

character; as a wonder the marvel of the event is emphasized. It might appear from the history recorded that Paul's ministry was not conspicuously marked by miracles. This text corrects any such misapprehension (*cf.* II Cor. 12:12 where all three terms occur; also Gal. 3:5, and see also the general application in Heb. 2:4). "In the power of the Holy Spirit" could be regarded as a further definition of the power mentioned in the earlier part of the verse, for the power of signs and wonders may not be abstracted from the power of the Spirit. But the teaching of Paul in general would militate against this restrictive interpretation. The power of the Spirit is, according to the apostle, the efficiency by which the gospel is effectual in all its aspects. Hence the analogy of this teaching elsewhere would indicate that he is referring to the inclusive agency of the Holy Spirit in virtue of which all phases of his ministry had been crowned with the success of which he dared to speak (*cf.* I Cor. 2:4; I Thess. 1:5, 6; 2:13). It is characteristic to intimate his dependence upon the Holy Spirit whenever he refers to the saving effects of the gospel. And it is also characteristic of him to make no disjunction in this regard between the working of the Spirit and that of Christ (*cf.* 8:9-11; II Cor. 3:6, 17, 18).

It is noteworthy how in verses 16-19a Paul weaves his teaching around the distinctive relations to and functions of the three persons of the Godhead. This shows how Paul's thought was conditioned by the doctrine of the trinity and particularly by the distinguishing properties and prerogatives of the three persons in the economy of salvation. It is not a case of artificially weaving these persons into his presentation; it is rather that his consciousness is so formed by and to faith in the triune God that he cannot but express himself in these terms (*cf.* vs. 30; Eph. 4:3-6).

19b-21 At this point Paul intimates the result of the commitment and enduement dealt with in the preceding context and he speaks of this in terms of the extent of his labours as minister of Christ to the Gentiles. We might have expected that the starting-point of his itineraries would have been stated to be Antioch in Syria (*cf.* Acts 13:1-4). But it is not likely that he has in mind precisely the *startingpoint* when he mentions Jerusalem but the south-eastern limit of his missionary activity. Furthermore, it would have been strange indeed, when mentioning the bounds of his ministrations, that he would have omitted the mention of

Jerusalem. He did preach the gospel there (*cf.* Acts 9:26–30) and since it was from Jerusalem the gospel went forth it was not only appropriate but necessary that he should say "from Jerusalem". The other limit is Illyricum. This is the northwest bound. Illyria was on the eastern shore of the Adriatic, comprising roughly what is now Yugoslavia and Albania and therefore north-west of Macedonia and Achaia, the scene of such intensive labours on Paul's part. It is uncertain whether "unto Illyricum" means that he penetrated into this country or simply reached its borders. He could have preached in Illyria on the journey mentioned in Acts 20:1, 2 or he may have made a preaching excursion into this territory during his stays in Corinth (*cf.* Acts 18:1, 18; 20:3). But of this we cannot be certain. The borders of Illyria satisfy the terms "unto Illyricum". "Round about" should not be understood as referring to the environs of Jerusalem. There is no evidence that Paul had conducted missionary labours round about Jerusalem to an extent that would warrant this kind of reference and, besides, since he is dealing with his ministry to the Gentiles in the territories extending from Jerusalem to Illyria, this restriction of "round about" to the environs of Jerusalem would not comport with the way in which his labours were "round about" in this whole area.[23] He says he "fully preached" the gospel. This means that he had "fulfilled" the gospel (*cf.* Col. 1:25) and does not reflect on the fulness with which he set forth the gospel (*cf.* Acts 20:20, 27). Paul had discharged his commission and fulfilled the design of his ministry within the wide area specified. Neither does "fully preached" imply that he had preached the gospel in every locality and to every person in these territories. "His conception of the duties of an Apostle was that he should found churches and leave to others to build on the foundation thus laid (I Cor. iii. 7, 10)".[24] And, in respect of what he considered to be his function, he

---

[23] Only here in the New Testament does κύκλῳ occur with μέχρι and this must be taken into account. It is *round about unto Illyricum*, not round about Jerusalem. It is true that Paul preached, according to his own testimony, "throughout all the country of Judaea" (Acts 26:20) and this might be construed as round about Jerusalem. But, for the reason just stated and also for the reason that Paul's ministry in Judaea could scarcely have been an extended one, it is much more in accord with the expression and with the known facts to take "round about" as referring to his missionary activities in the whole area specified.

[24] Sanday and Headlam: *op. cit.*, p. 409. The whole paragraph should be noted.

proceeds to say (vs. 23) that he had "no more any place in these regions".

In verses 20, 21 we are informed of the policy that guided the apostle in the conduct of his ministry and he elucidates for us the scope, on the one hand, and the limitation, on the other, of his claim in the preceding verse. It was his well-defined and studied procedure not to build upon the foundation laid by another (*cf.* I Cor. 3:10). This indicates the sense in which we are to understand "not where Christ was already named". He does not mean "named" in the loose sense of merely known or reported but in the sense of acknowledged and confessed (*cf.* I Cor. 5:11; Eph. 3:15; II Tim. 2:19). When a foundation is laid the church is conceived of as existing and in such centres it was his policy not to conduct his missionary labours. It would be an unreasonable application of this declared course of action to suppose that Paul would refrain from visiting a church that had been established by the labours of another or that he would refrain from all apostolic witness and activity in such places. He had visited Jerusalem on several occasions and had borne witness to the gospel there. He was at this time about to depart for Jerusalem in order to bring the contribution from the churches of Macedonia and Achaia and to cement the bonds of fellowship between the Gentile churches and those of Jewish composition in Jerusalem. He was determined to visit Rome. There is no contradiction. What he has in mind in verse 20 is that his apostolic activity was directed to the founding of churches and the edifying of churches he had been instrumental in establishing and not to the building up of churches that were the fruit of another man's labours. In verse 21 he draws support from Isaiah 52:15. The quotation varies slightly from the Hebrew text but with the transposition of one word is the same as the Greek version. This text is derived from a context in which the world-wide effects of Messiah's sacrifice are in view and the appropriateness of the application to the apostle's Gentile ministry is apparent. He conceives of his own work as the minister of Christ to be conducted in pursuance of this prophecy and, therefore, as not only in accord with God's design but as specifically demanded by this Scripture.[25]

---

[25] On the objections to verses 19–21 *cf.* the excellent treatment by Sanday and Headlam: *op. cit.*, pp. 408–410.

15: 22-29

22 Wherefore also I was hindered these many times from coming to you:
23 but now, having no more any place in these regions, and having these many years a longing to come unto you,
24 whensoever I go unto Spain[26] (for I hope to see you in my journey, and to be brought on my way thitherward by you, if first in some measure I shall have been satisfied with your company)—
25 but now, *I say*, I go unto Jerusalem, ministering unto the saints.
26 For it hath been the good pleasure of Macedonia and Achaia to make a certain contribution for the poor among the saints that are at Jerusalem.
27 Yea, it hath been their good pleasure; and their debtors they are. For if the Gentiles have been made partakers of their spiritual things, they owe it *to them* also to minister unto them in carnal things.
28 When therefore I have accomplished this, and have sealed to them this fruit, I will go on by you unto Spain.
29 And I know that, when I come unto you, I shall come in the fulness of the blessing of Christ.

22-24 In verse 22 we have a virtual repetition of what Paul had said at 1:13. The significant difference is that now he tells the reason why he had been so many times hindered from fulfilling his purpose to go to Rome. This is the force of "wherefore also". He was hindered by the necessities of fulfilling his ministry in the regions more adjacent. He could not leave until he had fully preached the gospel in the territories in which up to date he had laboured. "But now" (vs. 23) the case is different. Having fulfilled the gospel he has no more place for this kind of activity in the regions extending from Jerusalem to Illyricum. Hence he is now free to cast his missionary eyes on more distant horizons. It is not Rome, however, of which he is thinking as the scene of labours complying with the policy set forth in verses 20, 21. Not at all. It is all-important, in view of Paul's declared plan in verses 20, 21, to observe how Rome relates itself to this projected outreach of apostolic labour. It is the region far beyond Rome that comes

---

[26] The addition after Σπανίαν in verse 24 of ἐλεύσομαι πρὸς ὑμᾶς is not supported by sufficient authority.

15:14-33 PAUL'S GENTILE MINISTRY, POLICY, AND PLANS

within his ambition and, as subsequent considerations will show, Rome is envisaged as a resting point on the way. "Whensoever I go unto Spain"—this is Paul's objective and its relation to the principles enunciated in verses 20, 21 is patent. Whether or not Paul ever reached Spain is problematical.[27] But that he properly entertained the desire and hope is beyond question and there are indications in what follows that it was his intent, as soon as he had fulfilled his mission to Jerusalem, to be off on his journey to the western limits of Europe.

In verse 24b he intimates the kind of visit he planned for Rome. It was not to conduct the type of apostolic ministry he had fulfilled at Corinth or Ephesus. "I hope to see you in my journey", that is, on his way to Spain. It was to be, in his design, a passing visit,[28] though not by any means so brief or casual that he would not impart to believers there and derive from them that of which he spoke in 1:11-13. In this verse he expresses the benefit he hopes to derive from his visit as being "satisfied" with their company. The term rendered "satisfied" means to have full enjoyment of. The modification "in some measure" is not probably for the purpose of toning down the enjoyment he anticipates as if he were reflecting on the limitation placed upon the satisfaction derived from a human source but that he is again courteously reminding his readers that he will not be able to enjoy the full measure of satisfaction because his visit will only be a passing one.[29] Perhaps the most significant element in this verse is the clause, preferably rendered, "to be sent forth thither by you". "Thither" refers to Spain. He expects from the church at Rome a sending forth with

---

[27] Probably the strongest support for the supposition that Paul achieved his desire to go to Spain is that derived from The Epistle to the Corinthians by Clement of Rome who says of Paul δικαιοσύνην διδάξας ὅλον τὸν κόσμον καὶ ἐπὶ τὸ τέρμα τῆς δύσεως ἐλθών (V). On the basis of the expression τὸ τέρμα τῆς δύσεως J. B. Lightfoot concludes: "From the language of Clement here it appears that this intention (Rom. 15:24) was fulfilled". He maintains that the expression points to the western extremity of Spain. "It is not improbable also that this western journey of S. Paul included a visit to Gaul (2 Tim. iv. 10; see *Galatians*, p. 31)" (J. B. Lightfoot: *The Apostolic Fathers*, London, 1890, Part I, Vol. II, p. 30). The other early reference to Paul's visit to Spain is rom the Muratorian Fragment. The atrocious Latin of the manuscript is amended by Lightfoot to read: "Sed et profectionem Pauli ab urbe ad Spaniam proficiscentis" (*ibid.*). For a more cautious interpretation of these references *cf.* Sanday and Headlam: *op. cit., ad loc.*

[28] διαπορευόμενος has this meaning.

[29] *Cf.* Meyer, Gifford: *op. cit., ad loc.*

commendation and blessing comparable to that experienced earlier at the hands of other churches (*cf.* Acts 13:1-4; 14:26; 15:40). How close was the bond of fellowship between the churches and the apostle in the discharge of his specifically apostolic commission!

25, 26 Now is explained the reason why the journey to Rome is postponed and for what purpose he sets out for Jerusalem. He is going there on the ministry of mercy. It may surprise us that Paul would have interrupted his primary apostolic function (*cf.* vs. 16) for what is apparently secondary and concerned with material things. We think so only when we overlook the dignity of the work of mercy. We are reminded of this in that incident which perhaps more than any other reveals apostolic statesmanship in the worldwide missionary enterprise (Gal. 2:7-9). And we must read the appendix: "only they would that we should remember the poor: which very thing I was also zealous to do" (Gal. 2:10). Of this Paul was not neglectful. Hence, "I go unto Jerusalem, ministering to the saints". There is a further implication on which Paul will reflect later (vs. 31).

The contribution he brings to Jerusalem was from the saints in Macedonia and Achaia. The voluntary nature of the collection is implied in the words "it hath been the good pleasure of" (*cf.* II Cor. 8:1-5; 9:1-5). The word "contribution" is the same as that rendered in other cases by the term "fellowship".[30] It has been suggested that "make a certain contribution" should be translated "establish a certain fellowship", in accord with the more usual meaning of the word in question. There does appear, however, to be warrant for the meaning "contribution". So the translation in the version may be retained. But it is difficult to suppress the notion of fellowship as flowing over into the thought of contribution in this instance. It was the bond of fellowship existing between the saints that constrained the offering and it was calculated to promote and cement that fellowship.

27 This verse begins with the same terms as verse 26 and reiterates the voluntary character of the contribution. This is not

---

[30] κοινωνία means "participation" and "fellowship" and so the clause in question has been rendered: "*they have undertaken to establish a rather close relation w. the poor*" (Arndt and Gingrich: *op. cit.*, ad κοινωνία, 1; but *cf.* also idem, 3). *Cf.* TWNT, III, p. 809.

15:14-33 PAUL'S GENTILE MINISTRY, POLICY, AND PLANS

incompatible with the debt of which Paul then proceeds to speak. Charity is an obligation but it is not a tax. The obligation mentioned in this case is specific. It is not in the same category as a commercial debt incurred which we are under contractual obligation to pay. It is the indebtedness arising from benefits received as when we acknowledge our indebtedness to a great benefactor. The Gentiles were partakers of the spiritual things which emanated from Jewry and from Jerusalem and these spiritual things were of the highest conceivable character. The apostle is here enunciating what belongs to the philosophy of God's redemptive grace. "Out of Zion shall go forth the law, and the word of the Lord from Jerusalem" (Isa. 2:3b; *cf.* vss. 2, 3a). "In this mountain will the Lord of hosts make unto all peoples a feast of fat things" (Isa. 25:6). It is the Lord's servant, "a shoot out of the stock of Jesse", who "will bring forth justice to the Gentiles" (Isa. 11:1; 42:1). Upon Zion the glory of the Lord is risen "and nations shall come to thy light, and kings to the brightness of thy rising" (Isa. 60:3). "Salvation is of the Jews" (John 4:22). Paul had frequently in this epistle reflected on this relationship (*cf.* 3:2; 4:16, 17; 9:5; 11:17-24). So now he brings this truth to application in the concrete and practical. Gentiles should minister to the Jews in material things. The term "carnal" is not in this instance to be given any evil associations; it is used with reference to tangible, material possessions. And this ministry is accorded the sanctity of worship by the term the apostle uses.[31]

28, 29 Paul now returns to the design of visiting Rome on his way to Spain. There is a note of despatch in verse 28. "Having, therefore, accomplished this, and having sealed to them this fruit, I shall be off by you into Spain".[32] The contribution is called "this fruit". It was the fruit of the faith and love of the believers in Macedonia and Achaia and a token of the bond of fellowship existing between these believers and the saints at Jerusalem. In view of verse 27, however, it is likely that it is regarded as the fruit accruing from the "spiritual things" which emanated from Jerusalem. The gospel came from the Jews and went into all the world. An example of the fruit borne in distant climes is now being brought

---

[31] λειτουργῆσαι; *cf.* vs. 16.
[32] "I shall be off to Spain" is Barrett's expressive rendering.

back to Jerusalem in the supply of the wants of the poor saints there, an indication of the close relation between "spiritual" and material things. It is more difficult to understand what is meant by *sealing* to them this fruit. Since Paul represents himself as sealing the fruit, the preferable view surely is that the collections delivered to them at Jerusalem would seal to the churches there the fruit accruing from the gospel and would be to them the certification of the love which constrained these contributions.

In verse 29 there is the note of certitude. We may not say that the certitude applies to his arrival at Rome. There are the indications noted earlier (*cf.* 1:10) and to be noted later (vs. 33) that Paul fully recognized the sovereignty of God in this matter and that he did not know what God had in store for him (*cf.* Acts 20:22-24). He had well-defined designs, and he had solid hope that he would finally reach Rome. But the *certitude* pertains to the blessing with which he would come if God so willed, "the fulness of the blessing of Christ".[33] This is the blessing which Christ imparts and Paul is convinced that his presence in Rome would be accompanied by the *fulness* of this blessing. No term could more appropriately express the full measure of the blessing anticipated. We are liable to think of the rich blessing that would *accompany* his ministry. This is without doubt in view. But we may not restrict the thought thus. The terms indicate that he will come thither in the possession of the fulness of Christ's blessing. This evinces the confidence of Christ's abiding presence in the plenitude of his grace and power. And it is also the key to the boldness with which Paul had planned his journey to the seat of empire and to the limits of the west. Although we may not press the terms of the sentence to convey this meaning, nevertheless, we cannot exclude from Paul's total thought (*cf.* 1:12; 15:24) the assurance that the fulness of Christ's blessing would also be imparted to the believers at Rome.

15:30-33

> 30 Now I beseech you, brethren, by our Lord Jesus Christ, and by the love of the Spirit, that ye strive together with me in your prayers to God for me;

---

[33] The addition after εὐλογίας of τοῦ εὐαγγελίου τοῦ in ℵc, L, the mass of the cursives, and some versions may not be adopted.

31 that I may be delivered from them that are disobedient in Judaea, and *that* my ministration which *I have* for Jerusalem may be acceptable to the saints;
32 that I may come unto you in joy through the will of God, and together with you find rest.
33 Now the God of peace be with you all. Amen.

30-32 The estimate given of the maturity of the Roman believers (vs. 14) and the refreshment he expects from them on his visit (*cf.* 1:12; 15:32) would be added ground for entreating their prayers on his behalf. But it is characteristic of Paul to solicit the prayers of the saints (*cf.* II Cor. 1:11; Phil. 1:19; Col. 4:3; I Thess. 5:25; II Thess. 3:1). So he beseeches the Roman believers. "By our Lord Jesus Christ" could refer to the mediacy through which he directs his entreaty to them; he could not even beseech his brethren apart from Christ's mediation. But this does not appear to be the sense. It is rather that he makes Christ Jesus his plea for compliance with his request (*cf.* 12:1; II Cor. 10:1). The fuller title "our Lord Jesus Christ" adds force to the plea. "The love of the Spirit" is coordinated and would have to be interpreted as serving the same purpose. Expositors commonly regard this love as the love which the Spirit instills in us, the fruit of the Spirit (*cf.* Gal. 5:22).[34] But there is no good reason why it should not be taken as the love which the Spirit bears to believers.[35] Besides, since "the love of the Spirit" is coordinated with "our Lord Jesus Christ" there is good, if not decisive, reason for the view that the love of the Spirit to us is intended. As the plea is urged on the basis of what Christ is and, by implication, does, so attention is also focused on what is true of the Holy Spirit himself. This imparts a distinctive emphasis. In respect of the Holy Spirit, what could enforce Paul's request more than to be reminded of the Spirit's love? As God's love inspires and validates hope (5:5), so the Spirit's love should incite to prayer.

Paul's request is that "ye strive together with me in your prayers to God for me; that I may be delivered from them that are disobedient in Judaea" *etc.* The term "strive together" is suggestive of

---

[34] *Cf.* most recently Bruce: *op. cit., ad loc.*: "the love which the Holy Spirit imparts and maintains".
[35] *Cf.* Barrett: *op. cit., ad loc.*: "the genitive cannot be objective, and the clue is given by v. 5". It should be borne in mind that the love of God shed abroad in our hearts (5:5) is the love of God to us and the genitive is subjective.

the wrestling which prayer involves; it is to be persistent and earnest. Truly, as commentators observe, this is necessary because of the resistance offered to persevering prayer by the world, the flesh, and the devil. But there is something more germane to the nature of prayer indicated by the term "strive". It is that earnest and consecrated prayer will be persistent and will wrestle. It is a means ordained of God for the accomplishment of his gracious designs and is the fruit of faith and expectation. That to be prayed for is twofold and pointedly particularized. First, it is to be delivered from the disobedient in Judaea. These are the unbelievers. The sequel shows that there was good ground for the apostle's foreboding (*cf.* Acts 20:22, 23; 21:27–36). Although he could protest that he did not hold his life as dear to himself (Acts 20:24) and that he was "ready not to be bound only, but also to die at Jerusalem for the name of the Lord Jesus" (Acts 21:13) and, therefore, would not compromise the gospel to save his life (*cf.* Matt. 16:25; John 12:25), yet he did not crave martyrdom. Furthermore, it was in the interests of promoting the gospel that he sought to be delivered from the murderous plots of unbelievers and, besides, it would be contrary to all Christian principles to resign himself fatalistically to the ungodly designs of men. Hence his earnest petition to the believers at Rome. Though Paul could not have anticipated the exact course of events, we cannot but discover the answer to his own prayers and of those at Rome in the events as they developed (*cf.* Acts 21:31–33; 23:12–35). The second particular for prayer was that his ministration might be acceptable to the saints. This is surprising. Would a gift to meet the poverty of saints be unacceptable? The apostle had ample evidence of the suspicions with which his Gentile ministry had been regarded and would most probably have heard of the false reports circulating in Jerusalem (*cf.* Acts 21:20, 21). There was, therefore, ground for fear that the fruit of his ministry in Macedonia and Achaia would not be welcomed. In the esteem of believing Jews still "zealous for the law" and especially for circumcision the contribution would be marked by a ministry prejudicial to what they deemed precious. This is the situation Paul envisioned. We can readily sense his concern and therefore the need for earnest prayer to God that the contribution would be acceptable. What a violation of *fellowship* rejection would be! That the fruit of the gospel that went out from Jerusalem, the fruit of faith and love, the token of the bond of fellowship between

15:14–33 PAUL'S GENTILE MINISTRY, POLICY, AND PLANS

believers, a contribution to cement bonds of love and meet the needs of the saints should be rejected, what a tragedy! The repercussions for the cause of the gospel and for the fellowship of which the common redemption was the bond are what the apostle dreads. There is good reason to believe this prayer also was answered (*cf.* Acts 21:17–20).

The prayers to be offered had an additional design (vs. 32). It is that he might come to Rome in joy and together with the believers there find rest. Various factors would contribute to the joy of his contemplated arrival in Rome: the realization of his plans and hopes for many years, deliverance from his enemies at Jerusalem, the success of his visit thither in the grateful acceptance of the contribution, the fellowship with believers at Rome, and the prospect of continuing his apostolic labours in the regions beyond. The rest he hopes for is not that of leisure but the refreshment and encouragement this new fellowship would impart. Most significant is the qualifying expression "through the will of God". The term used for "will" frequently refers in the New Testament to the preceptive will of God, the will revealed to us for the regulation of life and behaviour (*cf.* Matt. 6:10; 12:50; John 7:17; Rom. 2:18; 12:2; Eph. 5:17; 6:6; I Thess. 4:3). But it also refers to the will of God's determinate purpose, his decretive will realized through providence (*cf.* Matt. 18:14; John 1:13; Rom. 1:10; Gal. 1:4; Eph. 1:5, 11; I Pet. 3:17; II Pet. 1:21; Rev. 4:11). It is in this latter sense the term is used in this case. There are two things to be noted. (1) In praying for the particulars mentioned, especially that of reaching Rome, there is the expressed desire that these may prove to be the determinate will of God. There is the prayer that God may bring these requests to pass and therefore that they may be his determinate will unfolded in his providence. (2) There is also the recognition that God is sovereign and that the coming to pass of these events is dependent upon his sovereign will. The apostle in this reflects his resignation to the will and wisdom of God. It was not part of God's revealed will to Paul that he would go to Rome. Hence the reserve of submissiveness to what God determined his providence for Paul would prove to be.

Paul did go to Rome but under circumstances and after delays which he could not have forecast. God answered the prayers but not in the ways that Paul had hoped for or anticipated. The lessons for us to be derived from these verses (30–32) are numberless.

33 God is called the God of peace because he is the author of peace (*cf.* vss. 5, 13). In view of the emphasis upon peace with God (5:1; *cf.* 16:20; Eph. 2:14, 15, 17; I Thess. 5:23; Heb. 13:20) we should infer that peace with God is primary. But we may not exclude what is the consequence, namely, the peace of God (*cf.* Phil. 4:7; Col. 3:15), the peace of heart and mind in stedfast confidence and tranquillity. It is noteworthy how often the apostle in his benedictions calls God the God of peace or invokes upon his readers the peace that is from God (*cf.* 1:7; 15:13; I Cor. 1:3; 13:11; II Cor. 1:2; Gal. 1:3; Eph. 1:2; Phil. 1:2; 4:9; Col. 1:2; I Thess. 1:2; II Thess. 1:2; 3:16; I Tim. 1:2; II Tim. 1:2; Tit. 1:4; Phm. 3). Hence in the benediction which closes this part of the epistle no formula in Paul's repertory could be richer. In the prayer that the God of peace would be with them there is included all of the blessing insured by the presence of the God of peace.[36]

---

[36] On the critical question pertaining to the benediction in this verse see Appendix F (pp. 262 ff.).

ROMANS XVI

XX GREETINGS AND CLOSING DOXOLOGY
(16:1-27)

A. PAUL'S OWN GREETINGS
(16:1-16)

16: 1-16

1 I commend unto you Phoebe our sister, who is a servant of the church that is at Cenchreae:
2 that ye receive her in the Lord, worthily of the saints, and that ye assist her in whatsoever matter she may have need of you: for she herself also hath been a helper of many, and of mine own self.
3 Salute Prisca and Aquila my fellow-workers in Christ Jesus,
4 who for my life laid down their own necks; unto whom not only I give thanks, but also all the churches of the Gentiles:
5 and *salute* the church that is in their house. Salute Epaenetus my beloved, who is the firstfruits of Asia unto Christ.
6 Salute Mary, who bestowed much labor on you.
7 Salute Andronicus and Junias, my kinsmen, and my fellowprisoners, who are of note among the apostles, who also have been in Christ before me.
8 Salute Ampliatus my beloved in the Lord.
9 Salute Urbanus our fellow-worker in Christ, and Stachys my beloved.
10 Salute Apelles the approved in Christ. Salute them that are of the *household* of Aristobulus.
11 Salute Herodion my kinsman. Salute them of the *household* of Narcissus, that are in the Lord.
12 Salute Tryphaena and Tryphosa, who labor in the Lord. Salute Persis the beloved, who labored much in the Lord.
13 Salute Rufus the chosen in the Lord, and his mother and mine.

14 Salute Asyncritus, Phlegon, Hermes, Patrobas, Hermas, and the brethren that are with them.
15 Salute Philologus and Julia, Nereus and his sister, and Olympas, and all the saints that are with them.
16 Salute one another with a holy kiss. All the churches of Christ salute you.

1-2 It is highly probable that Phoebe was the bearer of this epistle to the church at Rome. Letters of commendation were a necessity when a believer travelled from one community to another in which he was unknown to the saints. But if Phoebe conveyed the epistle there would be an additional reason. Besides, as will become apparent, Phoebe was a woman who had performed distinguished service to the church and the commendation had to be commensurate with her character and devotion. Cenchreae was one of the ports for Corinth. There was a church there and Phoebe was a servant of this church. It is common to give to Phoebe the title of "deaconess" and regard her as having performed an office in the church corresponding to that which belonged to men who exercised the office of deacon (*cf.* Phil. 1:1; I Tim. 3:8-13). Though the word for "servant" is the same as is used for deacon in the instances cited, yet the word is also used to denote the person performing any type of ministry. If Phoebe ministered to the saints, as is evident from verse 2, then she would be a servant of the church and there is neither need nor warrant to suppose that she occupied or exercised what amounted to an ecclesiastical office comparable to that of the diaconate. The services performed were similar to those devolving upon deacons. Their ministry is one of mercy to the poor, the sick, and the desolate. This is an area in which women likewise exercise their functions and graces. But there is no more warrant to posit an *office* than in the case of the widows who, prior to their becoming the charge of the church, must have borne the features mentioned in I Timothy 5:9, 10. The Roman believers are enjoined to "receive her in the Lord, worthily of the saints". To receive in the Lord is to accept her as one bound to them in the bond and fellowship of union with Christ. "Worthily of the saints" could mean "as a fellow believer should be received". But it is more likely that it means "as it becomes saints to receive a believer", the "worthily" reflecting on what becomes them rather than on what is owing to her. The particular commendation of Phoebe is that she had been a helper of many

16:1–16 PAUL'S OWN GREETINGS

and of Paul himself.[1] This specification of virtue is, no doubt, mentioned as the outstanding feature of Phoebe's service to the church and indicates that on account of which she was called a servant of the church. But this virtue is also mentioned to enforce the exhortation that she is to be given assistance in every matter in which she may have need. The kind of help rendered by Phoebe is not intimated. She may have been a woman of some wealth and social influence and so have acted as patroness. Her services may have been of another kind such as caring for the afflicted and needy. Under what circumstances she was a helper of Paul we do not know. But her help may well have been of the kind afforded by Lydia at Philippi (Acts 16:15). In any case Phoebe is one of the women memorialized in the New Testament by their devoted service to the gospel whose honour is not to be tarnished by elevation to positions and functions inconsistent with the station they occupy in the economy of human relationships.

3, 4 Prisca, on other occasions also named Priscilla, and Aquila Paul first met at Corinth (Acts 18:2). They had just come from Italy for the reason mentioned. They had given him domicile at Corinth (Acts 18:3). Later they accompanied Paul as far as Ephesus and they remained there (Acts 18:18, 19). There they instructed Apollos in a more accurate understanding of the gospel (Acts 18:26). They are mentioned also in salutations in two other epistles of Paul (I Cor. 16:19; II Tim. 4:19). By the time Paul wrote the epistle to Rome they had returned thither. This

---

[1] The contention of Russell C. Prohl that προστάτις means "one who presides" and is to be understood in the sense of the verb προίστημι (cf. 12:8) from which, he says, προστάτις is derived rests upon insufficient evidence. It is true that the masculine προστάτης can mean "ruler", "leader", "president" and the corresponding verbs προστατεύω and προστατέω have similar meaning. But προστάτης can also mean "patron" or "helper". The feminine προστάτις can have the same meaning. Besides, the meaning "president" does not suit in the clause in question. Paul says that Phoebe "became a προστάτις of many and of me myself". Are we to suppose that she exercised rule over the apostle? What she was to others she was to the apostle. The rendering that Prohl adopts "She was made a superintendent of many by me myself" is wholly unwarranted. Furthermore, the believers at Rome are enjoined to "stand by" or "help" Phoebe (παραστῆτε αὐτῇ) and the last clause in verse 2 is given as a reason to enforce this exhortation. "She herself was a helper of many and of me myself". There is exact correspondence between the service to Phoebe enjoined upon the church and the service she herself bestowed upon others. The thought of presidency is alien to this parallel. See Russell C. Prohl: *Woman in the Church* (Grand Rapids, 1957), pp. 70f.

should not be surprising. The Emperor Claudius had died and his decree (Acts 18:2) for this reason or for some other was no longer in effect. Aquila and Prisca were itinerant as the preceding references show and there is no reason why they should not have returned to Rome when the abovementioned restriction had been removed or relaxed. As the incident recorded in Acts 18:26 shows, they were well versed in the faith and Paul calls them his "fellow-workers in Christ Jesus". Since even the secular occupation of believers is in Christ Jesus it would not have been improper for Paul to accord this dignity to the partnership in tentmaking (Acts 18:3). But in view of verses 9 and 21 we must regard the cooperation as referring to joint labour in the gospel in the bond of union and fellowship with Christ. Here we have another example of the contribution made by a woman (Prisca) in the work of the gospel and of the church (*cf.* vss. 6, 12) within the limits prescribed by Paul elsewhere (*cf.* I Cor. 11:3–16; 14:33b–36; I Tim. 2:8–15). When Prisca and Aquila placed their lives in jeopardy on Paul's account we do not know. It may have been at Corinth or at Ephesus or elsewhere. Neither are the circumstances known. Laying down their own necks could be even literally interpreted. But this may also be figurative to express the extreme peril at the hands of persecutors to which they subjected themselves to save Paul's life. It may well be that so notable was this incident that it had been reported to all the churches of the Gentiles and that the gratitude of the churches for this act of self-sacrifice is alluded to in the latter part of verse 4. But, in any event, the fame of Prisca and Aquila was so widespread that to them not only Paul gave thanks but "also all the churches of the Gentiles". The data already adduced from Acts 18 are an index to the mobility of this couple as also to their devotion. That they should have returned to Rome is consonant with all that we know of their character and practice.

5 This reference to the church in the house as well as other references (I Cor. 16:19; Col. 4:15; Phm. 2) may not be restricted to the household (*cf.* Acts 10:2; 11:14; 16:15, 31; 18:8; I Cor. 1:16; I Tim. 3:4; 5:13; II Tim. 1:16). It was necessary and appropriate in apostolic times, as on some occasions today, for Christians to make their homes available for the congregations of the saints. It is not without significance that in our totally different present-day situation the practice of the house church is

16:1-16 PAUL'S OWN GREETINGS

being restored and recognized as indispensable to the propagation of the gospel. In a city like Rome or Ephesus (*cf.* I Cor. 16:19) there would be more than one such congregation. The fact that the church in the house of Aquila and Prisca is particularly mentioned in this list of greetings shows that it did not comprise the whole church at Rome. Hence there would be other *churches* and it would be proper to speak of the churches in Rome.

Epaenetus is called "beloved" as is also Ampliatus (vs. 8), Stachys (vs. 9), and Persis (vs. 12). There could not be any offensive discrimination in calling these "beloved" when others were not. There must have been a particular constraint of affection in these instances which the apostle would assume to be known or readily recognized by others. This can be detected in the case of Epaenetus; he was the firstfruits, that is the first convert, of Asia[2] unto Christ. The bond of peculiar affection is apparent.

6 Mary is another instance of a woman labouring on behalf of the church. There is no validity to the objection that Paul could not have had such intimate knowledge of affairs at Rome[3] so as to be able to particularize thus. He must have received much information from Aquila and Prisca who had just come from Rome when Paul first arrived in Corinth. The "much labor" suggests that Mary was one of the earliest members of the church at Rome and its organization could have been largely due to her influence.

7 Andronicus and Junias were kinsmen of the apostle. This cannot be proven to mean more than that they were Jewish (*cf.* 9:3). But they may have been more closely related as also Herodion (vs. 11), Lucius, Jason, and Sosipater (vs. 21). Since there are other Jews mentioned who are not called kinsmen (*cf.* vs. 3), those who are called kinsmen likely stood in a closer relation of kinship. It would not be necessary to suppose that they were all members of the apostle's *family*. When Andronicus and Junias shared captivity with Paul we do not know. His imprisonments were frequent (*cf.* II Cor. 6:5; 11:23) and on at least one occasion they shared this honour. "Of note among the apostles" may mean that they were apostles themselves. If so then the word "apostles"

---

[2] Ἀχαίας is not the proper reading. Ἀσίας is supported by P⁴⁶, ℵ, A, B, D*, G, and several versions. *Cf.* I Cor. 16:15 for Ἀχαίας.
[3] εἰς ὑμᾶς is to be preferred on both external and internal grounds.

would be used in a more general sense of messenger (*cf.* II Cor. 8:23; Phil. 2:25). Since, however, the term has usually in Paul the more restricted sense, it is more probable that the sense is that these persons were well known to the apostles and were distinguished for their faith and service. The explanation is ready at hand; they were Christians before Paul and, no doubt, were associated with the circle of apostles in Judea if not in Jerusalem. There are thus four reasons why they are selected for greetings.

8 Ampliatus was beloved "in the Lord". All the others mentioned as beloved were likewise. But it was not necessary to amplify in every case. "In the Lord" underscores the relation to Christ that alone establishes the bond of love which beloved in the Christian sense involves.

9 The derivation of the name Urbanus would suggest that he was natively a Roman. He is said to be *our* fellow-worker and was not therefore a companion of the apostle as Prisca and Aquila (vs. 3) and Timothy (vs. 21) who are called his own fellow-workers. Stachys is identified simply as beloved and, like Ampliatus, has no further commendation.

10 Apelles is distinguished as "approved in Christ" and is accorded this distinction because of peculiar trials and temptations perseveringly endured and proven thereby. Aristobulus is mentioned only because there were believers in his household. Like Narcissus (vs. 11) he must have been a man of station in Rome. J. B. Lightfoot maintains that he was a grandson of Herod the Great and a brother of the elder Agrippa and of Herod (king of Chalcis) and on intimate relations with the Emperor Claudius.[4] Those of his household need not have been more than servants or slaves. Although those of the household of Narcissus who are greeted are those "in the Lord", we need not infer that the absence of this restriction in the present instance means that all of Aristobulus' household were Christians. No doubt the same qualification applies in both cases, though mentioned only in one.

---

[4] *Saint Paul's Epistle to the Philippians* (London, 1908), pp. 174f. But *cf.* also F. F. Bruce: "Herod" in *The New Bible Dictionary* (London, 1962), pp. 521–523.

16:1–16 PAUL'S OWN GREETINGS

11 The name Herodion and the context in which the reference occurs suggest that he was of the Herod family or household. He was one of the kinsmen, therefore Jewish and, as suggested above, probably related in some way to the apostle. Lightfoot maintains that Narcissus is the powerful freedman by that name put to death shortly after the accession of Nero and therefore some years before Paul wrote this epistle.[5] Though deceased, his household would still go under his name as likewise in the case of Aristobulus.

12 Tryphaena and Tryphosa are supposed to have been sisters. Persis is also a woman. All three are said to have laboured in the Lord. The present tense used in the case of Tryphaena and Tryphosa and the past in the case of Persis should not be unduly pressed. The difference should not be construed as a reflection upon Persis' fidelity. She is called "beloved" and is said to have laboured *much*. In these two respects she is accorded an eminence not given to Tryphaena and Tryphosa. The distinction in tense may be an index to the reserve observed by Paul. He knew that Persis laboured *much* but is not able to say the same as of the time of writing. Or it may be that age or infirmity had overtaken Persis and that she was no longer active as she had been. Epaenetus, Ampliatus, and Stachys he calls "my beloved", Persis he calls "the beloved". It might have been indelicate to call her *my* beloved.

13 It may be that Rufus is the same person mentioned in Mark 15:21, the son of Simon of Cyrene. If so there was good reason for Mark's mention of his name. "Chosen in the Lord" does not refer to election in Christ (*cf.* Eph. 1:4) unto salvation. This would apply to all the saints mentioned in this chapter. It means "choice" and points to some eminence belonging to Rufus. The mother of Rufus was not *literally* Paul's mother. He means that she had performed the part of a mother to him. When or where we do not know.

14 The names listed in this verse and the brethren with them indicate a certain community of believers in a particular location or even vocation, all of the male sex.

---

[5] *Philippians*, as cited, p. 175.

15 Julia is most probably a woman[6] and may have been the wife of Philologus. It is not probable that she was a sister in view of this identification in the next greeting. The five persons mentioned in this verse and the saints with them formed a community and it may well be that here we have another example of a congregational group as in verse 5. This is more likely in this instance than in verse 14 because of the expression "all the saints that are with them" and the fact that both sexes are involved. The absence of reference to a church or to the church in a house does not militate against this supposition. There may not have been any one home extending this hospitality and the distinguishing eminence of Prisca and Aquila in this regard may have been the reason for the mention of their house in verse 5.

16 The holy kiss is enjoined not only in this epistle but in several others (I Cor. 16:20; II Cor. 13:12; I Thess. 5:26). Peter gives the same charge and calls it the kiss of love (I Pet. 5:14). We are advised of the custom of extending friendly greeting by a kiss in the reprimand of Jesus to Simon the Pharisee, "Thou gavest me no kiss" (Luke 7:45). There can be no question but the kiss was practised as the token of Christian love. Peter's designation makes this clear. But a kiss on its own account is the token of love and the hypocrisy of Judas is exposed by the question, "betrayest thou the Son of man with a kiss?" (Luke 22:48). Paul characterizes the kiss as "holy" and thus distinguishes it from all that is erotic or sensual. It betrays an unnecessary reserve, if not loss of the ardour of the church's first love, when the holy kiss is conspicuous by its absence in the Western Church. The final salutation at this point, "All the churches of Christ salute you", might seem more appropriate in verses 21–23 because these verses deal with the greetings of others rather than of Paul himself. But on closer examination we can see the significance of inclusion at this point. Paul is so identified with all the churches, particularly those of the Gentiles as the apostle of the Gentiles, that his greetings may not be dissociated from those of the whole church. His solidarity with the church universal governs his consciousness and as apostle of the Gentiles he represents all the Gentile churches in the conveyance

---

[6] "A common name, found even among slave women in the imperial household" (Arndt and Gingrich: *op. cit., ad loc.*). *Cf.* Lightfoot: *ibid.*, p. 177.

16:1-16 PAUL'S OWN GREETINGS

of his greetings. Another observation worthy of note is the plural "churches". We may not tone down the unity of the church. This comes to expression repeatedly in Paul (*cf.* 11:16-24; Eph. 2:16, 18-22; 4:2-16). But Paul is also jealous to maintain that in every instance where the saints are gathered together in Christ's name in accordance with his institution, there the church of Christ is (*cf.* vs. 5). Finally, this salutation, as F. F. Bruce observes, "is a strong argument for the Roman destination of these greetings. Why should Paul send greetings from *all* the churches to another church to which he was writing an ordinary letter? But at a time when one very important phase of his ministry was being concluded he might well send greetings from all the churches associated with that phase of his ministry to a church which not only occupied a unique position in the world ... but also, in Paul's intention, was to play an important part at the outset of a new phase of his ministry".[7]

---

[7] *Romans*, as cited, p. 276.

B. WARNINGS AGAINST DECEIVERS
(16:17–20)

16:17–20

17 Now I beseech you, brethren, mark them that are causing the divisions and occasions of stumbling, contrary to the doctrine which ye learned: and turn away from them.
18 For they that are such serve not our Lord Christ, but their own belly; and by their smooth and fair speech they beguile the hearts of the innocent.
19 For your obedience is come abroad unto all men. I rejoice therefore over you: but I would have you wise unto that which is good, and simple unto that which is evil.
20 And the God of peace shall bruise Satan under your feet shortly.
The grace of our Lord Jesus Christ be with you.

Though this passage differs in content and tone from the rest of the epistle we should not exaggerate the difference. Severity of mood and expression appears at various points in the epistle (*cf.* 2:1–5; 3:8; 6:1–3; 9:19, 20; 11:20; 14:15, 16). The warning note appears throughout. As Sanday and Headlam properly observe, this "vehement outburst . . . is not unnatural. Against errors such as these St. Paul has throughout been warning his readers indirectly, he has been building up his hearers against them by laying down broad principles of life and conduct, and now just at the end, just before he finishes, he gives one definite and direct warning against false teachers."[8] We need not suppose that these agitators and false teachers had actually invaded the Roman scene. Probably they had not. If they had we would expect direct encounter with them in the body of the epistle, as, for example, in the epistles to the Galatians and Colossians.[9] But

---

[8] *Op. cit.*, p. 429; *cf.* also F. J. A. Hort: *Prolegomena to St. Paul's Epistles to the Romans and Ephesians* (London, 1895), pp. 53–55.
[9] *Cf.* Hort: *ibid.*, pp. 53f. who says: "It is conceivable that just as St. Paul was on the point of finishing or sending his letter, fresh tidings reached him of impending doctrinal troubles at Rome".

16:17–20 WARNINGS AGAINST DECEIVERS

Paul was well aware of the existence of these heretics and, if their propaganda had not reached Rome, there was good ground for fear that the danger was impending.[10] The similarity of these warnings to those of Philippians 3:2, 18, 19 is apparent and Colossians 2:16–23 deals with the same or at least closely allied evil.

17, 18 The trouble-makers are by some regarded as antinomian libertines, by others an Judaizing zealots. These two viewpoints, though apparently antagonistic, are in reality and ultimate effect closely related. The person jealous for what God has not commanded soon sets more store by his own ordinances than by those of God. It might be pleaded that verse 18 favours the view that they were of the Epicurean variety. They are said to serve "their own belly". This characterization need not refer, however, to preoccupation with sensuous appetite. It may express the notion of self-service in contrast with the service of the Lord Christ (*cf.* James 3:15; Jude 19) and be virtually equivalent to earthly and sensual. Those condemned in Colossians 2:20–23 whose slogans were "handle not, nor taste, nor touch" (Col. 2:21) could thus come under the same indictment (*cf.* Phil. 3:19). On this interpretation of verse 18 the false teachers could well be Judaizing zealots. These were the apostle's opponents in many instances and they fit the description, "causing the divisions and occasions of stumbling, contrary to the doctrine which ye learned".[11] The word for "occasions of stumbling" is the same as, in the singular, occurs in 14:13. It does not appear that Paul has the same situation in mind.[12] In 14:13 a strong believer is for a weak believer the occasion of falling and this is a grave breach of love. But there is no suggestion of the gravity contemplated in the present passage.

---

[10] *Contra* to the supposition that the heretics had not yet reached Rome *cf.* Dodd: *op. cit.*, p. 242 who says: "He (Paul) knows, or has reason to fear, that the sort of people who have disturbed the peace of his own churches are at work in Rome. He has carefully avoided controversial references to them in the body of the epistle; but when it comes to the final admonition, he cannot refrain from an appeal to the Romans to beware of them."

[11] It may be that the heretics were of the gnostic variety and similar to those dealt with in the epistle to the Colossians (*cf.* especially Col. 2:4, 8 and Rom. 16:18). "They may have been associated with quasi-gnostic speculations... such as cropped up a little later at Colossae" (Dodd: *op. cit.*, p. 243).

[12] *Cf. contra* Barrett who says that "possibly the division between weak and strong is still in mind" (*op. cit., ad. loc.*).

We have here false teachers and propagandists. These are not envisaged in chapter 14. Hence the stumbling is that caused by false doctrine and falls into the category of the error anathematized in Galatians. The injunctions comport with an error of such character: they are to "mark" the proponents so as to avoid them and they are to "turn away from them". No such exhortations are appropriate in chapter 14. These teachers were skilled in the artful device of "smooth and fair speech", a common feature of those who corrupt the purity and simplicity of the gospel. Deceptiveness is the chief peril: "they beguile the hearts of the innocent". The term "innocent" means guileless and refers to the person not given to the wiles of deceit and craft and therefore not suspecting the same in others. The "innocent" person is the unsuspecting and thus readily ensnared by appearance. To the strategems of deception Paul refers in other passages (*cf.* II Cor. 4:2; Eph. 4:14). In view of verse 20 it is difficult to suppress allusion to the beguiling of the serpent (Gen. 3:1–6; *cf.* II Cor. 11:3; I Tim. 2:14).

19, 20 Verse 18 begins with "for" and gives a reason for the preceding exhortations. Verse 19 also begins with "for" but the connection is not the same as in verse 18. The apostle is concerned lest believers at Rome should have their minds corrupted from the simplicity that is unto Christ. The high esteem entertained of the maturity and devotion of the church there (*cf.* 15:14) only intensifies his zeal for the continuance of this fidelity. The fame of the Christian community at Rome had come to all the churches. He speaks of this fame as the report of their "obedience", a term characteristic of this epistle and adapted to the subject of which he now speaks (*cf.* 1:5; 6:16; 15:18; 16:26). The reputation of the Roman church and the crucial place it occupied would correspondingly aggravate the tragedy of corruption. Hence all the more reason for the urgent warnings and injunctions of verse 17. There is also another connection between verse 19 and what precedes. Paul is concerned not to insinuate that the false teaching had entered the church at Rome. He reiterates his assurance of their fidelity and he rejoices over them. Precisely for these reasons they must take heed and he beseeches them to do so. "I would have you wise unto that which is good, and simple unto that which is evil." Though this plea has analogies elsewhere (*cf.* Jer. 4:22;

16:17-20 WARNINGS AGAINST DECEIVERS

Matt. 10:16; I Cor. 14:20; Phil. 2:15) and the thought in general is plain enough, it is difficult to ascertain the precise meaning in relation to what precedes. It is obvious that good and evil, wise and simple are contrasted. If a preference may be proposed, the plea is that they would be wise in following what was good and immune to solicitations to evil, that the implied imperative is to the same effect as "hold fast that which is good; abstain from every form of evil" (I Thess. 5:21, 22). The terms "wise" and "simple" are used in order to emphasize the need for alertness and discernment in reference to the craftiness of the false teachers (*cf.* vs. 18a).

In verse 20a there is allusion to Genesis 3:15.[13] The designation "God of peace" (*cf.* 15:33; II Cor. 13:11; Phil. 4:9; I Thess. 5:23; II Thess. 3:16; Heb. 13:20) may well have been used here not merely for the reasons why Paul uses it elsewhere but also because of its particular relevance to the bruising of Satan. The latter envisions the conflict that is to issue in Satan's defeat. The preceding verses have in view the divisions caused by Satan's instruments (*cf.* II Cor. 11:12-15). It is God who bruises Satan and establishes peace in contrast with conflict, discord, and division. He is, therefore, the God of peace. The assurance given in this verse is the encouragement to give heed to the admonitions. Each element is significant. God will *crush* Satan, he will crush him *under the feet* of the faithful, and he will do it *speedily*. The promise of a victorious issue undergirds the fight of faith. The final subjugation of all enemies comes within the horizon of this promise (*cf.* I Cor. 15:25-28). But we may not exclude the conquests which are the anticipations in the present of the final victory (*cf.* I John 2:14; 4:4).

Verse 20b is another example of benediction inserted at the close of a subdivision of the epistle (*cf.* 15:33). It is similar to the closing benediction of several epistles (*cf.* I Cor. 16:23; Gal. 6:18; Phil. 4:23; I Thess. 5:28; II Thess. 3:18; II Tim. 4:22; Phm. 25). But, as noted elsewhere,[14] there are numerous instances of benedictions in the body of an epistle and the occurrence of this one here is not abnormal.

---

[13] Following the Hebrew but not the LXX rendering.
[14] See Appendix F (pp. 262 ff.).

C. GREETINGS OF FRIENDS
(16:21-23)

16:21-23

21 Timothy my fellow-worker saluteth you; and Lucius and Jason and Sosipater, my kinsmen.
22 I Tertius, who write the epistle, salute you in the Lord.
23 Gaius my host, and of the whole church, saluteth you. Erastus the treasurer of the city saluteth you, and Quartus the brother.

21-23 These verses are the greetings of others associated with the apostle. The name Timothy needs no comment. Lucius, Jason, and Sosipater are said to be kinsmen (*cf.* vss. 7, 11). In all there are six who are called kinsmen, not too large a number for the hypothesis that they were related to Paul by kinship and not merely of the Jewish race. In the case of Tertius there is direct salutation.[15] He was Paul's secretary. It is striking that this greeting should be inserted at this point; Paul is addressing his readers in both what precedes and what follows. Why Tertius' personal greeting appears at this point rather than at the end of this section we do not know. Paul's practice of using an amanuensis is attested in other epistles (I Cor. 16:21; Gal. 6:11; Col. 4:18; II Thess. 3:17). Gaius is undoubtedly the Gaius whom Paul baptized at Corinth (I Cor. 1:14) and there is good ground for thinking that he is the Titius Justus of Acts 18:7 into whose house Paul entered. Gaius was not only Paul's host but of the church. If Gaius is to be identified with Titius Justus, then his being host of the whole church would probably mean that his home was the meeting place for the assemblies of the believers at Corinth (*cf.* vs. 5).[16] But this could also mean that Gaius' home was open to all Christians visiting Corinth.

---

[15] "We have therefore in this little detail an instance of Paul's characteristic courtesy, and at the same time a strong proof of the genuineness of the passage: for what forger would have thought of introducing such an incident?" (Gifford: *op. cit., ad loc.*).

[16] If Gaius is to be identified with the Justus of Acts 18:7, then the reading Titius is to be preferred to Titus in the latter passage: Gaius Titius Justus being respectively the *praenomen, nomen gentile* and *cognomen* of a Roman citizen.

In this case he would be an outstanding example of the grace of hospitality (*cf.* 12:13). There are not sufficient reasons for identifying this Gaius with the person bearing the same name in any of the other instances (Acts 19:29; 20:4; III John 1). Erastus occupied a position of influence in the city. As in the case of Crispus, the ruler of the synagogue (Acts 18:8), this shows that the church at Corinth comprised men of social station. There is not sufficient evidence to identify this Erastus with the Erastus mentioned elsewhere (Acts 19:22; II Tim. 4:20). Quartus is called the brother. It is more likely that this means brother in Christ rather than brother of Erastus or even of Tertius. The fact that he is distinguished as "the brother", when all the others are brethren in Christ, does not require the ordinary use of the term "brother" any more than does the addition of "in the Lord" in verse 8 in the case of Ampliatus mean that others mentioned as beloved were not beloved in the Lord as well. All the others mentioned in these greetings (vss. 21–23) are not only mentioned by name but identified by some other addition. To end with no more than the name Quartus would be, stylistically if no more, abrupt.[17]

---

[17] The virtual repetition of the benediction found in verse 20 at this point found in D, G, the mass of the cursives, and some versions should not be regarded as impossible from the standpoint of internal evidence. The benediction in verse 20 would close the section devoted to Paul's own greetings and warnings (16:1–20). The benediction at this point would end the section devoted to the greetings of others, conveyed by the apostle (vss. 21–23), and then there would be the closing doxology (vss. 25–27). If such close proximity should seem strange we need but compare with II Thess. 3:16, 18. The question of text depends on the external evidence. The benediction is absent in P[46], ℵ, A, B, C, the Latin Vulgate and some other versions. In this instance, however, the suspicion can hardly be suppressed that a mistaken notion of incompatibility with the proximate benediction in vs. 20 may have exercised some influence in the omission.

D. DOXOLOGY
(16:25-27)

16:25-27

25 Now to him that is able to establish you according to my gospel, and the preaching of Jesus Christ, according to the revelation of the mystery which hath been kept in silence through times eternal,
26 but now is manifested, and by the scriptures of the prophets, according to the commandment of the eternal God, is made known unto all the nations unto obedience of faith:
27 to the only wise God, through Jesus Christ, to whom be the glory for ever. Amen.

25-27 This concluding doxology is longer than we find in other epistles of Paul. But we find rather close parallels in Hebrews 13:20, 21; Jude 24, 25. At the beginning of the epistle Paul had stated his desire to visit Rome and impart some spiritual gift to the end that believers there might be established. There is an appropriate connection with that aim and the opening words of this doxology. It is God who is able to establish and confirm the saints and of this Paul reminds himself and his readers. But there is a more proximate connection showing the relevance of the introductory words. In verses 17-20 he had warned against the seduction of deceivers and the paramount need is that believers be so established that they would not be the victims of Satan's craft. On God alone must reliance be placed. The confirmation which God gives will be, he says, "according to my gospel and the preaching of Jesus Christ". When he says "my gospel" (*cf.* 2:16; I Thess. 1:5; II Tim. 2:8) he means the gospel that was entrusted to him and which he preached (*cf.* I Cor. 15:1; Gal. 1:11; 2:2, 7; Eph. 3:6; I Thess. 2:4; I Tim. 1:11). "The preaching of Jesus Christ" could mean the preaching on the part of Christ through the instrumentality of Paul (*cf.* 15:18). But it is more likely the preaching concerned with Jesus Christ is in view. The gospel is essentially the preaching which has Christ as its subject; Paul preached Christ (*cf.* I Cor. 1:23; II Cor. 4:5). Thus the establishing is to be in accordance with the gospel of Jesus Christ whom Paul preached and there is no dissonance between Paul's gospel and the preaching of Christ. The term "preaching" is not to be understood as referring merely to the act of preaching. It refers to the *message* preached and so "the preaching of Jesus Christ" is virtually the gospel of which Jesus Christ is the subject.

It is difficult to be certain whether the words "according to the revelation of the mystery" are intended to specify another norm in accordance with which believers are to be established and thus coordinated with "my gospel" and "the preaching of Jesus Christ" or intended to assert that the "gospel" and "preaching" are in accordance with the revelation of the mystery. The latter alternative seems preferable. The gospel Paul preached is in accordance with the mystery revealed. Here "the mystery" is used to include much more than is denoted by the same term in 11:25. There it referred to a restricted aspect of God's revealed counsel (*cf.* I Cor. 15:51). Now it refers to the gospel message inclusively considered. But the term "mystery" has the same connotation as in 11:25.[18] The stress laid upon revelation appears expressly in the present instance as also upon the correlate of revelation, namely, that it had been hid from times eternal. If "times eternal" are to be understood as referring to the earlier ages of this world's history,[19] we have in verse 26 two considerations which do justice to Old Testament revelation, on the one hand, and to New Testament revelation, on the other. (1) The clause "now is

---

[18] *Cf.* comments *ad* 11:25.
[19] It is admittedly very difficult to ascertain the precise reference in χρόνοις αἰωνίοις. In II Tim. 1:9; Tit. 1:2 πρὸ χρόνων αἰωνίων could well mean "before the world began" and "times eternal" would thus be taken as referring to the ages of this world's history. In the present instance "times eternal" could designate the ages extending from creation to the coming of Christ. But this is not so certain. The expression could mean, to use Lagrange's expression, "The eternity of God". He appeals to πρὸ τῶν αἰώνων in I Cor. 2:7 and ἀπὸ τῶν αἰώνων in Eph. 3:9, a sense which, he says, is "indicated by the employment of αἰώνιος in speaking of God in v. 26" (*op. cit., ad loc.*). If this is Paul's meaning, then the thought is that the design was hid in the eternal counsel of God and implies the truth that this grace had been designed by God from eternity. Just as the mystery of election is enhanced by the fact that it took place in Christ before the foundation of the world (Eph. 1:4), so the glory of this mystery is shown by the fact that, though hid, it was not hid to God but was eternally embraced in his design. If χρόνοις αἰωνίοις has this import, then there is no overt reflection in this text on the relative concealment during the Old Testament periods. The relative fulness and expansion of the New Testament revelation would, however, be implicit in verse 26.

manifested", when taken in conjunction with the emphases on "silence" and "revelation" in verse 25, might create the impression that there had been no revelation whatsoever of this mystery in the Old Testament Scriptures. This impression, however, is decisively excluded or corrected by the words "by the scriptures of the prophets". These are the Scriptures to which Paul appeals repeatedly in this epistle for confirmation of the gospel he preached (*cf.* especially in this connection 1:2; 3:21; 11:25, 26). Hence the Old Testament was not silent on this mystery; it was the medium of revelation concerned with this subject. (2) Allowance must also be made for the significance of "now is manifested". There is no suppression of the emphasis upon the New Testament revelation in relation to the "silence through times eternal" (*cf.* Tit. 1:2, 3). The contrast is not absolute but it is *relative*, and this relative contrast must not be discounted. Again we must appreciate the pregnant force of the term "reveal" (*cf.* 1:17). In the Old Testament the ingathering of all nations had been foretold. This promise was given to Abraham (*cf.* Gen. 12:3, 22:18) and had been unfolded progressively. In the Psalms and Isaiah it is a refrain. But only with the coming of Christ and the breaking down of the wall of partition did this promise come to fruition and the implications become apparent. Thus the promise is revealed in fulfilment and operation. All the features of the history of revelation respecting the "mystery" are provided for in the terms here used by the apostle.[20] The "made known unto all the nations" makes clear what has just been said respecting the fulfilment which the New Testament brings. The prophetical scriptures were not the property of all the nations until the gospel went into all the world in accordance with Christ's command and in the power of Pentecost (*cf.* Matt. 28:18–20; Acts 1:4–8). With this worldwide proclamation these scriptures became the property of all without distinction and so *through their medium* the mystery is made known to all nations.

The great change in the ministry of the gospel and of the revelation concerned (*cf.* Acts 17:30) is "according to the commandment of the eternal God" (*cf.* I Tim. 1:1; Tit. 1:3). This points not only to the authority which God's appointment imparts to the

---

[20] *Cf.* the comments of Calvin: *op. cit.*, p. 328; Philippi: *op. cit., ad* 16:25; Bruce: *op. cit., ad* 16:26.

16:25-27 DOXOLOGY

universal proclamation of the gospel but also to the commission with which Paul himself was invested. It also has overtones of grace; it is by God's *commandment* that these overtures come to all men and they come, therefore, with the authority which God's command implies. The aim to which the mystery is directed is "the obedience of faith" (*cf.* 1:5). Though this is not most suitably taken as "obedience of faith unto all the nations", thus meaning *directly* that all nations are summoned to the obedience of faith, yet this thought is implied in the fact that the mystery is made known to all the nations. Wherever the gospel is proclaimed men are called to faith in it.[21]

"To the only wise God" resumes that with which the doxology began, "Now to him that is able "(vs. 25). In the latter, thought is focused on the *power* of God because this is specially relevant to the establishing of believers against all deception and compromise. Now at the close the *wisdom* of God is in the forefront (*cf.* 11:33; Eph. 3:10). The reason for this appears to be that the "mystery" with which verses 25b, 26 are concerned draws attention to and elicits the adoration of God's wisdom (*cf.* I Cor. 2:6-13). The appropriate designation is, therefore, "the only wise God". He is the only God and to him alone can be ascribed the wisdom exhibited in the unfolding of the mystery of his will. According to the reading followed by the version, this doxology presents an unfinished sentence. This should not be regarded as an objection. It is obvious that glory is being ascribed to God and we must not think so pedantically as to require neatly finished syntax. Paul's heart is filled with adoration and what we might regard as broken style does not interfere with the worship expressed. The question does remain, however: to whom is the glory ascribed, to "the only wise God" or to "Jesus Christ"? Other passages have been adduced to support the interpretation that this is a doxology to Christ. In II Timothy 4:18 the same form is used and is ascribed to Christ. It is not so apparent that the doxology is ascribed to Christ in other passages cited in this connection (Heb. 13:21; I

---

[21] No passage in Paul's epistles more than this one places in focus the distinction between mystery as something esoteric and belonging only to the initiated élite, on the one hand, and the Pauline conception, on the other. The features of this mystery as revealed set this distinction in the sharpest relief: (1) it is made known to all nations; (2) it is made known through Scriptures which are the property of all; (3) it is made known to all by God's command; (4) it is revealed to the end of bringing all to the obedience of faith.

Pet. 4:11). There is no reason why doxology in these terms should not have Christ as the object (*cf.* II Pet. 3:18; Rev. 1:6; 5:12, 13). But in this instance there is more to be said in favour of regarding "the only wise God" as the one to whom the glory is ascribed. This is the more frequent pattern (*cf.* 11:36; Gal. 1:5; Eph. 3:21; Phil. 4:20; I Tim. 1:17; I Pet. 5:11; Jude 24, 25).[22] Furthermore, "the only wise God", in apposition to the ascription with which the doxology begins (vs. 25), occupies, as in other similar doxologies, the place of prominence and we should expect that the closing words would apply to him.[23] We may justifiably sense an inappropriateness in the other supposition for it would mean that the titles which are particularly in focus in the earlier stages of the doxology are left without the ascription which expressly enunciates doxology. "Through Jesus Christ" could most suitably be understood as indicating the person through whom glory is ascribed to God and through whom God's glory is made known and extolled. The meaning would be, "to the only wise God be glory through Jesus Christ for ever".

---

[22] I Tim. 1:17 is particularly relevant.
[23] For ᾧ *cf.* Gal. 1:5; Heb. 13:21.

APPENDIX A

ROMANS 9:5

The interpretation of the two concluding clauses of this verse may be discussed, first of all, in terms of punctuation. There are three alternatives that have been proposed. 1. Place a period or colon after σάρκα and regard what follows to the end of the verse as having reference not to Christ but to God in the form of a doxology. 2. Regard the ὁ ὤν as having its antecedent in ὁ Χριστός and construe all that follows as applied to Christ and rendered, as in the version, "who is over all, God blessed for ever. Amen". 3. A third view had been proposed by Erasmus, namely, to take ὁ ὤν ἐπὶ πάντων with ὁ Χριστός and the remainder Θεὸς εὐλογητὸς εἰς τοὺς αἰῶνας as doxology to God.

It can be said in favour of both alternatives 1 and 3 that doxologies are usually by Paul applied to God in distinction from Christ (II Cor. 1:3; Eph. 1:3; cf. I Pet. 1:3). It is possible to take the latter part of the verse as doxology to God so that in this text the title Θεός would not be predicated of Christ. The following observations should, however, be made.

1. The form of doxology in the LXX and in the New Testament does not follow the pattern we find here in Rom. 9:5.[1] The form for doxology is rather εὐλογητὸς ὁ Θεός. In the LXX this latter form is very frequent and often in the form εὐλογητὸς κύριος ὁ Θεός. In Psalm 67:19 (68:19) we find κύριος ὁ Θεὸς εὐλογητός. But we have not sufficient reason to regard this as intended to be doxology. There is no corresponding clause in the Hebrew. In the following clause (67:20) we have doxology in the usual form εὐλογητὸς κύριος ἡμέραν καθ᾽ ἡμέραν, corresponding to the Hebrew (68:20) ברוך אדני יום יום. So the presumption is that LXX 67:19b is not doxology but affirmation. In LXX Psalm 112:2 (113:2) we find εἴη τὸ ὄνομα κυρίου εὐλογημένον, in III Kings 10:9 γένοιτο κύριος ὁ Θεός σου εὐλογημένος, in II Chron.

---

[1] C. K. Barrett properly recognizes this when he says that "if Paul wished to say 'Blessed be God', he should have placed the word 'blessed' (εὐλογητός) first in the sentence, as he does not" (op. cit., p. 179).

245

9:8 ἔστω κύριος ὁ Θεός σου εὐλογημένος, and in Job 1:21 εἴη τὸ ὄνομα κυρίου εὐλογημένον. But these are not exceptions to the pattern given above; the optative or imperative of these other verbs occurs first and is conjoined with εὐλογημένος. In the New Testament the instances are not as frequent as in the LXX but the same order is followed, whether it be with εὐλογητός or εὐλογημένος (Matt. 21:9; 23:39; Mark 11:9, 10; Luke 1:42, 68; 13:35; 19:38; John 12:13; II Cor. 1:3; Eph. 1:3; I Pet. 1:3). Rom. 1:25 and II Cor. 11:31 are not doxologies but affirmations that God is blessed for ever.

This preponderant usage of both Testaments constitutes a potent argument against the supposition that Rom. 9:5b should be regarded as doxology to God whether it be on the punctuation of alternative 1 or that of 3. The reasons necessary to support the thesis that Paul had here departed from the usual, if not uniform, formula for doxology would have to be conclusive. As we shall see later such reasons are lacking.

2. If the clauses in question were taken as ascription of blessedness to God after the analogy of Rom. 1:25; II Cor. 11:31, then we would expect the name Θεός or an equivalent title to precede, as in the cases just cited. That is, according to this pattern, ὁ ὤν would find its antecedent as ὅς ἐστιν in Rom. 1:25 and ὁ ὤν in II Cor. 11:31 in the person specified in the preceding context. But the only person specified in Rom. 9:5 is ὁ Χριστός. The argument in this case is not that ὁ ὤν could not introduce a new subject (cf. John 3:31; Rom. 8:5, 8)[2] but only that in this instance such a construction would be unnatural, abrupt, and contrary to the analogy of these other Pauline passages. Grammatically or syntactically there is no reason for taking the clauses in question as other than referring to Christ.

3. The interpretation which applies the clauses to Christ suits the context. In the words of Sanday and Headlam "Paul is enumerating the privileges of Israel, and as the highest and last privilege he reminds his readers that it was from this Jewish stock after all that Christ in His human nature had come, and then in order to emphasize this he dwells on the exalted character of Him who came according to the flesh as the Jewish Messiah".[3]

---

[2] See Sanday and Headlam: *op. cit.*, p. 235 to whom I am indebted for these references.

[3] *Op. cit.*, p. 236.

APPENDIX A: ROMANS 9:5

Without some predication expressive of Jesus' transcendent dignity there would be a falling short of what we should expect in this climactic conclusion.

4. With reference to the chief argument in support of the view that these clauses are doxology or ascription of blessedness to the Father, namely, that Paul never predicates Θεός of Christ,[4] the following considerations should be noted. (*a*) It may not be assumed that Paul never ascribes the title Θεός to Christ. In II Thess. 1:12 it is, to say the least, distinctly possible that τοῦ Θεοῦ ἡμῶν refers to Christ and that Θεοῦ stands in the same relationship to Ἰησοῦ Χριστοῦ as κυρίου. Likewise in Tit. 2:13, the same holds true of τοῦ μεγάλου Θεοῦ. In this case there is more to be said in favour of this construction than in II Thess. 1:12 (*cf.* also II Pet. 1:1). It may not be dogmatically affirmed that Paul *never* uses the predicate Θεός of Christ. (*b*) Paul uses several expressions which predicate of Jesus the fulness of deity. Perhaps most notable is Phil. 2:6 — ἐν μορφῇ Θεοῦ ὑπάρχων. μορφή means the specific character and in this instance is more eloquent than the simple Θεός because it emphasizes the fulness and reality of deity. To refrain from applying the predicate Θεός to Christ when he is said to have been originally and continued to be "in the form of God" could not possibly have arisen from any hesitation in respect of propriety and, if Paul should, on occasion, speak of Christ as Θεός, this is what we should expect. Of no less significance is Col. 2:9 where πᾶν τὸ πλήρωμα τῆς Θεότητος is said to dwell in Christ. This means "the fulness of Godhood" and no expression could express the fulness of Christ's deity more effectively. Again in Phil. 2:6 the terms τὸ εἶναι ἴσα Θεῷ refer to the dignity of Christ's station as the terms preceding deal with the dignity of his essential being and attribute to Jesus that equality which could belong to no other than to one who is himself also God. Other expressions in Paul could be adduced. These, however, place beyond any doubt the propriety, in terms of Paul's own teaching, of the predicate Θεός after the pattern of John 1:1 and 20:28. (*c*) Even if we were to discount the possibility of II Thess. 1:12 and the probability of Tit. 2:13 and regard Rom. 9:5 as the only instance where Θεός is expressly applied to Christ by Paul, this should not

---

[4] *Cf.* Dodd: *op. cit.*, p. 152 who, however, recognizes that Paul "ascribes to Christ functions and dignities which are consistent with nothing less than deity".

be regarded as an obstacle to what is on all accounts the natural interpretation of the clauses in question. We have just found that in Paul's teaching all that is involved in the predicate Θεός belongs to Christ. That he should have usually refrained from the use of the term Θεός as referring to Christ could be adequately explained by Paul's characteristic use of titles, that ὁ Θεός is so frequently the personal name of the Father and ὁ Κύριος that of Christ. But that he should on one occasion (as supposed at this point) have expressly used Θεός of Christ should not be surprising in view of what Paul's conception of Christ not merely allowed but demanded. In II Cor. 3:17 Paul says ὁ δὲ Κύριος τὸ Πνεῦμά ἐστιν. This is unusual and without knowing Paul's theology we would be staggered and ready to question the propriety of the predication. It is his conception of the relation of Christ to the Holy Spirit that explains it, not his characteristic use of titles. So in Rom. 9:5. (*d*) The clause ὁ ὢν ἐπὶ πάντων as an assertion of Christ's lordship is in accord with Paul's teaching elsewhere (*cf.* 1:4; 14:9; Eph. 1:20-23; Phil. 2:9-11; Col. 1:18, 19; for parallels *cf.* Matt. 28:18; John 3:35; Acts 2:36; Heb. 1:2-4; 8:1; I Pet. 3:22). Every consideration would show the relevance of appeal to Christ's sovereignty at this point. The arguments already adduced against the supposition that both concluding clauses refer to the Father would likewise militate against the proposal to apply this clause to Christ and Θεός εὐλογητός to the Father. The most natural rendering would, therefore, be "who is over all, God blessed for ever", so that "God blessed for ever" stands in apposition to what precedes.

We may thus conclude that there is no good reason to depart from the traditional construction and interpretation of this verse and, on the other hand, there are preponderant reasons for adopting the same.

APPENDIX B

LEVITICUS 18:5

There does not need to be any question but Paul in Rom. 10:5 makes allusion to Lev. 18:5 more directly than to any other Old Testament passage. He places the principle stated in Lev. 18:5 in opposition to the righteousness which is of faith and calls it "the righteousness which is of the law". The problem that arises from this use of Lev. 18:5 is that the latter text does not appear in a context that deals with legal righteousness as opposed to that of faith. Lev. 18:5 is in a context in which the claims of God upon his redeemed and covenant people are being asserted and urged upon Israel. In this respect Lev. 18:1–5 is parallel to Exod. 20:1–17; Deut. 5:6–21. The preface is "I am the Lord your God" (Lev. 18:2) and corresponds to the preface to the ten commandments (Exod. 20:2; Deut. 5:6). The whole passage is no more "legalistic" than are the ten commandments. Hence the words "which if a man do, he shall live in them" (vs. 5) refers not to the life accruing from doing in a legalistic framework but to the blessing attendant upon obedience in a redemptive and covenant relationship to God. In this respect Lev. 18:1–5 has numerous parallels in the Pentateuch and elsewhere (*cf.* Deut. 4:6; 5:32, 33; 11:13–15, 26–28; 28:1–14; Ezek. 20:11, 13). It is the principle expressly enunciated in the fifth commandment (*cf.* Exod. 20:12; Eph. 6:2, 3). Thus the question is: could Paul properly have appealed to Lev. 18:5 as an illustration of works-righteousness in opposition to that of faith? In order to answer the question it is necessary to deal with the three distinct relationships in which the principle "the man that does shall live" has relevance.

1. This principle has the strictest relevance and application in a state of perfect integrity. It is the principle of equity in God's government. Wherever there is righteousness to the full extent of God's demand there must also be the corresponding justification and life. This is the principle on which the argument of the apostle turns in the earlier part of the epistle. Just as sin—condemnation—death is an invariable combination in God's

judgment, so is righteousness—justification—life. It could not be otherwise. God's judgment is always according to truth. Perfect righteousness must elicit God's favour or complacency and with this favour goes the life that is commensurate with it. This would have obtained for Adam in sinless integrity apart from any special constitution that special grace would have contemplated.

This relationship could have no application to mankind after the fall. It can never again be in operation for man's acceptance with God and for the life that accompanies this acceptance. The only combination operative now in terms of simple equity is sin—condemnation—death.

2. The principle "the man who does shall live" must be regarded as totally inoperative within the realm of sin. It is this truth that underlies Paul's whole polemic regarding the justification of the ungodly and the righteousness that is constitutive thereof. Justification by *doing* is the contradiction of justification by faith. *Doing* has human righteousness in view, and the only righteousness that can be operative in our sinful situation is the God-righteousness which the gospel reveals (*cf.* 1:17; 3:21, 22; 10:3). It is this contrast that Paul institutes in Rom. 10:5, 6. In alluding to Lev. 18:5 at this point he uses the formula "the man that doeth . . . shall live thereby" as a proper expression *in itself* of the principle of works-righteousness in contrast with the righteousness of faith. We have no right to contest the apostle's right to use the terms of Lev. 18:5 for this purpose since they do describe that which holds true when law-righteousness is operative unto justification and life and also express the conception entertained by the person who espouses the same as the way of acceptance with God (*cf.* also Gal. 3:12).

3. It must be understood, therefore, that the principle "this do and thou shalt live" can have no validity in our sinful state as the way of justification and acceptance with God. To aver that it has is to deny the reality of our sin and the necessary provision of the gospel. But we must not suppose that doing the commandments as the way of life has ceased to have any validity or application. To suppose this would be as capital a mistake in its own locus as to propound works-righteousness as the way of justification. We must bear in mind that righteousness and life are never separable. Within the realm of justification by grace through faith there is not only acceptance with God as righteous in the righteousness of

APPENDIX B: LEVITICUS 18:5

Christ but there is also the new life which the believer lives. Pauls had unfolded the necessity and character of this new life in chapters 6 to 8. The new life is one of righteousness in obedience to the commandments of God (*cf.* 6:13, 14, 16, 17, 22; 8:4). In a word, it is one of obedience (*cf.* 13:8–10). So Paul can say in the most absolute terms, "If ye live after the flesh, ye must die; but if by the Spirit ye put to death the deeds of the body, ye shall live" (8:13). In the realm of grace, therefore, obedience is the way of life. He that does the commandments of God lives in them. It could not be otherwise. The fruit of the Spirit is well-pleasing to God and the fruit of the Spirit is obedience. In the renovated realm of saving and sanctifying grace we come back to the combination righteousness—approbation—life. The witness of Scripture to the necessity and actuality of this in the redeemed, covenant life of believers is pervasive. It is this principle that appears in Lev. 18:5 and in the other passages from the Old Testament cited above. "Fear the Lord, and depart from evil: it will be health to thy navel, and marrow to thy bones" (Prov. 3:7, 8).

APPENDIX C

THE AUTHORITIES OF ROMANS 13:1

Oscar Cullmann contends that "the late Jewish teaching concerning the angels ... of the peoples" belongs "to the solid content of faith in the New Testament"[1] and that on the basis of this faith "the existing earthly political power belongs in the realm of such angelic powers".[2] In Romans 13:1 the ἐξουσίαι, he maintains, must be conceived of, in accordance with Pauline usage, as *"the invisible angelic powers that stand behind the State government"*. "Thus as a result the term has for Paul a double meaning, which in this case corresponds exactly to the content, since the State is indeed the executive agent of invisible powers."[3]

As far as Pauline teaching is concerned Cullmann appeals particularly to I Cor. 2:8; 6:3. In the former passage the analogy, he says, is complete because "it is quite plain", he avers, "that by ἄρχοντες τοῦ αἰῶνος τούτου are meant both the invisible 'rulers of the age' *and* the visible ones, Pilate and Herod".[4] The latter passage, he says, "proves that according to the Primitive Christian view these invisible angelic powers stand behind the earthly states".[5]

It should be understood that Cullmann's argument is based entirely upon the plural form and upon the pluralistic usage of the singular, not upon the usage of the singular.[6] Furthermore, it is not the good angels that Cullmann regards as the invisible angelic beings lying back of the human agents but the evil angels who by "their subjection under Christ ... have rather lost their evil character, and ... now stand under and within the Lordship of Christ".[7] "Of them it can be said in the most positive manner

---

[1] *Christ and Time* (E. T., Philadelphia, 1950), p. 192. *Cf.* also revised edition (London, 1962). In the latter the quotations given and pagination are the same.
[2] *Ibid.*, p. 193.
[3] *Ibid.*, p. 195.
[4] *Ibid.*
[5] *Ibid.*, p. 193.
[6] *Ibid.*, pp. 194f.; *cf.* also pp. 209f.
[7] *Ibid.*, p. 196.

APPENDIX C: THE AUTHORITIES OF ROMANS 13:1

that although they had formerly been enemies they have now become 'ministering spirits sent forth for ministry' (Heb. 1:14)".[8]

In dealing with this thesis it is proper, first of all, to take account of those features of Paul's usage which might lend support to this interpretation of the ἐξουσίαι in Rom. 13:1. It is true that on several occasions this term is used of angelic beings, sometimes viewed as good and sometimes as evil (Eph. 3:10; 6:12; Col. 1:16; 2:15; *cf.* I Pet. 3:22). In the use of the singular there is reference to satanic authority in Eph. 2:2; Col. 1:13 (*cf.* Acts 26:18). In those passages which refer to the exalted lordship of Christ there is surely allusion to suprahuman agents (Eph. 1:21; Col. 2:10; *cf.* Phil. 2:9-11). In I Cor. 15:24, where the final subjugation of all enemies is in view, suprahuman authorities are likewise contemplated. It should also be observed that in such connections the term "authority" is coordinated with the term "principality" (ἀρχή) (Eph. 1:21; 6:12; Col. 1:16; 2:10, 15). In Tit. 3:1, which is closely parallel to Rom. 13:1, Paul uses "principalities" as well as "authorities" in designating magisterial agents.

But, secondly, while it is to be admitted that the term in question (ἐξουσίαι or the pluralistic use of the singular) has suprahuman reference in several instances, yet Cullmann's thesis is not borne out by the evidence. In criticism the following considerations may be pleaded.

1. Cullmann bases his argument upon the use of the plural.[9] But the use of the singular is not totally irrelevant to the question at issue. The argument must take account of the diversity that applies to the use of the singular. The latter is used frequently without reference to suprahuman agency.[10] To say the least, why should not the plural likewise be used without any allusion to invisible angelic beings? It is necessary to preface our examination of the evidence with this caution.

2. Cullmann is confident that in I Cor. 6:3 there is reference to invisible angelic powers. "For it is only on this assumption that it has any meaning when Paul justifies his admonition to the

---

[8] *Ibid.*, p. 198; *cf.* also by Cullmann: *The State in the New Testament* (New York, 1956), p. 66 and the "Excursus" in the same volume, pp. 95–114.
[9] See citations in n. 6.
[10] *Cf.* Matt. 8:9; 10:1; Mark 13:34; Luke 19:7; 23:7; John 1:12; I Cor. 7:37; 8:9; 9:4; 11:10; II Thess. 3:9.

Church, to avoid the State courts in trials among Christians, by reference to the fact that the members of the Church will judge the 'angels' at the end of the days".[11] This assumption is based on far too precarious exegesis. The appeal to the fact that the saints will judge angels is adequately, if not fully, explained by what lies on the face of the text. It is in effect an *a fortiori* argument. If the saints are to judge angels, how much more should they be competent to settle disputes pertaining to things of this life. This only exemplifies the arbitrariness of what Cullmann propounds as proof.

3. I Cor. 2:6, 8, to which Cullmann also appeals with such confidence, does not offer the support required. The rulers of this age who are coming to nought (vs. 6) and who crucified the Lord of glory (vs. 8) cannot be shown, on the basis of the New Testament, to be angelic powers. Nowhere else does the New Testament attribute the *crucifixion* to angelic beings. It does charge men and particularly the rulers with this crime (Acts 2:23; 3:17; 4:26–28; 13:27). It is significant that the same term for rulers is used (Acts 3:17; 4:26; 13:27) as is used in I Cor. 2:6, 8. The relevant evidence, therefore, would identify the rulers of this age as the human potentates who were the agents of the crucifixion. Although in Eph. 2:2 Paul uses this term ruler (ἄρχων) with reference to Satan (*cf.* John 12:31; 14:30; 16:11), apart from the text in question (I Cor. 2:6, 8) and Rom. 13:3, he uses it in no other instance. In the Gospels it is frequently used of human rulers (*cf.* Matt. 9:18; 20:25; Luke 12:58; 23:13; 24:20; John 3:1; 7:26, 48; 12:42). Thus the usage of the New Testament does not indicate that the rulers of this age in I Cor. 2:6, 8 are conceived of as invisible principalities. The usage points in another direction. Again, one of the main props of Cullmann's contention is shown to fall short of the proof claimed for it.

4. Though Christ triumphed over the principalities and powers (Col. 2:15) and wrought judgment upon the prince of this world (John 12:31; Heb. 2:14), yet in Paul's teaching Satan and the demonic powers are exceedingly active in opposition to the kingdom of God (*cf.* II Cor. 4:4; Eph. 6:12). According to Paul's teaching here in Rom. 13:1–7 the governing authorities are represented as God's ministers to promote good and restrain evil

---

[11] *Christ and Time*, p. 193.

APPENDIX C: THE AUTHORITIES OF ROMANS 13:1

and are, therefore, directed against Satanic and demonic influences.[12] Evil powers are represented as subjugated but nowhere are they credited with well-doing. Besides, if the "authorities" are angelic beings that once were evil and now subjugated to Christ and ministers of God, what possible principle of differentiation can be applied to this order of beings whereby this dual and antithetical role can be predicated of the same order of principalities? There is no place for this differentiation in Paul's writings. In the words of Franz J. Leenhardt: "These demonic powers are always presented by the apostle as evil and maleficent. Christ has fought against them and conquered them: He has not placed them in His service, but has rendered them powerless to harm the elect who in spite of everything have still to struggle against them with the strength which Christ the Victor supplies. How can we conceive of these powers as being converted and becoming servants of the good? How could believers be exhorted to obey powers which they have still to fight against? How could Paul himself, who has just mentioned (ch. 8) the powers which seek to separate the believer from his Lord, regard these same powers as the basis of a useful authority worthy of conscientious obedience on the part of the believer?"[13] If the "authorities" were regarded as unfallen angels there would be much more plausibility to the thesis in question. But this is not Cullmann's position. These are "demonic beings" who in the time before Christ *"were destined to be subjected through Jesus Christ"*[14] and now are in subjection to him, "elevated to the highest dignity by the function that is here assigned to them".[15]

5. I Pet. 2:13–17 is closely parallel to Rom. 13:1–7.[16] But Peter calls civil magistracy a "human ordinance" (*ἀνθρωπίνη κτίσις*). This characterization militates against Cullmann's thesis. For even though he recognizes that there is the State behind which stand the angelic powers this designation of Peter stands in opposition to any supposition of angelic composition.

6. In Luke 12:11 the terms "principalities" (*ἀρχαί*) and "authorities" (*ἐξουσίαι*) are used with reference to human rulers.

---

[12] *Cf.* Barrett: *op. cit.*, p. 249.
[13] *Op. cit.*, p. 329, n.
[14] *Christ and Time*, p. 209.
[15] *Ibid.*, p. 202.
[16] Cullmann calls it the "first exegesis of this Pauline passage" (*ibid.*, p. 197).

This clear instance indicates that the plural of both terms can be used for human authorities. It would require the most conclusive evidence to establish the thesis that when these same terms are used with reference to the political power, as in Rom. 13:1; Tit. 3:1, there are not only the human agents but also invisible angelic powers. The arguments advanced by Cullmann are not sufficient to establish his thesis. It is significant that notwithstanding the vigour of his contention the concluding word of his "Excursus" is that the thesis "is an hypothesis, and naturally we can never say with final certainty that Paul had in mind not only the secular sense of the word ἐξουσίαι, but also the meaning which he himself attributes to it in all other passages. I can only wish, however, that all other hypotheses which we necessarily must use in the field of New Testament science were as well grounded as this one".[17]

---

[17] *The State in the New Testament*, p. 114.

APPENDIX D

ROMANS 14:5 AND THE WEEKLY SABBATH

The question is whether the weekly Sabbath comes within the scope of the distinction respecting days on which the apostle reflects in Romans 14:5. If so then we have to reckon with the following implications.

1. This would mean that the Sabbath commandment in the decalogue does not continue to have any binding obligation upon believers in the New Testament economy. The observance of one day in seven as holy and invested with the sanctity enunciated in the fourth commandment would be abrogated and would be in the same category in respect of *observance* as the ceremonial rites of the Mosaic institution. On the assumption posited, insistence upon the continued sanctity of each recurring seventh day would be as Judaizing as to demand the perpetuation of the Levitical feasts.

2. The first day of the week would have no prescribed religious significance. It would not be distinguished from any other day as the memorial of Christ's resurrection and could not properly be regarded as the Lord's day in distinction from the way in which every day is to be lived in devotion to and the service of the Lord Christ. Neither might any other day, weekly or otherwise, be regarded as set apart with this religious significance.

3. Observance of a weekly Sabbath or of a day commemorating our Lord's resurrection would be a feature of the person weak in faith and in this case he would be weak in faith because he had not yet attained to the understanding that in the Christian institution all days are in the same category. Just as one weak Christian fails to recognize that all kinds of food are clean, so another, or perchance the same person, would fail to esteem every day alike.

These implications of the thesis in question cannot be avoided. We may now proceed to examine them in the light of the considerations which Scripture as a whole provides.

1. The Sabbath institution is a creation ordinance. It did not begin to have relevance at Sinai when the ten commandments

were given to Moses on two tables (*cf.* Gen. 2:2, 3; Exod. 16:21–23). It was, however, incorporated in the law promulgated at Sinai and this we would expect in view of its significance and purpose as enunciated in Genesis 2:2, 3. It is so embedded in this covenant law that to regard it as of different character from its context in respect of abiding relevance goes counter to the unity and basic significance of what was inscribed on the two tables. Our Lord himself tells us of its purpose and claims it for his messianic Lordship (Mark 2:28). The thesis we are now considering would have to assume that the pattern provided by God himself (Gen. 2:2, 3) in the work of creation (*cf.* also Exod. 20:11; 31:17) has no longer any relevance for the regulation of man's life on earth, that only nine of the ten words of the decalogue have authority for Christians, that the beneficent design contemplated in the original institution (Mark 2:28) has no application under the gospel, and that the lordship Christ exercised over the Sabbath was for the purpose of abolishing it as an institution to be observed. These are the necessary conclusions to be drawn from the assumption in question. There is no evidence to support any of these conclusions, and, when they are combined and their cumulative force frankly weighed, it is then that the whole analogy of Scripture is shown to be contradicted by the assumption concerned.

2. The first day of the week as the day on which Jesus rose from the dead (Matt. 28:1; Mark 16:2, 9; Luke 24:1; John 20:1, 19) is recognized in the New Testament as having a significance derived from this fact of Jesus' resurrection (Acts 20:7; I Cor. 16:2) and this is the reason why John speaks of it as the Lord's day (Rev. 1:10). It is the one day of the week to which belongs this distinctive religious significance. Since it occurs every seventh day, it is a perpetually recurring memorial with religious intent and character proportionate to the place which Jesus' resurrection occupies in the accomplishment of redemption. The two pivotal events in this accomplishment are the death and resurrection of Christ and the two memorial ordinances of the New Testament institution are the Lord's supper and the Lord's day, the one memorializing Jesus' death and the other his resurrection. If Paul in Romans 14:5 implies that all distinctions of days have been obliterated, then there is no room for the distinctive significance of the first day of the week as the Lord's day. The evidence

APPENDIX D: ROMANS 14:5 AND THE WEEKLY SABBATH

supporting the memorial character of the first day is not to be controverted and, consequently, in this respect also the assumption in question cannot be entertained, namely, that all religious distinction of days is completely abrogated in the Christian economy.

3. In accord with the analogy of Scripture and particularly the teaching of Paul, Romans 14:5 can properly be regarded as referring to the ceremonial holy days of the Levitical institution. The obligation to observe these is clearly abrogated in the New Testament. They have no longer relevance or sanction and the situation described in Romans 14:5 perfectly accords with what Paul would say with reference to religious scrupulosity or the absence of such anent these days. Paul was not insistent upon the discontinuance of ritual observances of the Levitical ordinances as long as the observance was merely one of religious custom and not compromising the gospel(*cf.* Acts 18:18, 21; 21:20–27). He himself circumcised Timothy from considerations of expediency. But in a different situation he could write: "Behold, I Paul say unto you, that if ye be circumcised, Christ will profit you nothing" (Gal. 5:2). Ceremonial feast days fall into the category of which the apostle could say: "One man esteemeth one day above another: another esteemeth every day *alike*". Many Jews would not yet have understood all the implications of the gospel and had still a scrupulous regard for these Mosaic ordinances. Of such scruples we know Paul to have been thoroughly tolerant and they fit the precise terms of the text in question. There is no need to posit anything that goes beyond such observances. To place the Lord's day and the weekly Sabbath in the same category is not only beyond the warrant of exegetical requirements but brings us into conflict with principles that are embedded in the total witness of Scripture. An interpretation that involves such contradiction cannot be adopted. Thus the abiding sanctity of each recurring seventh day as the memorial of God's rest in creation and of Christ's exaltation in his resurrection is not to be regarded as in any way impaired by Romans 14:5.

APPENDIX E

THE WEAK BROTHER

It has been common in our modern context to apply the teaching of Paul in Romans 14 to the situation that arises from excess in the use of certain things, especially the excess of drunkenness. The person addicted to excess is called the "weak brother" and those not thus addicted are urged to abstain from the use of that thing out of deference to the weakness of the intemperate. The temperate are alleged to be guilty of placing a stumblingblock in the way of the intemperate because by their use of the thing in question they are said to place before the weak an inducement or perchance temptation to indulgence of his vice.

It will soon become apparent that this application is a complete distortion of Paul's teaching and it is an example of the looseness with which Scripture is interpreted and applied.

1. Paul is not dealing with the question of excess in the use of certain kinds of food or drink. This kind of abuse does not come within his purview in this passage or in the other passages in I Corinthians. The weak of Romans 14 are not those given to excess. They are the opposite; they are total abstainers from certain articles of food. The "weak" addicted to excess do not abstain; they take too much.

2. The "weakness" of those who go to excess is in an entirely different category from that of which Paul treats in this instance. The "weakness" of excess is iniquity and with those who are guilty of this sin Paul deals in entirely different terms. Drunkards, for example, will not inherit the kingdom of God (I Cor. 6:10) and Paul enjoins that if any one called a brother is a drunkard with such an one believers are not to keep company or even eat (I Cor. 5:11). How different is Romans 14:1: "Him that is weak in faith receive ye". Is it not apparent what havoc is done to interpretation of Scripture and to the criteria by which the purity and unity of the church are to be maintained when the weak of Romans 14 are confused with the intemperate and drunkards?

APPENDIX E: THE WEAK BROTHER

3. Even when we consider the case of one converted from a life of excess and still afflicted with temptation to his old vice, we do not have a situation that is parallel to Romans 14. It is true that sometimes for such a person the cost of sobriety is total abstinence. Every proper consideration should be given and measure used by stronger believers to support and fortify him against the temptation to which he is liable to succumb. But his "weakness" is not that of the weak in the circumstance with which Paul deals. The latter is the weakness of conscientious scruple, the former is that of tendency to excess and conscientious religious scruple does not describe or define his situation.

4. There is the case of a person who has been converted from excess in some particular. It sometimes happens that such a person comes to entertain a religious scruple against the use of that particular which had previously been the occasion of vice and perhaps debauchery. Thus on religious grounds he becomes a total abstainer. He has made an erroneous judgment and has failed to make a proper analysis of responsibility for his former excesses. But the fact remains that on religious grounds he abstains from the use of the particular thing concerned. He is weak in faith and is thus in the category of the weak in Romans 14. The injunctions to the strong would thus apply in this instance. The past excess enters into this situation, however, only as explaining the reason for his religious scruple, and there is no ground for thinking that the origin of the scruples entertained by the weak at Rome was of this character. But the weakness, in the illustration given, is still that of wrongly entertained scruple. It is that religious scruple that the strong must take into account in their relations to this person and not at all his tendency to excess. There is no tendency to excess in the case posited.

It is obvious, therefore, that Paul's teaching in this chapter turns on scruple arising from religious conviction. This is the principle on which the interpretation rests and in terms of which application is relevant. To apply Paul's teaching to situations in which this religious involvement is absent is to extend the exhortations beyond their reference and intent and is, therefore, a distortion of the teaching concerned.

APPENDIX F

THE INTEGRITY OF THE EPISTLE

The question respecting integrity pertains almost entirely to chapters 15 and 16 of the epistle. Hypotheses divergent from the traditional view that these chapters belonged to the epistle Paul addressed to the Roman church have not always been based on the textual data. But, as the discussion proceeds in the last few decades, hypotheses and opinions advanced are to a large extent related to the textual variants. The most important data can be briefly summarized in order that various questions may be placed in focus in relation to the relevant evidence.

1. At 1:7 ἐν ‘Ρώμῃ is omitted by G, a Graeco-Latin manuscript of the tenth century. The margins of the minuscules 1739 and 1908 indicate that "in Rome" did not appear in Origen's text and commentary. There is also evidence in other Latin texts that "in Rome" had been restored to the corrupted text represented by G with the result that a combination of both is effected.

2. At 1:15 G again omits τοῖς ἐν ‘Ρώμῃ and what T. W. Manson calls the "patchwork" in D,[1] a sixth century bilingual, may well attest, as he and others suggest, that the ancestor of both D and G omitted reference to Rome at 1:7, 15.[2]

3. Preponderant evidence supports the ending of chapter 14 with verse 23. But in L, an eighth century uncial, in the minuscules 104, 1175, and in manuscripts known to Origen the doxology of 16:25–27 appears at this point after verse 23.

4. In the uncials A and P and in minuscules 5 and 33 the doxology appears after 14:23 and at the end of the epistle (16:25–27).

5. In G the doxology does not appear at all; but after 14:23 there is a space which probably indicated that the scribe was aware of the doxology and left enough space for its insertion. Marcion's text also omitted the doxology and ended with 14:23.

---

[1] T. W. Manson: *Studies in the Gospels and Epistles*, Manchester, 1962, p. 229.
[2] *Cf.* F. F. Bruce: *Romans,* as cited, p. 26.

APPENDIX F: THE INTEGRITY OF THE EPISTLE

6. In P[46], the third century papyrus, the doxology of 16:25–27 occurs after 15:33 and not at the end of the epistle. This is the only witness for insertion at this point. But the early date of P[46] has led some to attach considerable weight to this reading.

7. There is some evidence that recensions of the epistle came to an end with the doxology after 14:23. Particularly significant is codex Amiatinus of the Vulgate which from its chapter divisions and summaries would indicate that the final chapter, number 51, comprised the doxology which immediately followed what is dealt with in 14:13–23 as chapter 50.

It is not necessary to review a great many of the theories that have been propounded. For example, E. Renan's theory of a quadripartite epistle on the basis of what he alleges to be four distinct endings (15:33; 16:20; 16:24; 16:25–27) has been so thoroughly dealt with and in its main contentions so effectively refuted by J. B. Lightfoot (*cf. Biblical Essays* [London, 1893], pp. 293–311) that it would be wasteful expenditure of space to repeat the arguments. Suffice it to say that Lightfoot's masterful treatment of relevant data must always be taken into account in dealing with the questions at stake.

It needs to be stated at the outset that as far as the textual evidence is concerned there is no ground for disputing the genuineness of the text "in Rome" (1:7), "who are in Rome" (1:15), the doxology (16:25–27). The only questions requiring discussion are those that arise from the omission of reference to Rome in some authorities at 1:7, 15 and the different positions which the doxology occupies in the traditions referred to above. Though the doxology does not appear in G and though Marcion's text did not contain it, this does not give any ground for assailing its genuineness as Pauline.

It is not difficult to discover reasons for Marcion's recension, namely, the exclusion of all that follows 14:23. It is apparent that 15:1–13 is continuous with 14:1–23. But no texts in Paul are more antithetical to Marcion's depreciation of the Old Testament than 15:4, 8, 9. The same applies to 16:26.[3]

The evidence does indicate that a shorter recension of the epistle was in circulation. Codex Amiatinus, as referred to above, is an example of this type of text. Furthermore, Cyprian in his

---

[3] *Cf.* Manson: *op. cit.*, p. 230.

Testimonia, in which he gives "an arsenal of proof texts for various dogmas",[4] does not clearly adduce texts from Romans 15 and 16 even though some of these are directly germane to some of his headings.[5] Likewise Tertullian in his books *Against Marcion* does not quote from these two chapters even though, as F. F. Bruce observes, they are "full of potential anti-Marcionite ammunition"[6] and, after quoting 14:10, Tertullian also says that this comes in the closing section of the epistle.[7] This kind of evidence would favour the view that the shorter recension ended with 14:23 with or without the doxology of 16:25-27. The question arises: how is this shorter recension to be explained?

Scholars of the highest repute, without disputing the genuineness of chapters 15 and 16 as Pauline, have taken the position that Paul himself was responsible for the discrepancy between the longer and shorter forms in which the epistle was in circulation. J. B. Lightfoot took the position that Paul first wrote the epistle in the longer form, including chapters 15 and 16, and addressed it to the church at Rome. But since "the epistle, though not a circular epistle itself, yet manifested the general and comprehensive character which might be expected in such" and therefore "is more of a treatise than a letter",[8] Paul himself made it also available as a circular or general letter and thus omitted the two last chapters in order to divest it of personal matter and make it suitable for the churches in general. This circular letter, Lightfoot supposes, omitted the reference to Rome in 1:7, 15 and added the doxology which is now found in most manuscripts and versions at the end of the epistle but which, he thinks, did not belong to the original letter addressed to Rome.

It would not be prejudicial to the Pauline authorship of the received text of the epistle to accept this hypothesis. But on the premises assumed by Lightfoot there is one formidable, if not insurmountable, objection to the supposition. This objection has been advanced by several competent critics and is to the effect that 14:1-23 and 15:1-13 are so much of a unit that for Paul to divide his own work at 14:23 would be most unnatural. In the

---

[4] Kirsopp Lake: *The Earlier Epistles of St. Paul*, London, 1927, p. 337.
[5] *Cf.* Lake: *ibid.*, pp. 337f.
[6] *Op. cit.*, p. 27.
[7] *Cf.* Lake: *op. cit.*, pp. 338f.
[8] *Op. cit.*, p. 315.

APPENDIX F: THE INTEGRITY OF THE EPISTLE

words of Sanday and Headlam: "There is nothing in the next thirteen verses [15:1–13] which unfits them for general circulation. They are in fact more suitable for an encyclical letter than is chap. xiv. It is to us inconceivable that St. Paul should have himself mutilated his own argument by cutting off the conclusion of it."[9]

In view of the unity of 14:1–23 and 15:1–13 more reasonable would be the hypothesis that the shorter recension, ending at 14:23 and omitting reference to Rome in 1:7, 15, was the original in the form of a general epistle. When the other two chapters were added and the whole addressed to the church at Rome, the insertion of "Rome" at 1:7, 15 could be readily understood and 15:1–13 could be regarded as a necessary and fitting expansion of the theme dealt with in 14:1–23, especially of 14:13–23.[10] To this hypothesis also there is the decided objection that the elimination of reference to Rome in 1:7, 15 does not remove the definiteness of destination involved in 1:8–15. A circular or general epistle would include churches that Paul had visited and it is apparent that these verses have in view a community that he had not yet visited. The fact is simply that the omission of Rome at 1:7, 15 does not remove the notices in 1:8–15 which militate against the hypothesis of a circular Pauline recension.[11]

Since the evidence indicates that a text ending at 14:23 existed in the third century, how are we to explain this abridged edition of the epistle? For the reasons given above and in T. W. Manson's words, "It cannot be the work of the author".[12] Surely no hypothesis has more in its support than that the circulation in this mutilated form was due to the work of Marcion. We have Origen's word for it that Marcion cut out everything after 14:23.[13] There is no reason to doubt that Marcion's excised text could have exercised sufficient influence to explain the form in which the epistle was in circulation in certain areas. This may have been the text in the hands of Tertullian. But it is not inconceivable that Tertullian was acquainted with the longer text and yet

---

[9] *Op. cit.*, p. xcv; *cf.* also F. J. A. Hort's detailed analysis of Lightfoot's theory in *Biblical Essays*, as cited above, pp. 321–351.
[10] *Cf.* Lake: *op. cit.*, pp. 362–365.
[11] *Cf.* Hort: *op. cit.*, pp. 347–350 for his summation of the argument against two Pauline recensions.
[12] *Op. cit.*, p. 233.
[13] *Cf.* Bruce: *op. cit.*, p. 27; Manson: *op. cit.*, p. 233; and, for fuller defence, Sanday and Headlam: *op. cit.*, pp. xcvi–xcviii.

refrained from appeal to chapters 15 and 16 in his books against Marcion for the reason that Marcion did not include these chapters in the *corpus* of Paul's epistles.

There is still another hypothesis respecting the last two chapters of Romans, particularly as it concerns the doxology and chapter 16. For more than a hundred years it has been contended that 16:1–23 was not addressed to the church at Rome but to the church at Ephesus. This was the thesis of E. Renan. But the contention was not original with him.[14] The discovery of the papyrus manuscript P[46] has given new impetus to the hypothesis for, as noted, P[46] adds the doxology of 16:25–27 at the end of chapter 15 and in this respect is the sole witness to this location. On this basis T. W. Manson concludes that "we should regard P[46] as offering in chapters i–xv the form in which the epistle was received at Rome; and, what is perhaps more important, its text should be taken as descended from the pre-Marcionite Roman text of the letter".[15] But as Sir Frederic Kenyon says, "it would be dangerous to adopt this conjecture without confirmation, and it is possible that the variable position (*i.e.* of the doxology) is due to its being treated like a doxology to a hymn, and being read at the end of xiv. or xv., when xvi., which is mainly a string of names, was omitted".[16]

It is necessary now to pay some attention to the supposition that chapter 16:1–23 is a letter or part of a letter to Ephesus. Various arguments have been pleaded in support of the Ephesian destination. These have been well summed up most recently by F. F. Bruce, though not himself defending the hypothesis.[17] J. B. Lightfoot subjected the thesis of E. Renan to thorough analysis and has probably presented the case for the Roman destination more fully and competently than any other.[18] For succinctness and

---

[14] *Cf.* Manson: *op. cit.*, pp. 231, 234 for the references to R. Schumacher and David Schulz.

[15] *Op. cit.*, p. 236. On this view it would be only chapter 15 that Marcion struck from his text of the epistle and the references to Rome in 1:7, 15. Leaving Marcion out of account, then the main question would be to explain the two types of text, the Roman of fifteen chapters and what Manson calls the Egyptian of sixteen (*cf. ibid.*, p. 237).

[16] *Our Bible and the Ancient Manuscripts*, Revised by A. W. Adams, London, 1958, p. 189.

[17] *Op. cit.*, pp. 266f.

[18] *Op. cit.*, pp. 294–306; *cf.* also Lightfoot's *St. Paul's Epistle to the Philippians*, London, 1908, pp. 171–178. Though Lake deems the case for the Roman

APPENDIX F: THE INTEGRITY OF THE EPISTLE

persuasiveness no statement of the case for Rome surpasses that of F. F. Bruce.[19]

The most plausible argument for Ephesus is that concerned with the mention of Prisca and Aquila and the church in their house (16:3, 5). Paul first met Prisca and Aquila at Corinth. They had recently come from Rome because of Claudius' edict (Acts 18:2). When Paul departed from Corinth after eighteen months (Acts 18:11) or possibly longer (Acts 18:18), he was accompanied by Prisca and Aquila and when he came to Ephesus he left them there (Acts 18:18, 19). When Paul wrote I Corinthians from Ephesus (I Cor. 16:8) Prisca and Aquila were still there and Paul again refers to the church in their house (I Cor. 16:19). By the time II Timothy was written they were again in Ephesus (II Tim. 4:19); at least they were not in Rome. The argument for residence in Ephesus, when Romans 16:3, 5 was penned, rests on the relatively brief interval between the date of I Corinthians and that of Romans. On certain calculations it is possible that the time elapsing was too brief to allow for a journey back to Rome and the establishment of the kind of residence there that Romans 16:3, 5 presupposes. But it is compatible with the known facts to interpose a period of approximately a year and on other reckonings more than a year. Aquila belonged to Pontus. Prisca and Aquila came from Rome after the edict of Claudius. They left Corinth with Paul and stayed in Ephesus. These migrations are of themselves indicative of the mobility of this couple and there is no reason to suppose that they had not returned to Rome. In view of their having come from Rome and their occupation as tentmakers it would have been easy to set up residence and business there again. In fact, a branch business in Rome may have required their return. In F. F. Bruce's words, "Tradespeople like Priscilla and Aquila led very mobile lives in those days, and there is nothing improbable or unnatural about

---

hypothesis comparatively weak, except for the tradition, yet he adds: "Still, the fact always remains that Rom. xvi. 1–23 is an integral part of all MSS. of the Epistle which we now possess. Thus the earliest tradition which we have connects it with Rome, not with Ephesus. This is not everything, but it is a great deal. Probably it is enough to prevent the Ephesian hypothesis from ever being unanimously accepted, and rightly so, for it can never be proven fully" (*op. cit.*, p. 334).
[19] *Op. cit.*, pp. 267–270.

their moving back and forth in this way between Rome, Corinth and Ephesus".[20]

The case for the integrity of the epistle as that addressed by Paul to the church at Rome may be summed up in the following observations.

1. The evidence clearly supports the Pauline authorship of chapters 15 and 16, including the doxology of 16:25–27.

2. The Pauline authorship of the doxology would not be in question even if it were placed after 15:33. It would be a fitting conclusion at this point. In that event chapter 16 would be an appendix largely devoted to greetings.

3. The only authority favouring this location for the doxology is P[46]. This is not enough to pit against the preponderant evidence for 16:25–27. Besides, it is contrary to Paul's uniform pattern to close an epistle without a benediction. Since there is not sufficient support for the benediction of 16:24, it would be a complete departure from Paul's custom to end an epistle with 16:23. The doxology is, indeed, a departure from pattern in that it is doxology and not a benediction. But its consonance as to content with the epistle as a whole, the distinctive character of the epistle itself, the analogy of 11:33–36 as the conclusion to a well-defined segment of the epistle, and the occurrence of benedictions at 15:13; 15:33 and 16:20 are considerations which combine to show the appropriateness of such a lengthy doxology at the end rather than the customary brief benediction.

4. If the doxology were placed after 15:33, this would constitute an additional argument for the genuineness of 16:24 and would remove the anomaly of an ending without a benediction. But the evidence for the doxology at an earlier point is not sufficient.

5. There is no good reason for positing Ephesus as the destination of 16:1–23. Thus we may conclude that the traditional position as supported by the preponderant evidence must continue to be accepted.

---

[20] *Ibid.*, p. 268.

INDEX OF CHIEF SUBJECTS

Adiaphora, 192
Adoption, of Israel, 4f.; adoptive relation, 11
Advent, of Christ, 167 ff.
Age, "world", 113f.
Apostasy, 88, 192; of Israel, 68ff., 79f., 98
Apostle of the gentiles (see also Contents), 79f.
Asceticism, 173
Authorities, 147f., 252 ff.
Blessing, 134f.
Body, 110f.; of sin, 111f.
Calling, 20, 37, 88; effectual call, 19, 37
Church, body of Christ, 119f.; house church, 228f, 238
Circumcision, 205
"Communism", 120
Compassion, 25f.
Confession, and faith, 54f.; and good works, 56; with the mouth, 57
Conscience, 2, 154, 196
Consummation, 165ff., 169, 185 (see also Contents)
Conversion, of Israel (and the Gentiles), 79, 84, 96, 99, 102, 168
Counsel, 47
Covenant, 9, 26, 38, 52, 62, 89, 93, 100; Abrahamic, xivf.; 12, 43, 205f.; of the fathers, 5, 90, 99, 101
Creator, 108

Days, observance of, 172–178; the Lord's Day, 257 ff.
Death, believer's attitude to, 181f.
Decalogue, 161f.
Diaconate, 124f., 126
Differentiation, 42, 47, 67, 69, 71f., 73
Discrimination, God's sovereign, 12ff., 18, 26, 32, 69; of love, 129
Disobedience, 102f., of the Gentiles, 102; of Israel, 63f., 65f., 101
Divinity, of Christ, 245 ff.

Eating and not eating, 173–185
Edom (ites), 20ff.

Elect, of Israel, 94, 97; of the Gentiles 94f.
Election, 14–19, 21, 24, 26, 37, 42, 67–73, 101
"End of the law", 49f.
Eschatology, see Consummation
Ethics, 110, 162
Exhortation, 125, 200

Faith, 44f, 54, 55f., 58, 60, 63, 87f., 142, 196; and the exercise of gifts, 118f., 122f.; see also Gentiles; for "righteousness of faith", see Contents
Fear, 156
Foreknowledge, 68, 70
Fulness (see also Contents), 105

Gentiles (see also Contents), xv, 37f., 39f., 44, 62ff., 77; intimate association with Jews, 86f.; faith of, 42f., 87ff.; salvation of, 76f., 79ff., 85, 90
Gifts, 121–127, 130
Giving, 125f.
Glory, 35ff., 185, 204
Gospel, 55, 240f.
Gospel proclamation, and the Word of Christ, 58f., 61; those appointed to the task, 59
Government, in the church, 126f.
Grace, 50ff., 63, 69ff., 90, 102, 105, 117f.
Grafting, practice of, 85f.

Hardening, 28ff., 31, 72f., 87, 92ff., 95, 97ff.
Hate, hatred, meaning of, 21ff., 74 (note)
Heart, and religious consciousness, 55
History, redemptive, 90
Holiness, 112
Holy spirit, 2, 107, 110, 112, 120, 130, 213, 221
Hope, 131ff., 200, 207
Hospitality, 133f.

Ignorance, as an excuse, 49

269

INDEX OF CHIEF SUBJECTS

Incomprehensibility, of God's counsel, 104
Israel (see also Contents), xivf., 9ff., 17f., 23f., 37, 39f., 41ff., 44, 46, 48f., 53, 60, 62f.

Jews and gentiles, see Contents
Judaism, 146
Judgment, 102, 106, 142, 149, 168, 176f., 184f., 187, 250
Justice, 25ff., 30, 88, 153, 161
Justification, 50, 56, 250

Kingdom, God's, 93ff., 193
Knowledge, 48, 63, 209; God's, 105ff.

Law, 139, 164: Christ and, 50f.; "law of love", 160f.; Mosaic, 50f.; purpose of, 49f.; and righteousness, 43, 50ff., 249ff.; royal, 165 Legalism, 51f., 172f., appendix B Liberty, in Christ, 193, 195f.
Longsuffering, 33ff.
Lordship, of Christ, 6, 170, 176, 180, 181ff., 245ff. A, 258; the confession of, 55; and the worship belonging to God, 57
Love (see also Contents), 186, 192; character of, 128f.; of Christ, 191; electing, 69; of God for Jacob, 21f.

Magistrate (see also Contents), 137f., 140f.
Majesty, of God, 31
Mercy, 25ff., 28ff., 33, 66, 72, 95, 102f., 105
Ministry, 123f., 127, 210
Miracle, 212f.
Mystery, 92, 97, 241ff.

Norms, of conduct, 138f.

Patriarchs, as the "root", 85
Peace, 139f., 224, 237
Perdition, eternal, 192
Persecution, 134
Perseverance, 88, 132
Prayer, 132, 222
Predestination, 37
Prohibitionism, 188f.
Promise, 12, 14, 18, 24f., 38f., 42, 66, 205
Prophecy, in the apostolic church, 122f.

Redeemer, 99 (note), 110
Rejection, of Israel, 66f., 75, 81, 85, 87, 90, 100, 105

Remnant (see also Contents), of Israel, 40ff., 75, 78, 86, 93f., 97f., 101
Responsibility, human, 42
Restoration, of Israel, 79ff., 94f., 97ff., 100f., 168 (see also Contents)
Resurrection, 182, 258; "life from the dead", 82ff.
Revolution, 150
Righteousness, 71f., 194; election and, 72; of faith, 51ff., 101 (see also Contents); of God, 46, 48ff., 63, 73; of the Gentiles, 43; of Israel, 73; and law, 51f., 249ff.

Sabbath, 257ff.
Saints, needs of the, 133f.
Salvation, 55f., 72, 90, 102ff., 165, 167, 169; Israel's 79f., 98f., 101; of Jew and Gentile, 102; of Gentiles, 206
Sanctification, 109f., 116f., 143; practical aspects of, 128; "second blessing", 114
Scripture(s), 199ff.; Paul's use of, 25, 27
Seed, meaning of, 41f.
Sin, 113, 162, 250
Sovereignty, 27f., 30, 41, 107, 180; of Christ, 183
Stumbling-block, 187ff.
Sword, 152f.

Taxes, 154ff.
Teaching, office of, 125
Trespass (for "fall") of Israel, 76ff. 87

Unbelief, 87; and Christ's resurrection, 54; of Israel, 105; and revelation, 53
Unclean, 188f.
Union, with Christ, 1f., 109f., 188

Vengeance, 141–144

Weak and strong, see Contents, 260ff.
Will, Christ's, 201; of commandment, 114ff.; God's, 28ff., 31f., 34, 37, 41f., 47, 70, 72f., 106, 139, 149, 180, 193, 223; man's, 26, 42, 70
Wisdom, God's, 105f.
Wrath, 33ff., 88, 140f., 153

Zeal, 63; character of, 48f.

INDEX OF PERSONS AND PLACES

Abraham, xiii ff., 5f., 8ff., 24, 38, 65ff., 205f., 242
Achaia, 214ff., 218f., 222
Adam, 250
Adriatic, 214
Agrippa, 230
Ampliatus, 225, 229ff., 239
Andronicus, 225, 229
Antioch in Syria, 213
Apelles, 225, 230
Apollos, 227
Aquila, xi, 225, 227ff., 232, 267
Aristobulus, 225, 230f.
Asia, 225, 229
Assyria, 40
Asyncritus, 226

Baal, 65, 69, 72
Babylon, 59
Benjamin, 65ff.

Cenchreae, 225f.
Claudius, 146, 228, 230, 267
Colossae, 173, 178, 235
Corinth, 214, 217, 226ff., 238f., 267f.
Crispus, 239

David, 6, 65, 73, 132

Eden, 113
Edom, 17, 20f.
Egypt, 27f.
Elijah, 65, 68ff.
Epaenetus, 225, 229, 231
Ephesus, 217, 227ff., 266ff.
Erastus, 238f.
Esau, 8, 13, 16f., 20ff., 37

Gaius (Titius Justus?), 238f.
Galatia, 173, 178
Gaul, 217
Gomorrah, 40

Hagar, 13
Hermas, 226
Hermes, 226
Herod, 231, 252
Herod (King of Chalcis), 230
Herod the Great, 230
Herodion, 225, 229, 231
Hosea, 38

Illyria, 214
Illyricum, 208, 214, 216
Isaac, 6, 8ff.
Isaiah, 39, 73
Ishmael, 10ff.
Italy, 227

Jacob, 4, 6, 8f., 13, 16f., 20ff., 37, 40
Jason, 229, 238
Jerusalem, 208, 213ff.
Jesse, 203, 206, 219
John, 112
John of Patmos, 258
Judaea, 214, 221f., 230
Judas, 128, 232
Julia, 226, 232
Junias, 225, 229

Lucius, 229, 238
Lydia, 227

Macedonia, 214ff., 218f., 222
Mark, 231
Mary, 225, 229
Moses, 24f., 27f., 46, 50ff., 62, 73, 258

Narcissus, 225, 230f.
Nathanael, 9
Nereus, 226

Olympas, 226

Patrobas, 226
Persis, 225, 229, 231
Peter, 146, 149f., 168, 232
Pharaoh, 24, 27ff., 34
Philippi, 227
Philologus, 226, 232
Phlegon, 226
Phoebe, 225ff.
Pilate, 252
Pontus, 267
Prisca (Priscilla), xi, 225, 227ff., 232, 267

Quartus, 238f.

Rebecca, 8, 13f., 16, 20, 23f.
Red Sea, 28
Rome, xif., 121, 146, 174, 178, 204, 208f., 215ff., 226ff., 234ff., 240, 262ff.

INDEX OF PERSONS AND PLACES

Rufus, 225, 231

Sarah, 8
Saul of Tarsus, 66
Simon of Cyrene, 231
Simon the Pharisee, 232
Sinai, 5, 257
Sodom, 39f.
Sosipater, 229, 238
Spain, xii, 216f., 219

Stachys, 225, 229ff.
Stephen, 73

Tertius, 238f.
Timothy, 230, 238, 259
Titius Justus, see Gaius
Tryphaena, 225, 231
Tryphosa, 225, 231

Urbanus, 225, 230

INDEX OF AUTHORS

Adams, A. W., 266
Arndt and Gingrich, 35, 137, 160, 218, 232
Augustine, 49

Barr, J., 166
Barrett, C. K., 82, 94, 130, 159, 194, 212, 219, 221, 235, 245, 255
Barth, K., 16, 131
Berkouwer, G. C., 16
Blass and Debrunner, 3, 187
Brown, D., 84
Bruce, F. F., 3, 6, 16, 21, 96, 173, 221, 230, 233, 242, 262, 264ff.
Burton, E. De Witt, 3

Calvin, J., 4, 32f., 40, 49, 59, 66f., 84, 96f., 101, 122, 127, 140, 143, 155, 161, 194, 242
Clement of Rome, 217
Cullmann, O., 147, 252ff.
Cyprian, 263

Debrunner, A., see Blass
Delitzsch, F., 59
Dodd, C. H., 66, 167, 235, 247

Field, F., 78

Gaugler, E., 16, 66, 78
Gifford, E. H., 37, 63, 66f., 69, 73, 84, 196, 198, 204, 217, 238
Gingrich, F. W., see Arndt
Godet, F., 2, 33, 66f., 84, 131, 181, 194

Haldane, R., 67
Headlam, A. C., see Sanday
Hodge, C., 11, 21, 28, 38f., 66f., 84, 96, 122, 143, 194
Hort, F. J. A., 234, 265

Kenyon, Sir F., 266
Kittel, G. (TWNT), 218
Klassen, W., 143

Lagrange, M. J., 3, 34, 78, 82, 241
Lake, K., 264ff.
Leenhardt, F. J., 16, 61, 84, 167, 255
Liddon, H. P., 3, 11, 66f., 74f., 112, 119, 146, 150, 198
Lightfoot, J. B., 3, 114, 217, 230ff., 263ff.
Luther, M., 20, 66, 122

Manson, T. W., 262f., 265f.
Marcion, 262ff.
Metzger, B. M., 142
Meyer, H. A. W., 4, 6, 15, 38f., 50, 55, 66f., 82, 117, 127, 131, 150, 194, 217
Morison, J., 8, 16
Moule, H. C. G., 84
Murray, J., 149

Oesterley, W. O. E., 142
Origen, 262, 265

Philippi, F. A., 6, 11, 13f., 20ff., 31, 40, 52, 66f., 75, 78, 81, 84, 122, 131ff., 139, 159, 179, 191f., 194, 242
Prohl, R. C., 227

Ramsay, W. M., 86
Renan, E., 263, 266
Ridderbos, H., 16

Sanday and Headlam, 11f., 21, 33, 38, 66ff., 71, 82, 92, 98, 194, 199, 201, 214f., 217, 234, 246, 265
Schulz, D., 266
Schumacher, R., 266
Shedd, W.G.T. 122
Simpson, E. K., 183

Tertullian, 264f.
Torrey, C. C., 142

Vos, G., 82

Winer, G. B., 3, 115

INDEX OF SCRIPTURE REFERENCES
OLD TESTAMENT

GENESIS
2:2	258
2:3	258
2:7	111
2:17	111
2:21	111
2:22	111
2:23	111
3:1–6	236
3:15	237
3:19	111
4:26	57
12:3	206, 242
12:8	57
13:4	57
15:8–21	5
17:1–21	5, 205
18:10	11
18:14	11
21:8–12	13
21:12	10
21:33	57
22:18	206, 242
25:23	17, 20, 23
26:25	57
29:32	21
29:32	21
29:33	21
32:28	4
48:16	4

EXODUS
2:24	5
4:21	29
4:22	4
4:23	4
6:4	5
6:5	5
7:3	29
9:12	29
9:15	27
9:16	27
10:1	29
10:20	29
10:27	29
11:10	29
14:4	29
14:8	29
15:13–16	28
16:21–23	58
20:2	249
20:11	258
20:12	249
22:25	158
24:16	5
24:17	5
29:42–46	5
31:17	258
33:18	25
33:19	25f.
40:34–38	5

LEVITICUS
16:2	5
18:2	249
18:5	51f., 249–251
19:18	162
27:28	3
27:29	3

NUMBERS
6:27	39
12:6–8	122
14:28	185
15:17–21	85
24:19	27

DEUTERONOMY
4:6	249
4:37	16, 18
5:6	249
5:17–21	161
5:32	249
5:33	249
7:7	16, 52
7:8	16, 52
7:26	3
8:18	5
9:6	52
10:15	16, 52
11:13–15	249
11:26–28	249
13:1–5	122
13:16	3
13:18	3
14:1	4
14:2	4, 16, 52
15:15	52
18:15–22	122
21:15	21
28:1–14	249
29:4	73
29:9	52
29:29	52
30:11	52
30:12	51–54
30:13	51–54
30:14	51–55
32:9	52
32:21	62, 77n
32:35	141
32:40	185
32:43	206
33:29	52

JOSHUA
2:9	28
2:10	28
6:17	3
7:1	3
7:11	3
7:12	3
9:9	28

I SAMUEL
12:22	66

II SAMUEL
12:11	27f.
16:10	28
22:50	206

I KINGS
3:8	16
8:10	5
8:11	5
12:1	98n
18:24	57
19:10	68
19:14	68
19:18	68

II KINGS
5:11	57

II CHRONICLES
7:1	5
7:2	5
9:8	246
12:1	98n

274

INDEX OF SCRIPTURE REFERENCES OLD TESTAMENT

JOB					
1:21	246	3:4	142	51:7	78
5:11	27	3:7	137, 142, 251	52:7	59
41:11	107	3:8	251	52:15	215
		6:16	22	53:1	60
		8:1	53	54:9–10	99n
PSALMS		8:13	22	54:17	78n
1:1	129	13:24	21n	59:20–21	98ff.
1:2	129	16:4	108	60:1	99n
5:5	22	17:5	135	60:2	99n
11:5	22	25:20	136	60:3	99n, 219
11:6	142n	25:21–22	142	61:8	22
14:7	99n			62:1–4	99n
18:49	206	ECCLESIASTES		63:16	4
19:4	61	12:14	184	64:7	32, 57
19:7–11	116			64:8	4, 32
26:5	22	ISAIAH		64:9	32
28:2	133	1:9	41	65:1	62f.
28:6	133	1:14	22	65:2	62
28:7	133	2:3	219	66:18	210
31:6	22	8:9	78n	66:20	210
33:12	16	8:14	44		
37:5–13	142	10:5	40	JEREMIAH	
37:21	159	10:22	40, 70	4:22	236
37:26	158	10:23	40	11:16–17	85
67:19–20	245	11:1	219	18:1–6	32
69:9	198f.	11:10	206	31:34	99
69:21–23	73	13:15	78n	31:37	66
70:20	53	14:24	40	44:4	22
73:24–26	207	19:1	78n		
77:19	103	19:24–25	99n	EZEKIEL	
78:12–13	28	20:5	78n	1:28	5
79:6	57	25:6	219	10:2	142n
80:8–16	85n	27:13	99n	18:23	47
85:9–11	35	28:16	44f., 57	18:32	47
90:1	207	29:10	73	20:11	249
94:14	66	29:15–16	32	20:13	249
96:13	185	30:26	99n	33:11	47
98:9	185	31:4	78n		
105:1	57	31:8	78	DANIEL	
105:6	16	33:1	78n	5:1	74
105:25	28	33:20–21	99n	5:4–5	74
105:26–38	28	40:13	107	9:11	98n
105:43	16	41:8–9	16		
106:9–11	28	42:1	219	HOSEA	
116:3	58	42:25	88n	1:6	38
116:4	57f.	43:1	88n	1:10	38
116:13	57	43:20–22	16	2:23	38
117:1	206	44:1–2	16	9:15	22
125:4–5	88n	45:4	16	11:1	4
126:1–2	99n	45:9	32	14:6	85
135:4	16	45:17	99n		
136:10–15	28	45:23	184, 185n	JOEL	
139:21–22	22	46:13	99n	2:28	122
140:10	142n	48:1	4	2:32	57
		49:14–16	99n		
PROVERBS		49:18	185	AMOS	
1:20	53	50:10–11	88n	3:2	16, 68n

275

INDEX OF SCRIPTURE REFERENCES OLD TESTAMENT

3:12	41	NAHUM		MALACHI	
5:21	22	1:5–6	88n	1:1	17, 20, 22
				1:2–3	17, 20, 22f.
JONAH		HABAKKUK		1:4–5	17, 20, 22
2:2	58	1:6	27	1:6	4
				2:10	4
		ZECHARIAH		2:16	22
MICAH		8:17	22		
7:18–20	99n	11:16	27		

INDEX OF SCRIPTURE REFERENCES
NEW TESTAMENT

MATTHEW		21:42	44	15:21	231
1:21	162	21:43	76, 81	16:2	258
1:22	163n	22:14	17, 19n	16:9	258
2:12	68n	22:16–17	146		
2:22	68n	22:37–39	160	**LUKE**	
3:5	163n	23:30	133	1:6	115n
5:20	93	23:39	246	1:20	163n
5:42	158	24:6	49	1:23	155, 210
5:44	134	24:14	49	1:33	49
5:45–47	135	24:22	17	1:39	130n
5:48	116, 135	24:24	17	1:42	246
6:10	223	24:31	17	1:52	137
6:24	21	24:36	16	1:64	134
6:31–33	193	25:26	130n	1:68	134, 246
7:13	93	25:34	134	1:72	5
7:21	115	26:18	166	1:73	5
7:22	56, 167	26:52	153	1:76	106
7:23	56	26:54	205	1:77	48n
8:9	253n	27:34	73	2:14	47
8:12	76	27:46	201	2:28	134
9:16	164	27:48	73	2:34	134
9:18	82, 254	28:1	258	3:11	126n
10:1	253n	28:18	55, 180, 242, 248	4:13	166
10:15	167	28:19–20	242	4:21	163n
10:16	237			5:10	133
10:22	49, 56	**MARK**		5:22	175
10:28	192	1:15	166	6:8	175
10:34–36	139	2:21	164	6:27–28	134
10:37–38	21	2:28	258	6:35	159
11:23	53	3:26	49	7:45	232
11:25	166	6:25	130n	8:13	166
11:26	47	7:2	188	9:25	175
11:27	180	7:5	188	9:46–47	175
11:29	137	7:15	188	10:15	53
12:1	166	7:19	188	10:21	47
12:4	159	9:43	93	10:27	160
12:18	147	9:45	93	10:29–37	160
12:36	167	9:47	93	11:28	31
12:50	115, 223	11:9	246	12:8	56
15:24	205	11:10	6, 246	12:11	255
15:36	179	12:10	44	12:19	147
16:25	222	12:14	146	12:32	47
18:3	93	12:29	160	12:47	115
18:7	154	12:30–41	160, 163	12:51–53	139
18:14	115, 192, 223	12:33	115n	12:58	254
19:5	129n	13:20	17	13:3	192
20:25	254	13:22	17	13:34	93
21:9	246	13:27	17	13:35	246
21:31	115	13:33	166	14:9	140
21:32	106	13:34	253n	14:23	115n

277

INDEX OF SCRIPTURE REFERENCES NEW TESTAMENT

14:26	21	6:62	33	3:23			147
15:24	83	6:63	61	3:25			6
15:32	83	6:68	61	3:26			134
16:8	169	7:6	166	4:2			83
17:24	167	7:8	166	4:11			44
17:30	167	7:17	115, 223	4:19–20		147,	149
17:30	167	7:26	254	4:26–28			254
18:7	17	7:48	254	5:20			61
18:11	179n	8:9	2	5:29		147,	149
18:20	161	8:30–32	9	5:35			4
19:7	253n	8:33	146	5:36–37			146
19:38	246	9:22	56	6:1			124
19:42	33	9:31	115	6:4	123,	132,	155
19:44	166	10:17–18	182n	7:14			147
20:17	44	10:28	192	7:18			92n
20:21	146	11:9–10	44n	7:20			166
20:22	146, 155n, 156	11:25	82	7:51			73n
20:38	81	12:13	246	9:14			57
21:8	166	12:25	21, 222	9:21			57
21:23	154, 155n	12:31	254	9:26–30			214
21:24	92n, 153, 155n, 166	12:38	163n	9:31			156
21:25	155n	12:42	56, 254	10:2			228
21:36	166	12:47–48	61	10:14			188
22:37	49	13:1	49	10:22			68n
22:48	128, 232	14:30	254	10:36			55
23:2	155n, 156	14:48	167	11:4			228
23:7	253n	15:1	85n	11:18			83
23:13	254	15:13	163	11:29			124
24:1	258	16:11	254	12:1			166
24:20	254	17:4	204	12:2			153
24:38	175	17:8	61	12:25			124
24:53	134	17:12	159	13:1–4		213,	218
		20:1	258	13:2		155,	210
JOHN		20:17	201	13:10			106
1:1	247	20:19	258	13:16			4
1:12	5, 253n	20:28	247	13:22			115
1:13	115, 223			13:27			254
1:14	119	ACTS		13:43			88
1:16	164	1:4–8	242	13:46			76
1:47	4, 9	1:14	132, 155, 201	14:16			42
2:19	182n	1:16	163n	14:17			166
3:1	254	2:16	122	14:22		93,	132
3:3–8	193	2:17	122, 166	14:26			218
3:5	93	2:22	4	15:2			126
3:16	192, 202n	2:23	254	15:4			126
3:31	246	2:27	147	15:6			126
3:34	61	2:29	6	15:22–23			126
3:35	180, 248	2:36	55, 180, 182, 248	15:40			218
4:22	195, 219	2:41	147	16:4			126
4:34	115	2:42	155	16:15			227f
4:50–51	82	2:43	147	16:27			153
5:23	180	2:46	201	16:31			228
5:26–28	183	3:12	4	17:11			123
5:29	82, 183	3:13	6	17:24–31			61
5:47	61	3:17	254	17:26			166
6:39	167	3:20	166	17:30		42,	242
		3:21–24	122	17:31			167

278

INDEX OF SCRIPTURE REFERENCES NEW TESTAMENT

17:32	83	1:9	130	3:30			57, 205
18:1	214	1:10	115, 220, 223	3:31			66
18:2	146, 227f., 267	1:11	xi, 126n, 217	4:1			6, 45, 56
18:3	227f.	1:12	xi, 209, 217, 220f.	4:6			50
18:6	76	1:13	xi, 91, 216f.	4:7			50
18:7	238	1:15	xi, 262	4:8			50
18:8	228, 239	1:16	xii, xiii, 56f., 87	4:11			xiii, 6, 57, 205
18:11	267	1:17	xii, 48, 56, 194, 242, 250	4:12			6, 10, 37, 57, 205
18:18	214, 227, 259, 267	1:18	42, 88	4:13			xiii, 10, 12, 37, 50
18:19	227, 267	1:19	115n				
18:21	259	1:21	175	4:14			37, 50
18:25	106	1:24	29	4:15			37
18:26	106, 227f.	1:25	246	4:16			6, 37, 71, 205, 219
19:22	239	1:26	29				
19:29	239	1:28	29, 48n	4:17			6, 37, 205, 219
20:1–3	214	1:32	48n	4:19			11
20:4	239	2:1	234	4:20			11
20:7	258	2:2	234	4:21			11
20:17	126	2:3	234	4:23			205
20:20	123, 214	2:4	34, 105, 115n, 234	4:24			55, 205
20:22–24	220, 222	2:5	141, 234	4:25			55, 205
20:24	123	2:8	141	5:1			194, 207n, 224
20:27	214	2:9	147	5:2			131, 194
20:28	126	2:11	87	5:3			132
21:10–11	122	2:12	43, 192	5:5			221
21:13	222	2:13	43	5:6			166
21:19	123	2:14	43	5:7			163
21:20–27	259	2:15	2, 43, 139, 167	5:8			202n
21:27–36	222	2:16	167, 240	5:9			141
21:28	4	2:18	115, 223	5:10			55, 182
22:16	57	2:24	138n, 195	5:12			111
23:1	2, 154	2:27	195n	5:18			72, 83
23:6	83	2:28	9	5:20			71
23:9	33	2:29	9	5:21			71f.
23:14	3	3:1	4, 201, 205	6:1			42, 234
24:15	83, 200	3:2	4, 201, 219	6:2			66, 111, 234
24:16	154	3:3	101	6:3			68, 234
24:21	83	3:4	25n, 66	6:4			55, 83, 110, 183
26:5–6	48	3:5	25, 42, 141	6:5			55, 83, 183
26:17	79	3:6	25n, 31, 66	6:6			110f.
26:18	79, 253	3:8	234	6:9			55
26:20	214n	3:9	57	6:10			55, 83, 110
26:23	83	3:17	106	6:11			83, 110
27:33	92n	3:18	156	6:12			110
27:35	179	3:19	57	6:13			83, 111, 251
28:28	76	3:20	48n, 50	6:14			110, 251
		3:21	48, 50, 194, 242, 250	6:15			66
ROMANS				6:16			68, 236, 251
1:2	242	3:22	48, 50, 56f., 87, 194, 250	6:17			251
1:3	6			6:21			49
1:4	6, 55, 83, 248	3:23	57	6:22			251
1:5	79, 117, 210, 236, 243	3:24	71	7:1			68
		3:26	166	7:4			111
1:6	19n	3:27	43, 87	7:5			170
1:7	19n, 37, 224, 262	3:28	50	7:6			111
1:8	209	3:29	57	7:7			42, 66

279

INDEX OF SCRIPTURE REFERENCES NEW TESTAMENT

7:12	115	9:22	103, 106, 141	12:18	146
7:13	29, 66	9:23	105	12:19	145f., 153
7:18	115n	9:24	57	12:20	145f.
7:21	43, 115n	9:25	52, 76, 98	12:21	145f.
7:23	43	9:26	52, 76	13:1	252–256
8:2	43	9:27	66, 70, 98	13:2	137, 140
8:3	50, 115n	9:29	51, 66, 98	13:3	254
8:4	110, 163n, 251	9:30	48, 56, 63, 75	13:4	137, 140
8:5	170, 246	9:31	48, 56, 66, 71,	13:5	137, 140f.
8:6	83, 170		73, 76	13:6	137
8:7	134, 170, 196	9:32	46, 48, 50, 56,	13:8	128, 186, 189n,
8:8	170, 196, 246		66, 71, 73, 76, 87		192, 250
8:9	110, 213	9:33	46, 56f., 75, 87n,	13:9	128, 186, 250
8:10	111, 213		98	13:10	128, 186, 250
8:11	111, 213	10:1	80	14:1	201, 203, 260
8:12	83	10:2	66, 71	14:3	203
8:13	83, 113, 251	10:3	66, 71, 73, 87n,	14:4	60
8:15	5		194, 250	14:5	60, 257–259
8:16	11	10:5	83, 98, 249f.	14:9	55, 82, 248
8:17	11	10:6	73, 194, 250	14:10	4, 168f.
8:20	49n	10:18	31, 98	14:13	4, 44n, 60, 106,
8:21	11	10:19	76, 98f.		235
8:23	111, 200	10:20	76, 98	14:14	1, 159
8:24	131, 200	10:21	66, 67n, 73f,	14:15	4, 198, 234
8:25	131, 200		87, 98	14:16	234
8:28	15, 18f., 29, 37	11:1	4	14:17	56
8:29	15, 37, 68n, 202n	11:5	xiv, 17–19, 37	14:19	133, 198
8:30	19, 37	11:7	xiv, 17–19, 37,	14:20	44n, 198
8:31	42		72n	14:21	4, 44n
8:32	29	11:11	xv	14:22	119n
8:33	17, 19, 72	11:12	xiv, xv, 164n,	14:23	119n
8:34	182		168	15:1	174, 190
8:35	132	11:13	123, 210	15:2	190
8:38	3	11:15	xiv, xv, 168	15:5	136
8:39	3	11:16	6n	15:8	6, 51
9:1	47, 66	11:18	197	15:9	51
9:2	66, 80	11:20	234	15:14	48n, 236
9:3	66, 80	11:23	xiv	15:15	xi, 79, 117
9:4	xiv, 99, 101	11:24	xiv	15:16	79, 117, 155
9:5	xiv, 99n, 101,	11:25	xiv, xv, 137,	15:18	236, 240
	219, 245–248		241f	15:20	121
9:6	xiv, 66f., 97, 100n	11:26	xiv, 168, 242	15:22	xi
9:7	100n	11:28	xiv, 4, 6n, 17	15:23	xi
9:8	100	11:29	xiv	15:24	xi, xii
9:9	100n, 166	11:32	xiii	15:25	xi, 124
9:10	6, 68, 71, 100n	11:23	xv, 35, 254	15:26	xi, 47, 124
9:11	48, 68, 70, 71,	11:36	244	15:27	124, 133, 155
	72, 100n	12:1	56, 221	15:28	xii
9:12	68, 71, 98, 100n	12:2	56, 169, 180,	15:29	164
9:13	68, 71, 100n		194, 223	15:31	124
9:14	66	12:3	79, 210	15:32	115
9:15	50, 98, 102	12:8	227n	15:33	237
9:16	50, 102	12:9	159, 186	16:3	267
9:17	98	12:10	159, 163	16:5	140, 267
9:18	72f., 106	12:12	155	16:9	140
9:19	234	12:13	239	16:12	140
9:20	234	12:17	146	16:13	17

16:14	4	6:10	260	13:2	48, 119n
16:17	xii	6:13	111	13:4–7	162
16:18	xii	6:14	170	13:8	48
16:19	xii	6:15	68, 111	13:11	224
16:20	xii, 200n, 224	6:16	68, 111, 129n	13:13	128
16:21	xii	6:17	111, 129n	14:1	133
16:22	xii	6:18	111	14:3	125
16:23	xii	6:19	68, 111	14:6	96n
16:25	xii, 91f., 268	6:20	111, 113	14:20	237
16:26	xii, 268	7:4	111	14:37	122
16:27	xii, 268	7:5	166	15:1	240
		7:15	19	15:9–10	117
I CORINTHIANS		7:26	154	15:12–13	83
1:1	115	7:29–31	167	15:18	192
1:2	19n, 57	7:34	111, 130	15:19	132
1:3	224	7:37	106, 253n	15:21	83
1:5	48n	8:1	48	15:24	49, 253
1:8	49, 167	8:4	189	15:25	92n, 237
1:9	19, 37	8:6	107	15:26–27	237
1:14	238	8:7	189	15:28	49, 237
1:16	228	8:8	193n	15:42	83
1:20	169	8:9	44n, 253n	15:44	111
1:23	240	8:11	191f.	15:51	92, 241
1:24	19n, 104	8:12	198	15:54	111, 181
1:26	19n	9:4	253n	15:55–56	111
1:29–31	211	9:16	154, 210	16:2	258
2:2	106	9:24	26	16:8	267
2:3	88	9:26	26	16:15	229n
2:4	213	9:27	111	16:19	227ff., 267
2:6	104, 114, 169, 254	10:1	6, 91	16:20	232
		10:6	199	16:21	238
2:7	92, 104, 169, 241n	10:10	199	16:22	3
		10:11	166, 169	16:23	237
2:8	104, 114, 169, 252, 254	10:12	88		
		10:15	200	II CORINTHIANS	
2:11	130	10:16	134	1:1	115
3:7	214	10:17	119f.	1:2	224
3:10	117, 214f.	10:18	133	1:3	113, 200, 245, 246
3:12	200	10:20	133		
3:13	167f.	10:26	164	1:4	132
3:16	68	10:30	179, 193	1:8	91, 132
3:20	175	10:31	179	1:11	221
4:1	92	10:33	198	1:12	2, 154
4:5	151, 168, 170, 184	11:10	253n	1:13	49
		11:13	106	1:17	133
4:12	135n	11:26	92n	2:1	106, 186
4:16	110	11:28	115	2:4	102n, 132
4:17	106	12:1	91	2:14	48n, 211
5:3	111	12:2	3	2:16	83
5:4	130	12:3	55	2:17	1
5:5	167	12:8	121, 124	3:6	213
5:6	68	12:9	119n, 121, 124	3:13	49
5:11	215, 260	12:10	121, 124, 175	3:14	72n
6:2	68	12:26	135	3:17	213, 248
6:3	68, 252f.	12:27	120	3:18	114, 213
6:7	78	12:28	121, 126	4:1	123
6:9	68	12:29	121	4:2	2, 138, 154, 236

INDEX OF SCRIPTURE REFERENCES NEW TESTAMENT

4:3	192	13:10	88n	5:23–24	119
4:4	169, 254	13:11	136, 200n, 237	6:2	197
4:5	240	13:12	232	6:5	197
4:6	48n			6:6	133n
4:10	182f.	**GALATIANS**		6:8	113, 170
4:11–12	183	1:3	224	6:9	166
4:17	132	1:4	15, 114f., 169, 223	6:10	129, 131, 166
5:4	82, 181	1:5	244	6:11	238
5:6	111	1:6	19	6:16	9, 96n
5:8	47, 111, 181	1:8–9	3, 173	6:18	237
5:9	181	1:10	198	6:19	130
5:10	111, 168,f, 184	1:11	240		
5:11	2, 154	1:13	66	**EPHESIANS**	
5:15	83	1:14	48, 66	1:2	224
5:18	123	1:15	19, 37, 117	1:3	134, 245f.
5:20	59	1:19	159	1:4	15, 17, 19 72, 202n, 231, 241n,
5:21	4	1:20	2	1:5	5, 15, 20, 47, 115, 202n, 223
6:2	166	1:23	118		
6:3	123	2:2	15, 26, 240	1:6	15, 151
6:4	132	2:7	79, 205, 218, 240	1:7	35, 105
6:5	229	2:8	79, 205, 218	1:9	47, 92
6:6	48n, 128	2:9	79, 117, 205, 218	1:10	164, 166
6:7	170	2:10	102n, 218	1:11	15, 18, 20, 115, 223
7:1	130, 156	2:13	136		
7:4	132	3:5	213	1:12	35, 151
7:6	137n	3:9	134	1:13	207
7:11	130n	3:10–11	51	1:14	35, 151, 204, 207
7:12	130n	3:12	250	1:17	48, 201
8:2	105, 125, 132	3:13	4	1:18	19n, 82n, 105
8:4	124	3:16	6, 205	1:20	55, 180, 248
8:7	48n, 130n	3:17, 18	5	1:21	55, 180, 248, 253
8:8	130n	3:19	5, 92n	1:22	55, 180, 248
8:9	150, 198	3:20–21	135	1:23	55, 120n, 164, 248
8:16	130n	3:22	103		
		3:23	5	2:1	83
24		3:24	49	2:2	253f.
8:18	151	3:26	5	2:3	111, 170
8:21	138	3:27	170	2:4	35, 105
8:23	133, 230	3:28	5	2:5	71, 83
9:1	124	3:29	15	2:7	35, 105
9:11	125	4:1–3	5	2:8	56, 70f., 89n, 118, 165
9:12	124, 155, 210	4:4	5, 164, 166		
9:13	124f	4:5	5	2:9	56
10:1	137n, 221	4:9	173	2:10	56
10:17	211	4:10	166, 172, 178	2:12	5, 166, 200
11:3	125, 236	4:11	172	2:14	224
11:12–15	237	4:21–31	51	2:15	224
11:15	49	4:29	9	2:16	120n, 233
11:22	4	5:2	259	2:17	224
11:23	229	5:7	26	2:20	121f.
11:31	2, 246	5:8	19	3:3	2
12:10	47, 132, 197	5:10	197	3:4	92
12:12	213	5:13	19	3:5	92n, 121
12:19	1	5:14	166	3:6	77, 240
13:4	82	5:19–21	170	3:7	117, 210
13:5	115	5:22	119, 128, 207, 209, 221	3:8	35, 57, 105f., 117,
13:9	197				

INDEX OF SCRIPTURE REFERENCES NEW TESTAMENT

		1:11	151	1:16	107, 253		
3:9	130, 210	1:9	165, 221	1:18	120n, 248		
3:9	92, 210, 241n	1:20–25	181	1:19	119, 164, 248		
3:10	243, 253	1:23	182	1:23	88		
3:11	18	1:28	165	1:24	120n		
3:13	132	1:29	89n	1:25	124		
3:15	215	2:1	113	1:26	92, 169		
3:16	35, 105	2:2	136, 201	1:27	35, 92, 105		
3:19	48n, 164, 207	2:3	129, 163	1:28	116		
3:21	244	2:4	136, 163	2:2	92, 105		
4:1	19, 56, 110	2:5	198, 201	2:3	48n		
4:2	56	2:6	198, 247	2:4	235n		
4:3	–213	2:7	198	2:8	235n		
4:4	19, 120n, 213	2:8	198	2:9	164, 173, 247		
4:5	107, 213	2:9	180, 182, 248, 253	2:10	253		
4:6	107, 213	2:10	180, 182, 185n, 248, 253	2:13	83		
4:9	54, 183			2:15	253ff		
4:10	183	2:11	55, 180, 182, 185n, 204, 248, 253	2:16	172, 178		
4:11	121			2:17	172, 178		
4:12	120n, 123	2:12	88, 165	2:18	173		
4:13	48, 164	2:13	47	2:19	120n		
4:14	236	2:14	175	2:21	172, 235		
4:16	120n	2:15	11, 237	2:22	115n, 172		
4:17	1	2:16	83	3:1–3	183		
4:18	83	2:17	155, 210	3:10	48, 170		
4:23	130	2:25	155n, 230	3:12	17, 72, 113, 170		
4:24	170	2:30	155n	3:15	19, 120n, 224		
4:25	120	3:1	130n	3:18	49n		
4:27	141	3:2	235	3:20	172		
4:28	126n	3:5	4	3:22	125		
4:30	167	3:8	31	3:23	172		
5:8	170	3:10	83	4:2	132, 155		
5:9	209	3:12	133	4:3	92, 221		
5:11	133, 170	3:14	19n, 133	4:5	131		
5:16	131	3:16	135n	4:7	140		
5:17	115, 223	3:18	235	4:9	140		
5:21	156	3:1	49, 235	4:12	115f.		
5:23	120n	3:21	111	4:14	140		
5:26	54n, 61	4:2	136	4:15	228		
5:28	163	4:4	135, 207	4:17	123		
5:29	163	4:5	168	4:18	238		
5:32	92	4:7	207, 224				
6:2–3	249	4:8	129, 151	**I THESSALONIANS**			
6:5	125, 156	4:9	129, 200n, 224, 237	1:2	224		
6:6	115, 223			1:4	17, 19, 72		
6:10–18	170	4:11	136	1:5	213, 240		
6:11	170	4:13	119	1:6	132, 213		
6:12	253f.	4:14	133	1:6–10	141		
6:14	170	4:19	105	2:4	240		
6:17	61	4:20	244	2:8	47, 126n		
6:21	140	4:23	237	2:12	19, 193		
PHILIPPIANS				2:16	141		
1:1	124, 226	**COLOSSIANS**		2:13	213		
1:2	224	1:2	224	3:1	47		
1:6	167	1:7	140	3:3	132		
1:9	48	1:9	48	3:7	132		
1:10	115, 167	1:13	170, 253	4:1	1		

INDEX OF SCRIPTURE REFERENCES NEW TESTAMENT

4:3	115, 223	3:7	138, 195	4:22	237
4:7	19	3:8	124, 226		
4:13	91, 132, 200	3:9	2, 154, 226	**TITUS**	
5:2	167	3:10	124, 226	1:1	17, 48, 72
5:4	167	3:11	226	1:2	241n, 242
5:8	165, 170	3:12	124, 126n, 226	1:3	166, 242
5:9	141, 165	3:13	124f., 226	1:4	224
5:12	126	3:15	127	1:5	126
5:15	133, 138	3:16	92	1:9	125
5:18	115	4:1	166	1:13	88n
5:21	231	4:4	179, 188	1:15	2
5:22	129, 162, 237	4:5	179	1:16	56
5:23	130, 200n, 207, 224, 237	4:13	125	2:12	166
		5:8	118, 138n	2:13	166f., 247
5:24	19	5:9	226	3:1	49n, 146n, 253, 256
5:25	221	5:10	226		
5:26	232	5:13	228	3:3	135
5:28	237	5:17	126	3:8	126n
		5:21	17n	3:12	106, 130n
II THESSALONIANS		5:22	133	3:14	126n
1:2	224	6:1	197		
1:4	132	6:8–9	136	**PHILEMON**	
1:10	167	6:11	133	1	140
1:11	19n, 209	6:12	19, 56	2	228
1:12	247	6:15	166	3	224
2:2	167			17	133
2:6	166	**II TIMOTHY**		25	237
2:12	47, 168	1:2	140, 224		
2:14	19	1:3	2, 154	**HEBREWS**	
3:1	221	1:9	15, 18f., 37, 72, 241n	1:1	6, 122
3:9	253n			1:2	166, 248
3:16	224, 237	1:12	167	1:3	55, 248
3:17	238	1:16	134, 228	1:4	248
3:18	237	1:17	134	1:7	155, 210
		1:18	134, 167	1:9	201
I TIMOTHY		2:1	72	1:14	115, 165, 210, 253
1:1	242	2:8	240		
1:2	224	2:10	17	2:4	15, 213
1:5	2, 49, 154	2:19	215	2:10	107
1:11	35, 240	2:20–21	36	2:14	133, 181, 254
1:12	117, 123	2:22	57	2:15	181
1:13	66, 117	2:25	48	3:1	19n
1:14	66, 72, 117	3:1	166	3:6	88
1:15	66, 117	3:7	48	3:10	106
1:16	117	3:11–12	132	3:13	92n
1:17	244	3:16–17	199	3:14	88
1:19	2	4:1	170	4:1	88
2:1	110, 146n	4:5	123	5:14	175
2:2	146n, 152	4:6	166	6:1–2	83
2:3	146n	4:8	167	6:11	49, 130n
2:4	48	4:9	130n	7:3	49
2:6	166	4:10	169, 217n	7:25	82
2:7	1f.	4:11	123	8:1	248
2:8	175	4:18	243	8:2	155, 210
2:14	236	4:19	227, 267	8:5	68n
3:4	126n, 228	4:20	239	8:6	210
3:5	126n	4:21	130n	8:9	6

284

9:1	6	1:12	122	2:21	48n		
9:6	6	1:17	88	3:3	166		
9:14	83	1:20	166	3:7–8	167		
9:21	210	1:22	178	3:9	192		
9:26	166, 169	1:25	54n, 61	3:10	167		
9:28	165, 167	2:2	112, 165	3:14	166		
10:10	115	2:5	112, 211	3:17	136		
10:11	155, 210	2:6	44	3:18	244		
10:22	2	2:7	44				
10:25	167	2:8	44	**I JOHN**			
10:29	188	2:9	17	1:4	207		
10:33	133	2:13	49n, 147n, 154, 255	2:1	112		
10:38–39	147			2:14	237		
11:6	196	2:14	147n, 151, 255	2:17	114f.		
11:7	68n	2:15	147n, 255	2:18	166		
11:20	134	2:16	147n, 255	2:21	2		
11:34	153	2:17	147n, 156, 161, 255	2:23	56		
11:37	153			2:27	2		
12:1	26	2:18	156	3:1	5		
12:5	53	2:20	134	3:2	207		
12:14	113, 133, 139	2:23	142	3:3	200		
13:2	134	3:1	49n	3:14	83		
13:5	136	3:5	49n	4:1–6	12		
13:7	126	3:9	135n, 138	4:4	237		
13:17	126	3:11	133	4:9	83, 202n		
13:18	2	3:13	49n, 134	4:10	202n		
13:20	200n, 207, 224, 237, 240	3:14	134	4:15	56		
		3:15	134	4:17	167		
13:21	115, 240, 243f.	3:16	2, 134	5:11–13	83		
		3:17	115, 134, 223	5:14	115		
JAMES		3:20	147				
1:9	137n	3:21	2, 55	**II JOHN**			
1:21	147	3:22	49n, 55, 180, 248, 253	7	56		
2:5	17			11	133		
2:11	161	4:2	115				
2:15–16	142	4:5	170	**III JOHN**			
2:17	83	4:7	49, 168	1	239		
2:17–22	56	4:9	133				
3:9	134	4:11	243	**JUDE**			
3:15	235	4:13	133	3	118, 130n		
3:17	137, 139	4:19	115	6	167		
4:6	137n	5:1	133	19	235		
4:7	49n	5:3	137	23	22, 129		
5:3	166	5:5	49n, 137n	24–24	240, 244		
5:8	168	5:6	166				
5:9	170	5:11	244	**REVELATION**			
5:13	136	5:14	232	1:3	166		
5:20	147			1:6	244		
		II PETER		1:10	258		
I PETER		1:1	247	1:18	82, 182n		
1:1	17	1:4	133	2:2	197n		
1:2	15, 68n	1:5	48n, 130n	2:6	22		
1:3	83, 245f.	1:6	48n	2:8	83		
1:5	165f.	1:10	17, 19n	2:9	182n		
1:9	147	1:19	167	2:25	92n		
1:10	122	1:21	115, 223	3:1	83		
1:11	122	2:19–20	78	4:11	108, 223		

5:12	115n, 244	17:14	17	22:20	168
5:13	244	18:4	133		
7:14	132	20:5	83	II ESDRAS	
11:18	166	21:3	207	16:53	142n
13:10	153	21:27	188		
16:3	147	22:10–12	168		

REFERENCE -- NOT TO BE
TAKEN FROM THIS ROOM

ENNIS AND NANCY HAM LIBRARY
ROCHESTER COLLEGE
800 WEST AVON ROAD
ROCHESTER HILLS, MI 48307